Soulstream

Soulstream

The Mancer Epic

Book I

GEO IVERY

To order the Audio Book, contact:
Ivery Towers LLC
www.thesoulstream.com

123774

Contents

Acknowledgments

There are way too many people I have met on this long journey to thank, but for all of you that I don't mention here, just know that I still have you in my thoughts and my heart. The first acknowledgments go to my parents, for without you all telling me from an early age that the sky's the limit, I probably would have dismissed the thought of writing and drawing long ago.

Next I have to acknowledge my brothers—De'Nelle, Jerraile, Rahshae, Ka'Zhaun and Gabriel—who listened to all of my endless stories as we grew up, imagining ourselves as superheroes.

To my sisters—La'Quoia, Jalane, Nakayla and Jhourden—who stared at me with wide-eyed anticipation as I wove campfire tales, and to my adopted sister, AJ, who is the first person to read my novels when they were unreadable, I love you.

To my cousin Clarence, who always sees life as a new adventure we need to conquer, in style.

To my best friends from high school—Adam, Jody, Jodet, Justin, Ramon, Mieszko, Konrad, Sean, Crystal, Janice, Janelle, lil' Justin, and the rest of the D&D crew—even though most of us have grown apart in our separate corners of the world, this story would not exist without you. Maybe we can get together one day and play a little table top or live-action role playing, as in the good ol' days.

To my guild, The Forgotten Oath, Ian, Candelas, Flos, Mikey, Ying, Mick, Andreas, Abe, Ghando, Zeko, Rin, Alexey, Juan, Lori, Linda, Wayne, Talon, Ka'Zhaun and the rest of the Officers rank 4 and up, you guys and gals have always been there for me, and I love you all like family. Even though people think we're big geeks, I know we're all just über!

To all the friends I've met at jobs across the country, especially the call centers, I just want to tell you that, no matter what the bosses say, you all are powerful and worth more than you know.

To Susan Jaramillo, whose Virgo energy revitalized me with every smile, thank you so much for your support.

To the Jaramillos, who always welcomed me into their home as a son, I finally made it, just as you guys always said I would.

To Alejandro Otero, who reminds me that beauty is something we work hard to attain from inside and out, thank you for teaching me those lessons.

To the kids on the streets, you will never be forgotten, even the ones who have fallen. Now you are immortalized.

To my quirky editor, Dr. Paul Weisser, who believed in my story so much, we argued like son and father over the details. Thanks for making me look good!

To all of the dreamers, never let the colors fade and never let the haters prevail.

To all of you that I have not mentioned, again I love you and thank you for your support.

A special acknowledgment to Jodet Nanez, the cover artist for the 1st edition and my best friend, I love you bro and thanks so much for coming up with this cover to embody my vision. The new cover artist is Youness Elh, thank you for the excellent art.

Last but not least, I would like to acknowledge the love of my life Rieu Ivery.

THE FORGOTTEN OATH

The years went by, season after season, and the only things that made Isja realize he was getting older were the animals and trees around him. He had known he was immortal since the night he was first found by Gemini. Of course, he hadn't believed the mysterious stranger then. Naturally, no one in his right mind would have believed. Gemini had spoken of a war between Supernaturals on Earth that the human mind simply was incapable of understanding.

There were supposedly Magick users known as Witchbreed, hunters that were called Jreamers, shape shifters known as Spiraar, and blood drinkers known to the underworld as Vampyl. All of these factions were at war. Isja had found it hard to believe that he, a simple boy, was one of the most powerful of the Supernaturals, known as the Mancer.

It took him many years to cope with the fact that he wasn't human, let alone one of the most powerful entities on the planet. He was a simple farmer from a village near Carthage, who thought that he'd been blessed by the gods to be able to help his family the unusual way he did. Isja was able to speak to the land and the animals alike. The land gave his family more than enough food for them to flourish, but Isja had to leave because Gemini warned that there would be people hunting him.

Isja had watched, shaking, as the hunters slaughtered his innocent family and chased him deep into the mountains. Many seasons had passed since then. Isja had stopped counting two hundred years ago. That was another thing—all Mancers were immortal. Isja had not physically aged even one day since the murder of his family. He looked like any other eighteen-year-old boy from his homeland. His green eyes and pale skin complemented his sandy blonde hair, which flowed around his face and over his shoulders.

This was the beginning of a new season. Spring was upon the enchanted forest, in which Isja had made the oath to Gemini so many years before. It was on this very day that Gemini, who was considerably taller than the boy, made him promise not to leave except for a dire emergency. Isja remembered, laughing at what had been barren lands, but had become a plush and beautiful grove.

"What could ever reach me here, and why would anyone think to come to this place for a simple farmer?" Isja had asked the tall, dark man that cold night, so many moons ago.

"You must understand," Gemini had replied, "they are more capable than you credit them. You choose not to fight in the war, and that is your decision alone to make. Just don't underestimate them, and promise to stay here unless you need to come to me in an emergency."

Gemini had pointed to the Magick mark on a wall, the same wall that the boy was now watching a glistening waterfall rush over.

"I promise, Gemini."

Isja had hugged the man before watching him touch the rune on the wall and disappear.

As Isja turned around to look at the barren lands, it seemed as if, in the blink of an eye, this place had become hauntingly beautiful. It was a grove filled with animals that lived through their cycles, and thousands of trees that bore fruit and provided homes for the wildlife. The forest was touched by the sun and glowed like no other that Isja had ever seen. The moon sparkled across the lake in the middle of this grove like liquid silver.

The constant splashing music of the waterfall meant more than serenity to Isja. Sometimes he would sit next to his favorite tree, the oldest and first one he had planted in the grove.

Staring up at the sky, he thought, *I wonder if anyone, even Gemini, remembers me out here in my solitude.*

Many times, Isja wanted to die because of his self-exile, but death would not grant him that wish. The boy never knew illness, nor harm from any animal in the grove, as he slept in the open fields or beneath the trees.

This morning, he had awakened from a dream of the world outside his enchanted grove. He felt the world calling to him, to help in the war from which he had run away. Terrible pollution, corruption, and blood stained lands that were devastated war-torn continents away. Although he had never physically been to those places, he knew they existed.

Isja shook his head clear, trying to dismiss the dream. He stood up to sing a song to his animal and tree friends. The winds were kind to him, and his talented voice seemed to bring instant harmony across the grove:

> *There once was a boy who lived in the woods,*
> *Ignored Destiny's war 'cause he thought he should.*
> *He could heal with his hands, from the skies to the sands.*
> *And people were saved right where they stood.*

Isja sang his song as he walked through the forest. Panthers leaped gracefully from tree to tree, while small woodland squirrels brushed against his bare feet. These were only a couple of the many different types of animals that were residents of the enchanted grove. Deer, wolves, hyenas, antelope, and mice walked and hopped around him, understanding his mood. It made him smile to see their cheerful dances around his feet and crazy stunt flying overhead. Isja walked through the forest, humming and singing the song as he made his way to his favorite tree. He could barely remember his childhood, or even much of his hometown, but he did remember his relationship with the land and animals. This was when he was truly at peace.

During the centuries that Isja had lived in the grove, he had very few visitors. Some of them had stumbled in by accident, and others he had brought in for sanctuary. Each time before, the animals in the grove had become restless. As the boy reached his beloved tree and leaned his bare back against the bark, the birds that were flying high above the grove in their circular dance suddenly shrieked in alarm.

Immediately understanding that there was an intruder in the forest, Isja slid to the ground. But a second later, a bullet shattered the bark above his head.

The animals in the grove grew frantic, tugging urgently at the boy to move. Isja's heart pounded. For an agonizing moment, his legs failed to obey. Finally, scrambling to his feet, he looked directly through the trees an impossible distance away. There was an intruder—a sniper, with weapons the boy had never seen before. The war that he had purposely chosen to escape centuries ago had finally made it to his doorstep.

Isja looked toward the trespasser with a pleading expression. But the trigger was pulled, and a bullet aimed directly for the boy's face fired through the air.

A bird instantly dove from the sky to take the bullet, sacrificing itself for its friend. The animals on the ground around Isja tugged at him, again urging him to flee. This time, he darted through the forest as fast as his limbs could carry him—as fast as any of the deer or panthers running alongside him. He remembered to run toward the lake and the waterfall. The rune was his only salvation. Gemini would know what to do. Isja hadn't seen his mentor in many, many years, but this was his only hope.

With a newfound resolve, he ran gracefully through the enchanted woods. Bullets flying through the air either missed him completely or were stopped by other friends who jumped or flew in front of them, sacrificing themselves for his safety. With tears rolling down his eyes at the loss of his beloved forest friends, Isja made it to the edge of a high ledge. Below was the tranquil serenity of his Liquid Moon Lake.

He looked back quickly to see if the sniper were still in position. The plea on Isja's face turned into defiance as he saw the bodies of his fallen friends. The boy turned back to the ledge and jumped in the air, diving toward the lake as gracefully as the birds above. While still in the air, he could see his reflection in the perfectly clear water, his salvation just within reach. He would make it to Gemini and apologize for his neglect. He should have helped save the world from this evil when he had had the chance.

His gliding through the air brought a calm over him that was at once both peaceful and terrifying.

The sound of a bullet piercing the air was the last thing Isja heard. He felt a sharp pain as his limp body slammed into the beautiful lake. The waterfall splashed around him as his eyes lost focus, and blood stained the silvery waters.

"Target eliminated," the sniper reported into his microphone.

The signal was picked up by a top-secret satellite with the letters OZONE on its rotating transistor solar panels. The satellite forwarded the message in a nanosecond to a top-secret base.

"Guardian has completed his mission in Antarctica, sir," the Receptionist said, forwarding the message to the Commanding Officer.

"Bring him home," the Commander snapped. "Save the footage to his mission logs."

As soon as the Receptionist pressed the Save button, the file was intercepted by a ghost signal.

"Sir, there's been a breach!" she gasped.

The Commander stopped in mid-stride, turning with an angry, frustrated expression. "Find out who or what it is, and send the trackers. *Now!*"

A gasp came from the hacker who had just taken the information from OZONE. She shut her laptop and breathed heavily, her hands shaking.

"Are you ready for school, Cindy?" her mom asked from just outside the door.

"Yes, mom, I'm almost ready."

Her mother continued to walk down the hall without even turning the knob. Cindy turned back to her laptop and reopened it. Just touching her computer was all she needed to do to enter the virtual web. Her personal website and haven for Supernaturals needed to be updated.

In her androgynous online voice, Cindy announced: "Surge-Overload signing in. OZONE has killed another one of our kind. It's time we took the battle to them!"

Chapter 1

BLUE MONDAY

Sometimes even waking up was a chore these days for Blue. Why should today be any different? He hadn't really had the easiest life, but not the hardest either—at least, not until recently. All Blue could remember were bits and pieces from the night before. He rubbed his head and found it painful to even open his eyes. Normally, he would expect his parents to berate him with reasons why he shouldn't party so hard with his friends, and why his hangovers were the reason he couldn't concentrate in class. But this time was different. Something was horribly wrong. When he finally opened his eyes, he was sitting in a crater where his house used to be.

In a panic, Blue scrambled to his feet and looked around in horror. His confused daze, accompanied by a harsh and sharp headache, made him think twice about moving too fast. Almost falling over when he stood up too quickly, he caught his balance and regained his footing.

Surely, I didn't drink THAT much.

As the memories of the night before started to flood back to him, all he could do was stare blankly in disbelief as he recalled the events that had led to this bizarre scene.

✶

It began on a Monday. Nothing special about that. Blue hated it like most other Mondays, because it symbolized the end of his fun time.

He woke up and went into the bathroom after a long weekend of partying with Tommy and Guy. On most Mondays, Blue's parents woke him up, purposely extra loud and annoyingly happy, or occasionally sighing with disappointment—he was never quite sure which it would be. Over the last few years, they had come to realize that he simply didn't care.

Blue subconsciously prepared for the inevitable lecture that accompanied the abrupt end to his bliss. He dressed without showering and rinsed out his mouth, not to freshen his breath, but to get rid of the nasty taste of whatever he had drunk the night before. It had been taking a lot more alcohol recently to numb his senses, let alone get him drunk.

Blue was miserable this morning. His mother was outside his room, asking him to come to breakfast, sounding stern, yet oddly comforting. Wearing an old shirt, a pair of torn jeans, and worn-out leather biker boots, Blue grabbed his sunglasses and leather jacket before heading down to the dining table.

He almost dreaded the walk downstairs as much as the entire first day back to school every fall. Monday was indeed his least favorite day. As he expected, there was the usual humming from his mom as she prepared breakfast for the family. Dad was sitting across the table, reading his paper, with an obvious scowl of disdain as he glanced at Blue's clothing and recognized his condition. Blue's sister seemed to be the coolest of the bunch as she strolled in. She gave her mother a kiss on the cheek and her father a hug, then proceeded to get Blue a cup of strong coffee.

Of all of them, Charity was his favorite, but he would never tell her that. She gracefully walked across the room and sat down, sliding coffee to Blue the way he liked it. Her features were very much like his. Both had dark hair, high cheekbones, and olive skin. The only difference was that her eyes were green instead of his bright blue. She pouted as her dad started in on Blue with the usual barrage of complaints, not even looking up from his paper while he scolded, as if this were all rehearsed.

"Why don't you *do* something with your life? I mean, look at your sister. She's got her life together . . . , on the fast track to being the top of her class. Even though she's a year younger than you, she doesn't go out and make a mess of things like you and that hair."

He looked over at Blue to scan him up and down, never changing the scowl on his face.

"Daddy, I'm thinking of studying abroad," Charity suddenly interrupted, knowing where this conversation would lead, as she watched her brother stir restlessly in his chair. She smiled at him to calm his nerves and looked pointedly back at their easily distracted father.

Their mother stood next to the table, proud of her daughter's diplomatic approach.

"All of you please do not forget to eat every bit of breakfast," she said, "and don't forget, we have an important dinner tonight."

She shot a quick look at her husband, then looked at Blue and reached to fix his mussed hair.

"Six o'clock tonight, and don't be late!" she said in her special "mother" voice.

Blue deftly dodged her hand, but also understood that he shouldn't mess this one up.

Mom doesn't usually announce dinners, so she must have something pretty important to say.

Blue ate the food so fast that he almost inhaled it. Then, looking around, he said, "I gotta go."

His mom reminded him one last time, "Six o'clock!"

Blue threw a hand up as he walked away to let her know he had heard. Charity came running after him.

"Can I get a ride with you today?" she asked, slightly out of breath.

He threw her a blank look.

Why is she asking? She HATES my car.

Charity waited for them to get a safe distance from the kitchen. Then she said, "Before you say no, I don't think me and Johnny are gonna work out. I don't wanna ride with him today after what he tried last—"

She stopped as Blue turned to her with an angry expression on his face.

"What did that piss-ant of a jock do to you?"

His voice was a little louder than Charity liked, with her parents in the next room. Shoving him out the front door and closing it quickly behind her, she unintentionally slammed it shut.

"Look, he didn't get very far. I don't want you to go around acting like, well, *you!* Anger management doesn't top your good points, Blue." She smiled as she realized that she was being a bit harsher than she had intended. "I'm just saying, please give me a ride, and don't make a big deal out of this, okay?"

Her smile was much like their mother's, and irresistibly cute and comforting.

Blue nodded, and mumbled as they walked toward the driveway, "Get in."

His car was beyond loud, and typical of the guys in his circle, who drove fast and big cars from years before any of them were born. They obsessed over loud music—if possible, even louder than their engines. Every time Charity saw their obnoxious attitudes and reckless driving, she rolled her eyes. But today was different. Instead of regret, she felt more secure with her brother than with any other person in the world.

Today she didn't even mind his deafening car, so long as she got to go to school without seeing her boyfriend—*ex*-boyfriend as of last night.

The ride to school was Blue's normal style of driving—way too fast and way too close. However, his sense of direction and space was flawless.

How in the world does he drive this thing with a hangover and never get in an accident?

When they arrived at school, Charity was thrilled that they had survived, and swore to herself that she would ask her father for a car of her own as soon as she could.

Before they got out of the car, Charity grabbed Blue's hand as he turned off the ignition.

"You know what mommy's 'important dinner' is all about, right?"

Irritated, more by her grabbing him so suddenly than by the tone of her words, Blue glared at his sister through his dark shades.

Wanting to get the words out before her brother lost patience, Charity continued without a breath, "Mommy and daddy are getting a divorce."

As she whispered the last word, she looked as if she were going to cry.

Blue raised an eyebrow, since he thought that his family was damned near perfect. Then he smiled, unaware of his sister's probing stare. He was more amused by the irony of the situation than by anything else, but Charity was obviously terrified and didn't share his sense of humor.

"How can you just laugh at something like this, as if it doesn't matter?" She got out of the car and turned to look at her brother. "Don't be late tonight, Blue! Tommy and Guy are not as important as this . . . , and maybe we can . . . .

Her words trailed off as she sank into deep thought. Seeing her brother's sarcastic expression, she walked off defiantly.

Blue sat for a second, lingering on his sister's words until he dismissed them as pointless.

Mom and dad breaking up? Nah.

He wouldn't think about this conversation again for the rest of the day.

As always, Tommy and Guy were waiting for him in the back parking lot, smoking before school started. That was their routine, if they even bothered to wake up for school.

As Blue walked up to them, he saw a girl get out of a red SUV. Her hair was light brown, and her bangs were a soft shade of purple. Those long purple bangs sculpted her exotic face and sun-kissed skin, but the thing that captivated Blue was the girl's innocent and amazingly golden eyes. For the first time in his life, Blue was actually glad he had come to school early.

Kaery had just moved to the city. Her single mother was a businesswoman who sometimes had to relocate. That wouldn't have been so bad if she hadn't insisted on bringing Kaery along. As an only child, Kaery had gotten pretty much whatever she wanted. The only problem was that she didn't want much, just to fit in somewhere. This was almost the end of her freshman year, and her mother had just moved her again.

I just KNOW this is not gonna be good.

The first day at a new school is rarely the best. At least, she was now in the Golden State, so the weather had a good chance of being nice. Earlier that morning, Kaery had ignored her mother's latest lecture on etiquette and scheduling. Hearing it as often as she had, she now found it totally monotonous and rehearsed.

Her drive to school had been uneventful, but when her mom pulled into the parking lot and she saw all the new faces, Kaery almost had an anxiety attack. She regained her composure when her mom finally stopped talking. Maybe her mom noticed Kaery's uncomfortable situation momentarily, but that was short-lived.

Over the engine noise all around them, her mother yelled, "These fuckin' kids and their ridiculous antique pollution machines! I can't hear myself think."

A midnight blue muscle car drove by in that instant, with a guy at the wheel who took Kaery's breath away. Directly on the heels of her anxiety attack, sudden intrigue made her gasp uncontrollably.

"Is everything okay?" her mom asked, not really worried because she knew her daughter wasn't all that frail.

As she straightened her daughter's clothing, all Kaery heard was, "And stay away from those boys!"

It was almost a veiled threat.

Kaery smiled as she said, "I love you, mom."

The words were true and always brought a smile to her serious mother's face.

Kaery was pleased with herself for not getting caught staring at the boy in the muscle car. She couldn't help noticing his sunglasses and cool hair. As she got out of the car, she reached back in to get her backpack, smiled reassuringly at her mother, and turned around.

There he was! He was looking directly at her without moving.

Kaery's heart almost stopped. The moment was brief, since two guys who seemed to be friends came up behind to startle him. Kaery also heard herself being called by a familiar voice.

"Kaery! O-M-G! You made it!" Then, waving to Kaery's mom, "Hello, Mrs. Newcastle."

Ahlina was one of Kaery's oldest friends. Even with all the moves, they had stayed in touch over the Internet. Now she kept chatting without missing a beat as Kaery's mother drove away.

"You are *so* skipping class with me! There's this new laptop at the mall that I've gotta ghost-touch. One minute it's there, the next minute, poof!"

Tommy and Guy never really cared for school. The only reason they ever even showed up these days was because of their best friend, Blue. Most of the kids knew that Tommy and Guy were never serious and rarely said or did anything appropriate. Tommy was probably the smarter of the two hooligans, always coming up with ways to get something over on the next person or make a quick buck. Guy usually just went with the flow, being the "big guy" in the group, as some people called him. These two seemed to have a never-ending flow of alcohol and drugs, which seemed odd for two teenagers who never worked a day in their young lives, other than doing odd jobs for Tommy's crooked uncle, Ronaldo Medici, known to everyone as Uncle Ronny.

Blue had met Tommy and Guy during his freshman year. Now, in his senior year, he wondered how they all stayed alive, with all the partying they had done. They were like roaches that never die.

When his pals came up to surprise him, Blue already knew what they were trying to do, and swiftly intercepted their plan. Agilely, he sidestepped and watched the liquid splash in the spot where he had just been standing.

Tommy looked at Guy in disbelief, and then started laughing at how totally cool Blue was for dodging his prank. Tommy could hardly ever outsmart Blue, or catch him off guard, and this day was no different.

Still hungover, Blue walked past his friends toward the back of the school, where he saw the letterman's jacket of an all too familiar jock. Charity's ex-boyfriend was standing near the back door to the south hall, kissing some random girl. Blue rushed over to him in a blur, with Tommy and Guy right behind, because they were always up for a fight. His friends didn't know how he got across the parking lot so fast, nor did they care, as they gleefully anticipated the upcoming brawl.

Sitting in her room was a fairly typical event for Maia, who was also known for having nightmares. As a matter of fact, her dreams were so explicit and detailed that her parents sent her to therapy at the ripe age of seven. Not understanding why their daughter was having nightmares about blood and sacrifices, the religious family decided to keep all movies and TV shows away from her. Nevertheless, she continued to have strange dreams.

Maia had told them to her parents many times. The moment she woke up screaming, she knew she was out of the apocalyptic Incan city, where she was a male god who forced her people to perform Magickal rituals in pools of blood. The scene was so vivid that it didn't take Maia long to realize that these were memories of an actual past life. Although she begged her family not to believe she was crazy or possessed, every time she saw the heads rolling in her dreams and the blood flowing like warm red lava, she tried to persuade herself that those things were not real. But she knew they were.

Maia stood up and walked to the bathroom. She had already attempted to take her life many times, so her parents kept a strict, but loving, eye on her. They tried hard to understand her pain. The stuffed animals from her childhood still sat on her pillow as if they were monitoring every movement of the weary teenager. Maia looked at her stuffed audience, frowned, and went to start her bath. As she turned to wash her face at the sink, the mirror was not really her friend, although she was exotically beautiful.

In her past-life nightmare, she was a ferocious looking male with dark features and a foreboding presence. Sometimes she saw him looking back at her in the mirror. In this lifetime, she was a curvy female with fair skin and long, thick hair that she currently dyed blonde with black strips throughout. She stared at her body for a long time before finally looking back at the overrun bathwater. The tub looked like it was filled with blood, as if she were in her nightmare again.

Maia stepped back, terrified, knowing now that she must be hallucinating. To brace herself, she gripped the counter so firmly that she cut her delicate skin. Closing her eyes as if to wish the blood away, she stood still for a moment. When she opened her eyes, the bathwater was still pouring over the sides of the tub, but it was clear water again. Maia sighed in relief and slowly walked through the puddle at her feet to turn off the tap.

When she looked at her reflection in the tub, she didn't know what to expect. But then a drop of her own blood from her cut hand hit the water, and images instantly started to appear. First, she saw a group of children sitting around laughing with her, as if they had all known each other for ages. That caused tears to form in her eyes, for this was the first reflection in which she was truly happy. Her watery image was sitting in a group of people she had yet to meet, but they enjoyed her presence as much as she enjoyed theirs. She was not some horrible deity in this reflection, but simply a young woman in the near future.

There was a dark man in the background, who was monitoring the group with a calm expression. He had a serene smile on his face as he gazed directly at Maia. She suddenly felt more comfort from this scene than she had experienced from any book she had ever read or any memory she could recall. Her tears of joy turned into a full-on cry as her mother burst into the room, panicking as she saw Maia's blood on the floor.

Blue had sat in the principal's office many times before, so Charity wasn't surprised when she saw him there today. Except this time his fists were bloody, and he had a dazed expression on his face, as if he didn't know why he was sitting there, let alone who he was.

"Blue, are you okay? How could you do that to Johnny? Why are you looking like that? Answer me!"

Her words blended together because Blue didn't really remember much of what had happened. He just looked at his hands and saw the blood.

As Tommy and Guy swaggered into the lobby, laughing and cheering, Blue looked up to see their awed faces and forced himself to listen to what it was they were so excited about.

"Dude," Tommy said, "I don't know how you moved that fast, but one minute you were next to us in the parking lot, and the next minute you were making John Spankston's face look like hamburger meat!"

Guy chimed in, "His football buddies tried to help, but you must've kicked six of their asses before we even got over there! That chick he was hitting on ran screaming . . . ."

Guy's words trailed off when he realized that Blue's sister was dating the quarterback. Quickly trying to backtrack, he said, "I mean, the cheerleader was scared and—" He shut his mouth with a snap.

"Shut up, Big Guy, and shut up, Tommy," Charity said. "You idiots are such cases."

"That will be enough, Ms. Scarsdale!" a chilly female voice said from behind. "And you two get to class before I find somewhere for you to be!"

Charity looked shocked, since she was never called to the Principal's office, but she knew exactly whose menacing voice that was.

"Yes, Mrs. Hatcher," Charity answered respectfully as she shot her brother a glance.

Tommy smirked because he was used to Mrs. Hatcher's threats. "Nice outfit, Ms. Hatchet . . . , I mean, Hatcher."

Guy, not knowing what to say, added, "And *I* didn't beat 'em up today." He said this proudly, with a huge smile.

"Get out of my office!" the Principal shouted, obviously at the end of her patience.

This Monday was definitely not a good one. Blue sat through a lecture, more aware of the content than usual. He knew that Mrs. Hatcher was notorious for calling parents. He also knew that he would be in detention until graduation—if he even graduated at all. He got through the rest of the school day without much drama, catching a few glares from members of the football team, but no one was bold enough to bother him. He didn't, however, see the girl with the golden eyes.

After school, he purposely avoided his sister because seeing her would only remind him of the sermon he would be hearing later that night from his parents, so he drove around to clear his thoughts. When he pulled up to his house early that evening, he ran upstairs and locked the door behind him.

A little while later, Tommy and Guy were outside, texting him that they were drinking in Tommy's car down the street. Blue smiled and jumped out the window to hang out with his friends.

Maia sat wrapped in her mother's arms, staring blankly at the tub of water, thinking about the images she saw. She blocked out her mother's prayers to god, and didn't listen to her mother's fears of losing her. She was numb from sitting on the wet floor for who knows how long, and finally, gently tried to explain to her mom that she wasn't trying to commit suicide. Her mother didn't believe her at all. Maia could read her parents' expressions (and everyone else's) fairly easily.

"I'm not lying," she insisted.

In fact, she didn't even know how to lie, but she could always tell with uncanny accuracy if someone were lying to her. Her poetry had been confiscated by her parents many times to turn it in to psychiatrists and specialists to evaluate her. They had lied many times about taking it, before Maia told them bluntly, at dinner one night, that she knew they were being dishonest. Now her mother had that same expression on her face.

It was a simple pleasure Maia had these days, watching people squirm while she profiled them. As she walked out of the bathroom to change into something dry, her mother regained her composure and wiped away her tears.

"We've decided to send you away," her mother said with more control than she expected to have.

Now Maia understood the real reason why her mother had been crying in the bathroom. She knew that her mother was not only telling the truth, but actually believed that it was the best decision. Maia's prayers had been answered as she pretended to protest.

"How could you make a decision like that without my consent?"

Walking over to the window, she looked out at the sky and saw in the constellation of Gemini the man's smiling face—the one that had been reflected in the bathtub. Now she realized that she must have been in the bathroom for hours, since the day had passed her by.

Seeing her mother's tears welling up again, she walked over to her and said, "I understand, Mami. I'll get better."

At that moment, the doorbell rang.

"They're here for you," her mother said.

Maia walked to her closet. "I know. I'll be ready to go soon."

✳

Kaery hadn't done anything since she had woken up but think about how much she hated the first day at a new school, even though it was almost the end of her freshman year. She had way too many first days in her past. This year alone, her mother had already moved her to three different high schools all over the country. She had skipped the first half of the day, hanging out with her punk-rocker best friend, Ahlina, just waiting for the day to be over.

While Kaery was looking at the clock for the hundred and fifteenth time, the calculus teacher asked her, "Do I bore you? If I bore you, Kaery, then perhaps you'd like to go home instead?"

Without a moment of hesitation, Kaery answered the teacher with complete honesty: "Yes, you bore me. You bore *everyone . . .* , even your wife, I'm sure. I would much rather be skipping this class and shopping at the mall with my friend."

Not knowing how she could have been so rude, Kaery was too shocked at herself to apologize. The kids in the class gasped, then chuckled aloud as Kaery scrambled for her backpack and ran out of the room. The teacher was in complete and utter disbelief, but speechless.

Kaery walked down the hall, trying to make sense of how she could have been so vulgar to the nice teacher. She hadn't intended to be that blunt, but lately, she couldn't lie, no matter what she tried to say. As she rounded the corner, she saw the boy from the parking lot being lectured in the Principal's office. He was so handsome that she stopped in her tracks to stare at him. His blue eyes were so intense that she couldn't draw her gaze away. As he focused on what the Principal was saying to him, he subconsciously licked his lips, which made Kaery almost melt.

At that moment, an attractive Native American boy walked over to her to see what she was looking at.

"Wow, a grade A hottie!"

As he looked at Kaery, she somehow recognized his warm smile, even though this was the first time she had ever met him.

"I'm Scape," he said. "And, yes, I'm gay, so I'm not hitting on you."

Surprised by his honesty, she replied, "Nice to meet you, Scape. I was just looking at that gorgeous boy over there."

She put her hands over her mouth as she walked away from the embarrassing scene.

Scape giggled, looked back at Blue, sighed, and then followed Kaery. Instantly, they were the best of friends.

Maia was in control of her emotions as she walked downstairs with her pink and black bags already packed. She didn't know exactly why she was so confident in her decision to go with her parents' plan. She had always fought them tooth and nail on any of their other decisions, using reverse psychology and guilt against them until they broke down and either cried or walked away altogether.

Tonight was different, though. She was afraid of change, yet somehow felt that this was right. When she got to the bottom of the stairs, she saw an attractive, tall, dark man with long black hair pulled back neatly. His suit was impeccably cut and almost too perfect, but his energy was warm and inviting. Maia liked him right away, recognizing him from her visions in the bathtub and the sky.

As Maia stared into the stranger's eyes, he said to her, "Hello, Maia. My name is Gemini. We are speaking the language of Magick, so your parents will not hear or understand what we are saying. You know in your heart that what I am saying is true. You must decide whether to come with me or go with the priest from the church. If you choose to come with me, simply hug your parents and leave. If you wish to stay, then the priest will be here in a few minutes to take you to a facility. They are planning to exorcise a demon they believe possesses you, and I will be gone from your life."

Maia could see that her parents had not heard a word that Gemini had spoken. For many years, she had longed to talk with someone on her own frequency. From all the doctors, with all their combined knowledge, nothing compared to the tranquil and honest words of this stranger.

Expecting Maia to go off on a psychobabble rant, her parents relaxed as they saw their daughter shake the stranger's hand and stare into his eyes without saying a word. The relief on their faces was instantaneous as Maia turned to give them a final hug. Her parents looked at each other with disbelief. This was going much too smoothly for the daughter they had known, loved, and monitored for so many years.

As Maia left her home, she wanted to know everything this stranger had to offer her. She no longer allowed fears of the outside world to bother her.

How long have I been in that house, seeking their understanding?

Walking down the street with the stranger, she forgot the path back to her parents' home as the streetlights turned off in a rolling blackout.

Blue had been smoking and drinking with his friends in Tommy's car for hours, without paying any attention to the time, when he finally realized that maybe he should get home. His friends were passed out, so he didn't try to wake them. He simply walked back down the street, mentally preparing himself for the inevitable argument.

A pale man, smoking a cigarette next to a dark car, smiled at Blue as he walked past.

Blue couldn't help feeling uneasy, and almost stopped to say something to the older man, then thought better of it, and continued heading home. When he looked back, the man was gone. He shook his head, blaming it on all the alcohol he had been drinking.

As he approached the front door, he could hear his parents arguing inside, so he decided to go in through the upstairs window. It was easy enough to scale up the wall. He had done it dozens of times before.

Plopping down on his bed, he put his mp3 player's headset in his ears. He just didn't want to deal with his parents at that moment.

Suddenly, a sick feeling overwhelmed him. Then he heard a man's voice chanting. Unable to hear his music in the headset, he threw it across the room and rolled over the side of his bed. When he hit the floor, he swore he would never drink again. But his next thought was that the alcohol had nothing to do with what he was feeling. The chanting made his senses fly off in many directions. As he screamed out in pain, every electronic device in his room flickered, sizzled, and melted.

As he looked up, Charity was walking into his room, carrying a lockpick, and obviously annoyed.

"Are you okay, Blue?" she asked as she helped him up to the bed. "What are you doing in here? You look like hell . . . . No offense."

She looked around the room at the melted electronics, then back at her brother. His eyes were a brighter blue than usual, and his pupils were dilated.

"You've gotta stop hanging out with those losers," she said. "One day, they're gonna get you all killed. Haven't you ever heard, 'Say no to drugs'?"

Reaching into Blue's pocket, she pulled out his sunglasses.

"Here, put these on. You're already late for dinner. Mommy's been calling you for, like, thirty minutes." She started walking to the door, then paused. "Well, come on." She smiled cheerfully as she always did.

The chanting had stopped, but Blue was still breathing heavily. "I'll be right there."

When he finally trudged downstairs, he got to the dining room table and sat down with his sunglasses on, as if that were normal.

"Look at him," his father snarled. "Obviously drunk and stoned out of his mind. Got a call that he's a thug at school, too, and then he shows up looking like one! You always stick up for the low life. I'm just done with him and this whole damned house!"

As Blue's father shouted all this at his mom, he didn't care that Charity was crying.

Blue's mom, who was setting plates of food on the table, threw down a glass dish, breaking it into pieces.

"You and your bitter attitude are the thing that's destroying this family," she yelled, "not our son's friends. I've watched you try to break them down over and over until you have a daughter who's an overachiever, dating someone just like you, and a son who rebels for the sake of rebelling. You say *you're* done, but *I'm* the one that's done with *you*!"

Charity tried to clean up the broken glass.

"Can you two stop?!" she shrieked, her faced streaked with tears, and her fingers bloody from gripping the glass too hard.

The chanting was beginning again in Blue's head. He began screaming in pain as a giant migraine overtook his senses. His head felt as if it were being torn apart in a telepathic assault. His screams so alarmed his mother that she ran around the table to hug her child.

"That boy has definite problems with drugs and alcohol," his dad said, the scowl returning to his face. "He'll probably end up like your father!"

As Blue's mom glared at his father, all the appliances in the house started to explode. Blue's skin became icy cold, then sizzling hot to the touch. His mother immediately released her grip on him. The chanting in Blue's head was a man's voice that kept repeating the words *Release your power now!* Blue couldn't help roaring a war cry that sent shivers through everyone. Seconds later, a thunderous explosion disintegrated the house and everyone in it.

Everyone but Blue. He just sat in the middle of the crater, thinking about what had just happened. Scrambling to his feet in a panic he had never felt before, he had no idea what to do. As he ran through the streets completely naked, his mind was flooded with emotions. All around him, the streetlights were shutting down in a wave. Down the street, he saw something familiar. It was Tommy's car! As he approached, Tommy and Guy were both awake, sobering up from the explosion.

"Dude! Blue! What the fuck happened? Where are your clothes? Did you hear that bang?"

"Just shut up and drive!" Blue ordered, without answering his friend's questions. Looking back one last time, he saw the man in the black suit standing in the middle of the street, exposing his yellow teeth in a grotesque grin.

Chapter 2

YOUR LIFE

Being the most popular girl in school was only one of Sky's many perks. Her parents must have known that she would be as popular, beautiful, and talented as the open sky, because to onlookers that was exactly what she seemed to be. Sky usually started her day by going over the outfit that she had chosen the night before, and then making last-minute changes.

Her custom-made closet was the size of most master bedrooms, and the clothes in it were neatly folded or hung up, looking like stock in a department store. The flat screen at the entrance of the closet kept a log of everything within the confines of the amazing room. A state-of-the-art computer program linked to the closet allowed Sky to purchase unlimited amounts of clothing, most of which she had never worn.

She lived in one of the mansions on the upper west side, near the marina. Her father was the self-made trillionaire Samuel Bradford, CEO of Brain Technologies. Her mother was the heiress of a diamond empire that went back six generations. To the rest of the world, this only child was more than privileged, she was exalted.

Sky dressed in fashions that were slightly risqué. But because of her status, she set the trends not only for the other girls at school, but also for the local media. She rarely carried her own books, so she didn't even own a backpack. Her purse, however, was filled with luxury makeup and trinkets that were as futuristic as her closet, even though all she really used was her satellite-connected holographic cell phone, which her father had created especially for her.

Just before Sky made her regular morning call to her entourage, she took a deep breath. A moment later, her friends flocked to her side as she stepped out of her electric sports car. Since her crowd had all the most gorgeous girls in school in it, the clicking of stiletto heels preceded them as they walked up the stairs to the grand entrance of the school.

Sky strutted through the door with more confidence than the rest of her class combined. She was on top of the world, and proud of it.

Estar Rouge was not the most popular girl in school. As a matter of fact, there was nothing more she could wish for than to be Sky Bradford. Estar was tall and thin, and tended to hunch over to blend in with the other students without being stared at. Her low self-esteem was a quality she was reminded of every time she looked at Sky, who was obviously born to rule the world. And she had to look at Sky almost every day.

Estar tended to make friends with the school's outcasts, more for comfort than necessity. She had always wanted to be a popular cheerleader type with adoring boys and jealous girls, but she didn't have the coordination, the body, or the wardrobe. Estar would sit and dream that she was as beautiful as Sky. But she was pale, while Sky had a permanent golden tan. Estar covered her thin frame in marked down fashions that looked several sizes too big for her, while Sky had a swimsuit model body—long, lean, and lovely, clad in high fashion. These two ladies clearly had nothing in common, with the exception of good grades.

"Isn't it annoying how everyone falls at her feet?" Ahlina whispered to Estar as they stared at Sky, who was burning up the courtyard with her entourage. "I mean seriously," Ahlina continued, "she was probably conceived in a jar like those cartoon puff girls with their mad-scientist dad."

Estar tuned out Ahlina's jealous words, even though she knew that Ahlina was only trying to cheer her up.

"I don't think she's *that* bad," Kaery said to the two, surprising them as she sat down next to Ahlina, looking toward Sky. Ahlina opened her slanted eyes as wide as she could to give Kaery the "concerned friend" look. Kaery got the hint.

"You're just as pretty as she is, if not prettier, Star," Kaery said.

Ahlina's approving smile changed suddenly into confusion as Estar yelled at them, "No one's as pretty as her, so don't feed me that bull!"

Then Estar got up to leave, throwing her heavy backpack over her shoulder.

Kaery looked hurt as she grabbed her hand, saying, "You know I don't . . . can't lie. You *are* beautiful, Star."

Star was what her closest friends called her, and in the past year, when she was introduced to Kaery over the internet, she had come to realize that Kaery was the most honest person she had ever known, but she took no comfort in that truth at this moment. She was not on Sky's level socially, and she absolutely did not compare with her beauty. As she walked off in her uncomfortable hunch, the baggy clothes that were too big for her made her look even scrawnier than she really was.

Kaery watched her walk away, then turned back to Ahlina.

"Don't worry," Ahlina said. "Star's worshipped Sky ever since I can remember. I mean, we've known Sky most of her life, because her mother chose to let her come to a local school to keep her somewhat humble." Ahlina rolled her eyes as she said this. "I just don't know what's so special about her. I mean, yes, she's always flawless, and yes, she's always really nice, but there's something about her we're all missing."

Kaery looked over her shoulder at Sky, who walked right past Star without acknowledging her at all.

"Maybe you're right," she said.

✶

Loiza had to make his move. The intricate planning to get his nephew, Crux, away from this place was all he could think about. The dilemma was that they all belonged to one of the world's oldest and most powerful Gypsy families of thieves. The escaping part wasn't the hard part. The Petsha Family were masters of stealth, escape, and hiding their tracks, and Loiza Petsha had proved time and again that he was one of the best.

As night fell, he prepared himself mentally for what he was going to do. There was no other option but to betray his heritage and give his nephew a chance of a better life than his. There was no way he could allow his people to sacrifice the boy to appease one of the many gods they worshipped. It seemed wrong. This boy was special, and deep down Loiza knew that this was the right thing to do, even though it meant his own life would be forfeit once his people found out what he had done.

To his top-secret contact, he said over the phone: "I'll make the drop. You make sure he gets sanctuary."

With a bead of sweat rolling down his temple, Loiza hung up. There was no going back. The plan had to be fulfilled.

Like most Gypsy families, the Petshas were highly superstitious. The only things they weren't superstitious about were the Supernaturals they dealt with. The rest of the world simply couldn't understand. The Petshas were able to see things that seemed out of touch with reality. To even try to explain such things would be a breach of the oath they had taken with the Supernaturals long, long ago.

Loiza had been raised with a prophecy that went back to the beginning of the first Gypsy families:

A GOD WAS TO BE BORN AMONGST THE GYPSY PEOPLE.

Apparently, all the gypsies felt that Crux was this god. That sounded amazing, far-fetched and wonderful to anyone who didn't know the end of the prophecy:

IN ORDER TO SAVE THE WORLD, THE GOD IS TO BE SACRIFICED BEFORE HE IS A MAN.

This was the part Loiza didn't like. Doing his own bit of research over the years, and watching as his people tested the boy's abilities, he had realized one thing: Crux was a Mancer.

✳

Just as on every other morning, Sky enjoyed but hated her solitude as she went through a process of understanding and growing self-awareness. She had asked her mother to hire a yoga instructor so she could learn how to meditate, because lately it had become harder and harder for her to concentrate. But the yoga didn't help. She tried to give herself a routine, so that when she got around other people, she wouldn't seem so distracted.

Ever since she could remember, she had never been ill or cold. She never even felt uncomfortable unless other people were around her. On the other hand, she did get vertigo, as if she were seasick. Her mother wished desperately for her to get over this, so she sent her to a prestigious private school with "socially acceptable" students. She thought her daughter had a social anxiety disorder, and wanted nothing more than for Sky to at least appear to be normal.

Sky knew she didn't have social anxiety; that it was deeper than that. Although she had been born into a life of glamour and celebrity, she knew that she was different from everyone around her. She could hear the quietest of sounds, and when the weather didn't suit her, she would simply think of the perfect temperature, and it would be so. These were things she could not explain to her already concerned parents, so she kept them to herself. In their minds, she was the ideal daughter, and she wanted to keep it that way.

As she walked to her tennis class, she took a deep breath before walking out into the hallway full of whispering students. The sounds of their whispers were all too clear and much too loud. She had a hard time blocking them out, so with a smile on her face, she walked as elegantly as she could. Just as when she arrived at school in the morning, she breathed in and out and meditated for a moment.

There were certain people she felt an internal calm around, but her status and theirs were not on the same level, or even remotely close, so she sadly kept her distance from them. Instead, she was surrounded by the snobby aristocratic daughters of the local rich and famous. In reality, they had nothing in common with her, but to the public they seemed like sisters. These girls mostly hated each other and competed for simple things, like boys' affection and popularity. None of them came close to Sky's calm demeanor and shining smile. She had been queen of every dance since she started school, but all she really wanted was to have someone tell her that he truly understood what she was going through.

"I understand what you're going through, nephew," Loiza whispered into the frightened boy's ear. "You must trust me! This place is no longer safe for you."

He stopped his words abruptly, sensing that someone was near. Loiza had awakened Crux from his peaceful slumber and forced him to dress quickly. Crux hadn't known what was going on, but trusted his uncle implicitly. The timbre of his uncle's charismatic voice seemed to have an undertone of danger, which made Crux worry. The part that Crux didn't understand was why his uncle was using his infamous stealth skills within the Petsha camp. Crux had never witnessed these skills firsthand, so that was exciting, but he was also confused.

"Uncle, where are we going?" Crux whispered quietly, as he had been trained to do on stealth missions. He and his uncle even tapped each other's hands in a silent language that most Gypsy families spoke among themselves. Loiza tapped to be silent as they approached Crux's father's quarters. It was the most lavish of all the tents, with guards patrolling the perimeters. Loiza had himself trained most of these men, so he easily made it around them and scaled a tree to get a good view of the meeting inside. As he followed behind, Crux was amazed at his uncle's talents, although he still did not understand what was going on.

Loiza pointed to the window, signaling for Crux to listen closely. As the chill of the wind bit into his skin, Crux was uncomfortable with his bizarre situation, but did as he was told.

One of the diplomats, an esteemed trader in the Petsha family, was speaking.

"You know we have prolonged this ceremony, Besnik, for the respect we have for you and your wife. However, you also know as well as I do that the Mancer who is your son must be sacrificed to save the world . . . . Crux must die!"

Hearing this, Crux gasped, but his uncle, anticipating this, clasped his hand over his mouth. Tears ran down the boy's face and onto his uncle's calloused hand. Crux had known that he was a Mancer as far back as he could remember. No one in his family treated him any differently than the shape shifters known as Spiraar, or the blood-drinking Vampyl in their family.

This has to be a nightmare, he thought. *I must still be dreaming.*

It was all too terrifying for him to comprehend. So, still a child, he fainted.

Estar ran home after lunch, not caring that she was skipping the last few classes. Being at school had suddenly become too much.

"Why can't I be beautiful and famous like Sky?" she cried to herself. "I just want her life."

She went to her room to see the shrine she had built in Sky's honor, made of pictures she had taken and others she had found in magazines. She focused so hard on the images that her skin began to tingle. When she looked at herself in the mirror, she saw something that both frightened and intrigued her. Her hair was a brilliant red with spectacular blonde highlights. Her lips were glossy as cherries, and her eyes, which she had covered in glasses to hide them, intrigued her the most. Estar always hated that she had one eye sky blue and the other forest green. She wore plain nonprescription framed glasses and avoided people's gazes, so they couldn't see her eyes. Looking in the mirror again, she suddenly realized that her eyes were the most beautiful things she had ever seen. Taking off her glasses and baggy sweatshirt, she threw them on the floor.

"I am a star!" she whispered. "I am Star!"

Today was the first time Sky actually felt that she was completely in control of her unique talent. As she sashayed down the hall in her graceful stride, the whispers were somehow quiet, and she returned people's smiles. Then, all of a sudden, she felt the warmth from one of the outcast students. She knew this one was named Kaery, who had recently transferred from the east coast.

As Kaery reached into her locker, she didn't even see Sky. For that brief moment, Sky lost her concentration as a flood of sound and chaos entered her space. The whispers became thunderous; the simple hallway chatter exploded off the walls. Without a moment's warning, Sky lost control. Falling to her knees, she clasped her hands over her ears and began screaming, "Shut up!"

Every locker slammed shut, the hall went silent, and the confused students looked around at each other.

Kaery walked over to help Sky to her feet.

"Are you alright?"

Sky looked into the golden-hazel eyes of this girl she had tried to avoid. There was always that damned social status thing she had gotten from her mother.

"I'm fine," Sky said softly, trying to muster a smile as she looked around at the onlookers. "I'm fine." She smiled again, which seemed to wash away the concern of most of the crowd.

As Kaery took Sky's hand, she stared off into space, her eyes becoming even more golden than usual.

"You are a Mancer," she said in an otherworldly voice.

Not comprehending what Kaery was talking about, Sky pulled her hand away and charged down the hall. Looking back, she saw Kaery's still vacant expression turning vaguely her way. As the other students walked around Kaery, she stood still.

Sky kept walking. When she turned the corner into the girls' locker room, she put her back to the wall and sighed.

"What's a Mancer?" she whispered to herself.

Chapter 3

LATELY

One stupid odd job after another was all that Blue had to look forward to. Tommy and Guy dropped out of school when they no longer had any reason to go. Blue had been undercover with them ever since the accident. He never really bothered explaining to anyone what had happened that night, a year before. That whole time, he had been accepting suicide missions that Tommy's crooked Uncle Ronny had given him: drug deals, arms smuggling, prostitution rings, money laundering, stolen cars, human trafficking—you name it and this overweight slob, Uncle Ronny, was into it.

It's amazing this guy is still alive and hasn't been taken out by the competition, Blue thought to himself. He had watched as Uncle Ronny made one idiotic decision after another without caring for the consequences. "Oh, well. So long as he pays me, I guess I'm fine," Blue said to himself aloud.

Whenever Blue made decisions, he always heard the voices of his family in his head. They were always berating him, asking a series of questions without giving him time to consider: "What have you become? Why are you doing this to yourself? You know it was an accident! Please don't do this, Blue. Put the gun down and walk away!"

Blue tried to continue to clean his weapons as he felt the pain of his loss. No matter what he tried to do, he couldn't stop the voices. The only time they were shut out was when he was in the midst of danger. Somehow the voices only came to him when he was alone.

When Tommy walked into Blue's loft uninvited, Blue knew he was coming.

"Man, you were freaking off the digits last night when you beat the hell out of that Triad guy," Tommy said. "Uncle Ronny told me you saved a helluva load from being stolen by those assholes. You're already moving up pretty quick in the ranks, Blue."

Tommy plopped his feet on the table where Blue was cleaning his guns.

Blue stopped what he was doing and threw a cold look at his friend.

"Sorry, man," Tommy apologized as he lifted his boots off the table. "Oh, by the way, Uncle Ronny is pissed at the Triads and wants us to return the favor from last night."

As he stared down the barrel of a Tech 9, Blue barely looked interested. All of this was just going through the motions. He was bored with it all, but for some reason he was good at it. He may have been terrible at school, but this life was easy.

"What does your uncle need me to do?"

Tommy stood up, excited as he always was when danger was involved.

"Okay, so there's a boatload of money coming in on a shipment at the harbor. We're supposed to . . . , well, you know, take it." Tommy laughed at his own poor joke. "If we do a good job, then we'll be rewarded. And you know what that means . . . . VIP status, hoes, booze—"

"How much is he paying?" Blue cut in. "You know I don't care about the other stuff."

"Right. A lot more than usual. So, probably around fifty k."

Blue nodded.

"When's the drop?"

★

Crux watched as his uncle took out one patroller after another. Stealth wasn't the only thing his uncle was legendary for, because his assassination skills were topnotch. Crux didn't know how he had made it from the camp to whatever shipping dock this was. He guessed that he must have fainted. The patrollers weren't as talented as the Petshas. These were Asian henchmen with semiautomatic weapons and sunglasses at night. If Crux had to come up with a word for them, it would be *cheesy*.

Loiza signaled for Crux to use his abilities as two of the henchmen approached from the east. Crux had an uncanny aim. Because he could change probability, he could hit a target with a pebble from a hundred yards away without even looking at it. It wasn't how he threw the pebble that mattered. Crux could change the density and momentum of anything. So a simple pebble could come at the target like a bullet, with the weight of a train. This was one reason why Crux always had pebbles and coins in his little bag.

For a brief second, Crux stepped out of the shadows. It was already too late for both of the weapon-carrying goons, as pebbles knocked them out cold. Crux stepped back into the shadows, waiting for his uncle to signal him to another position. There was a ship approaching the docks.

Is this how he plans on me getting out of this place? I HATE boats.

Crux frowned, but he knew that he could not return to the camp that he had so recently called home. He was only twelve years old, but he had lived a life of mystery and crime since he could barely walk. He had seen dead bodies, but had never been in a situation where he had actually watched them die.

Loiza was carving his way to the ship, one henchman at a time.

Wait, there's another car arriving from the east of the docks, Crux thought to himself as he watched his uncle walk out of range of his whispers and into a position to see the car coming. Crux changed shadows without waiting for his uncle's signal.

From this new vantage point, he could see the whole shipyard. There was someone else waiting for Loiza—a woman lurking in the shadows. She had dark hair and a cat-suit that looked strictly government grade.

The approaching car looked familiar to Crux.

"This is a trap!" he gasped to himself.

It was another Gypsy family. The Shandor, a family known to have Vampyl among their ranks, were fast approaching.

What are THEY doing here?

Crux jumped down. As he hit the ground, he barely made a sound as he rolled over the way he had been trained to do. He crept silently from shadow to shadow, trying to get to his uncle's position to warn him. He had pebbles in his hand.

The car was now near the dock. Loiza heard it, but didn't know why a car would be coming here at this time of night—unless they knew about the shipment.

Has Surge-Overload betrayed me? Loiza wondered.

That was a possibility, but Loiza continued down to the ship. Something was definitely wrong. Loiza was in no position now to signal his rambunctious nephew. Hopefully, the boy would stay put, but Loiza knew better. He had to get Crux on the ship, one way or another.

When Loiza made a signal to the shadows, Crux understood, "Get on the ship, no matter what!"

Suddenly, Loiza darted toward the Shandor car.

Lately, nothing made any sense to Crux.

Maia had been sitting up for days at a time over the past few months with Gemini, learning about her inborn abilities. Gemini was kind and thorough, and spoke truthfully. He told her of things she was able to do in other lifetimes. Maia listened carefully, realizing that her visions were finally being recognized as actual events, not hallucinations. Lately, she had been getting used to the idea that she was a Supernatural, and the transition had been a lot easier for her to accept than even Gemini had expected. Maia had been a lot more receptive recently than she could ever remember being in her entire life.

Gemini was a tall, stoic figure with dark skin, and features that made him seem much more regal than his surroundings. He walked into Maia's room with a glide across the floor that made her wonder if she would ever be that graceful in her own entrances anywhere. His cool demeanor was part of the reason she trusted him. Maia had been able to profile people at an early age. She had a natural, easy, deep-seated feeling of trust for Gemini, even though she didn't know where it came from or why she should feel that way.

As his long charcoal coat flowed around him like a shadow, he prepared his mind for the daily lesson. Maia enjoyed these sessions more than anything. Gemini's voice was deep and borderline intimidating, but the tone set her soul at ease.

"Hello, Maia," he said, breaking the silence from across the room. "Today I'll go over information that we've touched on before in a little more depth. Please feel free to ask questions as we go along."

His smile made her wonder if that was what the teachers in public schools were like.

"You have been granted the abilities of Celestial creatures and beings," Gemini continued. "In the language of Magick, you are called a Celestiamancer. The ability to read the stars and the flaws of others are only two of the many abilities you possess. In the past, you were able to use the blood of living and dead beings alike to scry or open temporal portals. I will need your help to find some of the Mancers who may complement your abilities."

Maia nodded, then asked aloud, "Why do we need to find other Mancers to complement my abilities?"

Gemini was waiting for this question. "The key Mancers we find," he said, "are instrumental in saving the world from the peril it is headed toward."

"Right! Should have known . . . . Apocalypse."

As Gemini walked over to Maia, she instinctively sat up properly, remembering all the lessons from her parents on bad posture. She absolutely hated sitting up straight.

"Please make yourself comfortable," Gemini said. "The best way to gain control of your abilities is to lose the fear of them."

His words made Maia relax. She dropped her shoulders and went back to hugging her knees.

"So, what do you mean by 'lose the fear,' Gemini?" she asked.

Gemini stood still for a moment as if going into a trance, with his eyelids fluttering. When he opened his eyes, Maia could almost see her own reflection in the silver orbs.

She stood up from the chair she was sitting on, but when she looked around, Gemini and the whole room had vanished. Instead, she was in a forest, a very familiar forest. She almost felt sick. Maia hadn't seen this place since the night before she left her parents' home. She was now living the nightmare she had always dreaded, in full color and stereophonic sound. Maia walked through the forest, pushing her way to the pyramids—a path she knew so well.

Suddenly, she saw people, an exotic looking group, in a city filled with colors and patterns, all reflecting things they had seen or heard in the stars. Maia walked through the earthy streets, passing its many guards as if she were invisible. She was drawn instinctively to one place, her own chamber at the top of a pyramid. The realization of this made her shiver a little.

She walked up an ornate set of stairs, and then turned around to look at the city. All of the populace were now staring directly up at her. She almost stumbled backwards when she saw the vast audience, but kept her composure as she looked down into their eyes. They were true believers in her very essence. These were her followers. Some of the crowd were Supernaturals, but most were human. Maia was enthralled by their intelligent eyes and their trusting, yet anxious stares.

When she resumed walking up the steps to her chamber, she looked down at her own hands, expecting to see the calloused and dark rough fingers of the male form she had seen so many times in reflections within her nightmares. Instead, she was pleased to see her own painted pink and black nails and pale skin. As she climbed the last steps, her heart raced. She stopped herself, just shy of entering the chamber, reminding herself that this was only a requiem for a dream.

Maia somehow felt Gemini's presence, which put her more at ease. The music of drums, like a heartbeat, was rhythmically staining the very air behind her. She heard chanting of both male and female voices, mingled beautifully together. The choir gave Maia a feeling of power she had never felt before. She walked into the chamber with the music outside becoming more of a background sound. There were two figures standing inside, waiting for her. The male was interestingly handsome, with the long hair and smooth features of the natives. She recognized him at once, and the dagger he was holding, but she didn't remember his name.

The female was small in frame, and had bright green eyes and very light hair, unlike most of the natives. She held a chalice out toward Maia and began to speak: "This is going too far, Maia! I know you want to save the people, but taking them completely from the planet is probably beyond even our power, and is certainly against the Oath."

The male stood quietly, watching the two young women. The green-eyed one continued, though she seemed almost weary, as if she had tried to stop Maia dozens of times before.

"There is no need to spill more blood, as we already know the end of the world. The things we saw in the blood are destined to happen. There is nothing we can do about them."

Maia began to speak to the female in a voice that she recognized as her own, but the words flowed out as smoothly as if she had already said them: "Come with me to the star fountain. There I will remind you that we do contain the power to save our people, and so we shall!"

Maia walked past the two, whom she recognized as her Witchbreed sages, Ssiah and Scape. They followed close behind.

She passed through stone hallways that had been hand-carved and were glowing with the language of Magick. Words of prophecies and rituals surrounded her in a way that made her feel resolved and honorable in her intentions.

Standing in front of a stone altar, there was a young male with dark black hair and red eyes. The altar was just as ornate as Maia's own chamber, if not more so, decorated in jewels to mimic the countless constellations in the evening sky. The sunset made the altar glow, as if lit from within.

A young woman was lying on the altar, singing a song that filled the air as she stared straight upward into the sky. Maia heard her own voice become deeper, but she was so entranced by her own speech that she didn't bother to analyze it. She looked down the pyramid at the people, who were staring back up at her with their intense eyes, and singing their songs of praise.

Maia looked back at the altar and spoke: "As this human virgin does not understand what I am saying, because I speak the language of Magick, so shall the Soulstream grant my wish with that very Magick. I wish to save my people from this Veil of Ignorance that plagues the world and leaves my people defenseless in the war of future days. The blood has shown us the prophecies of the future peril of this world as we know it. You three . . . , Scape, Ssiah, and Ewm . . . , are my Witchbreed council, and shall grant my wish, for I am your Mancer."

She pointed at the two males and the young female as they looked back at her.

Ssiah began to speak, "But we are to respect human life, and these sacrifices—"

"Are for the greater good of the people, Ssiah," Ewm said to the green-eyed Ssiah. "We are here to serve Maia in his dominion, and if this is his wish, we cannot break the Oath."

They see me as a male!

The handsome Scape finally spoke: "Ewm speaks the truth, young Ssiah. We must comply with what Maia instructs. The stars have been read, and if he believes this is to be, then we are not to question him, but must make the sacrifice."

Scape's smile was intended to calm Ssiah, but her eyes filled with tears, and she felt alone. She did not miss that his glance was signaling her to stop her protest.

"Tonight," said Maia, "my people will be exalted and sent through the Soulstream to a world where they will be safe and powerful. That is their birthright! We shall start the ceremony, and the blood shall be their passageway. I am done with your questioning of my judgments. You will do as I say, Witchbreed, and do it now!"

The three figures bowed their heads as they prepared the rites for a spell that had never been done before in the entire history of the world.

Ssiah's tears stained the top of her hands as she drew with her fingertip the Enochian markings on the ground surrounding the altar. With every Aenjelhic rune she drew, the light reflected from the altar made it glow with starlight.

Ewm quietly said, "Scape, please pass me the dagger."

The tall handsome man reluctantly passed the dagger to the young male, keeping an eye on the Mancer, who was watching their every move.

Maia paid careful attention as Ewm carved runes into the very air above the young woman lying on the altar. The virgin's tears of joy flowed down her cheeks, but she never stopped singing her song as she stared faithfully into the night sky.

"Scape," Maia commanded, "it is your turn to call the elementals."

Scape stripped off his cloak, bathing his tattooed body in moonlight as the wind passed through him. His very skin transformed to the color of moonlight. The great silver orb gleamed brightly on the top of the pyramid as the people below continued their chanting, their voices blending with the rising winds over the land.

Maia stood before her people, reciting words of enlightenment and praise. As she stared up into the sky with tears streaking her face, she forced a temporal gate to open above her beloved city to take her people away. Happiness struck her almost as hard and fast as the pain in her back and through her chest. Falling to her knees, she watched her own blood flowing and splashing onto the runes of the altar as the dagger pierced her body.

As Maia's blood poured onto the Virgin, the young girl screamed and fainted.

"You were right, Maia," Ewm said to the fallen Mancer. "There must be a sacrifice for your crimes. And although this portal will take them away, it must be at your expense, not this innocent girl's."

As Scape pulled the dagger from Maia's back, Ssiah cried out and tried to come to the Mancer's aid, but was stopped by Ewm.

Scape spoke harshly to Maia for the first time: "You have exiled your own people to a world that is not their own. I hope you are happy, tyrant!"

He took Ssiah in his arms and held her close to his chest. Then he walked away with her into the air, his glowing skin still as beautiful as the moonlight reflecting off him. As he and Ssiah floated away, Ewm followed.

Maia turned to look at the cosmos one final time. The giant portal that seemed to take over most of the sky had been opened. She felt her life essence pouring out of her as her people were being sent by the hundreds through the brightly lit sky. The winds stirred around the pyramid as the failed Magick rocked its foundation, almost tearing it apart.

Falling onto her back, Maia smiled, knowing that although she had been betrayed, her people would be safe. Suddenly, the sky, usually a reflective pool of water to Maia, became unfamiliar as the stars changed places in the heavens.

Looking at her blood-soaked hands, she cried out in horror, "What have I done?!"

She sat up, trying not to scream as she looked around in a panic, holding her chest and gasping for breath. She was now in Gemini's lair.

"You see, Maia," he said, looking at her with a stern and disciplined face, "it is your turn to recognize that you have made choices that have resulted in the world you so tried to escape. It is also your turn to join the battle and help to atone for the crimes that were committed against the Oath."

Maia's tears and sobs were shaking her very existence, as she finally understood the meaning of her nightmares.

"I am paying for choices I made in another lifetime," she whispered.

Now she understood what she had to do. She must help Gemini destroy OZONE.

Chapter 4

CHANGES

Carry me away! was all Sky could think of as she felt the breeze touching her body while she lay on a lawn chair, tanning her lovely brown skin. Her large sunglasses blocked the sun from her eyes as she looked up into the clouds. It was such a beautiful day; nothing could ruin this moment.

She absentmindedly reached for her pink lemonade that was on the mini table next to her.

What?! Where's my drink?

She looked in the direction where she expected it to be.

This is impossible! How did I get up here?

The guesthouse was thirty feet below.

What's wrong with me? How can I possibly be flying?

Sky looked down at the lawn chair she had been lying on a few moments before. As soon as she saw it, she found herself lying on it back on the ground, right next to the mini table with her drink.

She quickly jumped up onto the grass, stared at the lawn chair, and then gazed back up at the clouds.

What the fuck?!

Recently, she had been hearing things from a little farther away, and seeing things in all directions at once. And now she had just been flying!

She had reached the point where she wanted to talk to her parents about everything.

"Sky! Your phone's ringing," her mother called from the house in her elegant West African accent.

Sky was startled by the sudden sound of a voice.

"That godforsaken phone your father made for you," her mother continued as she came outside, "has been ringing uncontrollably. I'm ready to toss it into the pool, even though I know its waterproof. . . . Are you okay? You look like you've seen a ghost!"

For the first time in her life, Sky actually didn't know what to say.

"Where . . . is my phone?"

She feigned a smile.

Her mother held it out, looking at her with something bordering on suspicion.

Sky grabbed it. As she did, it started ringing again.

I don't want mother to hear this!

When Sky touched the screen, a digital voice, neither male nor female, spoke: "You are no longer safe. This is a warning, Sky. They know what you are."

Sky's heart stopped beating for a second.

"Who are you?!" she screamed.

"Who I am is not important. They are coming to kill you, and you need my help."

Sky touched the screen again to end the call.

Her mother, looking utterly confused, stared at her as if she were deaf.

"It must have been a wrong number," Sky lied.

Her mother continued to look at her as if she were trying to read her lips.

"Mom, are you okay?"

Her mother shook her head, as if it were astonishing to be able to hear again.

"The strangest thing is, I couldn't hear a word you said."

"Mom, you need to go see Doctor Hills, and get that checked out right away."

Her mother nodded, and went into the house to call her physician.

Sky sighed, looking at her phone as if it were a dreadful thing.

Suddenly, the ring tone began to chime again.

Sky stood still, staring closely at the phone. Even though she knew she was alone, she looked around to see if someone were watching her. Then she thought about her father's security system.

She ran into the house and upstairs as fast as she could to the one place her father had no cameras, the sanctuary of her own room. Once again, she touched the screen of the phone, and watched as a hologram of a digital face, seemingly made of sand, said: "You know you're a Mancer, and so do they. It is time for you to leave."

Sky thought this was a prank, even though she knew otherwise deep down. And there was that word again.

"What is a Mancer?" she asked in a whisper.

The eerie digital voice said, without hesitation, as if it knew Sky: "A Mancer is a threat to the very fibers of our current society. You are able to do things others only wish they could. The secret society known as OZONE has no need for our kind, and so they eliminate the threats."

Sky yelled, "I don't believe you!" and hurled the phone across the room, where it landed by the closet. As she sat on her bed, a tear rolled down her caramel skin.

✸

Surge-Overload stopped touching her laptop. This machine was ten times more powerful than anything that Brain Tech had released on the retail shelves. Since before Surge-Overload could walk, she had been savvy about electronics. Her rocket scientist father was pleased that his genes had reigned supreme in the battle with those of his beautiful wife. The couple had tried to send Cindy to many different schools, but she had tested so highly that they decided she needed special programs of her own. She went to space camps and think tanks with her father. But something happened on Cindy's tenth birthday when she brought her laptop to the government building where her father worked. When she came home, she said that she didn't want to go to space camp anymore, or even to continue attending her own school.

Her father told her that this was her choice. Over the weeks that followed, Cindy wanted to wear gothic makeup and dye her hair multiple colors.

"Reynolds," Cindy's mother reasoned, "let her express herself and be as eclectic as she wants."

"Maybe you're right, Lisa. Let's hope it's just a phase."

Cindy stopped wearing her mother's favorite sun dresses and feminine clothing, preferring pastel camouflage and dark makeup. She also began to spend a lot of time alone in her room, building computers and never leaving her laptop farther away than an arm's reach. Cindy thought the world of her parents, even though she didn't identify with "Cindy" anymore. Her online persona was Surge-Overload, the anonymous cybergod.

She was able to do things online with just a mere thought, and fly through the ether as easily as most people sleep. Not being held back by any firewall or program that anyone could invent, she had hacked her way into virtually every government database in the world. During her hacking, which actually had begun simply for mere entertainment and kudos from her online fans, she came across files that were disturbing, to say the least. All of them belonged to OZONE.

The more Surge-Overload looked, the more she discovered that OZONE wasn't just a myth, but the most powerful secret society in the world. It made the other societies look like high school clubs. This was her most intriguing hack yet. Staying up for nights in a row, looking for everything she could find on OZONE, Surge finally came across horrible files of assassinations. These quickly became her obsession.

The thing about the murders that made no sense was that they were worldwide and went back for centuries, but didn't seem to have any connection between them. But Surge learned from these files that she was a Supernatural, like many others. But more than that, she was a Mancer. OZONE had been hunting Supernaturals since history books had been written, and that realization started Surge's personal quest against them.

She intercepted many of their assassinations by warning the targeted ones, arranging to give them sanctuary, along with new identities, or taking them out of the system altogether. Today, she tried to save three more confirmed marks on the assassination lists, including the infamous role model, party girl, and daughter of Brain Tech's CEO. Her father had links to OZONE, whether he knew it or not. One thing was for sure: his research had been funded by corporations secretly owned by OZONE, so he was being watched by many eyes. Surge-Overload was going for the ultimate hack—trying to find OZONE's list of assassins and get rid of them once and for all.

Change of plan . . . . They must kill EACH OTHER.

Star looked at herself in the mirror again, as she had for countless times today. Sticking her butt out and her chest up, she practiced her Sky Walk until her feet hurt. For a week now, she had skipped school, calling in sick by pretending to be her mother. All she had to do was think it, and her mother's exact voice flowed from her mouth.

This talent unnerved her at first, but then she began to love it, along with her other new ability to change her appearance. Star was a curvy bombshell, with flawless skin and radiant red hair with blonde highlights. But no matter how hard she tried, she couldn't change her unusual eye colors. Nevertheless, she had to admit to herself that they were absolutely breathtaking. The green one was a deep forest green, which made the blue one look icily exotic. Star wanted to show herself off to the world, and she was ready to do it tonight.

The first thing she did was march into her closet and throw out everything she owned.

I want a whole new life . . . , which means Estar Rouge must DIE *to the public.*

She knew this would hurt her mother, but she could never go back to being *that* girl. In Star's mind, the best way to be rid of her old life was to stage her own death. But before she did that, she wanted to have a little fun. Using Magick, she created a dress that revealed her long legs and shapely silhouette perfectly. This was going to be her outfit to the mall.

When Star arrived at La Galleria, she pushed opened the doors, and immediately felt the rush of wind. She loved how that made her hair spin and twirl around her face. As she walked past the shops, she kept the hair-breeze blowing—but only around herself.

The shoppers froze in awe of her. This was more attention than Star had ever received before.

This must be what it feels like to be Sky.

Although she was holding her head up high, she was nervous underneath. It took a special effort not to relapse into her usual slump. As she walked into the high-fashion boutiques, she gave no one a second glance. Money was no problem. She would simply pick up a business card from the counter, give it a kiss, and it would turn into cash. Pretty soon, she was walking out of the stores with bag after bag of beautiful clothing.

While she was strutting toward an elegant shoe store, a rugged looking young man started walking toward her. Star pretended not to notice him.

"Hey, Red!" Tommy said with a sly look on his face. "How are ya, babe? And why don't I know you?"

"That's not my name," Star said, as she kept walking. When she started to turn the next corner, she heard familiar voices. It was Kaery and Ahlina, skipping class.

"I swear," Ahlina said to Kaery as they walked out of a store, "I want all of those new Brain Tech laptops rolled up like Sushi. They're just that yummy!" She licked her lips.

"You already stole, like, three of 'em," Kaery said with a smile. "And refurbished them with those hacker upgrades from your online friend, Surge-what's-his-name. Why aren't you happy with the ones you have? I still don't know exactly what you did to them, but they seem to play your online games pretty nicely."

I can't let them see me like this, Star thought.

Spinning around to avoid them, she ran right into Tommy, dropping some of her bags.

"Yeah, Red, I *thought* you wanted me!" Tommy said with a leer.

"Um, yeah, sure. Do you have a car?"

Star said this in a new "bitch-girl" voice.

When Tommy pulled keys out of his pocket, Star grabbed his arm to walk out of the mall.

"Hey, you're pretty strong for a girl."

"Shut up, please."

Pulling her blanket over her knees, Sky sat up in bed. The phone was still on the floor where she had thrown it. She was too upset to think about anything beside what the prank caller had said to her.

Even if I traced that call, I'd probably never find that creep.

For the first time in her life, she was completely frantic.

The whispers at school almost made my ears bleed. And what's up with my silencing people as if I had a mute button? Poor mom probably even thinks she was deaf for a second. And just before that, I was flying through the fucking air!

These changes were not cute by anyone's standards, and Sky wanted them to stop.

I'm gonna tell dad tonight, that's for sure.

Suddenly there were footsteps out in the yard.

Who's outside? Dad's at work, mom's at Doctor Hills, and the gardeners have all gone home.

She could clearly hear someone walking on the grass, even though she was upstairs with her window closed.

Looking through the window, she admired the gorgeous hills of California. But then she saw a beautiful woman directly below, looking up at her.

Sky's phone began to ring behind her, but somehow she could see it even though she was still looking down at the woman.

"What's going on?" Sky said aloud, terrified.

The woman was staring up so intently that Sky had the feeling this stranger wanted to kill her.

Sky thought of reaching for her phone, but found it already in her hand without lifting a finger.

"Who *is* this?!" Sky yelled into the phone.

"It's dad, Sky. Is everything alright? Your mother seemed worried."

She could see his 3-D hologram on her phone screen.

"Hi, daddums. I just got a prank call is all."

Despite her attempt to sound calm, Sky was shivering and almost dropped her phone.

"What's wrong, Bunny? And why are you wearing a bathing suit at night?"

Stealing a look out the window, Sky saw that the woman was gone.

"It's nothing, daddy. I'm just . . . , I mean . . . , I was just, you know, sunbathing."

Mr. Bradford looked at his daughter fondly. "It's sunset, little girl. You may be capable of many things, Bunny, but even *you* can't bring the sun out for your own pleasure."

He began to laugh in his jovial way that made Sky automatically cheer up. She smiled at the hologram as if she were actually standing in front of her father. Then she peeked one last time to see if the stranger were anywhere in sight.

No one's out there.

"When are you coming home, daddums?"

"As soon as my work here is done, Bunny. Your mother called me from Doctor Hills' office. Make her take it easy when she gets home."

Sky smiled, but then suddenly felt she had to tell her father everything. Of all the people in the world, he was the most understanding.

"Daddy, I have something to tell you."

As she reached for her robe, her father's voice began to break up.

"Bun . . . , what's hap . . . ? . . . hear you."

Sky saw her father's face scramble. Then a digital, genderless face of swirling sand replaced his image.

"You didn't listen to me earlier," said the face, "but now you have no choice. The agents will be there soon to take you away. This is your last chance for sanctuary. I am Surge-Overload, and I mean you no harm. I am trying to help you."

Sky jumped at the loud shatter of her bedroom window, accidentally dropping her phone back on the floor. As she turned to see what had caused the crash, there was the beautiful woman, kneeling in the shards of glass! She was wearing a cat-suit that looked like something from Brain Tech's labs because it melded flawlessly with her body. She had chocolate-colored hair with raspberry highlights, and would have been ravishingly beautiful if she hadn't been carrying a machete. She rose from the glass and walked toward Sky.

"Who are you, and what do you want?" Sky yelled.

The woman, who was almost as tall as Sky, continued walking toward her.

Trying to keep some distance between them, Sky backed up into a wall.

The woman finally spoke—in a cold, regal voice that reminded Sky of her mother on a bad day: "You're the Mancer I'm here for, and you'll be coming with me!"

Sky thought of running toward the door, but before she could blink, the woman was in front of her.

She moves impossibly fast!

Sky was shocked.

"I'm no such thing!" she protested. "And I'm not going *anywhere* with you! My father will have you arrested if you lay a finger on me, so you might want to get out of here, because the police have already been—"

Her sentence was cut off as the woman darted toward her with the machete aimed at her throat.

Sky moved back, matching the speed of the assassin. Her focus was so sharp that she could hear the woman's breath. Another attack, this one meant to slice and disembowel her, missed its target as Sky backflipped out of the way, landing on the wall behind her and sticking to it like an insect.

The woman stopped attacking.

"And you say you're not a Mancer?"

Sky stared down at the woman, and only then realized that she was high up on the wall above her bed. As soon as she looked down, she fell to the soft thousand counts Egyptian cotton sheets.

The woman spun around, away from Sky.

She must have heard the footsteps in the hallway.

A Soldier burst through the door, complete with high-tech goggles and Brain Tech weapons. Sky was relieved that the police had arrived.

Dad's state-of-the-art alarm system must have been triggered when this bitch was walking around outside.

But Sky's smile was short-lived. As she was about to warn the Soldier of the assassin behind him, he aimed his large gun straight at Sky.

From behind the shattered door, and out of the Soldier's sight, the mysterious woman grabbed the gun and, with one squeeze, shattered it to pieces, along with the Soldier's reinforced gloved hands. He didn't have time to scream in pain as she kicked him in the face and buried her knife in his throat, all in one swift motion.

"We have to go! Now!" the woman yelled at Sky. "They're here to kill you!"

Sky couldn't even scream. Not knowing what to do, she stared in horror at the dead Soldier. She had never seen a dead body before.

"Grab some clothes now," the woman commanded, "and make it quick! They're here, and that's not good."

Sky ran into her closet, locked the door, and dialed her father's number on her touchscreen computer inside.

The digital face intercepted her call.

"You are making a mistake. The woman is here to save you. Go with her now, or the OZONE agents will destroy you and make it look like an accident or robbery."

The door suddenly opened, with the woman standing there.

Sky took some clothes off their hangers, and then pretended to fall to the floor so she could grab her phone.

The woman hauled her to her feet and pushed her over to the window.

"Jump!" she ordered.

"What? We're on the second floor. You may be suicidal, but—"

The woman unceremoniously tossed her out the window. As Sky saw the grass below, she thought, *I don't want to die!*

And then she landed softly on the ground.

When she opened her eyes, the woman was jumping down effortlessly from the window. Then she clutched Sky's arm and ushered her into the darkness of the trees.

"Be quiet!"

For a few long seconds in the dark, Sky and this strange, surprisingly feminine woman in her armored cat-suit stood totally still. Then Sky saw her mother walk into the house. Without warning, a man in dark gray armor with an *O* on his helmet rushed through the kitchen and tackled Sky's mother to the floor. As Sky heard her mother screaming, she could feel her heart racing and the wind beginning to blow in strong gusts around her. The only thing that stopped her from running to help her mother was the powerful grip on her arm.

"She will be arrested and profiled," the woman said with total certainty. "We have to move out."

Her grip on Sky was relentless.

She's stronger than any guys I've ever dated.

Sky watched helplessly as the Soldier handcuffed her mother. She had no choice but to escape the Soldiers that she knew were there for her.

Surge-Overload closed her laptop and sighed to herself. "That was way too close." She took a long swallow of the energy drink on her nightstand, and wiped a bead of sweat from her brow. "Why do some of them make my life so difficult?" Surge stopped talking to herself as her mother walked into the room.

"Honey, you are scaring your father by being up here all the time. He feels you need to go out and do things with the rest of the kids your age. There are those cute boys down the street."

Surge looked up at her mother as if she were crazy. "Mom, I'm fourteen. Shouldn't you be giving me the opposite lecture, like normal parents?"

Surge's mom tried to smile, but only started to cry. This was the first time in Surge's life that she had witnessed her mother cry. Her mother was rarely sad, so Surge knew that she was breaking her mother's heart.

"Okay, mom, I'll do whatever you want. Just stop crying, please."

Her mother's face lit up as she walked over to hug Surge. "Cindy, I'm not trying to change you, but I would like to see you out and about more. I have some nice camps you can go to. It'll be just like old times, remember?"

Surge only looked away as her mother hugged her lovingly.

"Yes, I remember."

Surge tried to sound cheerful, but failed. Her mother didn't even notice, but had stopped hugging her.

"Well, you'll love them, and I have them all planned out."

She walked out of the room, leaving Surge to shake her head as she thought about how her mother would tell her father the "good" news.

Surge sighed. Then her eyes widened.

"The shipyard!"

Chapter 5

CHASE ME

Loiza was dead. Crux wasn't sure of many things, but he saw his uncle die with his own eyes. He tried to think hard through misty eyes what his uncle would do in a situation like this.

Run for my life! Use all the training I've ever received.

Crux could barely walk straight after all the nausea and the pain from fighting the Shandor. That was the part that Crux didn't understand, but he came across two large shipping crates he could hide in.

Fairy, Possum, Snake, and Crow,
Catch a coyote by his toe,
If he hollers let him go.
My tarot told me to pick the best one over here.

Crux said the nursery rhyme out loud at times when he needed to make a choice. At the last word, he pointed to his random decision—a green crate. He picked the lock to wait inside.

This ship is my only way out of this mess.

Ever since Crux had been a small boy, he was reminded by his enchanted and "proud to be exiled from the world" family that he was special. The Gypsies were unlike other families who inhabited the world. They embraced charm and superstition as guidelines and a way of life. They ran with Supernaturals much more frequently than normal people did. Supernaturals were rare, and for the most part feared, but a lot of Gypsies were known for adopting them into their ranks as if they had been born there. Crux was actually one of the unique Supernaturals who were born into the order of thieves known as the Petsha. His mother was an expert herbalist and card handler, while his father was the king of his small mercenary family. Although the Petshas were a small band, they treated their cousins with respect and honor—within the Gypsy codes, of course.

The time had gone by so fast that Crux rocked back and forth on this ship, recalling the events from earlier that strange night at the docks. He had never witnessed his family fight another Gypsy until that night, and it disturbed him because it meant the prophecies his father and the circle had talked about must be true.

The Gypsy families must have a bounty on my head by now. I'll never be safe.

The bleeding wound he was holding on his ribs was proof of that.

Star sat in the passenger seat of Tommy's loud muscle car with her long legs crossed. He could barely drive without staring at them. Wanting to get as far from the mall as possible, she constantly reminded him to keep his eyes on the road. When they arrived at the chop shop, all she could do was sigh. A few dogs barked as she got out, as if they were going to tear their own flesh to free themselves from their chains.

Tommy got out of the car and tried to quiet them, but to no avail.

"Sorry, Red, they smell fresh meat," Tommy said, licking his lips as he looked Star up and down.

She couldn't do anything but purse her lips.

He's a twenty-year-old dropout. With manners like that, he's only had sex when he pays for it.

She rolled her eyes and walked past Tommy toward the dogs.

He tried to stop her with warning gestures, but as soon as she got within reach of the dogs, they stopped growling. Star just stood staring at them, and then walked her six-foot frame past them into the chop shop as if they were statues.

Tommy looked in disbelief at his guard dogs, while they cowered like puppies. Then he laughed aloud. "You see a nice piece of ass, and that's all it takes for you to submit?"

He shook his head in disbelief, and ran in after Star.

As she looked around the shop, she saw someone familiar, but couldn't quite place him. He had black hair and bright blue eyes. His expression was cold and uncaring.

Is he even going to look at me?

He was methodically cleaning some weapons on a metal table.

Tommy put his hand on Star's lower back. She had to admit that she liked the attention, but when she looked around at him, and down toward his hand, he quickly removed it, and started small talk.

"So, yeah, this is the hangout where we do our thing."

Star looked unimpressed. "What exactly is your 'thing'?" she asked mockingly.

She was definitely not going to sit on anything in *this* dusty place, but she had to admit there was something intriguing and exciting about these dangerous older guys. The smell of oil and rust was overshadowed by the smell of opportunity in the air. These were the guys who were going to help her stage her own death, even if she had to grin and bear the shady interior and Tommy's cheap cologne.

Star made a fan across her nose with her palm as Tommy moved in to kiss her. He instinctively checked his breath with his hand.

She walked toward the rusty stairs of the loft, only to be grabbed by Blue.

"That's *my* area," he growled, "and I don't appreciate company."

"Fine!" Star retorted, yanking her arm out of his grasp, and looking down to see if any grease or oil had gotten on her skin. She didn't know how Blue had moved across the warehouse that fast without her hearing or seeing him, but he was starting to annoy her.

"We have business, Tommy. Give her a ride home."

Tommy watched the sparks between these two almost light up the room.

"I'm not going anywhere," Star said defiantly, staring into Blue's eyes.

"I mean, she could stay with me . . . , right, Blue? She won't harm anyone."

Tommy knew the answer as he asked this, squinting as the last words left his mouth.

Star was thinking to herself, while tapping her six-inch stilettos.

That name, Blue. The boy Kaery was obsessed about a year ago! He's kind of cute in a tortured reject sort of way. So far, he doesn't recognize me. Good!

✶

Loiza had definitely recognized the car as Shandor property. The Gypsy family was known for their cursed Vampyl relatives.

I know why they're here. But how they know I'm trying to send my nephew away, I have no idea. One thing's for sure . . . . Surge-Overload had nothing to do with this. The Shandor must have been watching the Petsha camp.

The Shandor waited to make their move until Loiza and Crux were a good distance away. Loiza knew these Vampyl were very capable assassins. As skilled as himself, if not better. He would have to make a stand to save Crux if they were here for the reasons he assumed.

The Shandor's black car, with tinted windows that were as dark as the car itself, drove up and stopped abruptly after spotting Loiza, who purposefully walked out into the light. All four doors opened at once, and out came five dark-clothed figures.

Crux could see them from his vantage point, and waited for his uncle's move. He knew he would have to back up his uncle, if worse came to worst. That seemed inevitable, so Crux reached into his small pouches and grabbed a handful of marbles and small knickknacks, prepared to toss them like missiles at the Vampyl if they tried anything.

Loiza knew his nephew was watching him, and he also felt the presence of the stranger up on the docks behind him.

If she hasn't made her move yet, then she's not here to kill me.

A man with looks that could have been on a billboard in New York gracefully walked toward Loiza, keeping a reasonable distance away. As the others stood near the car, he began to speak.

"Loiza Petsha, what have I done to deserve such an audience? From the smell of fresh blood in the air, you've killed my entire shipping crew."

Loiza didn't speak, just kept eyeballing the Vampyl near the car.

"No worries, Loiza, they are not here to kill you, or you would be dead by now."

The man's voice was dripping with seduction, as if he were using his hunting voice on a senseless mortal. Loiza knew the Vampyl were predators. Their curse made them even more beautiful than they were in their mortal lives, and everything about them was meant to seduce and lure in victims.

Loiza broke his silence: "Chass, as one of the five families, I just want safe passage."

The beautiful man tilted his head slightly, then his icy blue eyes wrinkled as he began to laugh uncontrollably, losing his composure. The others behind him began laughing as well.

Loiza knew that Chass was one of the most infamous Vampyl murderers in all of the Shandor family. He was surrounded by mystery, like most of the ancients, but he tended to have a diplomatic approach to whatever he desired.

Chass stopped laughing. "You know as well as I do that I can't offer that." His face became more rigid as he turned to signal the other Shandor in their quiet Gypsy language.

Loiza did not miss the kill-on-command signal.

"I'll get right to the point, Loiza," Chass said, "because right now I am going against two things. One, you have leverage. And two, you have the sunrise on your side."

The other Vampyl seemed to shuffle their feet uneasily at the sound of the word *sunrise*.

Loiza noticed that two of the Shandor were not Vampyl, but he had been hoping to keep this little game going a little longer, so the Vampyl wouldn't remember the sunrise.

"About that leverage," Chass said, almost spitting out the words. "Where is the boy, Loiza, so you can lose your life with dignity?"

The time for diplomacy had passed, and Loiza knew it. He placed his hand behind his back to send a message that only Crux could see: "I love you, Crux. And this is for you. Get on the ship, no matter what happens to me."

Loiza reached down to his hidden pouch in the back of his jacket to pull out a blade. He knew they were faster than he was, but he had a serious purpose and a completely desperate determination.

As he dropped the dagger on the ground, Crux held his breath. It was suicidal to fight a Vampyl at night, but Loiza knew he had to keep his thoughts clear. Chass was known for his telepathy, among his other skills. But Chass didn't have time to warn the other Vampyl, as Loiza kicked the blade in the air and threw silver daggers with an accuracy only the Petsha masters could obtain, piercing two of the Shandor through the heart.

Chass dove out of the way with Vampyl shadow speed. Two of the Vampyl jumped away at the silver onslaught that was coming at them with deadly accuracy. One of them made her way to the side of the car and charged at Loiza. Crux barely saw her as she connected to Loiza's face with a punch that knocked him off his feet.

As Loiza twirled in the air, he connected a kick to her face that cracked the hard bones of her Vampyl body. When he landed on the ground, he reached into another pouch to throw a glass vial at the man charging him. The acid burned through the Vampyl's eyes.

Chass sat on the car, watching the fight with a smile on his face. With a lightning fast sweep kick, the woman tripped Loiza, then kicked him in the ribs, cracking a couple of them as he rolled across the ground.

The male with the burned face smiled terribly through a bloody grimace as he picked Loiza up and threw him against a crate.

Crux couldn't take any more. As he was about to throw his marbles, the strange woman who was perched above him jumped down and looked right at him, shaking her head and signaling him to stay put. Then she ran across the darkness with a speed that Crux recognized as Supernatural, even though she was wearing a black military armored cat-suit that was much too tight.

The female Shandor didn't see the attack coming. The armored woman jumpkicked the back of the Shandor's head, sending her flying toward Chass and crashing into the dashboard of the car. As she landed, Loiza looked up at her through the blood in his eyes.

Chass stood up, perturbed.

"I don't have time for you, Juno. And I don't have time for this."

He grabbed Loiza by the throat so fast that Juno had no time to react. As he snapped his fingers, a dozen more Vampyl leaped out of the shadows.

"Damn! Surge-Overload was right," Juno said under her breath.

Surge-Overload sat in her bedroom with her laptop connected to the ether, swimming through the digital energy at the speed of information, monitoring the cameras of the entire European shipyard.

I must have missed something. I never gave orders to kill the Triad scattered all over the docks . . . . But they're better off dead anyway.

She saw Juno in position, but it wasn't Juno who killed the guards. Someone else had done that. The Triad were known for human trafficking, as well as drugs and money laundering from sources that were hard to track.

Scanning the perimeter, Surge saw the unmarked and unregistered vehicle arrive.

"Surge-Overload to Juno . . . , come in!"

Juno pressed the secret micro-headset. "I'm in position."

"Where is the Mancer?" Surge asked in her anonymous digital voice.

"He's behind me in the shadows at a safe distance from his uncle. We have company, though."

Surge sent a mini-electromagnetic pulse that stopped the car from moving. Then she scanned the shipping yard with the cameras. But she couldn't get a lock on the boy, so she changed her vantage point to satellite view. The shipping yard was dark, so detection was difficult, but she could pick up the movement of multiple people in the shadows.

"Judging by their movement patterns," she said to Juno, "Vampyl are waiting in the shadows and slowly surrounding the shipyard. I'll cover you, but I need tracking rounds on all targets."

Surge switched to thermal view until she located Crux.

"Over and out," Juno said to Surge as she jumped down to run to Loiza's assistance.

Surge traveled through confidential government files, simultaneously gaining access to and overriding military motion-detecting impulse cannons, and electronically setting the Vampyl as targets.

"This is boring!" Star stated flatly, as she sat in the back seat of Blue's new car while they watched the shipyard. "What are we doing here?"

But rather than answering, Blue got out of the car, reached back to take his keys out of the ignition, and stalked off in the direction of the Marina.

Tommy turned to the back seat and muttered, "I think he's mad now."

"Does it look like I care?" Star said. She was enjoying the sunset through the windshield. "You never really explained what we're doing here, Tony."

"Tommy! My name's Tommy. And we're waiting for a shipment, is all."

Star crossed her arms and glared at Tommy, totally unamused.

He looked hungrily down at her legs for a long time, licked his lips, and said, "I know what we can do out here."

Star was suddenly very nervous. This was actually her "maiden voyage" as an attractive girl, so her senses were unprepared. She was beginning to melt for this bad boy. As she looked at his brown, product-gooey hair, his irritatingly adoring glances at her were having a strangely pleasurable effect on her.

When he leaned over to kiss her, she sat back, eager for her first kiss. Tommy was surprisingly gentle. But as soon as their lips met, an explosion rocked the pair of them as smoke rose from the shipyard.

"Blue!" they said simultaneously.

★

Juno pulled out a gun and began shooting at the Vampyl, as they jumped over the large crates and ran toward the car where she stood. She knew it was futile to shoot a Vamp at night, but she needed to buy time. The female Shandor pushed her way through the windshield, tearing her own expensive clothes. But she didn't seem to care, since she was angry beyond words.

Still holding Loiza up by the throat with one hand, Chass whispered, "Where is the Mancer?"

As a barrage of bullets flew through the air at his entourage, he lost all patience. Gritting his teeth, he squeezed harder.

Loiza couldn't speak, as Chass well knew, but Loiza did throw up the universal symbol for "Go to hell!"

The head Vampyl's eyes began to change to a blood red, glowing when light hit them from any direction. He reached back and jammed his hand into the body of his distant cousin, enjoying the grimace of pain etched on his face.

Crux couldn't hold back any longer. He saw his uncle in so much pain that his arms reacted all on their own. Concentrating on the marbles to make them weigh a ton, he threw his projectiles through the air. The first few destroyed everything in their path.

Chass could see Crux now. In his Gypsy tongue, he signaled for his entourage to go after the boy. Then he crunched Loiza's neck and tossed the body away like a sack of dirty laundry. As he ran toward Crux, he ignored Juno—a mistake, for she backhanded him with her gun.

The missiles were now hitting their targets with unrelenting explosive force. The Vampyl that were hit instantly became a pile of gore.

Crux continued to throw the projectiles until there were none left. His breathing racked his chest, and his eyes were moist with tears for his uncle. Most of the Vampyl had been destroyed. Juno killed a few more. Then one finally got close to Crux, the one Loiza had burned with acid. He would have been handsome if it weren't for the grotesque bubbling holes in his face.

Crux stepped back. Everything he had ever heard about fighting Vampyl suggested that the best plan was to wait until daylight.

They're much stronger at night, and they all have blood skills.

The twisty-faced undead was definitely not playing with Crux as he swiped at his face. The Vampyl was faster than Crux, and no doubt stronger than the preteen boy, but he was also untrained in the ways of Petsha resourcefulness.

Crux dropped to the ground, grabbed the blood-drinker's boot, and quickly concentrated on it, making it weigh as much as a truck. Then he somersaulted out of the way of the next attack.

A claw somehow caught Crux's side, but it didn't stop him from sprinting toward the ship. His uncle wouldn't want anything else for him. Without missing a step, he bent down and picked up small shrapnel and pebbles on the dock, tossing them behind him to slow the chasing Vampyl.

Juno continued to shoot her OZONE-issued gun with fiery shots that would have killed mortals. Most of the Shandor were hot in pursuit of the Mancer, who was launching high-impact rounds at them. Juno had no idea what he was capable of, but he seemed to be able to hold his own for now. Chass was a different matter altogether.

"I hate Vampires!" Juno yelled as she stood surrounded by three Vampyl, including Chass the fearless. He wiped blood from his lip with his Italian shirt, and smiled at Juno with a condescending grin as he tried to read her thoughts.

She grinned back at him, punching one of his entourage in the face while shooting off another's kneecap.

Chass's backflip kicked her in the face while causing a wall of darkness to form between them before he landed.

Juno knew this tactic, for she was an adept blind-fighter. Gracefully tumbling backwards, shooting every second of the way, she caught one Vampyl in the back of the head as he nearly pounced on Crux. Juno pressed her micro-headset, calling to Surge, "I could use that backup. I've marked them with bio rounds."

Within a second, lasers targeted two of the pursuing Vampyl, and in an instant they were torn to shreds by explosives they could neither see nor dodge.

"Locked and loaded, but not on all of them," Surge replied.

Crux reached the edge of the shipyard, but still had to make it across the water to the ship itself. This was easier said than done. But then he saw a ledge that he could jump from. He didn't need to turn around to know there were more of them behind him. Although his ribs burned from exhaustion, he scaled a large shipping crate and rolled on top of it while he got ready to run toward the ship. One of the Vampyl stood in front of him, stopping him in his tracks. The man looked like most of the Shandor that Crux had ever seen—extremely attractive, with pale skin, and eyes that could kill with a glance.

In a desperate bluff, Crux smiled happily, and sighed, "Great! The sun!"

He stood up straight and looked out over the ocean to where it met the sky. For a split second, the Vampyl looked out onto the horizon. When he turned back, Crux was kneeling. He had picked up a small piece of metal that he was concentrating on, although he doubted he could throw it fast enough at this close range.

But there was no other choice. He threw the metal at the Shandor's head, almost expecting the dodge as he looked down at the docks. When the Vampyl's head blew into bits, Crux was surprised. But with no time to ponder, he jumped off the ledge as the ship began to sail away. By concentrating his thought that he weighed as little as the breeze, he was carried by the wind over the water.

He rolled as he hit the deck, grabbing a piece of a chain, and spinning around to watch the explosions on the dock. But he stayed in ready position in case one of the Vampyl decided to jump after him. Crux continued to stare at the docks until he suddenly felt the warmth of the sun on his skin.

Looking for a place to hide and heal, he hurt with every breath, not knowing how much blood he had lost.

Blue had no remorse. He had a job to do, and no one and nothing was going to stand in his way. Placing the keys in his back pocket, he readied the weapons in his jacket. Then he walked directly toward the front gate that the Triads would be guarding. As usual, they were standing there with sunglasses on and dark suits with semi-automatic weapons on their hips. They didn't even see Blue before both of them were shot and lying on the ground. These murderers were some of the lowest. Blue despised them even more than he did Tommy's Uncle Ronny. They were gangsters who were known for trafficking young kids and foreigners, and then forcing them to do unspeakable things. Their drugs poisoned the streets, but they didn't seem to care. Blue figured the job really required a total sociopath.

The shipment had only been there a few minutes when Blue arrived. This was going to be quick and easy without Tommy as a distraction. That was the only reason he had agreed to the girl coming along. Blue had always been fast, but he didn't realize how fast until he was in the midst of danger, and his enemies were lying on the ground unconscious. But he had yet to kill anyone since the accident.

After knocking out a few more of the goons, and making his way onto the ship, he noticed three large crates, each one the size of a bus. Just as he was about to open one, he spun around and shot a Triad guard in the shoulder. He must have accidentally hit a generator, because a loud explosion sent a huge fireball into the air. Knowing his time was limited, Blue went to open another crate. The first one was empty. The second was filled with random cargo of no importance. The third and last was locked like the others, but the latch was easy to shatter. Inside, staring up at him, a wide-eyed boy was shivering, with blood on his clothes.

"Bastards!"

Sometimes Nina went to the water down by the docks for peace and serenity. These walks reminded her of the times that her father used to take her to the water when she was a young girl. This sunset was like many she had seen since she had first met Natasha. She just came to look her fill, and to try to forget the danger at home. In a lot of ways, Natasha was like her father, both good and bad. She probably hit out of love, but Nina didn't know why she was always the one who was bleeding.

She dipped her hand in the murky water to wash the blood where the glass had cut her.

That's the last time she'll ever hurt ME.

The only thing she was able to take with her from the apartment was her backpack, which she had been wearing on the night when she first met Natasha. It was at a sleazy bar she wished she had never gone to. Too much drama was not something that sat well with Nina. The glorious sunset and the serenity of the ocean calmed her nerves and brought her to a happy place.

As she sat placidly, explosions made her drop the cloth she was using to clean her cut hand. She stood up and quickly grabbed her backpack. This was the bad part of town. She had lived here long enough, and seen so much, that she couldn't wait to forget it all—starting with that damned bar.

✶

Blue stood still, looking at the boy, who was obviously scared and probably didn't speak English.

"This is not my problem," Blue said aloud to himself, slamming the crate shut.

The voice of his sister chimed in his head: "You know this is why you're here . . . , to save a life."

Blue tried to ignore the voice, but as he took a step, a bullet ricocheted off the crate.

As he dodged the bullet, he had his back to the crate, which was blocking the shooter's view of him.

That boy is gonna die if I leave him here.

Cursing his bad luck, Blue opened the crate and signaled for the boy to come out. Crux walked slowly. He didn't know who this man was, who was younger than Loiza, but seemed to have the same energy. Crux smiled a soft, sad little smile, and went to Blue's side. He had no clue how long he had been in that dark shipping crate, and he definitely didn't know how or why he was still alive. But meeting this stranger was no accident. Loiza had wanted him to have a better life.

Maybe this is it?

As he stood next to Blue, the gunfire continued. Crux soon realized that he was in just as much danger now as he had ever been. He peeked around the corner, but Blue quickly moved him back into position, away from the shooters.

"Are you crazy, kid? You're gonna get yourself shot. Let *me* handle this. Oh, yeah, you probably don't understand a word I'm saying."

Crux's silence frustrated Blue. But he checked his clips, and then, as he rounded the corner, he saw Tommy shooting one of the Triad in the head. The girl was kicking another in the balls.

With a broad grin, Tommy, called, "Hey, I saved you! You owe me one!"

Blue was going to smile back, but then saw a Triad behind Tommy. Crux threw a pebble that knocked the gangster out, almost killing him on impact. Blue looked pensively at the boy, while Star looked down at the fallen assassin.

"I totally think it's time to go," she said, stepping calmly over the bodies.

Crux stayed behind Blue as they ran off the ship to the docks.

"How much was in the crates?" Tommy asked. "I mean, was it drugs or cash? What was in the shipment?"

Blue turned his head as he walked, and simply pointed to Crux.

Tommy looked Crux up and down with a "Whaddaya mean?" expression.

Just then, a Triad's shots rang out again through the air. One hit Blue directly in the chest. He knew he was hit, but still managed to shoot the Triad where he stood.

Star and Tommy ran to help Blue, but he shook them off, as he kept walking toward the car, dripping blood with every step.

As Blue got into the car, he was stubborn as always, waiting impatiently for everyone to hop in. Knowing that a police chase was next on the agenda, he turned on his music and rolled away.

Chapter 6

AWAKEN

"Jayde, it is time to awaken the sleeping giants. Go retrieve them, and bring them to me."

Gemini's words were as much a request as a command to the Asian woman who was bowing in respect. She had served Gemini since before the fall of Egypt, so many thousands of years ago, and rarely contested his tactical requests. As Gemini turned to walk down the hall to Maia's room, Jayde was already gone.

Somehow, even in her sleep, Maia knew that Gemini was there, even though he was standing silently in her doorway. She woke up, smiling, knowing that he needed her. Although she hated the mornings, she didn't complain.

"What is it, Gemini?"

"As you know, we will soon have many visitors. I will need your help to find them."

Maia nodded, and he walked away down the hall. She dressed and prepared for the upcoming duties. Not yet fully awake, but trying to concentrate on the task at hand, she hurriedly grabbed the first thing she found to wear, and ran down the hall after Gemini. Her heart was pounding, because she had been preparing for this day for many months.

Now that it was finally upon her, it seemed as if all the time to prepare had gone by too quickly. Maia wasn't sure if she was up to the task.

Gemini was standing in silence in a room that could easily seat a hundred people. Its walls were marked with the Language of Magick. Maia now could read each rune easily. After she took a few lessons with Gemini, they were simple to pick up again. She had known them in her past life, so it was only a matter of relearning what she already knew. Everyone holds information from the past. Everyone has a Shard from the Soulstream. Maia was one of the fortunate ones, the Supernaturals, who could tap into the Soulstream at will. That was her fate, and she wholly accepted it, to atone for her crimes from another lifetime.

With a solemn look into Maia's eyes, Gemini simply said, "The time is now."

"Agent Guardian," the man said into the holographic monitor, speaking his own name. He was annoyed that he had to stop in this obnoxiously large hallway. Corporate artwork mingled with digital art, and cold sculptures lined the walls. He walked confidently down the corridor to his next checkpoint. They knew who he was miles before he got into the headquarters. He had completed so many missions in the years he had worked for this secret society, but that last mark was disturbing. Even if he couldn't prove it in the past, he had known about Supernaturals before he took the job of annihilating them. He was a little too good at his new job, and moved through the ranks easily, but he didn't do his work because it earned him the title of best assassin in the world. He couldn't have cared less about titles.

Guardian came from a small family in the suburbs of New York. He wasn't exceptional at anything in high school or college except sports. On paper, his life seemed fairly streamlined as he rose in the military and then received his job as a government agent specializing in counterterrorism. All of this meant nothing to him, since the public had no access to his records. Every so often, he still visited his family, but anyone who researched his identity mysteriously disappeared.

He had seen some terrible Supernatural things as a government agent, but he couldn't get validation from any of his peers or superiors. Nevertheless, he continued to do his job. Through investigations, he came across a vampire here or a shape shifter there. It wasn't until he was approached by his commander-in—chief that he was recruited into OZONE. Guardian had completed hundreds of missions across the planet, seeking and destroying the "ongoing threat to humanity," as his trainers called it. He had an abnormally heightened instinct to fight the Supernaturals, although he could not explain it, nor did he want to. It didn't bother Guardian that he had completed many tasks that were a little "iffy," but this latest mission was the most mind-rattling of all.

After he finally finished being bio-scanned into the overly protective underground citadel, his chest ached. Although he knew what that meant, his employer didn't. Guardian knew that he was different from other people before he took the position, but he never disclosed that on the application or on assessments for the job as Agent. He hated planes, but had decided a long time ago that he would go on whatever mission he had to, in order to destroy the threats to the planet. Unlike the other agents, he never came back with souvenirs, only bruises, wounds, and the strange markings that burned into his flesh every time he took the life of a Supernatural. His secret pains were his to bear alone undiscovered, and he preferred it that way. This scared him at first, but he believed that it was all worth it, in the name of honor and the greater good. At this point in his life, however, everything seemed to be speculation.

He knew the Supernaturals wore many different faces, and that some were immortal, but this latest mission felt different. The boy was an innocent. Guardian could feel deep within his consciousness that Isja was inherently good. This feeling tore at every fiber in his code of justice. And, as with all other Supernaturals that Guardian had ever destroyed, a piece of the victim's essence would be with him until he was himself dead. Ironically, this made him stronger and a lot more proficient at his job. As far as Guardian knew, he was human, but he was what the Supernaturals called a Hunter, or Jreamer, in their strange language, which he somehow understood.

Scowling as he walked past the receptionist and the armed guards, he tried not to scratch at the rune that burned his flesh under his Brain Tech armor. Guardian knew the procedure: three more retinal and cardio checks before he was allowed into the inner sanctum of the citadel. While thinking of the innocent look on the boy's face in the forest, he went through the motions. That memory would probably haunt him for many sleepless nights. Guardian was opposed to killing innocents, particularly children. By the looks of the Grove, the boy was probably an immortal, but he had no trace of evil or malice about him at all.

Regardless of his private ethics, Guardian completed the mission, and was welcomed as a hero when he opened the doors to the top-secret citadel known only by OZONE Agents. This organization, which technically did not exist, was actually more powerful than any government on Earth. It sat behind the scenes, using the militaries, religions, and world leaders of the nations as pawns to find the true threat: the Supernaturals.

Guardian's name had been changed when his rank became official. He was the most successful Agent in the entire organization, but he didn't brag about it. His skills were matched by only a few others. Two of those he had trained himself. They would probably take over the rank of Number One in the future, but Guardian didn't care in the least.

As he stormed to his reporting analysis room, he thought of the look on the boy's face as the plea for help touched Guardian's heart like a warm breeze. The thought of his oath to protect the whole human race tore at his conscience. He couldn't have aborted the mission, since another Agent was there. Juno would have turned him in for negligence, and his record would have been forever scarred. As far as Guardian knew, humans were somehow immune to even seeing Supernaturals, much less capable of fighting in this war against them—except for a very rare few. OZONE took it upon itself to kill any threat to humanity, including the

Witchbreed, Vampires, Were-creatures, and any other monsters or things that went bump in the night. Guardian prided himself on being the thing that bumped back, but now he found himself in turmoil. This boy had been different.

✶

"Now, *that's* different," Tommy said, after a long silence in the car. "The cops just passed us up as if they didn't see us leave the scene of the crime. This night is getting weirder by the minute, and all we have to show for a bust is some skinny kid."

He turned to look in the back seat with an aggravated scowl toward Crux. Then he looked at Star, gazing at her with glossy-eyed adoration.

As she looked out the window, Star tried to stay calm. She had been clutching the door handle, thinking of being in any car but this one.

Crux gazed silently at his three rescuers. He didn't know why he felt so safe, considering that these three misfits were not as skilled as the Petshas in getaways or stealth. Also, he still had a wound to attend to. The driver, who reminded him of his Uncle Loiza, was also bleeding, because he had just been shot. But for some reason, he didn't look fazed at all by the wounds. He was much more interested in getting out of this place. Crux clearly shared that desire. This was the first time he had ever been in an American car. That was nice, but he would be happier right now if he had some food. That crate had been his prison for quite a while.

As though she could read his thoughts, Star asked, "Have you eaten, boy? I can hear your stomach growling from here." Her tone was neither pleasant nor inviting, merely curious.

"He's fresh off the boat from Europe," Tommy said. "He doesn't look like he speaks a bit of English."

"Quiet," Blue said. "The cops are out of sight. Let's go."

As they drove off, Crux finally spoke to Star: "You are Glamouri, right, the Coven of beautiful Witchbreed? And yes, I *am* hungry." He held his stomach as he smiled up at Star.

She looked confused. "What's a Glamouri . . . , and what's a Witchbreed?"

Blue looked into the rearview mirror at the two in the back seat, listening carefully to their conversation.

Crux grabbed Star's hand. In an instant, her senses went into overdrive, and she closed her eyes as her memory flashed back to another time and place.

Blue turned the music down to listen a little better.

Realizing that he was being watched in the mirror, Crux turned back to Star just as she opened her eyes.

"The Magick you were using," he said, "it was Glamour. It is strong, and the ones who mastered it are the Witchbreed Coven, Glamouri. You should know that, since you used it on the car to hide from the police."

Blue looked in the mirror at Star, then said to Crux, "I don't know exactly what you're talking about, but I do know you were on a ship full of dangerous people. I'm not gonna ask what they did to you, or how you got in an illegal cargo shipping crate, but I will ask, why were you there?"

As he looked out of the window, Crux said, "I'm hiding from some dangerous people, who make those guys at the shipyard look like amateurs. Can we please get something to eat?"

Blue pulled into a fast-food drive-thru, turned off the music completely, and looking back at Crux asked, "What do ya want?"

Looking totally confused, Tommy asked, "How do you two know what he's saying? All I'm hearing out of his mouth is gibberish. But you guys are talkin' to him in that weird language of his."

Blue said to Tommy, "Are you high?"

"No, he's human," Crux answered.

Guardian didn't bother to review the mission data footage in the control center. Instead, he went to change into civilian clothing. As he walked into the unisex locker room, he saw one of his quest partners, Juno, walking toward him. She seldom spoke, but if anyone could give him a run for his money in a battle, she was the one. He nodded as she made her way past him, seeming rushed.

Probably on another mission.

Guardian couldn't put his finger on it, but he knew she had secrets. All the Agents did, but she seemed somehow different. She didn't talk much, and she was always on a mission.

I wonder if she ever takes the time to sleep.

Juno passed Guardian, and though they were colleagues, she simply looked in his direction as she headed out of the building. But she was held up by the recording department. According to them, the footage from the Antarctica mission had been stolen by a hacker. Juno had to recap what she saw, and it had to match Guardian's report to the smallest detail. For high-end missions, the Agents usually traveled in pairs or in groups of three. They rarely needed more than that.

This base is so sterile, she thought. *It reminds me of a hospital.*

The sight of Guardian, who was obviously hiding the fact from OZONE that he was a Jreamer, although she was sure they already knew, was an interesting dramatization that she wished she had the patience to watch unfold. Unfortunately, Juno had lost any sense of patience long ago. Of all the Supernaturals, OZONE preferred working with Jreamers, because their powers were far more predictable. Juno had been assigned to Guardian when he first joined OZONE, with the understanding that she was to report everything he did.

She never bothered telling him that OZONE was watching him. He was probably aware of it, but that was something she would never mention. When she left the building and headed to the docks, she made sure to use Glamour to conceal her exit. Juno admitted to herself that she was extremely good at pretending to be a human who hated Supernaturals. As far as she knew, and she could be wrong, OZONE didn't suspect anything, because her extensive record of success was almost equal to Guardian's.

✳

Sneaking out of the house was one thing, but this was ridiculous. Ahlina was practically kidnapping Kaery with an elaborate scheme all laid out. Kaery was reluctant to go, because clubs just weren't her thing, but Ahlina didn't really give her much of a choice when she came up with a bogus story for Kaery's mom and did all the talking while Kaery simply smiled at her mother. She was supposed to be sleeping over at Ahlina's, but that was just too boring for Ahlina, who always had a "better" idea.

"Your mom wouldn't understand, even if we told her Scape was totally gay," Ahlina said, while getting into her car. "Just because he's a boy, she would've said, 'Heck, no!' And you know I'm right."

Ahlina stuck her tongue out mockingly.

"Are you sure about this?" Kaery asked. "I mean, aren't they gonna check our IDs at the club?"

"What do I look like, an amateur? I was gonna wait for Scape to get in, to surprise him . . . , but, oh, well."

Ahlina whipped out three new identification cards.

Kaery grabbed them.

"I can't deny they look and feel authentic."

Without even looking at Ahlina, she handed the cards back to her.

"Keep yours," Ahlina said, grinning. "C'mon, Kaery, don't pout. I just wanna have fun. We've been doing finals all week, and I'm so over it. It'll be fun! It's the hottest place in Chinatown. Oh, and we have new outfits in the back seat." She reached for a small bag and tossed it to Kaery. "You can't get into the Forbidden City without looking forbidden." She giggled.

Kaery peeked into the bag with eyes open wide. "Oh, hell, no!"

Ahlina laughed as they pulled up to Scape's apartment. The minute she honked the horn, he came running out.

Jumping into the back seat, he sighed, "I'm completely shocked that my parents are letting me get out of the house on a weekday, but I guess luck is on our side. I gotta feelin' that tonight's gonna be a good night."

He sang the words along with the radio, playfully nudging Kaery's shoulder, which made her feel better.

Ahlina screamed, "I *love* that song!" and turned up the volume.

Jayde stared at the sign which said, "FORBIDDEN CITY," where Maia had said two Mancers were headed. Her eyes, the color of bright emeralds, glittered expectantly, and her long raven black hair flew around her fair skin in the wind as she perched high on the building across the street. Two of her strongest qualities were patience and intuition. Aside from Gemini, she was arguably the oldest living being on the planet. In another time and place, she was revered as the Goddess of Martial Arts and Spirituality. At that time, she was the most patient of Supernaturals, especially when it came to humans and their abysmal ignorance.

Now she chose to serve Gemini, because she fervently believed in his cause. In ancient times, she was well known for fighting, but had decided after many lives had been lost at her own hands, that she would turn to a life of peace and solitude. She heard story after story about friends who had chosen the same path, only to be murdered one by one. As the world's most infamous warrior, she felt that it was her karmic duty to right the wrongs of the past. Jayde momentarily pondered her training for the new Mancers. But first things first. She had to find them and bring them to Gemini.

Blending in with the angel statues next to her, she watched with her beautifully slanted eyes as the young people lined up outside the Chinatown nightclub. She enjoyed watching the young humans shine with innocence. There were scantily clad girls and macho guys, all with their high-tech cell phones, and vanity to match. Jayde could almost smell their colognes and perfumes over the salt water of the bay.

Then she realized that she only saw humans here. Usually in large crowds, there was an occasional Supernatural. Looking down at the forming line, she saw no such beings. There were a few men carrying weapons underneath their black jackets, while the music from inside the club blared. Jayde continued to profile the crowd with her heightened senses.

Looking more carefully, she noticed a marked vehicle down the street. Tuning out the music, she focused on the talk inside the car, which was a good fifty yards away. She heard the orders, "The bust will go down tonight. Uncle Ronny is goin' down. We have enough evidence to take him. We know he's inside his VIP area, and there are multiple bogies, all armed to the teeth."

Jayde stood up to glance down the opposite direction of the street. Multiple cars were making their way to an empty private lot. As she listened, she heard Mandarin coming from the cars: "Kill all of Ronny's men, and take that fat bastard out!"

This was not the place for any of the innocents to be, let alone the unsuspecting Mancers.

Jayde watched as an American car rolled up to the valet.

"They're here," she said to herself, as she jumped off the ledge of the skyscraper and landed softly on the deserted sidewalk, as if she had jumped only a few inches. Without stopping her movement, she walked toward the club, her pacifist side hoping that she could somehow avoid the inevitable battle.

Chapter 7

ENLIGHTENMENT

The nightclub had been Tommy's playground ever since he could walk. Even though his family was Italian, they owned clubs in all the hot parts of town. His Uncle Ronny was notorious in the underground, and pretty much had his hands in anything illegal. Tommy had never worked a day in his life at anything that taxpayers would call "upstanding." He had been exposed to crime very early, and felt right at home with the lowest that society had to offer. Tommy had a feeling that he should feel guilty for bringing Blue into this lifestyle, but his conscience had diminished along with his childhood innocence. He no longer believed in anything but money and Blue Scarsdale.

As they drove up to the club, Blue turned around to Crux. "Stay close to me, little one."

Tommy rolled his eyes, while Star noted the jealousy.

Crux smiled at Blue before turning his sunny face to Star. He noticed that her mismatched eyes were a lot brighter than they had been a few minutes before. Of course, until now, he hadn't been paying attention to much beside the burgers and fries.

Tommy said to everyone in the car, "Just follow me straight to the VIP lounge. Uncle Ronny will wanna know *exactly* what went on at the docks." He scowled at Crux as he said, "You better have a damned good story, or that will be your last meal."

Crux didn't understand a word Tommy said, but nodded anyway, content that the rumble in his stomach had been replaced by a brick of hamburger and fries. He looked at Blue, awaiting orders.

Star was staring out the window, horrified at the outfits of the girls on line.

Looking down at her bright red minidress, she said, "I can't go out there like this!"

Ignoring her, Tommy got out of the car to greet the bouncers, who were all pit fighters. As he heard people whispering his name, and as he got the royal treatment from the bouncers, he felt like a celebrity.

From somewhere in the back of her mind, Star remembered an ancient chant. Without conscious effort, she began to whisper the words, focusing on her clothes. Right in front of Blue and Crux, her outfit changed colors and turned into a short, backless haute couture dress covered with sparkles. Blue turned away from the mirror to witness the incredible transformation in the flesh.

Crux smiled at Star, while keeping his hands on his bag. She waved her hand over him and repeated the chant. Instantly, his torn short-sleeved shirt became an embroidered black-silver long-sleeved tunic, and his wool pants turned into shiny leather.

The twelve-year-old looked down, and then back up to Star. "You can't be serious!"

Star looked into the rearview mirror, smiling at herself. "I'm sure we'll turn some heads," she said. Then she looked at Blue's shirt full of bullet holes.

As she leaned forward to touch his shoulder, Blue caught her hand. "I don't need your fuckin' makeover, or whatever you just did." As he prepared to climb out of the car, he said to Crux, "Stay near me."

Crux slipped a small pouch into Star's clutch purse without anyone seeing. Then he quickly jumped out of the car and followed Blue.

As Star regally exited the vehicle, she heard gasps and people whispering to each other, wondering aloud who she might be. The overwhelming feeling of popularity raised her ego to another level. She could feel the envy seeping from the very pores of the girls in skimpy dresses, while they watched her walk into the club, just as Sky walked into school every day. Star kept a picture-perfect smile on her face and mused to herself, *Must be what Sky feels like.*

✱

This is just stupid and terrible! Sky thought to herself, looking around the room. *There's absolutely no signal for my phone, and that aggressive Soldier lady locked me in here. I swear, I HATE her!*

Her frustrations were beginning to get the best of her, so she sat down and stared at the door she had tried to open at least a dozen times.

It must be dead-bolted from outside.

"Great, I'm a prisoner!" she said aloud, still looking around the room for an exit. The dim glow from the older lightbulbs irritated her. She suddenly missed the fresh outdoors and people. "C'mon, Sky, you've been in worse situations . . . . Who are you fooling? No, you haven't. This really sucks." Her mind began racing, so she closed her eyes, trying to remember the meditation exercises her parents had spent countless dollars on.

As she focused on her surroundings, she began to see in all directions at once. Now she wasn't scared, but relieved that she could focus. The room was like a fallout bunker that Sky had only seen in movies or cable specials about serial killers. There was no sign of blood or life of any kind, since this room had a fresh coat of dust. The dim light was controlled by some unknown source. The door was too thick for even a grown man to rush, let alone the svelte, swimsuit-model Sky. She didn't even attempt to turn the latch.

I'll only break a nail.

Through the cracks of the door, and along the floor, she felt the breeze from outside.

Here we go! This is crazy, but if I could do it once, I should be able to do it again.

She closed her eyes and thought of floating on the breeze. At first, she thought she was just imagining things, since her eyes were still closed. Not only could she see the room in every direction at once, just as clearly as if her eyes were open, but the dim light was now brighter, too. As if she were a detective, she observed every detail of the small room. There were traces of her fingerprints and footsteps, along with a couple of hair follicles.

"How the hell is this possible?" Sky said aloud again.

She felt exhilarated as her senses were heightened and she floated around the room.

I AM a Mancer . . . , whatever that is. I feel like a freak, but I also feel so liberated and free. The irony is, it took being in this tiny room for me to accept what I am.

Sky smiled to herself, but then opened her eyes at the sound of a sliding dead bolt.

Before Juno had completely opened the door, Sky was in her face with the breeze. But Juno didn't seem the least bit surprised.

"It's time to go," she said.

Excited to leave the room, Sky took in a deep gulp of fresh air and followed Juno out to a little sports car.

"Mine's better," Sky said, without thinking twice about her egotistical comment.

Juno looked obliquely in her direction without turning her head, smirked, and just kept walking.

"What's your name again?" Sky asked with a bossy tone. She hadn't meant to sound that way, but she was desperate for information.

Juno unlocked the car and said simply, "I never told you . . . . I'm Juno. Get in."

Sky looked around, scanning the area, but knew she didn't have a clue where she was. Even though she was a track star, she decided there was no way she could outrun that car. Better judgment ruled against dramatics for the time being. She climbed in and buckled her seatbelt.

Juno paused for a second.

Why is she obeying orders so easily?

Then, as fast as the thought crossed her mind, Juno got in the car and drove off. She needed to make one stop before bringing the girl to her planned destination.

"This outfit is way too short, and my butt is almost sticking out the bottom. For the thousandth time, I'm not going in there like this, Ahlina."

Kaery was fidgeting uncomfortably in her short dress. Ahlina gave Scape a look, and he immediately understood the signal. Walking in front of Kaery, he looked her up and down. She blushed, well aware that there was way too much flesh showing.

They had been standing in this line after changing in a parking lot. Kaery had been stared at by many people by now, but Scape was actually admiring her.

"What are you looking like *that* for?" Kaery said, finding her voice.

Without stopping to think about his words, Scape answered, "Kaery, you look ridiculously hot, and you're gonna be the reason we all get in . . . , not those IDs Ahlina doctored up. And Ahlina is just not as endowed."

Kaery knew that his words swere sincere because no one had been able to lie to her for well over a year. The ironic twist was that *she* hadn't been able to lie, either.

Ahlina looked down at her own small breasts in the shiny top, and punched Scape in the arm. She was as slender as a teenage boy, without any curves at all, which she had always blamed on her Japanese and Chinese roots. Her hair was curly in the front and straight in back, which was also a bit odd. But she was comfortable with her looks, especially her beautiful green eyes, and felt like her individualism stood out even more in crowds full of people who all looked the same.

Kaery was still blushing at Scape's words, but before she could voice a protest, she gasped in shock, "Star?!"

Star was walking right into the nightclub with Blue and a little boy.

Kaery was so confused that she didn't know how to tell Ahlina and Scape, so all she did was point frantically at the entrance.

Scape and Ahlina turned around in the line to see who had Kaery all starstruck. But all they got was a glimpse of a sparkly dress and an extremely healthy wave of red hair with blonde highlights.

Scape turned back to Kaery. "Who was that, Milla Jovovich?

Ahlina added, "I don't know who it was, 'cause all we could see was the back of her head and legs that didn't end. But from this angle, she was gorgeous!"

"No, you don't . . . you don't understand," Kaery stammered. "It was Star! I don't know how, but that was our friend, Star."

As Kaery peered excitedly into the doorway of the club, Ahlina and Scape stifled their giggles and shrugged.

"As long as she wants to go in now, I don't give a damn *who* she thought that was," Ahlina whispered to Scape, twirling her finger around near her temple in the "crazy" signal.

Scape laughed out loud, then got out his new ID.

The bouncers here were exceptionally scary. Even though they wore high-end suits, tailor-made to fit their big frames, they all had scars on their faces and fresh bruises.

"They're all mixed martial arts fighters in the underground pit fighter scene," Ahlina said to her friends. "I've only been to a couple matches, but I sure didn't like all the blood. And those bloodthirsty mobs reminded me of ancient Rome."

As they approached one of the large men, they handed over their fake IDs. He looked Ahlina up and down, then Scape, and finished with a long look at the surprisingly curvy Kaery. After doing a double take, he opened the rope to allow them access.

As they passed the scary man, Kaery blushed, but Ahlina pushed her into the club and walked around the corner to the counter where the entrance fee was collected. Scape handed her some money, and she paid as fast as she could to escape the judging eyes of the register girl, who figured they were all sixteen, but didn't say anything, since they had gotten past Bruno.

As the threesome walked into the open room, they saw a luxurious lounge full of high-fashion trust-fund babies, plus a mix of the city's famous and infamous. The décor was like nothing Kaery had expected from the looks of the place outside. She forgot she was in a shiny silver dress until she saw her reflection across the room. That's when she remembered her friend walking into the club.

"Guys, we have to find Star," she shouted, trying to compensate for the high-energy, blasting technomusic.

Ahlina pretended not to hear Kaery, although she had. She was already dancing, and pulling on Kaery and Scape to dance with her.

Scape looked at Kaery with an expression that would have melted her heart if she hadn't been so intent on finding Star.

"You two go ahead and dance," she said. "But I'm serious. I'll find Star and show you."

Following her instincts, Kaery headed toward the back of the club.

✲

Maia's eyes opened wide as she held her breath until she realized she wasn't breathing.

Gemini stood silently looking at her.

"They're all in danger," Maia finally mustered the strength to say.

She had been meditating for quite some time, and the techniques Gemini taught her had brought her more enlightenment with each moment. The Mancers that she was supposed to find were none other than kids her own age, doing reckless things that led them to a dark place full of pain and bloodshed.

After watching Maia's reaction for a long while, Gemini asked, "Is Jayde there?"

"Yes. She just got there."

"Then, they're not in danger." He started to walk out of the room, then turned and said, "I feel rather sorry for anyone who gets in Jayde's way."

Burying any sign of nervousness for failing Uncle Ronny, Tommy walked into the VIP room as if he belonged nowhere else. He knew that there were some things his uncle tolerated, but failure was not among them.

I'm not gonna end up like Guy.

He remembered how his best friend, who was a pit fighter, had botched a job, and Uncle Ronny had sent the mourning family a care package on the holidays. What they didn't know was that the fresh exotic meats were their beloved Guy.

That's when Tommy realized that Uncle Ronny was not to be disappointed.

Grabbing a glass of champagne, even though he thought the stuff was gross, Tommy laughed nervously.

Uncle Ronny took note, watching his brother's son walk in as if he owned the place. This was typical behavior for his family, but Uncle Ronny had already been told that the job at the docks had gone well, so he allowed the celebration to last a few more seconds before he stopped Tommy.

"Tommy-boy, whatchoo got for me?"

Uncle Ronny was enormous. His forehead seemed to always have beads of sweat as if his body never regulated its temperature. His high-fashion clothes always had some part of dinner speckled on them, but no one was bold enough to tell him about how disgusting he looked—or smelled. This man was one of the most feared people in the city, but not because of his looks or his physical prowess. He had employees for that. Uncle Ronny was notorious for his wild-card tactics and strategies when it came to dealing with competition.

Tommy was still laughing at an imaginary joke when Blue and Crux walked in behind him.

Uncle Ronny acknowledged Blue with a nod and a wave, then looked down to Crux, who was dressed like some celebrity's brat. As soon as the thought of celebrity entered his mind, Star walked into the VIP room behind Crux. Uncle Ronny took his stubby arms from around the two girls near him, and spit out his champagne. It was as if he had never seen a woman before, although he was currently surrounded by two beautiful sluts.

As he stood up to introduce himself, he completely forgot about his companions on the couch, who were squinting at Star with hatred and jealousy in their eyes.

Their envious glares only fueled Star's ego, as the fat criminal reached out to kiss her hand. But repulsed by his odor and the pasta sauce on his face, she flinched.

Tommy noticed this, so before his uncle had time to react, he stepped in to hug Star's waist. "This is Red . . . , my fiancée."

Star could barely hear what Tommy had said over the blaring club remix in the background.

Did he say fiancée?!

But before she could open her mouth, Uncle Ronny was introducing himself.

"I'm Uncle Ronny, and it's nice to meet you, Red."

"That's not my name," Star objected. "I'm Star."

Blue and Crux watched the family members ogling Star like a piece of steak. As Blue was about to walk out the room, Uncle Ronny stopped him.

"So this is the little lady you all brought to a job that I specifically said was secret?"

Blue looked upset as Uncle Ronny swung around to direct his malicious attention at Tommy.

"I can tell you did your normal work, because the docks are torn to pieces. But answer me this. What in the hell happened to discreet and secret?"

Blue didn't know what to say, so he said nothing.

Crux couldn't understand anything that was going on, but he did read the tension in Blue's face. This was quickly becoming one of those scenes where Crux was looking around for the exits.

But the only ones he saw were guarded by the huge brawlers in suits that reminded Crux of cheap Shandor knockoffs. The best way to run was the way they had come in, which would mean taking on the dozens of fighters at the entrance. They were very much like the goons at the docks. Their cologne made Crux slightly nauseous, but he wasn't quite sure if it was the smell, or the fast food he had inhaled earlier, which sat in his stomach like a rock.

Uncle Ronny reluctantly turned his attention from Star and got down to business. Tact was not one of his qualities because he really didn't know what it was. He walked over to Crux and reached out to rub the boy's head, but Crux evaded him easily and slid behind Blue.

"Who's the squirt?" Uncle Ronny asked. "He seems to be taking a liking to you, Blue. He also looks European, like the shipment that was supposed to be here tonight."

"Uncle, I have an explanation," Tommy said tentatively. Then he shot a look at Star, who slapped his hand off her. Shaking his hand from the sting, he continued, "We got to the docks, and the Triad had three shipping crates and—"

"Spare me the details, Tommy. You know I don't got patience for that shit."

Uncle Ronny wiped sweat off his forehead with his sleeve, but beads reformed instantly in their place. His cologne didn't cover the foul aroma that seeped through his open-necked shirt, exposing his curly-haired barrel chest.

Star frowned, totally grossed out by the sight of this disgusting man. She turned to leave, but Uncle Ronny snapped his fingers in a way that reminded Crux of Chass, the Shandor Vampyl. He had recognized this man as a criminal from the instant he walked into this den, but he knew without a doubt that this was a villain capable of great treachery.

A bouncer blocked Star's path. Backing away from him, she said, "What's your deal? I just want the ladies' room."

As she held her clutch purse like a weapon, Crux kept his eyes on her intently, then looked over to Blue.

"The girl has nothing to do with this," Blue said. "Tommy never said anything about the job being either a secret or discreet. He only said to steal the cargo and get it back to you."

Blue's calm voice put an end to the tension. The bouncer glared at Star, then at Blue.

"Let her go to the bathroom," Uncle Ronny said, "but don't let her leave the club."

The bouncer stepped aside as Star stomped past him, looking back briefly, and then flipping her hair, disgusted, as she walked through the door into the blaring music.

"Now, back to you all," Uncle Ronny said, sounding like a slithering snake. "So, where's the shipment?" His eyes darted from one to the other, checking for any hint of a lie.

Motioning toward Crux, Blue said, "He's all that was there."

But he stayed close enough to the boy to protect him in a worst-case scenario.

Crux looked up at Blue, surprised.

Uncle Ronny began screaming at his sluts, "Get out!" Then he looked with rage at all the random VIPs in the room. "Out!"

When the last one had gone, he turned back to Blue, his face as red as the pasta sauce on his suit.

"Where are the diamonds? I have trustworthy information that the shipment was supposed to have Gypsy diamonds from the Shandor." Uncle Ronny stepped up to Crux and got right down in his face. "Look, you little bastard Gypsy thief, where are my diamonds?"

As Blue reached to take the fat man's hand off the boy, who was struggling to get free, he was met by a ringed backhand from Uncle Ronny. Blue immediately fell backwards to the floor, spitting blood.

Keeping a fast grip on Crux, Uncle Ronny said to Blue, "I put up with you, little punk, because my nephew said his pyromaniac buddy who killed his own folks needed a job. But don't ever think you can put your hands on me. See, I figured only someone who was that messed up would fit in right at home here, and you've done great."

Uncle Ronny walked over to Blue and kicked him viciously in the stomach three times.

Tommy winced at every kick, remembering Blue's gunshot wounds. But he was too afraid to stand up to his psychotic uncle.

"Stealing from me is where you went wrong," Uncle Ronny howled, as he kicked Blue in the ribs. "Where's the goddamn shipment?"

Jayde walked across the street and stepped up to the sidewalk. "I need to get in," she said, as she approached the tower of a man in front of the rope.

He turned from flirting with the next attractive girl in line to look at the beautiful image of Jayde, who was dressed in soft leather pants and a cotton top that hugged her body. But the monk bandages on her arms and the China bangs covering her eyes made him think twice about letting her in.

"Sorry, chick, but you—"

He didn't finish his sentence before Jayde hit a pressure point in his left kidney, leaving him paralyzed on the ground.

The girl next in line began screaming, so Jayde turned to the others in line, and shouted, "Go home! It's not safe here!"

Then, walking into the club, she passed the register girl, who pressed an alarm after yelling at Jayde to stop.

Jayde quickly scanned the room, looking for the Mancers. Before she could get a complete panoramic view, a fist came straight for her face. But she dodged it so easily that the fighter thought he had swung at the wrong person. His fist slammed into his buddy's ribs, breaking them.

Somehow, impossibly, Jayde was behind him. She kicked him in the back of his knee, dropping him to the floor in pain. Then she saw two Wicasht on the dance floor, completely oblivious to the danger around them. Reading their energy patterns, she immediately realized that even though they weren't enlightened, they were definitely Witchbreed.

Kaery walked into the bathroom, frustrated that she was mistaken about seeing Star. But when she looked in the mirror, her jaw dropped, "Star! It *is* you!"

Star turned around to see her friend staring at her, dressed in an outfit that made Star take a step back.

"Why does everyone keep looking at me like that?" Kaery whined. "And what happened to you. My god, you look . . . , well, great! Is this why you've been skipping school lately?"

"Kaery, shut up. Did anyone ever tell you that you ask too many questions without giving people time to answer?"

But she was so relieved to see her friend that she stepped over to Kaery and hugged her hard. Kaery stood completely stiff, shocked that the standoffish Star was hugging her. Looking up into her friend's face, Kaery became aware of Star's six-inch stilettos.

"How do you walk in those things?"

"Practice. But that's not the real issue right now."

Star grabbed Kaery's hand and pulled her over to the door, cracking it open to reveal the bouncer, who was standing there with his back to the door, watching the dance floor.

As the music invaded the bathroom, Star quickly shut the door.

"We're kind of in trouble," she said.

Blue heard his sister's voice. "Get up and get out of there, Blue!"

Uncle Ronny kicked Blue in the ribs one more time before Tommy shouted, "Uncle, he's telling the truth! There was nothing there! I checked myself."

Uncle Ronny knew he had to be lying, and punched his nephew in the mouth, breaking a tooth.

"You see, that's exactly why I killed your father! He lied to me one time too many. Up until now, you never made that mistake. Now I have no choice but to believe you're in the scam with your little friends here."

At that moment, a bouncer ran into the VIP room, yelling, "The alarm's been tripped at the front desk!"

"Go handle it. Why are you interrupting my meeting?" Uncle Ronny said with bloody knuckles and sweat pouring down his face.

"But, sir—"

"Don't question me!"

Uncle Ronny yanked Crux's hair as the bouncer ran out of the VIP room. Crux climbed agilely up the fat man, and punched him in the throat. Uncle Ronny slipped on his brass knuckles as fast as it took Crux to punch him, and slammed his fist into the boy's chest. Uncle Ronny had been one of the most vicious pit fighters in the city long before he decided to monopolize the crime syndicate. Crux flew across the room, shattering a table and all of the martini glasses on top of it.

Blue raised his head and fought through the pain in his chest. He drew himself upright and assumed a fighting stance. With a loud roar of laughter as he saw this, Uncle Ronny coughed and wheezed himself into convulsions.

But then, without warning, or so much as a battle cry, Uncle Ronny ran across the room at Blue. Even though he was in dire need of medical care, Blue was much too fast for him. He dodged Uncle Ronny's attacks with smooth reflexes, then returned the attack with his own series of punches and kicks that shook the fat man and put him on the defensive. With spectacular spin kicks, he got Uncle Ronny again and again, then grabbed a piece of the broken table and held it up against Uncle Ronny's throat.

"Don't do it, son," his parents' voices murmured in the back of his mind.

"Shut up!" Blue screamed out loud, surprising the injured crime boss. The lights flickered as Blue reached back to jam the metal spike through the fat man's skull. But Crux grabbed the rod, and suddenly it was heavier than anything Blue had ever lifted. He dropped it to the floor with a loud thud, and then looked down at Crux.

"Don't do it," Crux said.

Blue let go of Uncle Ronny's wrinkled suit, and put his arm around the boy, ready to walk out of the room. They turned their backs on the defeated man. Blue knew it wasn't worth it, and listened to the boy's wisdom. Hearing the cocking of guns behind them, Blue instantly regretted putting Crux in this situation. Uncle Ronny fired two of his favorite guns, shooting Blue in the back before Blue could shield or push Crux out of the way.

Crux spun around, and landed on the ground in a sitting position with his legs crossed. Then he threw shards of glass from the table at Uncle Ronny. One of the shards shattered the bullet aimed at Crux. The other shards hit the man with enough force to permanently cripple his hands. As he cried out, Crux stood up, and Tommy picked up his uncle's guns.

Blue pleaded with Tommy, "Please, Tommy, just come with us."

"I can't, man. Remember what I told you I had to do if I ever found my father's killer?" Tommy said this quietly, holding the guns at his side as he spoke to his best friend. Tears were running down his face to the point where he couldn't even see Blue's features. He wiped away the tears with the back of a shaking hand, and said, "I don't have anything else to live for, Blue, and you know that."

"Please, Tommy Boy!" Uncle Ronny pleaded before Tommy shot him in the leg.

"Blue, get out of here," Tommy said, smiling sadly. "You know they'll be in here in a minute. I'll take the blame."

Blue walked over to his friend and hugged him. "Thank you."

"No worries. And, Blue, I got to save you twice in one day, after all these years of you saving me."

Tommy wasn't smiling anymore, but he was content nonetheless.

Blue turned and walked out of the VIP room with Crux. They both barely winced as they heard the shots from Uncle Ronny's guns.

The clubbers all ran out into the street as soon as the shooting began. Jayde parried and sidestepped sloppy punch after punch, causing one bouncer after another to drop in agony. As they tried to attack her, they only succeeded in slicing each other and crushing each other's ligaments.

Jayde made her way to the two Witchbreed teens in the middle of the dance floor, who were still dancing and not paying any attention at all to the chaos around them.

"Ahlina, get out of here!" a familiar voice said, stopping Ahlina in her tracks. "Oh, my god!" she said, spinning around. "How did you know I was here?"

Jayde looked over at the front door. "There's no time to explain. Get your friends out of here *now!*"

As Blue walked into the main club, he saw Jayde surrounded by half a dozen men. With a speed that reminded him of his own movement, she was a flurry of attacks and flips, as well as pressure point takedowns. It looked as if she were teleporting across the small space and taking on all of them at once. When the last of them fell to the floor, she looked directly at Blue and Crux.

"This way, Ahlina," Jayde said, reaching for the thin girl's arm.

"Wait! Wait, I said! Wait! Kaery's here!"

Walking to the bathroom, and kicking open the door, Jayde said, "We don't have time for this."

Just then, ten bouncers backed into the room, fighting an enemy from outside. Gunfire began to fill the air. Jayde realized that the only way the entire group could make it out safely was to go through the back.

When Star and Kaery came out of the restroom, they saw dozens of injured pit fighters, moaning on the floor.

Kaery's eyes widened at the sight of Blue. "You?!"

Blue looked into the honey-colored eyes from long ago, and in an instant was brought back to a better time. He didn't say a word, but only kept gazing into her eyes.

Scape and Ahlina both stared, with their mouths open, at Star.

"You can't be serious!" Ahlina said, looking Star up and down.

Star smirked.

"O-M-G," Scape sputtered, putting his hand over his mouth.

"I'm sorry to break up this little reunion," Crux said, as the gunfire got closer and closer, "but we need to get out of here!"

He didn't wait for anyone to follow, but just ran back through the VIP room to the back door.

Jayde agreed with Crux, and simply said to the others, nodding her head toward him, "Get out of here!"

Everyone hurried through the VIP room, treading gingerly over broken glass and pools of blood. Crux made his way to the back alley, and the others swiftly followed. Jayde stayed inside the club to fight off the gunmen.

When Star saw Tommy's body, with his hand pointing a gun at his own head, she acted as if she weren't affected, but she had to fight back tears.

Blue suddenly came to a complete stop, shocked to see the carnage of the body of his best friend, the three bouncers, and what was left of Uncle Ronny. He knelt down to leave his mp3 player in Tommy's hand.

"Goodbye, old friend," he said. "I won't forget you."

Jayde rushed through the room. "It's time to go, Aegis," she said.

Blue somehow knew she was talking to him. He got up and ran after her.

Juno and Sky arrived at the docks at sunset. After a thorough investigation, Juno concluded that there had been a heist. Someone must have tipped off local gangsters that the Triad had a shipment. There were two males and one female, judging from the stiletto heel marks. They had taken the boy in a U.S.-issued muscle car, and one of the males had been bleeding. An explosion like this was more than likely caused by a lucky shot to a generator—unless Surge-Overload had something to do with it. The remaining Triad who was injured, but not killed, reminded Juno of the Mancer's work at the European docks. Juno kept tracing the steps, as though she had missed something.

Sky sat impatiently, handcuffed to the car. "You know you can go to prison for, like, a long time for kidnapping, right?"

Juno glanced briefly at her, and decided almost immediately to just ignore her. She followed a blood spatter away from the explosion, reached down to grab a bloody cloth, and almost stopped moving when she touched it.

"Nina!" she gasped.

"Mom, this is embarrassing!" Surge whined to her mother. She was used to giving orders and saving people, although her parents knew nothing about that. Growing up a lot faster than her parents gave her credit for, or would ever know, she stood rooted to the spot, rolling her eyes.

"You've got to be kidding me . . . , a dress?!" Surge looked at herself in a mirror. "I said I would do what you told me to, but I only asked for my computer. If I put on this stupid dress, and I promise to go to your camps, is that cool?"

After careful consideration, her parents whispered to each other. Each moment was a torture for Surge. So much action was happening right now in the world that being disconnected from her computer was almost killing her.

"Okay," her mom said, "you can bring your laptop . . . , on one condition."

Her dad picked up where her mother had paused: "You have to go to work with me, like you used to after camp."

Surge never really thought about how good she had it in the science labs of her father's company. She smiled as she said, "Of course, daddy." She knew she would have access to priceless information. "Can I get on my computer now, please?"

"Welcome, all of you, to the beginning of your Enlightenment," Gemini said, as Jayde ushered the kids through the doors and closed them firmly.

Chapter 8

SHUT UP AND LISTEN!

They arrived at the old warehouse in silence, the events of the evening still fresh in their minds. Kaery was too nervous to speak, since she feared she would say the wrong thing. Ahlina was also surprisingly quiet and Kaery noticed her glancing a few times at the mysterious woman driving behind the wheel. The punk-rock girl's odd demeanor was enough to make the hair on the back of Scape's neck stand up. Crux fell asleep, leaning against Blue, who just stared distractedly out the window. Star reached over and turned on the radio.

A while later, as they were getting out of the car, they stopped dead in their tracks to stare at the old building. Every face showed lines of worry or anxiety.

Blue had been all over town, but he didn't know a lot about the warehouse district, other than that it had been abandoned for many decades. The last time he had come here he was with Tommy and Guy, when they had to break into a chop shop for Uncle Ronny and torch the place.

Ahlina distinctly remembered a rave she had once come to in this area.

Star had never been here, but the eeriness of the place intrigued her.

As Crux wiped his tired eyes, he squinted at the building, while Jayde walked toward it, saying, "All of your questions shall soon be answered. Come with me."

Her strong walk received silent kudos from Star. Kaery believed her, and was actually as intrigued as Star. They both walked forward, and Scape followed, with Crux at his side.

"Come on!" Crux said. "This is a sanctuary. You can tell by the runes on the building."

Blue looked at the warehouse, not knowing what in god's name Crux was talking about. He studied Crux for a moment as the boy almost skipped his way after the Asian woman, who had wiped out most of Uncle Ronny's bouncers single-handedly. Blue couldn't help sharing the interest the girls had. Besides, he had an urge to make sure the kid was going to be okay, so he reluctantly followed.

Arriving at the door, Jayde placed her hands on specific parts of a rusty metal door that looked as if it were going to fall over at the slightest touch. Blue noticed the broken windows and the bullet holes on the side of the wall near the door.

Star watched her step as she said to Jayde, "You're not some over-elaborate killer or something, are you?"

Ahlina looked at her gorgeous redheaded friend and said, "Shut up, Star. And just when did you become Sky, by the way?"

Star spun around and looked down at her petite friend. "First of all, don't tell me to shut up when I'm asking a legitimate question. Second, we don't know her, so this could be some stupid trap that we see those dumb people in movies fall for."

Before Star could continue, Jayde replied pleasantly, "I'm not here to kill you, or you would be dead already. I'm here to show you what you need to see. Now come in, please."

As she pushed the door open, no one moved. They were all shocked as they looked in with disbelief. Inside was a Japanese pagoda-style courtyard. The stone garden was so neat and well managed that it looked like something on a magazine cover.

Scape was the first to walk through the door. Immediately, he was overwhelmed by the beauty of the stone garden. The walkway was a wooden bridge leading to a large wooden archway.

Star looked quizzically at her friends' expressions and automatically started walking inside.

Kaery knew that what she was looking at was impossible. *There's no way this exotic place is inside a dilapidated warehouse in the middle of a rundown industrial district. What was in those drinks?* But she followed Star anyway.

Ahlina and Crux walked in side by side, passing Jayde.

Blue stood for a long while, watching the others walk over the wooden archway.

Jayde stood patiently, and then murmured, "It is nice to see you again, Aegis."

"What did you call me? And what are you talking about? I just met you, lady."

"Yes, of course you did." Jayde smiled, then bowed with respect as he walked into the building and shut the door behind him.

Blue was about to ask Jayde if he had met her before this night, but suddenly the warehouse door didn't exist any longer. Instead, there was a small Japanese gate with a field beyond it. Jayde was gone, but the kids were still walking toward the pagoda. Blue looked all around for the toned Asian woman who was obviously a martial artist. She was nowhere to be found, so Blue decided not to let too much distance get between him and the others.

As they walked through the archway, Ahlina said, "Isn't this all just a little weird? I mean, how did we end up here? And, trust me, I haven't even had that much to drink."

Scape giggled. "Yes, you did. In the car, when we were getting dressed, fool."

His giggle was stopped by a punch in the arm as Ahlina continued, "You know what I mean. I'm not drunk, and we end up in a miniature Tokyo after almost being shot to death."

Crux said quietly, "This is a sanctuary of someone very powerful. I can feel it."

"Who is this kid, anyway?" Ahlina asked Star. "I thought you hated kids! Why are you hanging out with them in clubs, of all places? I mean, I heard of messed up babysitters, but this takes the cake!"

"His name is Crux," Blue said, walking up behind them. "And she wasn't babysitting him, she was saving his life."

"For the record," Star said, "I still totally hate kids, but this one's alright, I guess." She messed up Crux's choppy Mohawk with her hand.

Kaery whispered to Blue, "I thought you were dead." She almost slapped her hands over her mouth after she said that, but the warm look that Blue gave her made her stop moving completely.

"Yeah, a lot of people did," he said. "I'm surprised you know who I am."

Scape giggled again, dodging another of Ahlina's predictable punches to the arm. "Are you kidding me, Blue? She knows everything about you. We had to hear about it every day up until a month ago or so." Kaery punched Scape's other arm. "Ouch! It's true." He chuckled as he rubbed his arm under his tight green shirt.

They suddenly found themselves at the entrance to a huge castle.

"Okay," Scape said, summing up all their thoughts as they looked up at the looming doorway, "now I will definitely say the creepy factor is here."

"Where are we going, and why won't you say anything to me?" Sky whined to Juno, as frustrated as she could be. "And, you know, you might need some hand sanitizer after picking up bloody hobo rags in a dirty shipyard." Sky reached into her bag to find the sanitizer, surprised to discover her holographic cell phone that she had almost given up on in the bunker.

Juno arrived outside a building that Surge-Overload had told her was a safe place. She got out of the car and looked at the old warehouse. With little inspection from a distance, she could see runes of Magick written on the building. She knew it was a ward, and only people who were invited would be able to see the building, let alone affect it in any way. It might as well be invisible to the world. Knowing this was the right place, she got out and walked over to Sky's door.

"Oh, no!" Sky exploded. "You don't expect me to get out of the car and go into that biohazard firetrap of a building, where some axe murderer probably has my name on some coffin?!"

"Get out! They won't let anything happen to you."

Juno gave this reassurance reluctantly. She didn't feel that she owed this brat any explanations.

"Oh, now you can talk?" Sky retorted, crawling out of the car. Her miniskirt and mismatched high heels made her look as if she were trying to set a new trend. Sky was furious that she hadn't been able to bathe since the day Juno kidnapped her.

Where are my parents? Will they ever find me? The thought nearly made her cry. *But I'll be damned before I cry in front of THIS bitch!*

She hated Juno for dragging her around like this without communicating. She would almost rather go with the Soldiers who attacked her home. And then she remembered that they had actually tried to shoot her, whereas Juno had saved her.

"Who's that?" Sky asked as she looked at the entrance of the warehouse.

Juno was already walking toward the woman. "I have the drop. Do what you will. I've done my piece."

Jayde retorted sharply, "You will be done when Gemini says your work is over."

Sky looked at both of them, listening to every word from twenty feet away as if she were standing next to them. As soon as she had the thought, she was standing next to Juno, asking, "What *is* all of this?"

Jayde held out a welcoming hand. "Come with me, Sky. You will be safe now." She pushed open the door, as Juno walked back to the car.

Sky almost asked Juno where she was going, but at this point she was happy to be rid of her, even though she didn't know who this Asian woman was in front of her. After watching Juno speed off, she peeped cautiously inside at the Archway.

"What in the—?"

While speeding across the Bay Bridge, Juno called Surge-Overload on her micro-headset. "Drop completed."

"Good. Expect your payment in approximately thirty seconds in the lost accounts worldwide."

"No, I don't want your money," Juno said. "I need your help locating someone. I found her DNA, so I know she must be nearby. Will you help me?"

Surge was almost taken aback in her room, since she had never known the hard-edge brawler of an assassin to ask for anything. As far as Juno knew, Surge was some mastermind old man in his basement. She had contacted Juno some time ago, when she found that Juno was accessing OZONE files similar to the ones she was hacking into. Juno did a great job covering her tracks, but she couldn't hide anything from Surge.

In the anonymous voice she always used over the ether, Surge stuttered into the microphone, but quickly regained her composure. "What . . . , what is it that you need my help with?"

"I need you to find the owner of this DNA. I'll upload a file of it soon."

"I'm on it as soon as you send it," Surge replied with total confidence.

★

As the kids walked through the castle, they heard footsteps. They stopped to look at each other as Blue took over point by moving to the front. Crux reached into his bag and then remembered something. He glanced at Star, who was trying to figure out where the footsteps were coming from.

The castle reminded everyone of a different time and place. The serenity only made them all feel even more alien as they glanced at one another to remind themselves that each one wasn't the only uncomfortable soul.

Star moved out of Crux's reach as she whispered to Blue in an obnoxiously loud whisper, "Who *is* it?"

Blue shrugged, then waited as the woman walking toward them approached.

"I hope that wasn't supposed to be a whisper!" Sky said, looking as confident as ever in this unfamiliar castle. "And what are *you* all doing here?"

"I think we all can ask you the same thing," Ahlina said, looking confused.

"This night is getting weirder and weirder," Scape said to Kaery. "Or should I say morning?" He pointed at the sunrise through the open window, which led to another garden.

Kaery quickly glanced at the sun, then back to Sky. "I'm sorry, but how did *you* get here? And do you know where we are?"

"Some annoying government lady in a cat-suit, and I was going to ask you all how *I* got here because, frankly, I don't have a clue. An Asian woman with green eyes, who smelled like orchids, walked me through some corroded warehouse, and poof! I'm in some place surrounded by the outcast club of my high school. Great!"

Star stood, almost starstruck, not saying a word. She just looked at Sky's outfit and wondered how she put together such innovative collections so effortlessly. Now, standing next to Sky, she was about the same height, maybe a little taller. But Sky's presence filled the small courtyard.

Ahlina watched Star eying Sky the same way she did in school. Then she said, "You're such a spoiled ass brat, Sky. You think 'cause you rule the school and the paparazzi, like Gaga, that you can rule this place as well?"

"I didn't mean it like that," Sky apologized sincerely.

Kaery put her hand on Ahlina's shoulder to stop her from opening fire on Sky. "I think it's time we all just tried to figure out where we are," she said, "and why we're here. You're more than welcome to join us, Sky, so you're not alone."

"I guess. Sure," Sky replied, ignoring the glare from Ahlina, as if the thin Asian girl were a flea.

"I have done as you requested, Gemini. Aegis and Crux are here, as well as Kaery, Ahlina, Star, and Scape." Jayde said this reverently, kneeling and looking at the ground.

Maia's head perked up from her concentration at the mention of Scape's name. "Can I greet them, Gemini?" she asked eagerly.

Gemini didn't move, sitting in his crossed leg position, his back straight and eyes closed. "Bring them to me, Maia."

Hopping to her feet and walking out of the circle, she almost ran out of the room.

Gemini opened his eyes. "Jayde, as you know, there is no such thing as coincidence to Supernaturals. How they all came to be here at the same time is something to ponder, but the lesson must be taught regardless. I must prepare them."

✵

As Maia made it down the hall, she anticipated seeing the face of one of her Witchbreed council who had betrayed her in ancient times, although she carried no grudge from that lifetime. Normally, Mancers do not get their memories back, but she was one of the special ones who had undergone Gemini's tutelage. She was anxious to see some of her people again.

I know it's impossible, since most of them are on another plane of existence altogether.

But she kept her cool as she walked around the corner to see them all standing and looking at her impatiently.

"Who are you?" Kaery asked, unconsciously grabbing Blue's arm, since she was startled by Maia's presence. Blue looked down at Kaery, who was fixated on the Latina with blonde hair and black strips running through it.

"I'm Maia, and I will be your escort to my Mentor."

"I mean, what's going on here?" Sky interrupted. "Because my dad—"

"Your dad is *what*?" Ahlina reprimanded. "So rich that he can mysteriously teleport you back home to your safe and cuddly thousand count Egyptian cotton sheets?"

Ahlina's bitter words were even felt by Star, who stayed quiet, watching her idol closely.

"You know," Sky retorted, rolling her eyes at Ahlina, "I'm not sure what your childhood trauma was, but I'm going to need for you to get over it, or get medicated. I didn't ask to be here, and your malicious verbal attack is so last season." Then to Maia she said, "Can your 'Mentor' get us home, please? Those of us who have one?" She looked down at Ahlina and sighed.

"His name is Gemini, and he is this way." Maia searched for Scape in the crowd. He looked a lot like he did in his past life, but his features were even more handsome now. His essence was not yet enlightened, so he probably didn't remember her.

Scape noticed Maia's long look at him, and felt the nostalgic undertone in her glances. He shook off the overwhelming sense of déjà vu and just stood there smiling.

Sky and Ahlina were still glaring at each other all this time.

Jayde joined them at the imposing, dark oak door to a chamber where Gemini was meditating. She or Maia would occasionally join him there to reach a calm state and a higher sense of self.

The halls in the castle had a cool breeze that smelled of spring. Because the sun was not warming the breeze, Sky thought of a temperature that she liked, and the breeze around and near her suddenly felt like a sunny afternoon in southern California near the beach. She did it so unconsciously that Scape had to look at her to see if she noticed that she had done anything.

Jayde nodded to Maia, signaling that she was free to go handle other business now.

The kids all watched as Maia started down the hall, and suddenly disappeared in front of them, like stars twirling and separating, and then gone on the cool breeze. They knew they had to follow Jayde, even though they had a million questions. The smooth stone floor was almost as reflective as a mirror in the large room they were being escorted into.

"Welcome, all of you, to the beginning of your Enlightenment," Gemini greeted them as Jayde ushered the group through the doors.

Gemini was sitting when they entered. But suddenly, with no visible effort, he was standing. His dark skin reminded Sky of ancient Egypt. His long dark cloak floated around him for a moment, then settled down like night falling on a mountain. The tall man smiled as he looked over each and every one of the young Supernaturals.

His voice is so inviting, his eyes so beautiful, Sky thought with a smile. But then, remembering that she was among strangers, she put her guard back up.

Those beautiful silver gray eyes scanned the youngsters, then looked at Jayde.

"I send you to find two Mancers," Gemini said, "and you come back with four Wicasht as well. If I were paying you, I would offer you a raise."

His smile brought Jayde back to much happier times. As she left the room, she closed the door softly behind her.

"I know you all have questions," Gemini said. "And they will be answered. But first, I must tell you who and what you are."

Everyone looked around at the others, then back to Gemini with puzzled expressions.

"I will get right to the point. You are all undoubtedly Supernaturals. You can second guess my words if you like, for that is your choice. But know that I only speak the truth. Kaery can validate that, if you would like to ask her."

As he looked straight at Kaery, his white teeth and warm energy made her retreat to the shy side of her personality.

"I don't know what kind of scam this is," Star exclaimed, "or how dumb you think we are. But there's no way I'm going to sit here and accept all of this as reality!"

"I agree!" Sky added, slowly walking to stand beside Star. "You're all crazy to believe this is more than a trick."

"Shut up, and listen to what he has to say!" Blue shouted, disgusted with both of them and their pouts. "We can at least give him that."

Gemini stood patiently, nodding in approval. Then, pointing at Star, Scape, Ahlina, and Kaery, he said, "You four are known as Wicasht, or the derogatory Witchbreed. You're able to use Magick much as humans use science, but on a much grander scale."

"See, he's already starting the crazy talk," Star said, annoyed and crossing her arms.

Kaery turned to her and said, "Shut up, Star! He's telling the truth."

Gemini continued as if there had been no interruptions at all: "Witchbreed are the first of the Supernaturals." Then, pointing at Sky, Blue, and Crux, he said, "And you three are like Maia, Jayde, and me. We are Mancers."

His look toward the kids was calm but serious. Then he turned around and took a few steps away from them, speaking with his back to them.

They all stepped closer, hanging on his every word.

"Reality," he continued, "through the eyes of Supernaturals, is not easy to comprehend, let alone explain in mundane words. However the story is told, the facts remain the same. There are a series of events that have led all of us to this very moment . . . . Let's start from the beginning. There is an infinitely vast amount of energy and consciousness that has been named many things . . . , Heaven, Valhalla, Utopia, and God, or some other transcendental realm or supreme being. Supernaturals know the true name, which can be translated as the Soulstream . . . . The Soulstream is responsible for the creation of all life, death, or anything inside or outside those complex realms. As a matter of fact, all life shares a shard of the Soulstream. Being infinite in wisdom, intelligence, power, and consciousness, the Soulstream limits how much any given individual can access it without suffering consequences. The only beings that can access the Soulstream at will, and subconsciously, have been named Supernaturals. They have an outlook and understanding of the universe and its many complexities far beyond mere mortal comprehension. These Supernaturals do what they must to protect their secrets, as well as things or beings under their care, such as humans, anima, and elementals."

Kaery was mesmerized. *Every single word he is saying is the utter truth!*

"In the early beginning of history on Earth," Gemini said, "Mancer and Witchbreed came together in the decision that humanity was too naïve, and cast powerful Magick into the universe to enlighten the human populace on Earth. This went against the very balance of things, and the purpose of humans being on the planet. In an instant, humans were connected to the Soulstream as the Mancer and Witchbreed have always been. They were able to use powerful Magick they had no training for, or control over, and disaster struck as the Earth was nearly torn apart that cataclysmic day. The Witchbreed then made a decision to reverse the spell before the Earth was destroyed completely, and to replace the

Enlightenment spell with a Veil of Ignorance, forever returning humans back to the disconnected simple beings they were. Humans are no longer able to comprehend Magick or to see most events or things touched by Magick. Spells are not perfect, and as a result, many glitches occurred. Some humans are still able to tap into the Soulstream, and even though it is only on a minor level, it is nonetheless leftover Enlightenment backlash, which creates new Supernaturals."

So, THAT'S how my people are able to see Supernaturals and understand the language of Magick, Crux thought.

"Now," Gemini continued, "some of the most powerful Supernaturals within all realms are Mancer, Witchbreed, Spiraar, Jreamers, Avatars, Crono, Aenjelhn, Dehmn, Vampyl, Dampyl, Psiel, Magii, Innates, Fae, Draconi, and Undead. Between all of these Supernaturals, there is, and always will be, a clash of light, median, and dark!"

As Gemini stood in front of his audience, he watched the wheels turning behind their eyes.

"The war is unforgiving," he said, "and it is upon you all. The feelings you have all encountered up until this point are very similar. Learn from each other, and learn from your enemies."

After taking in several large gulps of air, and trying to fathom how their lives had brought them to this point, they all looked at each other, realizing that this wise man was not only telling them the truth, but had explained to them something they could not refuse as reality.

Chapter 9

WHERE DREAMS START

(On Pangaea, 250,000,000 B.C.E.:)

"Humans have been on this planet for only several thousand years," Gemini said to the council of Supernaturals in front of him. "But we already see that they are a lot more innocent than we originally expected. The planet is young, and all one large continent, filled with lush vegetation and fresh resources. The prehistoric beasts that run rampant along the lands live harmoniously in an endless cycle of peace and instinct. The humans have small cities all over the continent that are ruled by the Mancers, and taught by the Wicasht. The Jreamers protect the borderlands, and act as patrols, along with enforcers of peace and order."

"Ignorant is more like it," a familiar deep voice came from the hall outside, getting closer with each syllable.

Gemini had been on the planet since before the trees had grown, or the water was drinkable. Many Mancer had come together with Wicasht to purify the living planet and its atmosphere. Nevertheless, Earth was still in the beginning stages of its hundred-billion-year life.

"As you all know," Gemini continued, "we come from the Soulstream, just as they do. They chose to be innocent, and we chose to be enlightened.

It is our duty to protect the Oath of Balance we all took, and not cast this Spell of Enlightenment."

"You need to allow room for change," Anshar said aloud, purposefully, as he looked around the room. His blue-gray eyes pierced the members of the council, drifting over the world's most powerful. "This is a place of endless possibilities, and none of you are taking advantage of it."

Anshar was confident in his approach to the Great Council as he strutted across the formal circular room to the center podium where Gemini was making his plea.

Coolly turning his gaze from Anshar back to the probing eyes of his audience, Gemini continued, "If we do cast this spell, then we may disrupt the world's peace and balance, thereby tainting the human experience."

"They deserve much more than to live like the animals and dinosaurs at our gates," Anshar argued, smiling charismatically at the council. "No offense to those of us who love the anima. Without our help, the humans would be no different from them and have no purpose."

Receiving nods of approval from the thousands of Supernaturals whispering among themselves in the circular room, Anshar seemed to have them wrapped around his manicured fingers—wrapped through lies and deceit. He had won this debate many times before the traditionalist council.

Gemini was still willing to give the Great Council the benefit of the doubt that all of them were not corrupted by Anshar's lies.

"I agree with Gemini!" Kaery's voice boomed above the crowd, shaking the very foundations of the building. "I believe this is a mistake, and so does my Coven."

"Excuse me, Kaery," a council member named Kumarbi spat in her direction, "but you gave up your role as the head of the Anu, Oracles of the Soulstream. So therefore you have no Coven, no more than a Banshee." His staff was glowing at every fiery thought that ran through his head.

Kaery stood up. "I apologize to the Great Council for Kumarbi's lack of respect for my new Coven, the Coven of Unity. We have all come from the traditional Covens that fill this very room, and we are the future of the Witchbreed, as the humans call us. All of us should be unified, or we shall have conflict, which I believe is being caused by Anshar!"

"Those accusations are enough to have you put on trial, Kaery," Anshar retorted, his smile gone deadly. "I would choose my next words very wisely from here on."

Ahlina tugged at Kaery's soft light purple robes to coax her to sit.

The Great Council members whispered together as they cast suspicious glances at Kaery.

Not at all happy that she was being threatened, she sat down next to Ahlina.

Anshar, along with his Coven, the Sinchimes, are definitely up to something foul. Only Gemini is normally bold enough to confront them like this. As an exile from my former Coven, I have nothing else to lose.

She had said her piece, although she wasn't sure if it helped or hurt Gemini's cause.

Gemini looked at Maia, the Goddess of Oracles, who was not particularly happy at the moment with her most favored Coven, the Anu. Rising from her throne, she said, "The stars are changing as we speak. It would seem a great shift is happening."

But then she was abruptly interrupted by Anshar, as he saw the worry in her face.

"You see!" he said. "It has been prophesied in the very stars that change is needed! We have already made a decision about casting the Spell of Enlightenment on the humans. They deserve the right to be more connected to the Soulstream. It is not our right to withhold it from them! We must order the Wicasht Coven of your choice, your majesties, to cast the Spell tonight, as per the prophecies."

Anshar spoke powerfully. Afterward, he looked at Aegis and Sky, bowing respectfully. As he had uttered his words, the Great Council of Supernaturals whispered their concerns to each other.

Aegis clenched his fist and slammed it on his throne, causing the entire Council to turn their heads in his direction.

"I'm tired of the same argument between so many supposedly 'enlightened' beings," he said. "I was chosen to lead the Supernaturals of this planet, so I've made up my mind. Sky and I have come to a decision, and this is simply regurgitating the same old information. As far as we are concerned, this matter is already in the works."

The Council sat silent as he spoke in a booming voice. His very energy shifted the vibration of the room, making all the Supernaturals feel uncomfortable. He knew he had their attention, since he had the power to destroy most of them with only a thought or a gesture.

Placing his hand on top of his wife's, he said, "Sky, I would like you to appoint the Coven that will be casting the Spell of Enlightenment. Then we'll move on to the next order of business."

Sky looked at her powerful husband and nodded. Scanning the room, she looked over many Witchbreed, knowing that most of them were extremely powerful and capable. But she also felt uncomfortable around Anshar and his Coven of Sinchimes, though they had been asking her for many years for the right to cast a powerful spell across the planet—a spell that, according to them, would ultimately make the planet thrive. Sky looked at the smug smile on Anshar's face and turned her gaze back to her husband.

"Blue, I have an answer for you," she said, calling him by his pet name.

As his blue eyes softened for his beautiful wife, his shining armor lit up as well.

"I know which Coven shall be the successors of the Spell of Enlightenment," Sky said proudly, and loud enough for the entire gathering to hear, although she spoke in a voice that was not strained.

Star almost thought it was Glamour, but knew it was just one of Sky's many abilities to be able to control the audible sound in the area so that everyone heard her.

The fourteen great Covens sat forward on the edge of their seats, listening closely. Some of them dreaded the task of performing a spell of this magnitude. There were a few Covens, including the Celidor, the Fenyang, and the Sinchimes, who were smiling, prepared to take charge of such a prestigious spell.

The spell was supposed to be a work of art, since it was an engineered creation of the most powerful Magicks the Coven could conjure to perform the Mancer's task. It was extremely dangerous, and a huge responsibility, so whoever was chosen would be the one whom Sky believed was the most qualified, and therefore the most powerful Coven in the Great Council.

The many Mancers in the room stood by, watching this as spectators, enjoying the drama.

As Sky stood, the ground shook, and the very air in the room became refreshingly light, as the breeze showed her power over the elements. She demanded attention, since her words would shape the very future of the planet.

"The Coven that I believe is most qualified to conjure the Spell of Enlightenment," said Sky with a smile, "is the Coven of Unity!"

With a shocked expression on her face, Kaery said, "I'm sorry. I don't believe I heard that correctly." She said this aloud without realizing she was talking.

Ahlina's expression matched her own as Kaery asked again, "Did she just say our Coven is performing the Spell of Enlightenment?"

Ahlina nodded.

Sky was able to hear every whisper of everyone on the continent, so no one in this room was an exception. "Yes," she said, "the Coven of Unity will be the successors of the spell!"

"I humbly apologize for interjecting," said Anshar, "or questioning your most wise words, my Goddess, but the Coven of Unity is less than a thousand years old. They are barely able to hold their tongues in a court like this. They all abandoned their traditional roles in their respective

Covens." He motioned to the entire Council, then continued, "I highly doubt they are capable—"

"You are mistaken, Anshar!" Sky interrupted. "Do not overstep your boundaries, Witchbreed. I am Queen, and I have spoken! Kaery and her young Coven are to cast the Spell of Enlightenment *tonight*."

Sky's suddenly placid smile and black diamond eyes pierced through Anshar. As he bowed in submission, his face lost color, and his brow formed a bead of sweat. "Yes, your Highness, I apologize once more." He lowered his gaze to the floor and took steps backward until he had left the room.

Anshar's glare at Kaery had not gone unnoticed by many of the Great Council, most of whom agreed with his frustrations. They had been around for much longer than the renegades who had formed the Coven of Unity. Kaery's Coven was not liked by many of the Wicasht Covens, but the Mancers seemed to favor them.

Anshar's Coven, the Sinchimes, stood up and followed their diplomat out of the room, some throwing disgusted looks toward Star, Kaery, and Scape.

The young, red-eyed boy, Ewm, looked away from the Celidor and leaned toward Khenebu, whispering, "Our old Covens will never forgive us, will they?"

"I fear we are beyond forgiving at this point," Khenebu replied. "We are favored by the Mancers, and now have a job to complete." He looked at his former Coven, the Fenyang, known for their technologically advanced weaponry.

Heaven, sitting next to Ewm, said, "Some of our Covens are more forgiving than others. Mine wished me well in accepting the bond between you all." Her thick purple hair and the sound of her voice from three vocal chords were mesmerizing.

Sky looked archly toward the Sinchimes Coven as they left the room. She considered reprimanding them for their blatant contempt of Blue's court, but decided instead to congratulate the Coven of Unity for being the most favored Coven of all the Wicasht. She knew she had angered many in the chamber, but she had observed this Coven closely for hundreds of years, and never had another Coven spoken so greatly of each other and of their intentions for a peaceful and powerful world. The Coven of Unity might be young, but they had saved many kingdoms time and again with innovative spells that none of the traditional Covens displayed. As far as Sky could see, they were the future.

Although Blue questioned their loyalty to the Mancers, he backed Sky's decision.

Kaery and her small Coven of nine sat in the hall long after everyone else had left. They remained silent as the echo of Sky's words rang through their ears. Kaery was dumbfounded by the fact that her Coven had been chosen over many others that were more prestigious and more qualified. Ordered to perform a spell they were opposed to, they weren't really sure how they would cast it.

Gemini walked into the Great Council room and looked at the young Coven for a while. His relaxed manner gave them time to pull themselves together.

"I am sure," he said, "all of you are nervous and secretly believe you may fail. I am here to tell you that I have spoken to Maia, who says you will succeed in your Magick."

Kaery sat up, beaming her gratitude at one of the wisest mentors and Mancers on the planet. She had collaborated with him on many occasions about strategy, and he was the one who had told her to follow her heart by forming this small band of Witchbreed, as they had been nicknamed by the other Covens and humans.

Walking over to Kaery and gently touching her cheek, he said, "You are strong, and shall continue to be. Listen to your heart, and the rest shall follow." He walked away, but then turned back to look into the eyes of the nine Witchbreed. "Remember this well," he said. "There is no Magick you cast that you cannot *un*cast." He did not smile as he said this, so everyone took his advice very seriously.

"I understand," Kaery said.

Gemini walked out of the room and into the throne haven of Sky and Blue, where the Queen was speaking with a Mancer named Ninala.

"Your baby will be so blessed and beautiful, Nina," Sky said, patting Ninala's pregnant belly. "I'll make sure he has an entire Kingdom to himself . . . . Why, hello, Gemini."

Smiling with respect at Gemini, Ninala said, "I will go to Juno now and tell her of your great blessings, Sky. Thank you."

As Ninala walked past Gemini, she touched the immortal's hand, sensing the love and respect emanating from him, but also the worry for her life and that of her baby. While she walked out, her smile slowly turned into a worried expression.

Sky was so certain that the spell would be successful, but Gemini did not feel the same way.

Blue strode into the room after a meeting with his most powerful Mancers. Before realizing that Gemini was there, he took off a piece of his ornate armor.

"Crux will take the front lines in battle," he said, "in case something goes wrong with the spell."

Sky looked quickly away from Gemini toward her husband, floating across the room as easily as most people breathe.

"Nothing will go wrong, my love," she assured him. "We have spoken to all of the Oracles, and this must be done. The humans shall share in our power. The planet will be unified much like the Soulstream."

Sky helped Blue to take off another piece of his armor.

"I'm sorry to intrude, Aegis," Gemini said. "I was just coming to ask if I may witness the spell itself, so that I may aid the young Coven of Unity, if need be." His words were genuine but calculated.

"As you wish," Blue said, raising a hand to touch his wife's beautiful brown skin. Then, looking sternly at Gemini, he added, "Make sure nothing goes wrong, because we have an army of restless Supernaturals!"

Gemini took the hint and walked out without another word.

In Gemini's lair, all of the kids were holding hands as their eyes opened. Then they simultaneously gasped and fell instantly asleep.

"Jayde," said Gemini, "take the Witchbreed to their homes and watch over them. Now that we know they are here in this time and place, we know what we must do."

He gazed fondly at the Supernaturals as they slumbered on the stone floor. Jayde lifted two at a time with ease, and walked quietly out of the room.

"We started this war," Gemini said, "and we must atone for what we've done."

Chapter 10

WHAT IF . . .

Sky woke up with a raging headache. Her thoughts automatically brought her to the dream she had just had. Not allowing herself to wake up completely by keeping her eyes closed, she wondered why her dream was so elaborate.

And just how long have I been sleeping?

The rays of sunlight beaming through the window made her reach up on autopilot for the blinds she had been pulling for the past eighteen years. But to her surprise, there were no blinds where they should have been. Also, she didn't smell breakfast made by their chef, Lupé. Reluctantly, she opened her eyes from the strange dreamscape she was still trying to understand.

Without realizing it, she let out a loud scream. Her voice was so shrill that it broke the window near the bed.

That's definitely not MY window!

Sky sat up, looking around the room as if she were trapped in a nightmare. Still unbelieving as well as stubborn, she whispered to herself, "This is all a dream. I'll wake up any second, now that I know I'm in a dream."

"Nice try," Maia said sarcastically, trying to hold back a laugh. "But reality doesn't work that way, even for someone like you."

"You're the psychic girl from my dreams! What's going on? Where am I?" By now, Sky was in a near panic.

"Yes, I'm the 'psychic girl' from your dreams. You just woke up after four days of sleeping in Gemini's lair. He's actually waiting for you in the meditation room, so you might want to get dressed."

Maia said all this politely with a smile, then shut the door to leave Sky to her own pondering.

This CAN'T be right. My life was perfect. My parents are great. Oh, my God, my poor mom! And dad must be worried sick! What the hell am I wearing? Oh, the same outfit I put together the day that psycho lady kidnapped me. Well, she did kind of save my life, but still, I don't understand how I ended up here. I remember that day at school, and the whispers. I remember the flying outside the house. The dream, it was so real! I was some sort of Queen or Goddess, and Blue was my husband. Now, that's just WEIRD. Maybe that psycho lady, Juno, drugged me, and this is the aftereffect. When was the last time I ate? God, I need a bath!

As Sky got out of bed, her feet touched the cold stone floor. Looking down, she saw a polished reflection of herself. The room was fairly large—not modern like her room back home, but more like something out of medieval France. The mirrors on the wall and the armoire smelled of preserved smoked rosewood. The jewels on the top of the armoire matched the dresses that were hanging in the wardrobe. Everything seemed familiar, but Sky couldn't really put her finger on why. She walked across the room, getting used to her bare feet on the cold floor. A breeze was blowing into the room through the broken window. Sky stopped for a moment to make it change directions. Instantly, the wind left the room as quickly as it had come. Even the temperature changed to ensure her comfort.

When Sky made her way into the bathroom, she saw one of her favorite objects: a large marble claw-foot bathtub. Without any hesitation, she turned on the water. There was jasmine bath oil on a shelf nearby. Sky looked at herself in the mirror for a long time.

What if this is still a dream?

Walking back to the tub, which was full now, she put her hand in the freezing water, which within seconds became hot. Watching the bathwater steam up from the tub, Sky smiled.

If this is a dream, go for it!

She slipped out of her small skirt and high-fashion camisole, took off her Victoria's Secret underwear, and slid into the bath, relaxing every muscle as the water glided around her skin as if it were welcoming her home.

The jasmine scent of the bath oil brought Sky to such a point of relaxation that she almost fell asleep again. Sinking underwater, she noticed she could still hear as well as if she were out in the air. While she moved around in the large tub as if it were her mother's womb, her thoughts wandered back over her short life.

I've been so blessed, compared to everyone else. What if it hasn't all been coincidence? Maybe this dream is trying to teach me something. Whatever, it feels amazing. I know this is impossible. I can even breathe underwater.

So long as she continued to believe this was all a dream, Sky was totally relaxed. Eventually, she floated out of the tub, with beads of water levitating off her soft skin back into the tub. Not a drop fell onto the stone floor as Sky went over to the wardrobe, excited about putting on new clothes.

They're outdated, but the fabric is so luxurious, and the craftsmanship is impeccable.

There was a bright green-and-blue dress that stood out more than the others. The smell of silk, woven in the sixteenth century, brought nostalgia to Sky, which scared her almost as much as the Council Meeting in her dream had.

As she tried on the dress, she thought, This could be tailored in a couple of places, but it's beautiful, nonetheless.

As Sky put on the dress, she decided to give it an update. Looking at herself in the mirror, she began shredding the silk. Her rips were so precise that the dress soon looked like a deconstructed haute couture piece of work from one of her favorite designers. The breeze danced over her skin as Sky spun around to admire herself. Smiling with pride, she suddenly saw Maia judging her from the doorway.

"Please continue to pirouette like some cartoon princess on a ballet stage. Don't mind me waiting for you for the past few hours since I woke you up."

Sky stood still with perfect posture as if she were too proud to be embarrassed by this intrusion. Somehow, though, she knew that Maia's critical eyes could look straight through her.

Could it really be HOURS?!

"Gemini and Jayde are in the meditation room, waiting to brief your royal highness," Maia said, while waiting with her hands on her curvy hips.

Appreciating the exquisite features of the petite Latina, Sky tried to remind herself that this was just a dream, even though everything felt completely real. As soon as she thought of moving into the hall, she was there in an instant, as though carried by the wind.

I LIKE this dream! I can do anything I want!

Maia looked at Sky with amazement as the beauty floated down the hall, then followed her as fast as her feet could carry her. Maia knew from Gemini and Jayde's training that she herself was not one of the Mancers who was gifted with many physical powers. Rather, she had the powers of Angels and Celestial Beings.

That's ironic, considering that my parents thought I was possessed!

The funny thing was that, in every story Maia had ever read about Angels, all of them had wings and flew around.

And here I am, out of breath, chasing a socialite brat who can fly at will!

Maia constantly wished she could unlock the skills within her, but as Jayde had promised, that would all come in due time.

The chamber looked exactly like the one in the dream, large and ominous, but there was Gemini, sitting in silent meditation. Sky didn't want to disturb him, knowing how hard it was to calm down for a proper meditation.

Then she thought to herself, *What if I'm NOT in a dream?*

She shook off the thought as she looked down at the reflection of herself floating above the stone floor.

Nope! Still dreamin'!

As soon as she thought about touching the floor with her outstretched toe, a hand grabbed her so fast that she didn't have time to react. Gemini was looking at her calmly.

"It's time you stopped pretending this is a dream," Gemini said. "Your denial is the result of being raised among humans. But that shall soon pass."

"What are you talking about?" Sky asked, trying to pull her arm from the grip that was like velvet-covered steel. "And what's up with you being so strong?"

"You shall soon be strong as well," Gemini said, walking Sky to the center of the room as he eased his grip, but still did not release the girl completely.

Sky had no choice but to follow along.

If I'm dreaming, why don't I have more control than this?

Maia opened a door just in time to see Gemini and Sky in the middle of the room. She caught her breath, trying to regain her composure. Maia had been home-schooled, so she never had the chance to be what Sky was—popular.

If I weren't so intimidated, I'd like to get to know her a lot better.

Knowing what was coming, Maia wondered if Sky were fully prepared for it.

✶

This was the most grueling but clichéd thing that Blue had ever done.

Why in the hell am I climbing a mountain? And how in the hell is a twelve-year-old boy, who's half my weight, BEATING me?

Blue was ready to give up. The sweat rolling off his skin onto the mountain path reminded him that he was definitely not in as good a shape as he had thought. By human standards, his physique was athletic, since he had made sure to do his daily exercises, even when he was working for Uncle Ronny. The thought of Tommy was enough to make Blue regain his focus and run even harder.

"C'mon, Blue!" Crux called. "We've been at this for the past four days, and you always want to give up around the same time."

Crux was still jogging in place, not even sweating. As he watched Blue running clumsily up the hill, he thought, *He looks more like a berserker than a runner!*

Crux stepped out of Blue's way, seeing that his friend was actually speeding up. As Crux thought about weighing less, every step and skip became more like a leap, and he was soon on Blue's heels.

Anticipating that Crux was catching up, Blue began to push himself even harder toward the top of the mountain. With the checkpoint just in sight, he picked up his pace.

Crux giggled to himself as he tossed a small stone at Blue's right foot, focusing on the pebble weighing a few pounds—just enough to throw his competitor off course a bit.

When the pebble hit its target, Blue tripped and rolled over on the dusty path, his momentum taking him toward the mountain edge at a frightening speed. In a panic, he tried to reach for something to catch himself, but, failing that, rolled right over the cliff.

Knowing that this was the end of his tortured existence, Blue couldn't help thinking of his dead family. But suddenly, his arm was clasped by a small hand.

I don't know how Crux is doing this, but I don't give a damn!

Blue looked down to the long drop onto the rocks below, then up to his grinning savior.

"What are you laughing at?" Blue yelled. "Get me up!"

With as much ease as it would take him to lift a sheet of paper, Crux dumped Blue unceremoniously back onto the trail.

Dirt was never more inviting than it was at that moment. Blue scowled at Crux as he jumped to his feet and ran toward the mountaintop.

Crux was about to apologize for the stunt until it dawned on him that he was going to be beaten this day. He tried flicking deadly pebbles at Blue, but this time the young Eurasian was ready and dodged his attacks.

As Blue triumphantly reached the top, Jayde was suddenly standing in front of him.

"Whoa!" he cried, trying not to crash into her. "Where did *you* come from? Did you see that? I made it to the top this time!"

Blue was so excited that he didn't react to the palm strike that hit his chest like a train, cracking his ribs. All he remembered was flying off the cliff, looking up to see Jayde holding Crux back. Crux was screaming like a friend who wanted desperately to save him.

Why did she hit him over the edge?

This was his second brush with death in less than five minutes. This time, there was an uncomfortable silence, not even his family's voices. Blue knew with certainty that he was going to die. As he crashed against stone and boulder, rolled down the mountain, and slammed into everything in his path, he listened in horror to the sound of his bones being crushed and pulverized. He had done some stupid and suicidal things in his time, but this was by far the worst.

Chapter 11

LOST TRAIL

"This is impossible!" Surge said aloud to herself.

It had been a week, and there was still no response from the sanctuary or its keeper. Surge had been waiting for correspondence or some other type of communication from Jayde. Even though Sky Bradford was the last person on the planet that Surge would have thought was a Supernatural, this was confirmed by Juno. Jayde had taken her, but then fell off the map as if she had disappeared.

By now, Surge was tired of looking for her, as she monitored the media and heard the news that Sky had been abducted. The kids at school held memorial services, as if Sky had died, demonstrating that she was a lot more popular than she probably gave herself credit for. Already, kids were starting to riot in their school because of her loss. And in schools across the country, kids put up countless blogs and videos online, begging her kidnappers to return her safely. Surge laughed at quite a few of her biggest fans' video blogs: some of them crying and asking her parents to donate her closet to them in the same breath.

Surge finally gave up on her hunt for Sky, just hoping the girl was fine. She moved on to her next order of business: the DNA sample that Juno had uploaded matched a baby in an Oregon hospital named Nina

Waterford. Surge-Overload searched everything she could on the girl, reading at the end of the report that she was presumed dead as of May 12th, two years before. Surge shrugged.

Apparently, this Nina Waterford died in a car accident, along with her parents, at the age of nineteen.

"Juno, I have the file you were looking for. It'll be uploaded before I finish this sentence. Surge-Overload. Over and out."

Juno smiled in the middle of the secret transmission to her micro set, looking at the partner she had been paired with. As he noticed her smile, her face changed back to its concentrating professional mode.

"Why were you smiling?" Agent Narles asked her, knowing he would never get an answer from his deadly new beautiful partner. All of the rumors about her were true. She was unpredictable, but one of the best in the world at what she did.

Another call had come in on a Code 2 this week. Narles was always excited to get Supernatural marks. This was a suspected dangerous Coven of Witchbreed in the sewers. Although he had only fought a couple of Supernaturals in the past, he was as confident as a decorated pilot from the U.S. Air Force.

I'm more than capable of taking out any perp that my new employers give me.

OZONE had recruited him not long after his wrongful discharge. Narles had been close to committing suicide mere seconds before the call came in from an OZONE Receptionist. He took it as a sign from God that he should stay alive. For the past six years, he had been assassinating for them and had an excellent track record. Laying his life on the line for the call of duty was what Agent Narles lived for.

Juno strode past the tall man and jumped into the sewers, landing on the wet tunnel below, instantly pointing her guns in all directions. The coast was clear as she continued to walk through the perimeter.

How the hell does she jump that far down gracefully with no rope? It must be her gear.

He followed her as fast as he could with his spelunking cable and Brain-tech armor to soften his fall in case he slipped.

Narles was a lot of things, and being a dedicated Soldier was definitely one of them. He took his job very seriously, and had no qualms about reprimanding anyone. The hierarchy at the base had told him to secretly spy on Juno and send in transmissions. She had been on and off the grid too many times in the recent past, so there were minor gaps in her reports. Although nothing was out of place, it was protocol to shadow the Agents, just in case.

Juno knew his intentions. Narles was fairly attractive for a human. What he lacked in intelligence, he made up for in heart. Juno had seen many Soldiers like him and knew that OZONE bred his kind like steroid cattle. She could hear him following her in his best stealth performance.

There were some minor alarm traps that Juno sidestepped or disarmed in the dark, putrid tunnels. She almost thought of leaving a few for Narles to disarm himself or be caught in some nasty dramatics, but she couldn't find it in herself to care about such vindictive things as she thought about Nina's blood sample.

Now that it had been confirmed that Nina was alive in this lifetime, or at least had been, Juno smiled in the dark as she performed her perimeter sweep. Sensing the presence of Witchbreed nearby, she signaled for Narles to scout another area, since she didn't want him to find them.

Narles got the signal and dashed down a random tunnel. His senses on edge, he looked all around for traps, and was proud when he found and disarmed three separate ones. Then he suddenly realized that he was deep within the sewers, and his partner was patrolling another area altogether, according to his GPS.

Peeking around a corner, Juno saw six young kids playing video games and laughing together. They seemed like any other kids, but with her Supernatural sight, she saw Magick written on their young bodies. There were three boys and three girls, none over the age of thirteen.

These were definitely Wicasht. Juno readied her clip, then walked into the room, pointing the guns at the backs of the kids' heads.

"You have one choice to make if you want to live," Juno began as the startled kids dropped what they were doing and turned to give her their full attention.

"You're a cop?" the oldest boy asked. His dirty, dishwater blonde locks were secured under a baseball hat, hiding his eyes.

"Hell, yeah, she's a cop! Look at her outfit!" said the oldest girl, who happened to be thirteen.

"Leave this place now," Juno said. "The agents are after you, and the only way to find sanctuary is to run to the nearest internet source and wait for your guide."

"Pagan, what should we do?" a skinny boy asked, as a little African American girl wrapped her arms around the blonde boy's leg.

Obviously, Juno thought, *the blonde boy is the leader of these kids.*

Narles was closing in on Juno's location, his guns already locked and loaded. He didn't care what age or gender these beings were. According to OZONE files, all of them were extremely dangerous and capable of terrorist destruction. That was all he needed to know, as his heart raced.

Juno's position had been compromised because she had been standing in the same spot for too long. He knew these were the key indicators that she had found the marks.

I'll be damned if I let her take all the glory! Who does she think she is, sending me off in the sewers to get lost while she cleans up another quest on her own?

Not appreciating the rookie treatment Juno was giving him, he ran a little faster toward her.

OZONE had planted a secret GPS tracking device in Juno's new suit, which Narles had access to via his 3D holographic GPS.

She may have thought she could lose me, but I'm a lot more cunning than she gives me credit for. I'll prove it to her.

This was it. It was time for him to get promoted and work with the likes of his idol, Guardian. He was going to take down the marks with his custom-made hollow points. As he turned the corner on top of Juno's location, his eyes widened behind his goggles.

✶

Surge-Overload heard the entire conversation through Juno's micro set. She was multitasking at the same time, looking through Top Secret OZONE files.

There's NEW technology!

Her heart raced as she read up on the Aeon-nanotechnology. This was meant for the Soldiers and Agents of OZONE to adapt to the environment or the abilities of the Supernaturals through microscopic bio-cybernetics. Brain Tech was a busy place, and this was their latest and greatest invention.

I wonder what Sky would think if she knew that her beloved father had engineered the bio-warfare that could destroy us all? The world would be better off with this little bit of technology snatched up and erased from the database.

All backup files and any mention of them automatically "ghost touched" them, as the hackers called it. One minute something was there, and the next it was gone, like a ghost. Surge was proud of herself for stealing the file, until she realized . . . .

This is a trap!

✶

Guardian sat in the Control Panel with the Receptionists and his Commander-in-Chief, his eyes fixed on the hundreds of monitors in front of him. He was more than adept at computers, thanks to the gruesome training that OZONE required of all their Agents. The Receptionists were a special kind of Agent, however, and Guardian soon realized they were humans who could use Magick. His confusion startled him somewhat, but he watched as the Techno-mages tried to track the location of their most dangerous terrorist, a Supernatural hacker named Surge-Overload, who had been hacking into their systems for the past few years. They profiled Surge-Overload, suspecting that he was a middle-aged Witchbreed man, who was highly adaptable, and extremely powerful in techno-Magick. Every Receptionist in the room had a personal infatuation with, and a vendetta against, Surge-Overload, knowing that this would be the bust that would make one of them the most powerful hacker in the world, and the most trusted OZONE Agent. After all, the field Agents were grunts to these guys.

Guardian could feel the shift in power and influence within OZONE. He also knew that he was part of a dying breed of heroes. He had done his job so well that he had almost knocked out all the competition. It seemed that, these days, all he was sent to do was search and destroy. Because of all this technology, which minimized the risks and possibilities, he seldom had to conduct real investigations.

The Receptionists calculated the risks involved in every mission, based on highly classified information about all of the Mission files of all Agents in the field. They knew what the Supernaturals were capable of, and annihilated them accordingly.

"Surge-Overload is running from us, sir!" Receptionist Deme reported to the Commander-in-Chief.

"Don't lose the scumbag! Track his location, and send Guardian to take him down."

"Yes, sir! Receptionists, infiltrate your best Ether labyrinths!" Deme commanded the dozen Receptionists in the room, as Guardian watched, completely confused.

Surge-Overload flew through firewalls like a cannonball through paper, crashing systems along the way, and exploding computers all over the OZONE network. This resulted in major losses for OZONE, which made her glad. She was determined to teach them a lesson. Usually, she ventured through their system virtually undetected, but now she knew for a fact that there was Magick at play here.

The traps are much too elaborate and intelligent.

She had never before encountered an enemy like this, and, to be honest, she enjoyed the challenge. They were only fractions of nanoseconds from cornering her into Ether labyrinths. These were temporary jail cells in which programmers sent hackers while they tracked physical locations or completely destroyed hackers' connections to the web.

Twice, Surge tricked her trackers into their own Ether labyrinths.

I have valuable information, and I'm going to take it out of here, once and for all.

She could no longer afford Soldiers chasing Supernaturals all over the globe. There were powerful Agents out there, and Surge wanted the list of their names.

When she was back at the portal she had come through, she decided to leave her own Ether mine behind. Any techno-mage who decided to follow her would meet catastrophic consequences.

Surge sent out a small beacon to lure her enemies. The virtual world was different as she navigated through this Ether and electronic realm more easily than her physical body had ever allowed. She knew the ins and outs of the place, the way a child knows its sandbox. As two of her pursuers quickly approached, she watched with amusement. Although she was playing a deadly game, this was fun for Surge. Anyone who went through this trap would be hit with an electromagnetic wave that would follow them back to their point of origin and forever destroy all of their electronics—hence Surge-Overload's name. The end result would be a massive and explosive meltdown.

Deme sat in his chair, connected to his monitor, as his palms and fingertips seemed to meld with the keyboard he was touching. His most trusted Receptionists were in this room, and they were extremely close to trapping, and possibly destroying, Surge-Overload. Deme's ego swelled with joy as two of his best techno-mages found the portal that Surge-Overload had run through.

Oh, no, it's a reverse trap! "No! Don't go through!"

It was too late. As the two Receptionists ran through the portal, Surge watched their virtual images get snared, and a ripple effect of electromagnetic force followed their trails back to the OZONE labs. She laughed to herself as she imagined the damage she was about to do.

Deme instantly commanded his techno-mages to put up their best shields and block the incoming onslaught. Many mainframes and files were lost, and computer screens literally exploded when the electromagnetic wave hit the Control Panel. The two techno-mages who were trapped dropped to the floor, as if their memory had been wiped clean.

Deme set up powerful barriers, but even he was knocked away from his machine with blistering hands, and a new respect for the hacker they had underestimated.

"What the fuck just happened?" the Commander-in-Chief demanded.

Guardian had watched the whole battle through the monitors. All he could perceive was that this was no ordinary hacker. Surge-Overload was OZONE's greatest threat at the moment, and if this were the best team against him, then maybe Guardian's job was still secure.

Juno gave the kids more than ten thousand dollars, plus an untraceable cell phone that she told them to use on their way. Then she fired a few random shots into their lair long after they were gone and turned around to search for her spy of a partner.

Narles had been anticipating his next few kills. As he gracefully rolled in the filthy sewage to turn the corner, he found that he was only aiming his guns at a wall that had been spray-painted with graffiti.

"OZONE SUX!" it blared, with a tongue sticking out of a happy face.

Narles was upset. Somehow his GPS had been hacked and redirected. Throwing his goggles down, he screamed aloud in anger and frustration. Then he shot a few rounds in the air and at the wall.

Chapter 12

ONE OF US

Gemini's firm grip made Sky shrink to the edge of fear. Knowing that she hadn't been taking all of this very seriously up to now, she had been trying to think of anyone she knew who would.

This is the stuff of movies or someone else's life, not mine. I refuse to believe it. Gemini said I was in denial, but what exactly does that mean?

If she thought she was going crazy before, now was not the time to reevaluate that theory. As she followed Gemini toward the center of the large room, she was beginning to worry more than she had expected.

Maybe I don't WANT the answers to my questions. Maybe I want to live a nice, normal, superficial life with a bunch of people who have no idea who I am, but smile in my face as if they adored me. Mom said to be careful what I wish for, as if she were on some stupid "Get well" card. Why is he grabbing my arm so hard, and how do I get out of this place? Better yet, where IS this place?

When Gemini got to his destination, he turned to face Sky. Looking into his eyes, she saw that he was not there to hurt her, but to show her something. After a long, hard stare, he released her arm.

"You have lived that life long enough," he said. "It is time to embrace who you really are. You have felt the constant struggle within your own soul, as if you didn't belong. Your mind wanders even when you are surrounded by people. Your true nature is screaming and pushing you to do something more, although you have no idea what it is you're supposed to do with your life."

As he spoke, Sky's wall of defiance evaporated into a film of vapor.

Am I that transparent? How could he know exactly how I feel? This has got to be a dream or some kind of trick.

"You see, that's your problem," he said. "You think too much . . . , like *them*. The humans."

"I *am* human!" Sky protested futilely, as if she didn't believe it herself.

"Don't blaspheme!"

This was not a threat, but more of a warning.

Reaching out his hand, palm up, he said, "If you are prepared to find out who you truly are, then simply take my hand."

Sky fought an internal battle for a few moments before reaching out to touch him. She flashed back to the time she was a little girl and almost drowned. But instead of dying that day, she thought about breathing, and she did—underwater. She tried to explain it to the lifeguard who jumped in to save her, but he just thought she was in shock and lucky to be alive.

She also thought about how she had never taken a martial arts class, or even fought anyone. But when Juno came for her, she moved as if she had been fighting for her whole life. She reached out to Gemini, hoping to finally get the answers to the questions she had been asking herself time and again. As her hand slid into his smooth palm, a voice called from behind her.

"Are you sure she's one of us?"

Maia asked this in a hopeful tone.

Gemini looked at his twin self holding Sky's hand, as the two of them floated in the air. The girl was already deep in a trance.

Maia was almost startled at the sight of the two Geminis. She had only seen them in the same room once before, when they were training her to use her powers. As far as she could tell, these two were identical. Even energetically, they shared the same bright beacon within, yet they were two completely different powers. She felt that the one next to her could level the building, while the one across the room could inhale all its oxygen.

"She is one of us," Gemini said. "It will take great effort to make her see what you saw, the truth of why you're here. Once she knows that, she will be instrumental in destroying OZONE once and for all." Gemini spoke confidently to his trusted pupil. "Jayde is having similar issues, I'm sure."

Blue's wounds were so severe that he was certain he must be dead. He had never been religious, but somehow he found himself thinking of his family in heaven. Their voices, which he had so loathed when they were alive, were quiet now, leaving him feeling hollow and forgotten. But his pain reminded him that he was definitely not dead—yet.

I guess I got what I deserved. I killed my family. I failed my best friends in the world. I've done so many wrong things, and now look at me. Always fighting against everything and everyone, and look where it got me. I don't regret anything, though . . . , except not having more control of my own destiny. This all feels so much like someone else's life, and I'm just looking at it from a distance. Maybe depression was a bit of it, and maybe stubborn pride was a huge part of it, but either way, I'm a waste of time now.

God, I was a fool to think I was invincible. I mean, after I got shot, I barely put pressure on the wounds and kept walking around like it was nothing. Somehow I felt like my family saved me, because the wounds were completely healed by the time I arrived at the Forbidden City. Shit, it even confused me, so I wasn't going to say anything to Tommy. Poor Tommy! I should have protected him a lot more, but he made his choice in the end. Is this what those people on the ER dramas feel like? Hell, no! No one on Earth has ever felt like this. I know it. It hurts so much, I can't think without lightning bolts of reality striking every limb.

I know this sounds like a cliché, but if someone is up there and can hear me, I promise I'll change. I will protect the boy and his innocence. He doesn't deserve my fate or Tommy's, and if anyone can hear me up there, please, send some painkillers! Oh, my God, it hurts to even laugh in my own head. That's what I get for not taking all of this seriously. It's too late now anyway, so why not laugh it off? Damn! I fell from the top of a mountain and probably hit every rock on the way to hell.

I can actually move an arm? Oh, hell, no. Those are my bones in separate places. I can't even scream, it hurts so bad. I know my mouth is open, and I can only guess that's blood I just coughed up. This is pathetic, but I want to get one more chance. I know this time I'll do things differently! My head feels like it's gonna explode from the pressure. I can barely see through my own tears, but the sun is overhead, and that sting in my eyes feels a lot better than any other part of my body right now.

Wait! Is my arm moving? Yes, it is! I'm NOT paralyzed! I'm wiggling my toes . . . , like those guys in the movies always do. Damn, it hurts! Well, at least I'm not completely dead. Oh, it's gonna suck when the animals come to feed on me. Stop being morbid, Blue! Think of something beautiful, like Kaery, and those golden eyes . . . , Sky and that incredible body . . . , even that hot-ass one, Star, in her own bitchy way.

I don't belong here. What was that crackling sound? It must be one of the other broken bones in my body. Think of something else.

That dream . . . , or maybe that flashback . . . , from Pangaea is a good start. I still don't know how, but it was me, and that was my kingdom. If some palm reader or crystal ball psychic had told me that I was a king in a past life, I would've laughed in her face. My life has been so useless. Self-pity is pathetic, Blue, don't do it. God, I sound like my own sister nagging myself. If I could only move, I would kick my own ass. My other hand is stinging like I placed it on a stove. Damn, I'm screwed! This is what they mean by not realizing what you've got till it's gone.

I don't understand, but somehow I feel guilty for all of them. Not just my family, and not just Tommy, but everyone. That sounds beyond screwed up, and I'm so not a saint or anything . . . . What was that popping sound? I already fell, so why am I still crackling like some kind of cereal? Maybe it's just my senses returning. This is totally fucked. I've done some stupid shit, but this takes the cake. I seem to say that every time I get myself in a bind.

Damn! I just remembered I was married to Sky! Now, that's a scary thought. I can't picture me married to myself, let alone a high-maintenance hot chick. But I gotta admit, it felt like love. She loved me in that lifetime. Good thing it was then. I don't know what I could've said to get someone like that to love me . . . , but, damn, it must've been good.

My spine feels like I've been crammed into a shoebox. The clouds up there are relieving my eyes from the sting just long enough for me to see the mountain's silhouette. Damn, that was a long fall, and I hate heights! What the hell was I thinking, running up the damned thing? Oh, yeah. My ego and pride again. Stupidity really killed the cat, not curiosity this time.

Ugh! My knee and neck feel like they were snapped in half. All I can think about is some council of robed assholes who stared at me for the answers to the fate of the world. I know it was me who failed them all. I made the wrong decision. What was the question, and what was it they needed my guidance for? Damn, I just heard myself laugh, and that fluid in my lungs is definitely blood. I can taste it. What's that burning smell? How long have I been here?

Man, this really sucks. God, if you can hear me, I swear I'll change, and it may sound messed up, but please don't let me be broken forever. I just wanna help the boy and kick his ass for almost killing me up there. Ouch, it hurts to laugh. Why don't I ever take anything seriously? Even my own prayers are ridiculous. It's not like anyone's listening. That taste on the back of my tongue is hideous. What is it, bile? Maybe I should settle down a little.

Maybe if I close my eyes for a while, I'll wake up and things will be okay again. That's so stupid, I know, but I just want OUT! I broke my leg that time in Colorado, when I was snowboarding with Josh, and he almost killed us with that snow machine. Good times! He always wanted to be a stuntman, even though we were only ten at the time. Who thinks of breaking themselves like this on a daily basis? A real bad-ass, I suppose.

Holy shit! What was a Spell of Enlightenment? It keeps coming into my head like a throbbing headache. Why am I thinking of that man with the yellow teeth the night my family died? He's got something to do with this, I know it. So I guess those gut feelings I had all these years were right, and I only acknowledge them now when I'm dying, like some fucking victim. There are signs all around us, and I just wasn't paying attention.

Gemini talked about some place called a Soulstream, and I knew he was telling the truth before Kaery said anything. Damn, she's hot! She was there at the Council meeting. I just wish I could remember what happened after that. I can only see explosions and blood raining from the sky in my memories. Now, that's just messed up . . . , memories of some other lifetime. I would so much rather forget.

Just a little sleep, and I should be okay. I know this is the last time I get to sleep again, but, hey, I don't regret shit. My life may have been one stupid thing after another, but it was mine. Just close your eyes, Blue. It will all be okay. What's that vibration like an Earthquake? And that hum? Whatever. My luck, it's a boulder about to crush me and finish the job. It's not like I can see, anyway, through the tears or blood or whatever's crusted in my eyes.

I know this is my fault, and I accept that. At least, I died by the hands of a hot lady. Okay, that sounds like something Tommy or Guy would've said. I can hear my own gurgling laugh through fluids in my mouth and lungs. Yeah, it's time to just laugh at the irony of it all, and die like a man . . . . I just wish I could change things.

✸

Sky's toes touched the floor as she opened her eyes with a long gasp. Looking around the room through tear-filled eyes, she saw Maia and Gemini standing near the door.

"You were right," she said, incredulous at the words that were coming out of her mouth. "I *was* a Goddess."

Chapter 13

LOOK BEHIND YOU

(Egypt, 14,000 B.C.E.)

Waking up in a bed of soft and velvety sand was all she remembered many moons ago. The sands of this hot desert would normally sting the eyes and flesh of anyone who dared walk through them, but not her. She drifted through them in a simple dress, her bare feet carrying her the long distance she had to travel. Nothing would get in her way. She would make it to the place in her dreams. The wind whirled around her body, inviting her to dance with it.

The sand was kind to her and did her bidding. Not one grain dared to come close to her beautiful face. The hood over her head was quite pointless. The sun dared not burn her brown skin. She walked forth, knowing this was the last part of her long journey. She forgot who she had been before this, but she would never forget who she was now, and she would not look back.

Walking over the last sand dune, she spied a small village of humans. They looked so plain, but happy in their mundane existence. She smiled as she went forward.

This may be going against every forgotten oath that I have ever taken, but I know what I will do. These shall be my subjects, and this shall be my new kingdom.

Sky walked down the hill to the village, where she crowned a young boy as the king of these beautiful lands. He didn't know it that day, but he would appear in the history books as the first pharaoh.

Sky looked up to the stars with a smile. She brought rain and prosperity to a people who had lived off the land humbly before her arrival. She unraveled jewels and minerals from the depths of the earth, which the people would wear as their own birthright. Her chocolate skin was envied and admired. They called her Isis.

She blessed their children and gifted them with many treasures. In a place that was once one of the harshest in the known world, she provided flawless, beautiful weather. Her Magick was unrivaled, attracting many strangers to her land. These strangers brought Magicks from far-off places, along with the intelligence and wisdom of the ancients. Slowly but surely, they formed a court for the pharaohs. Her people were truly blessed, for no one was foolish enough to even think of harming them.

The kingdom prospered so much that she wept joyful tears whenever she thought of how beautiful it would become. Many pharaohs had lived and died under her blessings, and she was worshipped lovingly and loyally by all.

She always had a vision that these people would be the most enchanted in the world, for she swore to herself that this vision would come true. She pulled forces from the far winds and the corners of the Earth to be her audience in her beloved court.

After hearing his name on the winds, one of these nights, Gemini arrived with his long dark cloak floating around him as it always had. Like everyone else in these lands, he knew he was being watched. The ever-scrying eye of the Goddess was in the air. Gemini could feel her presence in every grain of sand as soon as he entered her domain. After whispering his good intent, he heard a slight giggle in the air as confirmation that she had heard him. As the desert's fiery winds parted around him like a wave, there was a cool, clear blast of fresh air that escorted him toward the Goddess.

After he trekked a long distance over a high dune, he saw a temple that reminded him of the pyramids of ancient Pangaea. They were much larger than the humble ones the Mancers dwelled in long ago. Realizing that she was a formidable Mancer, who had made a decision to be the ruler as her birthright, Gemini smiled as he took steps forward toward her court.

He was greeted by one of the most organized battalions of humans and Supernaturals he had ever seen. They had found a way to live among each other with mutual respect. Not since long, long ago had Gemini seen the likes of this kingdom.

The battalion surrounded him in formation. At close range, he could see that even the humans of these lands had changed. They were not as affected by the powerful spell that the rest of humanity had endured—the Veil of Ignorance, which had been cast by the Coven of Unity many centuries past.

Gemini walked into the elaborate temple, which had markings that were both the language of Magick and a simple language the Goddess had created for her people to pass on information throughout the ages. He could see that she was indeed intelligent and wise. As he entered the main court, he noticed that this was no ordinary temple. To the human eye, it must have looked like a large fortress, but the pyramid was layered far beneath the ground as well, and was probably two times, if not three, as large underground as it was on the surface. He could tell all this by the Magick markings on the walls.

The Goddess graced her own court after many theatrics and a display of the finest entertainment the world had ever seen. Supernaturals and humans alike worshiped the very air she breathed. Adorned in jewels from deep within the Earth, and painted with runes of powerful Witchbreed, she floated across the court, touching the eyelids of her favored followers. The battalion of high priests was graced by her Magick. Gemini would not have believed it if he hadn't seen it with his own eyes, but here, with sheer will alone, she was able to break through the Veil of Ignorance, granting her human populace the ability to see Magick almost as well as the Supernaturals did.

As she floated toward him, she smiled at Gemini.

Suddenly, one of the battalions charged her with incredible speed and cunning, giving Gemini only a brief moment to warn her. He was an assassin, no doubt.

Before the words *Look behind you* could form in Gemini's mouth, Sky had already moved at the speed of thought, and was behind the unlucky assassin, whispering in his ear. His expression went from focused to painful contortion. His body floated in front of her as an example of betrayal and disloyalty, writhing in an invisible torture rack as he was tormented by unseen forces. Like a wineskin, his body burst in a thousand different directions in front of the entire court.

His patriotic fellow high priests ran to remove his remains as they all felt his betrayal and were ready to lay down their lives.

The Goddess looked at them with the kindest smile, to remind them that they were still in her loving favor.

This was all new to Gemini. He had never seen such dramatics in a Mancer court go by so flawlessly and unscripted. The event was cleared up as soon as it happened, and Sky floated toward him, smiling. He had yet to see her walk on her own court floor, which was spotless, reflecting the electric torchlight on all the walls like the constellations of the night.

Looking up at the ceiling, Gemini immediately realized that a Witchbreed spell enchanted it, for one could see deep within space, as if there were neither ceiling nor reflective ozone on this planet. He had a direct view into the infinite. This was an understanding that the rest of the world had yet to comprehend or witness.

This was most impressive, as Sky well knew as she formally greeted her guest.

"I have waited for this day for quite some time, dear Gemini." Her soft-spoken words were melodic and sweet.

A brief nod and smile came from the silent Mancer.

At his approval, Sky spoke again: "I apologize for the interruption just now. I have spies of other nations who wish to see my Kingdom at their feet. Sadly, these are nations I have personally helped to grow, as mine has. It would seem Mancers have not changed in so many millennia." Sky reached for the cloaked arm of her guest. "Please come with me, and I will show you my palace."

Sky guided Gemini through the pyramids, showing him the underground facilities that worked as both a haven for the exalted Supernatural members of the court and as a place of deep study.

"I would like to embrace the visions of all my people," she said, "into a cohesive kingdom of minimal violence and freethinkers."

As enlightened as this sounded, Gemini knew the folly of her ways.

"I understand," she said, "that you think what I am doing is déjà vu . . . , reminiscent of a failed spell cast long ago. I assure you, I have been monitoring other worlds across the universes that live harmoniously with both the ignorant and the enlightened."

When Gemini was not swayed by her argument, she began to become slightly annoyed, not accustomed to being questioned or defied. Readjusting her approach, she showed Gemini the Magicks that her beloved Covens had worked on.

He looked through the scrying mirrors, watching other worlds with conflict and harmony alike.

But she's right. They live together nonetheless.

"I am impressed by the view of the distant planets, Sky," he said, calling her by her ancient name—not Isis, as her people called her. "You have accomplished much in your time in these lands after being asleep for so long. However, I implore you, please remember that *this* is our planet, and we must not neglect the needs of the people here and now. Our needs as Supernaturals are not important. The human experience is the most cherished and should be treated as such."

"Ever the wise Gemini," she responded, "I have not and will not forget. Please tell me that I have your blessings."

Sky's gorgeous brown face was softer than he had seen before she asked for his validation.

With a warm smile, and a step closer to the Spheromancer, Gemini relented a bit. "As long as you do not bring the rules of those worlds to this one, and as long as you protect your kingdom as you have thus far, you have my blessings, Sky."

(Gemini's Lair today)

"You knew I would fail, didn't you?" Sky said to Gemini, accusingly.

"You were infatuated with yourself and what you could do. In the end, you failed to protect the very people you loved." Gemini said this calmly. "You have seen the rise and fall of your own Kingdom as I saw that sad and fated day, but we will speak of that later. My point was to show you what you are capable of. It is a forbidden technique of Magick that not many of us can do. I felt I had no other choice but to show you the truth." Walking over to the sobbing Sky, Gemini lifted her to her feet and said gently, "You still have my blessings."

Her smile lit up the room as she hugged the tall man.

*

Blue sat up coughing, then looked down at his hands. His head was still fuzzy, and he was not able to understand how he was alive. But he flexed his hands open and closed as if this were the first time he had ever seen his own flesh. His clothes were a bloody mess, but his skin was only slightly scarred. To look at him, it would be hard to tell that he had even fallen off a bike, let alone a high mountain. There were a few minor scars on his arms and legs, but nothing else. He felt a slight sting of pain, but nothing he couldn't tolerate.

"I have another chance, I see."

✳

Crux came running along the trail as fast as he could, tears falling freely down his face as he gracefully jumped from ledge to ledge. He had just made a friend, and couldn't bear to lose him.

Uncle Loiza's dead, and now this. It's not fair. Why did Jayde push Blue over the edge? I don't know the first thing about medicine, aside from bandaging, but I hope Blue can hold on long enough for me to help him any way I can.

Catching his breath, Crux stopped in his tracks. Panic fled and confusion followed the happiness that soon filled his heart as he jumped onto Blue's pain-streaked body.

"Nice to see you, too, Crux."

Chapter 14

CALL OF DUTY

After a long day, Guardian parked his car outside his condo. The building was nothing special, but it wasn't supposed to be. A perk of working for OZONE was that he didn't have to pay a mortgage or rent on any of the six places around the world that he loosely considered home.

Gazing down the street, he determined that everything was okay. Then he scanned the building, and after being satisfied that he didn't have any unexpected visitors, he turned the key and walked into the lobby with a grocery bag in his free hand.

"Hello there, Tim!" Mrs. Saint Marshall, his senile neighbor, greeted him. She always called him by her son's name, the son who had died in Vietnam. She was having a tough time finding the key to her door.

She's probably locked herself out again.

Guardian put down his grocery bag and opened her door. Just inside, in a bowl on the table next to the door, were her keys.

"You're all set, Mrs. S."

"You were always the sweetest boy to me, Tim."

Guardian smiled at her, picked up his bag, and walked two flights up. In front of his door, he pulled his keys out of a pocket in the customized holster made by McCallaway in the Armory Department. When he put the key into the lock, he noticed that the doormat in front of his condo had been moved slightly. Sniffing the air, he smelled the faint aroma of cigarette smoke. There was an intruder.

Guardian set the bag down slowly and pulled out his customized OZONE gun, which was equipped with ultraviolet rounds, antimatter pulse rounds, and his favorite hollow points.

Kicking the door open, he aimed the gun in all directions.

Then, walking slowly into his quaint living room, he saw the culprit. Agent Grin, the yellow-toothed Psiel from the Tracker Department, was leaning against a wall.

Guardian didn't put his gun away, but instead pointed it directly at Grin's head.

"You know for a fact that you're not gonna shoot me, so put that thing away, Guardian."

"I will when you tell me how you found me, and what you're doing here."

"It's my job to find people. You know that."

Agent Grin turned around with his stained teeth proudly exposed. The man's thin features and slicked back hair reminded Guardian of some trashy drug dealer from L.A. OZONE used him because he was a psychic, and a good one supposedly. Guardian knew that Grin was responsible for some of the most notorious quests in the files.

As Grin spoke, he kept his smile: "I'm assigned to you in a duo until we find Surge-Overload."

Guardian let out a sigh as he rolled his eyes and put his gun away.

Ignoring Guardian's disdain, Grin said, "I'm sure you're aware of the damage that hacker did when he attacked our base. The media were shut down in seven countries for twenty-six hours!"

Guardian looked bored. As he grabbed his groceries, he scanned the hallway in both directions.

"Don't be so paranoid. No one knows you're here. The neighbors seem to think you're a cop . . . , or maybe an accountant, depending on the neighbor. And one of them thinks you're her dead Soldier son. Your cover hasn't been compromised."

"It better not have been."

"Was that a threat?"

"You bet your gingivitis it was!"

Guardian threw his jacket down on the table, revealing his holster and high-tech guns.

"Touché, Guardian!"

Grin made himself comfortable in Guardian's favorite chair. Pulling out a pack of cigarettes, he slapped it on his palm. "Do you mind?"

Guardian didn't bother to answer.

"I don't have to be a psychic to know *that* look," Grin said. "I'll be going now. Just know that the protocol states that if you have any info, share it . . . , and I'll do the same. The bounty incentive is three times the usual, so let's make this bust quick."

Grin stood up. His ill-fitting black suit was more than slightly wrinkled, and the permanent cigarette smell on his clothes made Guardian wish for air purifiers.

"I know you'd rather be with your other partner, Juno, but she's got other duties at the moment. You'll just have to deal with my beautiful smile until this quest is completed. I'd rather be solo on this, but it's a Code 2, so that's not an option." As he walked to the doorway, Grin inspected the damaged door with his thin pale fingers. "A key would've been just as effective, Guardian."

His laugh sounded raspy and full of phlegm.

Guardian suppressed a grimace as Grin turned and went down the hall.

After closing and dead-bolting the door, Guardian walked to the bedroom to take off his shirt. He glanced in the mirror at the scars on his body, then went into the bathroom, half hoping a hot shower would wash them off. But he knew better.

Juno looked over Surge-Overload's file on Nina for the hundredth time with an obsessive focus. She knew that if she went to the OZONE base, her search would be monitored. But she didn't have much of a choice if she wanted to keep Nina off the radar.

According to the files, Nina had died years ago. But Juno knew that wasn't true, since fresh blood had been found at the site of a delivery gone wrong. More than likely, Nina had witnessed the explosions, and then dropped the rag that was nursing a wound on her left hand.

If this is the same Nina . . . , and I feel in my bones it is . . . . After all this time, she's still accidentally cutting herself.

Juno smiled at the thought, anticipating what she must do. Setting a pulse into the small hotel room would disrupt any frequency within a few feet of her—except for the special channel that connected her to Surge-Overload.

"Juno calling in! I need you to help me a little more."

✶

Surge knew she had only a few minutes before her mom came into her room to take her to some dance camp. She had kept up the charade so as not to cause any ripples in the family that might bring unnecessary attention to her precious work. She put her virtually undetectable micro set into one ear and spoke with the anonymous vocal scrambler automatically in place: "Let me guess . . . . The girl? Nina?"

"Yes. I need more information."

"I figured as much. The file is short, but what else do you need?"

"Can you cross-reference any camera footage from the night at the docks?"

"I already have that footage, Juno. It's yours in two seconds. Is there anything else?"

Surge heard her mother opening the door.

"No. Juno . . . , over and out!"

Surge slammed her laptop shut and spun around to show her mom a girly outfit that she had bought at the mall. Her mother was happy to see her daughter in something feminine, even if it was a plaid skirt with safety pins all over it and zippers in weird places, over a pair of torn jeans and combat boots. Her eye shadow was plaid as well. She had obviously spent time on it.

"You look . . . nice, Cindy," her mom said, beaming at her.

Surge almost laughed out loud.

There's no way she likes this style.

"Thanks, mom, but I know you're not into Cyberpunk-goth, so no need to lie."

"Well, what's wrong with your pretty sun dresses?" Surge's mother asked kindly.

"Mommm!"

"Okay, I won't try to dress you, but I don't want you to be made fun of at camp, so I bought you a couple of outfits and put them in your bags downstairs." She smiled hopefully.

"Sure, mom. But I can't promise I'm gonna wear 'em."

"That's fine, Honey. Just remember to smile and be nice to the girls . . . . Oh, and, Cindy . . . , only an hour a night on that computer, okay?"

Surge agreed with a sigh.

Maia gazed at the stars, as she did every night. But this time, she saw something different.

I've gotta tell Jayde or Gemini!

Running as fast as she could, she navigated through the large castle, looking desperately for someone to share this latest revelation.

Just then, Jayde came into the hallway. Maia would have run right into her if Jayde hadn't redirected her at the last moment.

Looking around alertly, Jayde asked, "Are you okay? Is someone chasing you?"

"No, that's not it," Maia said, out of breath. "We have to save the girl! If she dies, we'll fail!"

Chapter 15

TEST

This was one of those times when Maia wished she didn't have her special abilities. She was so panicked that she couldn't even formulate the words correctly. Her palms were sweaty, and she felt like the world was crashing to an end. She knew that she could be a little dramatic at times, but this was different. She was truly fearful, and had to express herself. Usually, she waited and watched the world go by, the way her parents had, preferring to psychoanalyze everyone she came in contact with, until they felt uncomfortable.

Maia knew that this was a test of her willpower. She had an epiphany, and was sure it was a call to action. She had seen a shift in the stars, and immediately knew that a chain of events had been set in motion.

If one thing changes too far off course, then the entire plan to destroy OZONE will most definitely fail . . . , and miserably. Probability and reality are tricky things.

"Jayde," she said, "you-mus'-peepare-'em-find-girl-Union-Square-downtown-San-Francisco-eight-o'clock-P.M.-four-nights!"

She said these words so fast that Jayde only caught them because of her acute hearing.

Maia then said, more slowly this time, "They must be ready for a battle that could end very badly if they are not completely aware."

From the shadows, Crux listened silently to the words of the pretty Hispanic girl as she ranted to Jayde. Not wanting to interrupt the conversation, all he could do was take mental notes. He had no idea where in the world he was, but he was going to find out one way or another. Every time he had asked Jayde, she had always replied, "You're in a safe place." This had never set his nerves at ease, although he was fairly certain that she was telling the truth. He had been undergoing Jayde's grueling training for the better part of a week, and just today he had watched Blue almost die.

If Blue were human, he would be dead by now without a doubt.

Crux's first instinct was to run away with Blue, so he eavesdropped a little longer.

"What else was in your vision?" Jayde asked sternly.

"There will be OZONE Agents there, and Vampyl looking for Crux," Maia said, staring vacantly into space.

Crux suppressed a gasp, as if Loiza had just put his hand over his mouth. The mention of Vampyl instantly terrified the twelve-year-old. His normal cheerful spirit seemed to drain from his body, along with the blood from his face. Standing still, contemplating what to do next, he thought his first reflex to run might still be his best option.

"We must prepare them even more than you have already," Maia continued. "The OZONE Agents are going to be looking for someone very important to us. She is going to be the Mancer in Union Square."

"Yes, I understood that part. What must the children do?"

"They must know the truth and deal with it as soon as possible. Otherwise, Gemini's plans are forfeit!" By now Maia was in tears. "You can't do it alone, or the girl will surely die. I have seen it. You must train them, Jayde, or the plan is doomed!" Then Maia's voice sounded haunted as she said, "I have to go as well . . . , and many people will die."

"You have not had any combat training, Maia. That is not your strong suit." Jayde looked the frail girl up and down.

"You think I don't know that?" Maia shot back. "If I don't go, then the plan is doomed!"

"We shall start tonight," Jayde said, walking past Maia and down the hall to the room where she had left Blue.

As she approached him, she snatched the eavesdropper by his collar. Crux had no choice but to proceed down the hall with her.

Maia walked at a distance behind them, trying to regain focus on the here and now.

✶

"This is not a dream," Gemini said. "It is your life from this point on. The truth is, you were both born in the middle of a war. There have been many losses of life on both sides. I am not proud to say that I am one of the few responsible for the world as it is today."

Gemini looked long and searchingly at Sky and Blue.

Sky felt that Gemini's words were accusing her for some decision she had made in another lifetime. Her frustration affected the temperature of the room, which began to rise.

"What exactly are we?" Blue asked Gemini. "I mean, you keep going on about these Mancer things, and I'm not sure if that means aliens, or what. But we're obviously not normal. Look how she's turning this room into a sauna!"

Before Gemini could answer, Jayde came into the room, thrusting Crux in front of her. The boy stumbled forward, with Maia following a few feet behind. As Crux dusted himself off, Sky took the opportunity to lower the temperature in the room.

Gemini cleared his throat. "You were all revered and worshiped as gods in another lifetime," he said. "Your meeting in this one is no coincidence. You should know that coincidence does not exist. The power unleashed within even one of you can be devastating. Jayde and I have taken it upon ourselves to find you and teach you to embrace your heritage and birthright. You are Mancer, and you shall rule."

Sky broke the somber mood. "So you expect me to go all 'movie montage' with some thug, an emo girl, a punk kid, crouching tiger, and tall creepy guy in a cloak? No offense. Oh, and what happened to the loser club from my school?"

Maia sighed. "This is going to be a lot harder than the stars could have ever prepared me for."

"She may be bitchy about it," Blue said, "but what did you do with Kaery and the others?"

"I'm hungry!" Crux added.

With a quick glance at each of them, Jayde boomed, "Gemini has been trying to explain to all of you that this is deadly serious. The Witchbreed kids are safe. I made sure of that . . . . Aegis, I pushed you off the mountain to unlock the ability within you that you used to your advantage in other lifetimes."

"Why do you keep calling me Aegis?" Blue asked, puzzled.

Maia answered, "She called you that because Aegis is your name . . . , written in the stars. It means armor of the gods."

Jayde was losing patience. "It is the name by which you introduced yourself, long ago. But that is not the point. The point is that you all need to understand your roles in this war. You have many enemies."

Sky rolled her eyes. "Yeah, some I was born with."

"More true than you know," Gemini added. "Jayde is right. It's time you were all tested on your survivability. Jayde, prepare the trials!"

Jayde bowed low and left the room, moving as elegantly as a panther.

Once she was gone, Crux leaned over and whispered to Blue, "They said there were going to be Vampyl there. Vampires are not a good thing. We need to get out of here. Fighting them would be suicidal."

"We can hear everything you say with that ridiculously loud whisper!" Sky snapped with a sigh.

Gemini looked at the group, then said, "Yes, Sky, I expect you to work with the rest of them. But first you must all conquer your own insecurities, and then learn to collaborate. There are lives that depend on it. Many lives."

As Gemini finished his speech, he turned to Maia, who had come to his side.

"I have to go with them to the next mission," she said. "A girl must be saved who will alter the tides of war."

"I need to get confirmation of one thing before we start the test," Gemini said. "Is Ninala alive?"

Maia looked first to the stars, then into her palms, and back up to Gemini.

"Yes."

Chapter 16

WEAKNESS

Sometimes things happen and you wonder why and how. However, I'm slowly but surely getting used to the fact that there is no coincidence. We chose to be in the flesh we are in, and we make our own destiny. Our spirit burns our very bodies like a battery. Then we return to the Soulstream from which we all came. This is my revelation and my truth. My name is Maia, and these are my thoughts as I witness the people I call friends, but who are really more of a family than I have ever known.

Blue tries his best to stay calm and cold. His attitude is much like his spirit, calm before a storm. His first trial started when Jayde knocked him off a mountain. He had no idea that he could regenerate his body, and then be twice as tough the next time he was attacked. This ability is called Aegis, the armor of the gods. Blue used it in past lives and was formidable with it, not to mention his other abilities, which he has yet to control. He is supposedly able to open temporal gates to the Soulstream itself, but I have yet to see that. His weakness is his lack of control. Basically, I believe he is a ticking time bomb, but Gemini seems to think otherwise. He says that Blue will be focused power. I have yet to see him focus on anything besides protecting Crux—and looking at Sky's butt.

Blue may be tough, but he can still be killed, and he's learning to live with the pain.

I'm not the only one who thinks Sky is a snobby brat, but it's true that something about her makes me want to like her. She has been privileged for eons by humans, and therefore treats others like they should continue to constantly pay attention to her. Her Spheromancer abilities are gaining in power every day. She can literally control weather, and even gravity within a small sphere around her. Her greatest weakness is that she doesn't believe in how powerful she truly is. Denying who she is only frustrates Gemini and Jayde, who constantly reassure her that this is all real. Her radius is getting stronger, but only because she is in the presence of such powerful Mancers and those Witchbreed kids, who also aided in her awareness. When they left, she instantly became significantly weaker. This one is not invulnerable by any means. If you can touch her, she's pretty much squishy.

The boy, Crux, is so sweet to me, but he is hiding deep scars and damage from a life among rogues and thieves. His entire existence on this planet has been in the midst of war, which means that he has spent more time on the field than Blue, Sky, and I combined, even though he's only twelve. I'm not exactly sure what all his abilities are, besides the ones on the surface, but I know that he can change the density of inanimate and animate objects for short periods of time. He also has minor probability shifting abilities, which make him seem very lucky. His quirky sense of humor and endless appetite are the signs of a growing preteen, but his indecisive nature and lack of trust make for a sketchy ally. His weakness is the very thing he uses in most of his stunts, the earth. Like humans, he can easily be harmed by stones. He doesn't regenerate like Blue, and he can't heal himself, like Sky or me.

Jayde is a martial artist to her very soul, quite literally. She is a Metamancer, meaning she can change the metabolic rate of every cell in her body. She has complete mastery of her physical self and uses the Soulstream to do fantastic things with her body. Watching her beat up on Blue was fun for the first couple of days, but now I pretty much expect to watch his bones break and his nose bleed. Jayde's weakness seems to be the vibration that Blue creates when he begins to open a temporal gate. His own ability hurts him as well, so he stops mid-try almost every time. Most of us are uncomfortable when his vibration hum starts, but Jayde is almost paralyzed. She has something deep within her that she has not shown me yet, and she does a great job of hiding it.

Gemini is an ancient Mancer, much older than Jayde, but he doesn't look a year over thirty. His body shares two souls. I have seen him split into two beings on a couple of occasions. One seems to have flaws that the other doesn't, and vice versa, but they combine into one of the most powerful forces I have ever known. I wish he didn't have the ability to block my profiling.

I have so many weaknesses, I don't know where to begin. Besides my mental ailments from torturous nightmares, and being sheltered beyond words, I suffer from feelings of inadequacy and low self-esteem. Sky calls me "emo," which I'm guessing is some sort of pop culture reference, considering it's her defense mechanism to shut people down by using banter they don't understand. I know I shouldn't be dealing with simple things like low self-esteem when the world needs people like me, but my human ties to this world always remind me that I am not some all-powerful god, the way I was in a past life. I'm able to read the future and its ever-changing script. I'm also able to find almost anyone on the planet with only a glance at the sky, or my palm, or sometimes a stone. I've used my other powers to heal both Blue and Crux from intense damage after sparring with Jayde.

This morning is the second day of training. The first wasn't so great. I feel like we failed the test when we all got floored by one of Jayde's simplest attacks. Even though I totally saw it coming, the next thing I knew, I was on the ground, holding my head and my butt from the impact. I didn't feel so bad because Sky was right next to me, and Crux was on top of her. Blue was used to the abuse by that point, I think, and just got up and wiped himself off.

Sky made me laugh when she decided she was going to come to combat training in a Victorian dress and high heels. Jayde made her see the folly of her way with a blur of attacks. I still don't know how Sky blocked one, let alone dozens, of punches and kicks that were thrown her way. I'm pretty sure it was her ability to move at the speed of thought within her invisible sphere. She was backed into a corner, and the dress was torn when it snagged on a piece of the wall. Jayde was able to knock Sky to the ground. I believe it was the first time I had ever seen her hurt. But she had healed her own wounds before I walked over to see if I could help. She just looked at me like I was there to insult her. Maybe I'm not the only one dealing with some issues of self-esteem?

Oh, god, now it's time for ME *to spar with Jayde. I don't know why this is all necessary! Oh, yes, I do. We have to save the girl in Union Square in three days. I know that I've been with Gemini for a year, three months, and four days. Oh, wow, I just did that. I can only imagine that if it's still feeling to* ME *like all this is happening too fast, then the others must be on the verge of anxiety. Mancers have something like a time paradox. In general, we aren't affected by time the way humans are. Days sometimes feel like a few minutes. Maybe I haven't grown so much? I've reverted back to my old habits of profiling everyone around me and being just as harsh on myself. No, I think I need to use my powers to survive, or Jayde wouldn't let me live it down. I don't want to fail in front of the rest of them, even though I've always failed at anything physical. Who am I kidding? I fail at a lot of stuff. Not really, but I guess I should go easier on myself. Oh, okay, here she comes.*

I used to blame my critical analysis on my personality type, but now I know I was way off. It has to do with some of my other powers. I can find anyone's weakness almost as easily as looking at their hair color. It's very strange how my point of view is quite literal. Jayde looks like a constellation of stars to me. Even her hair swims around her like swirling dark matter, or some strange comet belt. She has some bright force within her that almost makes me lose focus on the task at hand.

When she talks, she tells me to pay attention, but it's hard when I can see what she's going to do, seconds before she does it.

Damn, she's speeding up her attacks slightly, and the stars that make up her constellation are shifting when she moves in for her attacks. How did I dodge that? Oh, yeah, my body is reacting to my thoughts of what she's going to do. I feel so out of shape because I'm already out of breath. Sky is looking at me. Do I look fat? I am such a girl. Maybe I've been hanging out with Sky and Star too much. Ouch! She shifted her attack while I was waiting for the other one to take effect.

"Ouch!" Crux whispered, nudging Blue as he watched Maia fall to the ground for the tenth time. "This is just mean. She's so delicate. By the looks of her, I don't think she's fought a day in her life. Hell, she may have never fought in a past life, either." Crux laughed to himself.

Blue put his hand on Crux's shoulder and chuckled. "Pay attention, Crux. You wouldn't want people to think you're some insubordinate little punk, and I'm some useless thug, would ya?"

Blue turned his focus to Maia, realizing that she was probably the group's weakest link.

I only hope she can pull it together in time for this mission.

Sky sighed as she looked at Jayde's moves with a new intensity, totally ignoring the boys. Crux elbowed Blue in the thigh, still chuckling to himself every time Maia got hit. Sky noticed that Maia's moves weren't nearly as graceful as her own. She was barely dodging most of the blows with pure talent alone, much as Sky did when she was sparring.

Maia could see the moves coming before they happened, so she made a quick series of rational decisions about what she would do next. In the time it took her to spot a weakness and react, most people wouldn't have blinked once. She was really amazing to watch. Sky tilted her head as Maia went down for the twelfth time.

She's stalwart, that's for sure, Sky thought to herself. *I wonder why she's pushing herself so hard. This is just a sparring session, but she's fighting as if her life depended on it. The battle looks like a Kung Fu movie. Intriguing!*

Maia fell to the ground for the thirteenth time, but popped right back up. Her butt hurt a lot, but she was fighting through the pain, trying hard not to show weakness to the probing eyes of the kids on the sidelines. Sky was staring quite hard at every move Jayde and Maia made, which made Maia quite nervous.

"Focus, girl!" Jayde shouted in a frustrated voice as she threw a punch meant for Maia's stomach. Seeing the move coming, Maia tried to duck, which resulted in a direct hit to her lip. Sliding across the ground and slamming into a stone, she could taste blood in her mouth.

"Enough!" Jayde snorted, and turned away.

Maia sat on the ground, feeling a surge of energy that she had never felt before. As adrenaline rushed through her body, she started smiling behind the hair that was swinging in front of her face. Glaring at Jayde as she stood up, she announced, "We're *not* done!"

Jayde spun around, focusing on Maia like a laser. Then she remembered Maia's past life.

Blood is the key!

Maia was glowing. Her energy level had been renewed, even though most people would have been exhausted by this point.

Maia gazed back at Jayde from twenty feet away. As she glanced down to rearrange the stars within her own energetic constellation, all the pain left her.

"Jayde, I hope you're ready for round two! I can see your weakness now. It's some sort of Dragon constellation within you. So *that's* what you're hiding . . . , another personality within you, like Gemini, but wilder and more primal. All of a sudden, I see things a lot clearer."

Maia's light brown eyes began to glow fiercely as she stared deep within Jayde. In a flash, she was in Jayde's face with her own set of attacks. For over a year now, she had been training with Gemini, learning how to control her skills and take ownership of her powers. He had once told her that she would someday be able to move like a Celestial. Until now, she had no idea what he meant.

Maia kicked at Jayde and swung her fists at her, mimicking her fighting style as if she were mirroring Jayde's essence. It was now Jayde who was on defense. Maia struck at her constellations, trying to reach for the Dragon stars within her. She was being blocked by strategic parries and strikes, but Maia didn't feel pain as she matched Jayde's blocks with more attacks. Her hands began to glow as she tried to rearrange Jayde's energy the way she did her own.

Jayde stomped the ground, which caused her to float backward, gaining space between herself and the newly enlightened student.

I'm beginning to see why Gemini chose this one.

Seeing the distance between herself and her combat instructor widening, Maia decided to launch a surprise attack. With a single thought, she was in the air above Jayde's head, floating on a brisk breeze with the sun behind her golden hair.

When Jayde looked up, twisting her body into a defensive stance at the last moment, Maia was upon her, punching downward toward Jayde's heart.

Can she REALLY see my secret? Jayde wondered as she blocked the punch, but felt her energy waning.

The control that Jayde normally had was interrupted by a vibration pulse that she had only felt from Blue.

Has this girl somehow mimicked Blue's temporal vibration and used it against me?

Blue squeezed Crux's shoulder slightly as he watched Maia fly around the small Japanese courtyard like the sun's rays that were shining overhead.

Jayde's being on the defensive is something I'm sure she never saw coming.

Crux winced from the slight sting of Blue's crushing grip. As he noticed that Maia was glowing, his jaw dropped in awe.

Sky tried to keep her composure, but had to smile as Maia struck Jayde across the chest, sending her flying through the air a good thirty feet.

"Whoa!" shouted all of the kids simultaneously.

A steady clap came from behind them as Gemini walked into the courtyard, smiling at Maia. "You are finally focusing on your strengths, and not your weaknesses," he said. "I applaud you."

Maia looked down at her glowing hands. Almost as fast as she blushed, her glow vanished, and her palms became soft again. Looking over at Jayde apologetically, she thought, *I wonder if I've really hurt her. She's more like a juggernaut than anything I've ever known.*

As Jayde stood up gracefully and bowed to her, Maia blushed again.

While Jayde walked off, the kids ran up to Maia, slapping her happily on the back.

I guess this is what Gemini meant when he said I would make friends. I'm not sure what just happened, but I know now that blood is part of my ability list. I knew it was in a past life, but to be engrossed in it this way is scary, because it felt like a high I've never felt before. They aren't looking at me like some crazy psychic girl anymore, but a real member of the team. This is the best day of my life! I just want to get better, and I hope that we save the girl in time.

Chapter 17

KIRARI

(Ancient China)

"I don't think you should be trying to hide your fighting power from the Emperor," Ahlina said. "And if I were you, I would be bringing tons of money back home to our parents, so they can stop worrying. You're always talking about honor, but you never bring honor to the family name with your fists."

Ahlina was angry as she held her swelling right eye. Normally, her glittering green eyes were only matched by her sister's.

Jayde was walking quietly next to her.

"Aren't you going to say anything, Sis? I mean, those bandits almost sold me off to a brothel, and you barely arrive in time to beat them all to a pulp . . . , as usual."

"If you would learn to fight the way I told you, then you would be able to save yourself," Jayde retorted, trying not to laugh at her frustrated baby sister.

"Sometimes, Jayde, I swear you're just hollow inside. Don't you ever want to leave this Forbidden City?"

Ahlina was asking her sister this question for the millionth time.

"I have no reason to leave this place, Ahlina. It's our home and has been since the Ice Age. Zalomoni is the home of the Supernaturals who chose to continue to live a peaceful existence. There are not too many of these cities left in the world. Why would I leave?"

Jayde was not looking at her sister as she spoke. Her long, black, intricately braided hair was swinging in the wind as she walked. Many Supernaturals had had this conversation with her, but Jayde had shut them all down, because she had taken an oath to protect this city that was lost to the world.

"You would leave, Jayde, to use your skills for the greater good of the world, *that's* why! It isn't fair to be cooped up here in the mountains, pretending the world doesn't exist just because of the Great War that happened at the beginning of time."

Ahlina had cut her hair like a boy's long ago, to defy the elders, who had told her that women should act a certain way. She had always been a rebel, so leaving such a formal place was definitely true to her nature.

"Ahlina," her sister said, "you are Wicasht, and I am Mancer. We have a responsibility to the world to protect our own kind. Supernaturals are outnumbered by humans. It is a grand design to balance the power, but Zalomoni decided long ago, like a few other sanctuaries, that we would let them be, and work to preserve our own culture. We still have humans here, but they are conditioned to live among us. You're not going to change my mind about leaving, little sister. And I suggest you stop fighting Jreamers in the tournaments for money."

Ahlina crossed her arms and pouted all the way home. The temple where they lived was one of many ornate and systematically placed golden palaces. But theirs happened to be the Temple of Kirari, one of the last Dragons on Earth, and Guardian of the Forbidden City, Zalomoni.

Ahlina knew the story like the back of her own hand. In another lifetime, she had been a founder of the Coven of Unity, although she had yet to meet any other members in this life. She had helped to cast a Spell of Enlightenment that ended terribly. One of the results was the destruction of the beautiful Pangaea, which had been broken up into eight continents. Humans only knew of seven, however, since one had been claimed by Supernaturals. At the end of the Great War, most Dragons had decided to leave this realm and open portals to other realms of existence, which they now claimed as their homes.

Ahlina knew that all of these tales were true history, because all Witchbreed are enlightened with the true accounts of their past lives. But her own past life handicapped her freedom. Her sister was a powerful Mancer, who trained all of the Soldiers and citizens of Zalomoni to use their bodies and weapons to protect their homes. The rest of the world had yet to discover the martial arts, which Ahlina thought had been a selfish decision by the elders.

For Ahlina's blasphemy against the Oath of Zalomoni's secrecy, the elders had ordered her to teach the children about the Great War, a task she loathed even more than hiding in the mountains. Her students had been a mixture of unenlightened Supernaturals and humans, so, to entertain herself, she made all of her stories of the Great War sound more and more fantastical every time she told them. If someone had told these stories to her, she would have dismissed them as rubbish. But ironically, the students loved her and her tales. In fact, she was their favorite teacher.

It was when the kids loved her most that Ahlina looked to the sky, wishing that something would change to allow her to leave this place and rejoin her Coven. Zalomoni felt more like a prison than a sanctuary.

At this moment, as she kept pace with her powerful sister, thinking of different ways to argue her point, she gave up the argument for the time being.

Jayde had compassion for her little sister, knowing that she was longing for adventure. She couldn't relate to the bond that the Wicasht had to each other, although she figured that this was the real reason why Ahlina wanted to leave.

The world outside is much too dangerous to let her go out there.

As the sisters passed through the golden gates that led into the Temple of Kirari, Ahlina got the wildest idea, which changed her mood completely.

I know how to escape, and I'll do it this very night!

As she ran happily up the stairs and out of sight, Jayde shook her head, used to her rambunctious sister's mood swings.

At that moment, a captain of the guards approached Jayde.

"I apologize for interrupting your majesty, but we have a problem. The Spiraar tribe to the east is stirring near the great wall of Zalomoni. Our scouts say they may attack at any moment."

"Thank you, Guardian. I will meet with the elders to address the next tactical steps. Please tell them to expect me."

Jayde had personally trained this man how to fight. He was a Jreamer—the Supernatural version of a knight or hunter. Jreamers were born with the strength, speed, and agility of many humans. Some of them had even more abilities, but that was rare. Guardian happened to be one of the rare ones. His loyalty was undying, and his skill was extraordinary. Jayde knew that her messenger would fight through hell itself to deliver her message, so she turned away without a worry to find her sister.

Ahlina was on the top floor of the temple, out of breath from the thousand stairs she had just run up. Her heart was racing with fear at the same time that she was excited. She placed her right palm on the door that had been reinforced with enchanted gold and silver. It was several feet thick, so that even Jreamers could not break it down with sheer force. This was one of the rare times that Ahlina said a silent prayer to the stars that she was Wicasht. Reading the Magick written on the door, she needed only a moment to decide to cast a disruption pulse to open it.

"You know as well as I do that you are not supposed to be here, Ahlina!"

Ahlina dropped her hands to her side, turning guiltily toward her sister.

"I just want to see the statue, Jayde. I want to know what the ancient Dragons looked like. If I'm stuck here, why can't I get that one wish?"

Jayde eyed her sister cautiously, knowing that she was up to something, yet feeling that she couldn't deny Ahlina yet again.

"Fine. Move to the side and allow me to open the door. But after you see the statue, we must go. Do you understand?"

Ahlina lowered her head in a bow, which was disturbingly unlike her. Jayde could not remember the last time she had seen her sister bow to anyone, even the elders. She stopped for a moment to study Ahlina again. Finally, she placed both palms on the door, and as easy as pushing a feather, the giant portal opened.

Ahlina stood still for a second, admiring her sister's strength and power. The air pressure almost knocked her off her feet, and then pulled her into the room like a vacuum.

Jayde could sense her sister's racing heartbeat. "You must calm your nerves," she said. "A Dragon is present, and he reacts to fear. Even though he is in a slumbering form, he can still sense us. He only awakens fully when he is needed to save the city."

Ahlina took in a deep breath as she thought of freedom, which always put her at ease. Her heart rate lowered as she remembered that this was the same meditation her sister had taught her so long ago to control her chaotic powers. Ahlina glanced down at her bandaged right hand and wrist, then looked back to her sister and nodded.

As they entered the dark room, the candles and torches along the wall were covered in dust and cobwebs, looking as if no one had lit them for hundreds of years.

Jayde walked toward the wall to grab a torch, then began a chant that seemed more formal and respectful than necessary. Ahlina had heard this hymn many times before, but had never paid attention or bothered to learn it. It was melodic and calming like a lullaby. As Jayde sparked a flame on the torch, she continued singing.

Now Ahlina saw thousands of candles lining the walls. She was also aware of the Mancer time paradox, knowing that Jayde would light each and every candle, one by one, as she sang the monk hymn.

This is going to take forever!

Ahlina raised her bandaged right palm toward her sister, aiming it at the fire. Then, with her left hand, she applied a small amount of pressure as she shouted, "Burst!"

A ball of energy flew out of Ahlina's hand toward Jayde, whose lightning fast reflexes allowed her to dodge the sphere, which then collided with the small flame on one of the candles. The reaction was an explosion of light and heat that engulfed the entire room, lighting most of the candles, but melting many others. The room was instantly filled with smoke.

Jayde waved the smoke away from her face and glared at her sister. She was used to Ahlina's chaotic powers, but had been hoping she wouldn't attempt to use them in this place.

Trying to avoid Jayde's judgmental gaze with a shrug, Ahlina coughed slightly and smiled. "I was just trying to help," she said meekly.

Jayde was about to lecture her sister, squinting through her slanted eyes. But then Ahlina turned and gasped in awe at the statue of the large stone Dragon in front of her.

"By the Soulstream, it's beautiful!" Ahlina whispered in the presence of such magnificence. "I never thought one would be so big. How did we get it in the Temple?"

"We built *around* Kirari," Jayde said proudly. "Our family became the keepers of this great protector, who has not awakened for thousands of years. So, you see, there are more reasons why we are bound to Zalomoni than just sheer pride."

Ahlina took a step toward the large stone Dragon, staring at its glistening scales and powerful muscles. She had vivid memories of Dragons, but had never seen one up close in this lifetime. Somehow it seemed a lot larger in real life than in her head. She took another step closer to Kirari, but as soon as her foot touched the dusty stone floor, a firm grip held her shoulder, locking her in place.

Jayde stopped her sister from moving, saying, "That is as far as you will go. Kirari must not be awakened for any reason that is not dire. Do you understand?"

Ahlina nodded, still staring at the Dragon through her choppy bangs. Her thin frame looked like an ant compared to this magnificent creature. She had heard that most people could not come within a hundred yards without suffering from a paradox and having to flee. Even Supernaturals were not immune to Dragon paradox, but somehow Ahlina was fine. Jayde had trained herself to resist it. Ahlina, however, stood as if she were looking at a beautiful mountain range.

Noticing her sister's calm body and spirit, Jayde released her hand. But no sooner had she done so than there was a booming explosion outside that shook the foundation of the Temple.

Using her uncanny hearing, Jayde focused on roars and howls outside, as well as shrieks and weapons being drawn.

"We're under attack!" Jayde shouted. Turning to leave the room, she ran toward the large door, stopping just before she left. "Don't touch anything!"

Ahlina bowed toward her sister, keeping her head down until Jayde was gone. When she could no longer hear her sister's faint footsteps, she turned back to the Dragon and smiled.

"You're my ticket out of here!"

(Gemini's Lair now)

Jayde sat on the mountaintop in silence, listening to the sounds of the forest for miles, which brought her an inner peace. Needing to control the burning in her chest, she opened her eyes and coughed, clutching the cloth and skin right above her heart. She controlled her breathing as she remembered her focus. Jayde had to completely concentrate on the here and now. The wind passing through her long hair, and the sun shining on her fair skin, combined with the altitude's barometric pressure, helped her to achieve her goal.

Unknowingly, Maia had almost unlocked a great threat to the kids—a threat that Jayde had not seen since the destruction of the Forbidden City, Zalomoni.

Now, after so many years, her sister from that time was again showing her face. Ahlina was reborn and living among humans. She got what she always wanted.

Jayde looked at the horizon and smiled to herself. "You did have a point, little sister. I do have responsibility to the world, and I will bring honor to our family. I will show them how to fight."

Chapter 18

KNOW YOUR PLACE

Blue lay down on his soft bed, thinking about the recent events.

Today was such a long day. I'm coming to terms with this whole Supernatural thing a lot easier than I had suspected. Jayde is one tough chick. I would hate to be on her bad side. She kicks my ass constantly, but she was right. The more battles I've been getting into, the less it hurts. I could swear my bones were supposed to break again a couple of times . . . , although it still hurts every time I try to meditate and do what Gemini said about focusing on the Soulstream.

I'm still confused about what the Soulstream is, besides the energy pool all life comes from . . . , so I'm guessing heaven or God or something. Oh, well, it hurts like hell when I try to focus on pulling energy from it. Gemini said it was normal, and I would get used to it, so I guess I'll just have to believe him. Right now I'm exhausted from my head to my feet, and even my muscles hurt. I don't think I've fully recovered yet from the fall off the mountain. Damn, how does THAT sound? I fell off a mountain. I think that was all I needed to tell me that I'm not exactly normal.

Sky, on the other hand, is having some issues with coping. She's probably going through withdrawals from her high fashion closet and fan club at school. It would suck to lose so much, though. As far as I know, Crux is a runaway with nothing. Maia was adopted by Gemini, and her parents were happy to give her away. My folks and friends are dead. So Sky's the only one with collateral outside of here. I would have a hard time letting go of a celebrity life, too.

Damn, this bed feels good! I don't even have the strength to take my shoes off. I've never felt this tired, but for some reason I welcome it because I haven't heard my family's voices in some time now. I just have to lie here for a bit, and I'll be okay.

"I'm proud of you, brother," Charity said in a cheerful and pleasant voice.

Blue sat up and saw her standing in front of his bed with lock picks in her hands.

She looked down at them and giggled, "Sorry . . . , old habit."

"This can't be real. I mean . . . , you're *dead!*"

Blue looked intensely at his sister. She certainly seemed very much alive.

"Of course, I'm dead, stupid! I'm in your dream. But that's not the point. I'm here to tell you that mom and dad are proud of you. They understand what happened, and who you are."

Blue's face turned from confusion to interest. "How are they?"

"As good as most dead people . . . . They're at peace. They fulfilled their purpose for being on Earth. Now they're back in the Soulstream with the others."

"Is that supposed to be a joke?"

"No, it's reality. Stick with Gemini. He knows what he's talking about. If you don't take your destiny seriously, then the world is doomed. Sorry to hit you with such heavy stuff, big bro, but it's the truth."

Charity looked at Blue with those bright green eyes that reminded him so much of their mother. Sitting on the bed next to Blue, she placed her hand on his. "Stay with Gemini and save the girl."

"I don't know what you're talking about." Blue reached to touch his sister's hand and was comforted when the flesh was actually there. "Tell them—"

"I know, and so do they."

Charity's smile was so forgiving that Blue felt a wave of warmth over his face and chest.

"Wake up!" said a male voice from his sister's mouth. Crux was holding Blue's arm. "Wake up!"

Blue bolted up, still exhausted, and holding Crux's hand.

"Were you crying?" Crux asked. "You grabbed my hand as soon as I sat down. I tried to wake you up." He smiled in the moonlight that was illuminating Blue's bedroom.

Crux's Mohawk is looking shaggy and freshly cut.

Blue released the boy's hand and wiped his own face. "What? Why are you here?" He tried to regain his masculinity, and figure out what the boy was doing in his room, fully dressed in his fighter gear.

"We have to get out of here!" Crux whispered. "I'm tired of suicide missions, and I think we need to find our own way. All this predestined war stuff is old and scary." The more passionate Crux got, the louder he spoke.

Blue tried to suppress a smile as the boy paced back and forth.

It must be his nature to run. After all, he's a Gypsy.

Crux and Blue had become very close during the small amount of time they had spent together. Crux was the little brother that Blue never had. The remnants of Charity still lingered fresh in Blue's mind. He wanted to empathize with and protect the boy, but he knew that this was the safest place on the planet for either of them, with a secret society of assassins and—from Crux's story—Vampires and Gypsy thieves on their trail.

"Blue, are you listening? I mean, we really have to get out of here and find someplace safe like . . . , I don't know, Switzerland." Crux said this with an enthusiastic smile.

Blue just laughed. "Crux, I'm sorry, man, but we're away from any other people. Don't you think that's safer than any city full of OZONE contacts and informant possibilities? Dude, they rule everything: media, religion, government, medicine. You name it, and they have their hands in it and sign the payroll checks. That may not sound like a lot to you, but, trust me, that's pretty much the whole world." Blue ruffled Crux's hair. "Now go back to bed, bro."

Crux's spirit seemed broken a bit. As he pulled away and stood beside Blue's bed, he put his lock picks back into his pocket. Blue smiled at the irony of Crux entering his room the way his sister always had.

"Stop thinking I'm some kind of joke," Crux protested. "I know how to take care of myself, and I don't want to be thrown into another suicide mission because of some stupid old guy's prophecy."

"I promise I won't let anything happen to you, little man. Just trust me."

Crux gave Blue a tiny, half-hearted smile as he turned to leave the room. His small bag flopped on his back with every step he took toward the door.

"I hope you're right," Crux said over his shoulder as he closed Blue's door. In the hall, he whispered to himself, "I wish I could stay."

"Do you have to play that rock music so damn loud?" Grin shouted to Guardian, trying to speak over the blast. As he reached toward the radio, Guardian drew his gun.

Turning down the volume with a button on the steering wheel, Guardian continued to look forward down the road, driving as fast as he normally did.

"What do you want?" he asked.

"I get the feeling you want any excuse to shoot me," Grin said, looking at Guardian's custom-made gun.

"Wanna test that theory? I dare you to touch my radio." Guardian said this without bothering to look at his passenger.

"Listen, I know you don't want me here, and that's fine, because I would much rather be in my own car. At least, I can smoke in it."

"You insisted on me giving you a ride to the base, so this was *your* choice."

"Yeah, but I also said I wanted to bond a little if we're forced to be partners."

Guardian sighed. "You know I think you're disgusting, right? How's that for bonding?"

A phlegm-filled laugh and slight cough filled the air as Grin barely kept his composure.

"What's your problem with me, Guardian? Is it because I killed those kids, or is it my methods of turning people's brains to mush? Or are you just jealous of my good looks?"

Guardian did not acknowledge the last question, but was waiting to address the other ones Grin had asked. "Since you asked, yeah, I think you're a scumbag for what you do to children. Especially File 244519b. Did you really have to mutilate those kids? And how in the hell do you live with yourself?"

"I see you've thought hard about this. So what? I accepted a mission, knowing that I would be killing Supernatural children. And, yes, I enjoyed every slice and cigarette burn on their flesh. As far as I'm concerned, I shouldn't feel guilty because they aren't even human. Remember, we are OZONE Agents, and we do as we're ordered. I just so happen to like my job. Do you?"

Feeling his muscles twitching, Guardian stopped himself from punching the villain next to him. A slight chant entered his head: *Who are you trying to protect? Who are you trying to protect?*

Guardian smashed Grin in the face, shattering his front teeth with the gun. Then, swerving to the side of the road, he stopped the car, opened the door, and kicked the psychic out onto the dusty side of the freeway.

"Don't ever use your powers on me again, Psiel, unless you wanna end up in a worse place than you left your victims!"

Guardian's gun was pointed at Grin's bleeding face.

With a long screech and a cloud of dust in the air, Guardian drove off.

Grin sat in the dirt, laughing his phlegmy cackle while pulling out a cigarette.

"Touché, partner. I see you killed a boy, as well."

Grin continued his sour laugh as he lit the tobacco.

✶

"I'm inside the base. I have to be quick about this, though. What files did you want from here?"

Juno was speaking into her micro set as she walked into the empty research room in the OZONE underbase.

"Just go to the computer and place the external drive in. I'll have what I need in seconds. Remember to watch the door. I can't control cameras inside that place without them knowing it's me. Not while I'm doing this."

"Fine, but make it quick."

As Juno placed the external drive cord into the computer, she couldn't help searching for Nina Waterford in the system. A small file showed up with a report of the accident. Nothing was in the file that Juno hadn't seen before. She quickly closed the screen when Narles walked into the room.

"Lose him!" Surge-Overload's voice said, impatiently.

Juno stood up and walked toward her newly assigned partner. "What is it that you need?"

"Well, I haven't seen you since the sewers. Protocol says we're supposed to inform each other of any contact with the marks, and regroup at the nearest checkpoint if we haven't heard—"

"Don't give me a lecture on Protocol, bitch! I helped write that book, rookie. What do you really want?"

"I just want to know why I was left in the dark in the sewers, and why you always seem to treat me like a rookie."

"I treat you the way I see fit. Don't ever question my word. You know my numbers on the board, and you know I don't miss my targets.

If there had been someone or something to kill, I'm more than capable. Got it?"

Juno was now looking directly into the hazel eyes of the six-foot-tall Soldier, making him feel smaller than her—although, even in her boots, she was actually two inches shorter.

"Done!" Surge said into Juno's micro set. Finally, they had access to the inside from a remote satellite. *She's good!*

Juno got the point, but she was currently into putting this jackass in his place. Grabbing his shirt, she pushed him against the door, out of the camera's view. "I'm a higher rank than you! Do I make myself clear, Soldier?"

"Crystal clear, ma'am," Narles muttered through gritted teeth.

Juno released his collar and straightened it for him. "This little conversation is off the record. Got it?"

"Yes, ma'am." By now, Narles was standing at attention.

"At ease, Soldier! Now be gone."

Juno turned away from Narles and walked toward the computer.

Narles squinted his eyes into narrow slits as he looked in the direction she was heading. Seething with contempt, but knowing his place, he stalked out of the room and down the hall toward the Quest review chamber.

"What was *that* about, Juno?" Surge-Overload said into the micro set.

"Just another one of the new pretty boy recruits, who takes his job much too seriously. Nothing for *you* to worry about."

Juno grabbed the external drive port and put it into one of her many hidden pockets. Then she left the room and walked out toward the exit of the underbase.

Narles peeked out of the Quest review room to see if Juno had left yet. Then he went down the hall into the computer lab. Approaching the computer that Juno had been using, he found it locked.

"Dammit! I can't get in. I need to ask my buddy Deme if he can recover what she was looking at."

Chapter 19

BOUNCE

Crux made his way down the hall to the outer chamber. As far as he knew, everyone was either asleep or meditating. He wasn't exactly sure what age-old immortals do. The one thing he did know was that he wasn't sticking around. This palace in the mountains seemed too much like a crazy carnival that Crux didn't want any part of. The long halls were shining after a hard day of chores, which had included Crux and Blue waxing the floors.

I'm used to things starting out nice and smooth, but turning out terrible, and all of a sudden, I'M the sacrifice. Wow! I sound like Maia and her endless maudlin phrases. Gosh, did I just use a Gemini word, "maudlin"? I've been hanging out with these guys too long. They're all growing on me, but I have to go.

Being around Mancers, everything looks brighter and tastes better these days. I've never been around another one until recently. Well, everything also got weird with the flashback of Pangaea, where I was a General of an army of Supernaturals. Blue was the King of the entire world, pretty much. These are things that should come with instructions or warning labels when you're born. Not like Witchbreed, who become enlightened and regain all of their memories. Mancers have to relive and relearn all of their mistakes and try to do better the next time around.

This whole War thing has been getting on my nerves. The training from Gemini and Jayde is worse than anything the Petsha family could come up with. I mean, seriously, you would think they were training us for the Apocalypse. Okay, I just got a shiver down my spine. I'm sure that's what it's for now.

That's the door to the most snobby girl I've ever met. No, come to think of it, Star may have her beat by a little. I'll have to be extra quiet walking past her door, because she can hear freaking EVERYTHING . . . . *I'm almost out of here. Sky's actually not so bad, but she does need a reality check. This life isn't a choice. It's something she is.*

"Crux, what are you doing creeping around like a thief in the night?" Sky's voice rang through the halls louder than he could have possibly imagined. "I mean, seriously, you're gonna have to break old habits."

He almost stopped breathing, but turned with a loud "Shhhh!" Looking down the large hall both ways, he whispered, "I was trying not to wake you."

Crossing her arms and looking him up and down, she answered in a slightly lower than normal voice, "From the looks of it, you're bouncing."

"What's bouncing? I'm not used to all of these American terms."

"Bouncing . . . , bailing . . . , skipping out . . . , ghost . . . , adios . . . , hitchhiker . . . , going vagabond. Get it?"

"Yeah, I get it, and I'm just . . . , um . . . , practicing my stealth on Jayde's orders. Do you wanna join me? She said it's going to be another five-day training session."

Crux knew how much Sky hated chores and training.

"No way in hell," she said. "I'm going back to sleep. Or, at least, I *wish* I could, without having dreams of Pangaea and the Great War we started."

"Excuse me, Sky, but last time I checked, you and Blue ordered the Coven of Unity to cast a spell they didn't want to cast in the first place, and the world went up like a marshmallow in a bonfire."

"Shut up! No one asked you, anyway. Go do your stupid chores, or train to death, or whatever it is you're doing around here."

Sky said this as she floated backwards without consciously realizing she was doing it, and shut her door without touching it.

Whew! That was way too close. I have to bounce now, or they'll all know I'm running away. Okay, I have my bag, and now I have to get my diamonds back from Star. If I could only figure out how to get out of this place. I just hope we're not on some island! I swear, if I have to get on a ship, I'll definitely come right back and happily wax the floors. A simple jump through the window, and tuck and roll as I land. That was perfect Petsha form on that landing.

Before I get ahead of myself, let me use an old Shandor trick to find out where Star is. Okay, place the map on the ground and put a couple of rocks on the corners so it doesn't blow away in this breeze. Where's that pushpin? Found it. Okay, focus on Star and throw the pin in the air. It should tell me where that spoiled brat is.

When he tossed the pushpin gently into the air, the breeze didn't even stop it from falling onto the map and sticking in the city—San Francisco.

Great! I have to make it to the city we just left. What kind of luck do I have?

Tucking the map neatly into his pack, Crux tightened the straps on his shoes and zipped up his new jacket. Placing a scarf over his mouth, he ran as fast as he could, and then jumped between branches and through shadows, as he had been trained to do. He felt exhilarated as he continued his trek southbound.

"How long are we going to let him take this little trip?" Jayde asked Gemini as they stood on top of the Pagoda, looking down at the youngster making his break in the moonlight.

"He will be fine. He is just afraid. It is probably safer for him to be lost here than on the mission with the others, anyway. His skills are advanced for his age, but OZONE and Vampyl are going to be present, according to Maia."

Gemini answered in his usual confident tone as he watched Crux jump from branch to branch.

"Let's just hope he doesn't figure out how to make it out of here."

Did I really agree to this camp? Am I really going to sing campfire songs with chipper girls in pink-and-yellow T-shirts? Is my mom out of her fashionista mind? Sometimes I wonder how dad even got a date with her, let alone found anything in common. He's such a typical rocket science geek in all of his brilliance, a nice guy and all, but she's so the opposite. Mom was a so-so fashion student in New York, and now works as a consultant for Couture Inc. It just baffles my mind how clueless they are about the world in general between the two of them. I love them to death, though.

Please, don't let this camp director talk to me. Oh, no! She's making a beeline to me. I'm gonna act like I don't see her and just keep playing this MMORPG. If she interrupts my boss raid after I promised Soul Goddess and the Mad Hatter, I will totally tank for them. They can't possibly make it through this boss raid without my über hacks. No, here she comes with that ultra-cheery smile. It makes me wanna wretch. And please don't let her say anything about my black-and-green eyeliner.

"Hello, Cindy Alastar. I met you a little earlier at the opening 'Hooray for Sunshine' song ceremony." The young camp director, Rainbow, was trying her best to get Surge's attention with her bright smile.

Maybe if I act like she doesn't exist, she'll go away, Surge thought to herself, while typing to her friends in chat on the game. While awaiting her fate of a horrid camp song, she hurriedly shut her laptop. Looking up at the girls with disdain, she put her computer gently in her backpack.

"That's not the spirit, Missy. I think it's time for a 'Hooray for Happiness' song." Rainbow signaled for the others to come over to stand around Surge. Dozens of peppy girls ran over and started humming.

Oh, my god! Surge thought. *I'm gonna die if they do what I think they're gonna do. Try not to throw up. Why can't I bounce to some remote island right now?*

★

"Who did you say was sitting at this computer, Agent Narles?" Deme asked with a puzzled expression on his young face after inspecting the computer that appeared to be wiped of all memory.

The teenager had been handpicked from Mensa after scoring marks on exams that surpassed most of his class. He was the prodigal son of a Wall Street hedge fund tycoon and a spiritualist from Salem, Massachusetts. At age nine, he had hacked into the Pentagon. It was suspected but never proven that Deme tipped his father off on many accounts. When the authorities knocked on his New York penthouse, his father happily allowed them to take his only son, so long as the dirt didn't affect his income, and he didn't go to prison.

"I told you, sir, it was Juno." Narles hated reporting to an officer so young, but he knew his place in the greater scheme of things and didn't like disorder. He was undyingly loyal, and hoped that OZONE saw his efforts for what they were.

"Castia hæsito inritus irritus progentius!" Deme said, touching the computer monitor after lighting incense that smelled like almonds and rosemary.

Narles didn't understand what Deme was doing or if he had just cursed in Latin, but he stood silently at attention, staring at the computer monitor. Deme appeared to be in some sort of trance. His eyes were open so wide, with a blank expression on his face. The screen was changing faster than Narles could comprehend.

I ʜᴀᴛᴇ these techie guys!

The more Narles thought about it, the more he hated that he hadn't been given a different partner. He didn't have anything against women, aside from the fact that he didn't respect them after his ex cheated on him. He would much rather be partnered with the number one, Guardian.

When the screen stopped, there was a name on it: Nina Hall.

Who's that? Why was Juno looking for her? According to the file, she's dead. Deme is freaky. I met him the day of my interview with OZONE. That's how I knew this was the highest job on the planet. Serving and protecting the world from terrorists, and being paid to kill, is the greatest perk of this job. I don't have any friends, so it's easy to skip around without anyone missing me. I saved Deme once, so he's always been nice to me. Why isn't he moving? He outranks me by four ranks easily, so I can't speak until he talks again. Say something, you freak!

Deme gasped and sucked in a deep breath. When his eye color returned, all he could say was, "Surge-Overload!"

Chapter 20

TACTICS

A thunderous explosion woke everyone up. Blue jumped to his feet and put his boots on so fast that he forgot to grab a shirt as he ran out of the room. After the haunting dream about the Great War, he jumped to conclusions, figuring that the Supernaturals were here to kill everyone. He would welcome death more if it weren't for his sister's visit last night in his dream.

Wiping her eyes as she tried to fathom what was going on, Maia bumped into Blue, still wearing her pajamas. She realized he was as lost as she was.

Sky somehow had time to put on a Victorian-style dress that she must have remodeled when she was bored. However, she was barefoot, and had a confused expression on her face that matched Maia's and Blue's. With her hair in a ponytail flying in the air, she followed behind them.

The three of them were scrambling to make sense of the rumble in the ground, when suddenly the explosive force hit them like a wave, stopping them in their tracks.

Sky raised her hands to prevent the meteoric force from blowing them all off their feet.

Blue looked at her in awe, then screamed in panic, "Where's Crux?!!"

"Don't worry about him," Sky shouted. "He's doing some stupid training thing for Jayde for the next few days on stealth. What the hell is attacking us?"

"Not what, but *who*?" Maia said, pointing up to the mountain that Blue had fallen from. She didn't care in the least that she was in her pajamas, but stood staring at the cause of the explosions. Large boulders were flying through the air, crashing onto the courtyard and into the Pagoda.

Jayde was simply palm-striking them as she had done with Blue a couple of days before. Barely jumping out of the way, he shuddered as the boulders flew directly at them.

This is a test. It has to be, or is Jayde really trying to kill us?

Blue rolled on the ground, scraping his arm until it bled.

Sky moved to the side as if she were dodging cars in traffic.

Maia walked through the field, looking up to the stars. She yelled back to her friends, "Follow my every step."

Blue looked at Sky, then back at Maia.

She must be crazy if she thinks we're gonna walk through this onslaught of meteors. Those stones are big enough to squish any one of us like little bugs.

Blue went out on a proverbial limb. Running toward Maia, he figured, *If I'm gonna die, I might as well do it saving someone. I'm just thankful Crux is nowhere near this place. Maybe he was right about leaving the suicide missions.*

Sky took a step back, screaming while dodging shrapnel from exploding stone fragments. "You go right ahead," she shouted to Blue. "And tell me how that goes!"

Maia felt Blue behind her. In the calmest voice she had under the circumstances, she said to him, "I'm going on faith here, so don't kill me if you die. I can see the meteors before they fall. You have to follow me closely, though, and we should make it there before Jayde knows what hit her."

"Okay, I guess I get it," Blue said, following her every step as she had directed.

Like a miracle, all of the stones somehow flew right past them, leaving the two totally untouched.

Blue watched in slow motion as stones rushed by their heads, too close for comfort.

This has to be one of the most dangerous things I've ever seen.

Stones on the side of the mountain were tumbling down so hard that the ground was shaking. The cool breeze became filled with dust and fear.

Sky placed her back to the wall as she watched Blue and Maia scramble from one place to another, sometimes only inches from death.

What can I do here? she wondered. *I don't want to be the useless one.*

Looking around, she saw her opportunity: *I can send this breeze right back in Jayde's face, filled with dust, and end this deadly target practice.*

Jayde was flowing with graceful steps from one strategically placed boulder to another. She had made Blue, Crux, Maia, and Sky move them up the mountain one by one for almost an entire day before making them fight her again. She knew she was being tough on them, but it was necessary. The kids would certainly die if they didn't work together. And this was just the beginning. She would attack them all at once if they got up the mountain without being gravely injured. At this moment, Maia was using her premonition to guide her comrades up the mountain.

A smart tactic, Jayde thought. *But how would they handle a little shockwave to the ground?*

Jayde switched her fighting stance and focused on the Soulstream working through her, changing her own footsteps to that of the mountain itself. Now every step was earth-shattering. She stepped from one boulder to another, shaking the mountain's very foundation.

Maia fell off balance and twisted her ankle, but Blue caught her before she could fall down the path. He didn't know what else to do.

Every time he even *thought* of using the explosive energy within him, he got flashbacks of his family. It also hurt more than the time he fell off the mountain. Gemini told him to control that pain, along with the anxiety, but it was easier said than done. Blue felt that he would kill everyone around him if he unleashed that pent-up energy, but he might not have a choice soon if Maia couldn't guide them on the path. He pulled Maia behind a tree to hide.

Sky, who could see the peril as it was happening, flew through the missiles being flung her way. As they entered her space, she decided to try something different. She would do some flinging of her own. When a boulder flew directly at her, she stopped moving, trying to concentrate on her space. She felt the breeze around her, like a nice, fluffy blanket. Her hair flew up, and when she opened her eyes, she stopped the boulder where it was, making her hair drop as everything around her was frozen. Even the shrapnel was caught in midair like a paused movie.

"It's time we went on the offensive!" she called.

When Blue saw a boulder about to smash Sky, his eyes widened, and he could feel his palms tingle like static. His heart raced, and every cell of his skin opened with a fiery mist pouring through. He tried to remember Gemini's training about energy control, but only between thoughts, not wanting to let go. He almost screamed in frustration, but he could hear Maia saying, "Focus on the point you want to connect to, and it will be."

At that very moment, the boulder was only a few feet from Sky. Blue thought about the boulder with every fiber of his being. A hum entered the air like a vibration that could make the oceans ripple. Blue saw the boulder as it flew through the morning wind, and before he could stop it, a wire of pure light and energy burned through his skin. The string of light sprang coiled into existence and destroyed the large stone, disintegrating even the dust in the air.

Sky stood staring at Blue. His body was glowing as if a light engulfed it. The small stones around Sky dropped to the ground. She felt some of the pebbles falling on her feet. Looking up to the top of the mountain, she saw Jayde spinning in a martial arts form, ready to slam her palm against another boulder. Sky barely saw Blue run up the mountain in a blur. She flew toward Maia with the speed of thought.

"Are you okay?"

Maia shook her head, and, through blurry vision, felt her senses return. "Yes, I'm okay . . . , I think."

She looked at her palms and placed her hand on her ankle. Sky watched as a soft light touched Maia's skin, and then disappeared as fast as it came.

"I'm okay now, for sure," Maia said.

Both young women saw Blue destroying boulders with his strings of light coiling through the air like whips of pure energy.

Sky looked at Maia questioningly. "What's going on?"

"He made a choice. He chose to use his powers through the pain."

Sky kept her eyes on Blue as he went to strike Jayde. She grabbed Maia and said, "We can't let him take all of the glory. Let's go."

Without knowing that she was carrying Maia through the air at her speed of thought, Sky ran as if she were on the ground.

Maia looked down and thought to herself, *So this is what it feels like to fly.*

Blue suffered through the surge of raw energy tearing the fibers of his body, but he also knew he had a quest to complete—ensuring that the lives of his friends were not compromised. He swung at Jayde with speeds only she could match. She changed her stance, ignoring the boulders while blocking the lightning fast punches and kicks. Grabbing Blue by the leg as he threw a high kick, she easily tossed him to the ground. The slam sent up a minor dust cloud at the same time that Sky was starting another series of punches and kicks directed at Jayde.

Maia was telepathically instructing Sky where to attack and what Jayde's weakness was. Jayde struck and lunged back toward Sky, who dodged by flying backward toward the edge of the mountain. As Jayde focused on Sky, Maia communicated with Blue to strike Jayde's heart. Blue flew faster than Maia could see and punched Jayde in the chest.

But his fist barely made contact before Jayde redirected Blue, throwing him off the mountain for a second time.

When Sky saw Blue flying through the air, she jumped after him, diving toward the ground with defiance. Blue was out of her range, so she feared he would hit the ground before she could get to him. But when she thought about catching him, she was immediately holding him close. They both stopped an inch from the ground. Blue's glow was gone, and his eyes were intent on hers. They were suspended in the air as if gravity did not exist. For a long moment, they just stared at each other. Blue's bare chest was warm to the touch. Sky hadn't realized his muscles were so firm. She softly eased them both to the ground.

Watching this, Gemini leaped off the Pagoda. His coal black cloak was floating around him, and his dark shoes barely made a dent in the grass as he landed.

"It would seem," he said, "that you are ready for your final test . . . . Me!"

Chapter 21

LUCKY KNIVES

"Sir," the Receptionist reported to Deme, "she took files on some random empathic stones from the forests all over the planet. We filed them as Magick artifacts in the archives. Correction, she just took the stones from the archives and is making her way out of the facility. Should I send Agents or Soldiers to stop her?"

"No, don't get in her way. Keep an eye on her. She's in league with our biggest threat. And who knows for how long that union has been in place? Interrogate her partner in secrecy, though. I want to know everything." Then, to a Psiel Agent, he said, "Torture him if you have to."

"Yes, sir," said the Psiel Agent named Zeer, who turned on his heels and walked out the door with a devilish smile.

"Don't lose her position," Deme commanded to a Technomage on his left. "She will lead us to Surge-Overload one way or another." He subconsciously squeezed his shoulder while staring at the wall of computer monitors and holographic screens in front of him, all focused on finding Juno. Deme spoke more to himself than to anyone else when he said aloud, "Juno, you have made a fool of me for the last time."

"I'm making my way out of the building," Juno said into her micro set while loading her custom-made OZONE gun. "But I suspect they know my position by now. Things are much too quiet for OZONE. I can't speak on this frequency again, so this will be my last transmission for some time."

All OZONE Agents specialized in weaponry, and Juno happened to specialize in many of them. Her skills were rivaled by few on the planet. She anticipated a battle by now, but when it didn't come, she continued her trek through the underbase to her vehicle.

I will find Nina, no matter what!

Surge was tired of the songs, and the utter stupidity of it all. She called her mother to pick her up.

I can't stand the overly cheerful songs of these way too pretty to be real girls, anyway.

As she sat on the outskirts of camp, reapplying the eyeliner that they had made her take off, she cursed her fate for ending up there in the first place.

How did mom ever go to this ridiculous camp for so many years? The way she talks about this place, you would think it was a magickal wonderland. To me it's Hell on Earth.

She had just received Juno's transmission, but couldn't answer because she was being escorted by the camp director, Rainbow Ebullient. Even her name annoyed Surge, but she just sat in silence as the lady went on and on about femininity and happiness.

"You are a very special young lady, I can feel it, and you should embrace your special skills. I'm sorry to hear that you're so sick, you can't continue at camp." Rainbow said this in what seemed like a genuine tone. She didn't like being ignored, and when Surge whipped out her laptop and logged into her normal sites, Rainbow asked, "Cindy, are you listening to me?" Her tone now had changed to frustration underneath the cheer. Again, she asked, "Cindy, will you be coming back to camp next year to cheer with us on girl power? Cindy? Cindy, are you listening?"

Without knowing what came over her, Rainbow grabbed the laptop and threw it as far as she could, shattering it into pieces. Surge looked into the fiery eyes of the camp director, seeing that something was completely wrong with her. Rainbow's right eye was twitching, and her posture was changing into a hunch as she breathed heavily.

"O-M-F-ing-G, lady! Are you serious? You totally need therapy." Surge said all this without thinking.

"Don't take that tone with me, you ungrateful little gothic bitch!" Rainbow said with an infuriated tone that was almost a scream.

Surge stood up and took a step back. All of her senses rang "danger" as the camp director took a step toward her. The look in Rainbow's eyes showed that she was consumed with rage. Surge looked around for a place to run.

"Help!" she yelled out, but no one answered back. "It's not that serious. Okay, so I hated singing your dumb songs, and I really don't like sundresses and pastels. But, really, why are you freaking on me?"

"You come out here and disrespect my camp with your snotty attitude, and you think anyone here will help you?"

Saliva was dribbling down Rainbow's chin.

Surge could swear the woman was possessed. It showed when a glimmer of the madness tried to spill out of Rainbow.

"What's your childhood trauma, lady?" Surge said. "Back up, please."

As Rainbow got closer and closer, a car rolled up. It was the taxi that Surge had ordered. Grabbing the pieces of her computer, she ran toward the vehicle, looking over her shoulder.

The cab driver got out of the car and asked, "Is everything alright?"

Surge looked back at Rainbow, who was wiping her face. She seemed almost pretty again.

What kind of Jekyll crap was that?

"Thank you, we're fine, kind sir," said Rainbow. "I was just grabbing the bags for our young Cindy here, who'll be going home to rest because she's ill."

Rainbow lifted Surge's bags as if they weighed nothing and began to walk toward the car. Surge could barely roll them, let alone pick them up.

Standing next to the taxi, staring at Rainbow with tears in her eyes, Surge looked petrified. Rainbow walked casually past her, without so much as a glance.

The taxi driver smiled flirtatiously at the camp director as he reached for the bags after opening the trunk. But then he dropped the bags to the ground, not realizing how heavy they were. Pretending he had slipped, he looked at Rainbow in a much different light now.

Surge hurriedly got into the car and tried to close the door behind her, slamming it on Rainbow's hand.

"Now, that's just not nice of you, little girl," Rainbow whispered through the window. "I don't know what you are, but you're not like the other girls. I can smell it all over you. We'll meet again, you better believe it."

"Are we all done, ma'am?" the driver asked, walking toward Rainbow.

She yanked her hand out of the crack of the door, scraping off her skin.

Surge watched in horror as the camp director simply hid her hand behind her back, while blood gushed onto the ground. With the other hand, she produced cash for the driver. He seemed not to notice, happy with the large tip, as he flirted a little more and got into the car smiling.

As the car drove away, Surge locked the door, staring back in disbelief at the camp director.

Did that really just happen? Mom is so not going to believe me.

As the director waved her bloody hand in farewell, Surge looked down at the pile of parts in her lap, and sighed.

How am I gonna contact Juno now?

✴

"I hate partners," Guardian muttered to himself as he walked into the OZONE underbase after being scanned in. He watched a Psiel and two Soldiers grab Juno's partner, Narles. The man seemed confused and upset at the treatment he was receiving.

"I was just doing the right thing, I swear! I didn't do anything wrong! Why are you treating me like a terrorist?"

As Narles looked up at Guardian, shame overwhelmed him, making him angry that he was being embarrassed in front of one of his heroes. All he wanted to do ever since he heard that Guardian was the top Agent in OZONE was to work with him. There were thousands of amazing Agents in the organization, but Guardian's numbers and successes topped the charts. They were rivaled by Agents like Juno and 99, but they were *not* Guardian. The look in Narles's eyes indicated that he was staring at his long lost love.

Narles was quickly reminded that he was being detained when a titanium poly-steel club slammed against his neck.

"Keep moving, Agent Narles. Don't resist," the Psiel Zeer said. "No need to make this worse on yourself. We simply have questions."

Narles looked at the Psiel Agent through the stars in his vision. "I already told you that Juno was looking for a Nina Hall. That's all I remember."

He tried to stand up straight and look back to see if Guardian had seen him get hit. But Guardian was already on his way, out of sight. Looking disappointed, Narles followed his interrogators without any further resistance.

"Oh, you will love me after our little 'talk,' Agent Narles," said Zeer. "Trust me."

Guardian walked around the corner, thinking to himself, *What kind of trouble have you got yourself into now, Juno? And who is Nina Hall?*

✳

Juno had her gun ready, and one hand on a secret blade, awaiting an encounter from some random OZONE assassin. This was not a secret society you could just leave. Like any of the other stories you hear about secret societies or gangs, death was the only way out. Juno realized her position, but she was so close to the one person she had looked for, for what seemed like thousands of years. She thought to herself with every step about the mistake she must have made.

Narles! That piece of shit rookie partner. I know they're watching me, but I don't care anymore. The files say that these stones were found in Oregon, and that's where I'll look. I changed the names in the file a little with Surge's help, but that won't keep them away for long. They'll be on her trail soon, once they find out she's alive. I can feel her presence on each stone as if we were in Greece again. Nina, I'll find you!

Juno scanned her car. There was no bomb, and no one had touched the vehicle, which could only mean one thing. She was closer to her goal than she realized. OZONE didn't ever let people leave this smoothly. If they wanted to play this game, then she knew what she would do next. She dared not call Surge-Overload, but she knew that he was her only chance at pinpointing Nina from an Eagle Eye view. Satellites were not easily hacked, but somehow Surge had Satellite views. First, however, Juno had a long drive ahead of her.

I know what I'll do. I'll lose them. Since I'm already compromised, I might as well go all out. There's a Port Rune near the forest where these stones were found. That will be our escape. Damn OZONE for cursing me and keeping me captive all these years! So much blood, so many tortures, so many innocent lives lost. God, I was a fool! I was so angry.

Juno drove faster, almost double the speed limit, as she wove in and out of traffic, holding on to the stones she had gotten from the archives.

These are my closest connection to the truth. I will make amends for my crimes against my own kind.

✱

I think I'm lost!

Crux removed the small scarf that was acting as a mask against the wind. As he rested, he took a bite of the rations in his pack.

I know which way is North by the stars. A simple navigation. All Petsha know that. What I don't know is where the hell I am. I also don't know where on the planet I am.

He slapped himself on the head.

I don't know, and this place is getting creepy. I heard some explosions come from Gemini's place, but I can't go back now. Whatever is attacking them is probably after me. I can't let the Shandor bring me back to the Gypsies. My life is already forfeit if that happens.

He took his map out of his pack.

Okay, so the old Tarot reader once told me I could alter probability. I didn't know what she meant until I threw knives blindfolded in exactly the targets, just because I thought of it. That same ability has served me well ever since. Not even the Shandor knew I could do that. They only knew about my ability to change the weight of objects. God, I miss my dad! He was so understanding of my powers and told me to embrace my destiny. He also told me to embrace my true self and never compromise my spirit. Who would've thought he would be plotting for my own sacrifice, like in some ancient story? I mean, who sacrifices their first-born sons anymore? Goes to show how disconnected from the world my people are, even though they're still part of it.

Focusing on his current location, Crux threw the pin in the air. It fell on the map near Miyako in Japan.

Okay, I wasn't expecting that. I have to get out of here. I've always found my way. Maybe that probability thing was just a fluke. Maybe it was just luck. The Tarot lady always said there's no such thing as coincidence, and we make our own luck. She might have been crazy because she did like Absinthe a lot. Damn, this is stupid! I just wanna get outta here!

He threw a pebble into the wind.

The targets at the camp . . . . That's it! Maybe that's the trick. My daggers will show me the way.

He kissed his lucky throwing knives, focusing on a way out. Then he spun around and threw the daggers. The three of them flew through the forest and slammed into a tree. Crux followed closely behind, picked them out of the bark, and tried again. All three once more flew in the same direction, but deeper into the woods.

It's working! I WILL *get out of here!*

Guardian walked into the Control Panel to see Deme obsessively staring from screen to screen and whispering to himself in what seemed like Latin, although Guardian knew better.

"You needed me here?" he said, breaking the uncomfortable silence.

Deme continued to stare at the screens, looking at all surveillance of Juno's car driving through traffic as only other trained top OZONE assassins could. He didn't take his gaze off the screen as he cross-referenced the files Juno was researching with the stones.

"It doesn't make sense unless the girl is Supernatural," Deme said, deep in thought. "But she's dead. We have the files and the reports to back it up . . . . Unless she's *not* dead, and Juno has been covering her tracks. If that's the case, we have to go over every file and mission you and Juno have ever submitted."

Deme seemed to be talking more to himself than to Guardian.

"What are you talking about?" Guardian asked, coming directly to the point.

"We got a call from Grin that your behavior has been a little sporadic. He believes you should be analyzed."

Deme glanced over at Guardian.

"Grin's a fucking idiot! And I'll tell him that to what's left of his face."

"Maybe so, but he's an efficient idiot nevertheless. He also tends to believe you're Supernatural, and have secrets you're hiding from us. What do you say about that kind of idiotic and blasphemous talk?"

Deme said all this while staring at his monitor.

Guardian now realized that this was an interrogation and saw the room for what it truly was. There were three Technomages staring at their screens, as if they were in trances. There were also four heavily armed Soldiers standing at attention, posted strategically around the room. Deme had his back to Guardian, wearing clothes that, to Guardian's eye, were an indication of his age. His baggy pants and embroidered shirt were not as professional as the clothes of the typical OZONE Agent, but Deme didn't have to prove anything to anyone. The world didn't know he existed, and he was in sole charge of the most powerful machines on the planet.

Guardian was puzzled. *I could instantly kill everyone in this room, including Deme, and they know it. So, if I'm a suspect, why would they interrogate me in this place, so close to their most prized intel?*

"Don't look so defensive, Guardian!" Deme said, laughing delightedly, which made him seem even more like a child. "Did you really think I would take the word of that cancerous fool?" His laughter stopped abruptly. "I have a mission for you that will be approved by our Commander within seconds. Okay, it's already approved." Deme took his hands reluctantly off his computer and walked over to a Technomage who was focused on his own screen. "Any progress?"

"No, sir. Surge-Overload has not made contact through the device since this morning."

"Thank you, Shadow Harvester. Keep working on it."

Deme returned his gaze to Guardian, looking him over thoughtfully.

This is the best assassin in OZONE . . . , roughly six feet tall, and built like a mixed martial artist. This man has trained many of the assassins in the field, literally writing the book on how to capture, annihilate, incapacitate, and neutralize Supernaturals. I guarantee, he's already calculating his next move.

Deme continued to probe the impenetrable armor that was Guardian's subterfuge.

He's not the most feared assassin for no reason. He has tricks up his sleeve. There's something very peculiar about him, for sure. He's the topic of many OZONE private meetings. Apparently, he's a Jreamer, and doesn't know that about himself, based on all reports. How egotistical of him to believe he's just GOOD at what he does, and not give his gifts the credit for his success. Jreamers are the world's best hunters. They are Supernatural, most definitely, and OZONE has many among its ranks in higher levels, including the Commander.

It wasn't Deme's place to expose information, even if the subject was Guardian. Deme looked at the razor-blade sharp spikes of Guardian's hair.

His all-American looks help him in undercover missions, no doubt. He can easily go from rugged to polished, as he practices the art of disguise. This Agent is deceptively dangerous, but I'm not worried. I know how to handle him.

"According to our calculations," Deme said, "we should be intercepting an extremely high-level enemy of the state. You are to kill Surge-Overload."

Chapter 22

BONDS

Blue had been awake for some time now. Water rushing over his body in the shower had been pouring onto his aching muscles and bruised skin for hours. He knew this only because of the sun's position in the sky. Usually, he would have something to do to occupy his mind, like polishing guns or, lately, cleaning the already pristine floors of the Pagoda. Although he was still not sure how he had gotten there, and Crux's mission had been taking a very long time, he felt he would rather not question his teachers at this point. He used to ignore the ones back home, but now all he could do was think of how screwed up his life really had become.

I guess I thought I had it bad back when dad used to yell at me, but now I find out I may be the cause of the Apocalypse! Not every day does a guy get told he's responsible for how crappy the world is. I'm homeless, but somehow I'm supposed to fix the world we live in? Add that to the fact that I can't stop thinking about Kaery, and how she looked at me. But yesterday, when Sky was so close, she felt . . . , well . . . , GOOD. And on top of the fighting, and broken limbs that heal way too fast, I have a little adopted brother . . . . Oh, yeah . . . , for the first time since the accident, my family's been quiet.

I'm not exactly sure why I'm the guy these people need in their crusade against the modern-day lifestyle. I mean, even if I help kill the president of OZONE, or whatever the leader's called, what next? Do we go into the Dark Ages again? On top of all the madness, I don't even know how I'm supposed to fight a group of people who technically don't exist, with powers I don't know how to control. Yeah, I'm screwed. So is the world, if it has to depend on a high school dropout . . . .

Damn, my muscles ache! But it's a lot better than when I felt the Soulstream running through my body like it was gonna burn me alive, from the inside out. Not exactly my idea of cool. Maybe I'm afraid to be alone. Maybe I need to be medicated. Oh, no, I won't pull a 'Sky' and go to Denial Land. I know for a fact that these bruises hurt like hell, and how the Soulstream felt . . . .

One thing about the Soulstream that felt so familiar, and strange at the same time, was my family. I could feel them around me, telling me that I'm doing the right thing. When dad actually approved of me, I was ready to take on the world! Even Tommy and Guy were there, helping me. Gemini and Jayde have given me more than I can ever repay. Anytime I focus on the Soulstream, though it hurts like a bitch, I can still revisit my family in a peaceful place. I owe it to all of them to at least try to help fix the world, however I can.

I've been lying in this bed for hours, Sky thought, *and I can't stop thinking about Blue. How he tried to save me even though I was perfectly capable of stopping that boulder. Still, he totally tried to save me. I can't believe I jumped off a mountain for him. I didn't even know if that would work, but I couldn't handle him dying, or even hurt. I just wanted to protect him. He's so not even my type. I mean, Tyler was cuter than him, and he actually had a trust fund. Oh, wow! I sound like a superficial bitch. What they were whispering about me is so true. I wonder what Blue thinks of me. I was married to him in another life!*

Sky gazed up at the ceiling, which was hand-painted with a mural of a forest and naked humans, Angels, and anthropomorphic beings.

The attention to detail reminds me of my room back at the mansion. I remember staring at the walls for hours when I couldn't sleep. Daddums even made a revolving graphic picture frame that changed images with my emotions. It was kind of a mood ring, programmed to make me happy when I felt sad . . . , usually by showing a picture of something funny from my childhood. People always spoiled me . . . . I know Maia gives me disapproving looks, as if I don't belong here. I don't really want to be here, believe me. My life was perfect! Well, maybe perfect from the outside looking in.

Now I'm some Supernatural thing they call a Mancer, and I guess I'm responsible for this messed up world we live in. I don't know what to do, but Gemini and Jayde seem to. How long have we been here? Oh, my god, Prom Night! Okay, I did it again. Superficial talk even in my own head! I tried so hard all through high school to be so perfect, and excel at everything. Was I cheating with my powers all along? No way. I didn't even know what I could do. More honestly, I was afraid to find out what I could do.

After looking at Egypt in that flashback, I know I was kind of a big deal. No way can I do all that stuff I did back then. Seriously, that was like the most epic thing I've ever seen! Single-handedly starting the Egyptian culture makes this life seem kind of miniscule. I can't believe I'm even entertaining the thought of that dream being reality. Like, I need a shrink or something.

If I told the Prom committee what's been going on with me, I bet the girls in school would treat me like the outcasts. Oh, my god, the outcasts! What happened to THEM? *We've been so busy training and almost dying, and training again, that I totally forgot about them. Except for the dreams every night. I wonder if I'm the only one having them. I kind of doubt it. Blue looks kind of tired every time I see him.*

I wonder if Kaery, Ahlina, Scape, and Star are back in school. Damn! Star totally grew up and became beautiful! Her skin and eyes were amazing. Okay, enough again with the superficial! I'm making myself sick. But I can't help it. I was born into a family that gave me everything. I'm tired of trying to justify who I am to everybody, even to myself.

What did Gemini mean by him being our final test? I wonder if I'm the only one nervous about this stupid test. Is he gonna go all Donkey Kong on us like Jayde, and drop boulders, or is he gonna push us all over a mountain? Or maybe drown us? God! I hate deep water! My mind's all over the place. It seems every time I go to sleep, I see that Great Council judging me. It's scary to see the world go from peaceful to, as Crux would say, "a marshmallow in a bonfire." Wait! Where is that little scrub? I haven't seen him since that night he was creeping around, and it's not likely he's still doing a mission.

Oh, well, I need to find something to wear and meditate. Maybe now that I know I can fly, I can work on antigravity yoga. Okay, terrible joke, but now I'm interested to see if I can do it. Funny, I've never had brothers and sisters, but I can say that these guys make me feel a lot more secure than I've ever felt. I feel strong!

I feel so weak, Maia thought. *I was barely able to do anything yesterday but walk through a bunch of rocks. Blue channeled his old powers and went all "Zeus" on Jayde and the stones. Even Sky was able to dodge them like some kind of ninja.*

I twisted my ankle. Talk about embarrassing and lame. I mean, I wonder what Blue thought of me when I fell like some damsel in a horror film. I'm completely pathetic. I have to get used to not saying that stuff out loud, because Crux would definitely say something. Speaking of that boy, he's been quiet for the last couple of days. I know Blue and Sky said that he was on some secret training, but over the year I've been here with Gemini and Jayde, they never sent ME *on some outdoors mission or training until recently.*

Maybe they think I'm completely weak and ridiculous, like some stupid oracle, and that's it. I'm getting better at my healing, though, and that telepathic link was a new skill I just focused on using. I suppose I'm unlocking old skills, like the rest of the Mancers in our little crew. I have to say that it was inspiring, watching Blue and Sky connect to the Soulstream as if they had been doing it their whole life. Blue's weakness and strength is in the pain from the Soulstream. He uses the pain to focus on the task at hand.

The stars sure were vague, speaking of our little group. They tell me that we all need to meet in San Francisco in a little over a day, or we miss our opportunity to take over OZONE. I'm not sure how or which Mancer is going to be there to turn the tide, but if she's just as powerful as Blue and Sky, then we are dealing with a major one from the past. Too bad Mancers don't get their memories of past lives, the way Witchbreed do. Otherwise, I would know which Mancer we're looking for and feel a little more useful to the group.

"Jayde, it's time," Gemini said, opening his eyes after a meditative state. She was standing over him as if she were guarding the Dragon Kirari. "You were right about your test yesterday, and we *are* running out of time. I must show them the final test before they embark on a mission they cannot come back from."

She bowed humbly, and then left the domed room, heading down the hall toward the first door, Maia's room. When she knocked, she did not have to wait long for Maia to answer. The girl was in her pink cashmere pajamas, looking as if she had been hoping it were someone else.

"Sorry to disappoint you," Jayde said. "I'm not Blue." She noticed Maia's cheeks blush. "But I am the messenger. Gemini needs you to meet him in the courtyard now."

As she walked away, Jayde thought, *The girl had better control her emotions if she's going to help our mission.*

Walking in her calculated, confident steps, Jayde came to Blue's room, smaller than the others, but he had chosen it, and it fit his personality.

Of all these kids, he had the humblest spirit, which had aided him in the battle against her yesterday. He was closest to bringing out Jayde's true fighting style.

She caught herself almost off guard from his attacks. She hadn't been challenged like that in centuries. As she knocked, she didn't realize she was smiling when Blue opened the door, naked, with a towel around his waist and wet from the bath.

"Let me guess," he said. "Gemini is ready for us. Cool! Let me grab some clothes. Where does he want to meet us?"

As Jayde turned her gaze respectfully from his naked body, she could see he had a problem that had plagued him for many lifetimes. The Mancer females were not the only ones attracted to him. Most Supernaturals and humans were. He wasn't Jayde's type, but he was her student in this lifetime, nevertheless. She empathized with Maia's dilemma, but she had more control than anyone in the world, rivaled only by Gemini, and maybe one other.

"Be in the courtyard in five minutes."

After leaving Blue to his wardrobe, she arrived at Sky's room. Expecting another underdressed Mancer, she raised her hand to knock. To her surprise, when Sky opened the door, she was fully dressed in another one of her high-fashion ensembles that she had put together from the closet. These were her clothes from another lifetime, but she butchered them, making one think she didn't like them. No wonder she got along with the Glamouri Coven so well in other lifetimes.

"I got it," Sky said. "I heard you down the hall with Blue."

Jayde was impressed. The girl's radius was expanding. It used to be fifteen to twenty feet. Now it seemed somewhere between twenty and thirty.

Bowing respectfully, Jayde turned and continued on her path toward the courtyard.

Crux must be running out of food by now. I must find that boy and talk him into coming back to the sanctuary. At least, this place is protected by Magick.

✷

"Okay," Crux said aloud, "so my daggers have led me to this cave overlooking nothing. Great! This is just great. By the Fae, I hope my luck really hasn't run out. Wait! Something feels different about this cave."

A bright smile covered his face, and a feeling of hope rejuvenated his bones and sore muscles.

"It feels like Magick."

He tucked his daggers into his pocket and pulled out of his pouch a handful of small pebbles that he had found on the trails leading here.

"Supernaturals have the inborn ability to sense other Supernaturals if they allow their senses to work," Uncle Loiza used to say when he would blindfold Crux.

Those words ran through Crux's head now as he walked into the dark cave that smelled of sea salt, even though it was high in the mountains. Crux knelt down, and felt sand. He put some pebbles back in his pouch after scoping the cave, slightly disappointed that he didn't see any sign of danger.

The sand was definitely not from this island. Crux smiled when he smelled the familiar beach sand. Dusting his hands off, he looked around the cave desperately, searching for the Magick he sensed. After feeling the walls with his bare hands, scaling them like reading Braille, he gave up and sighed.

Okay, so obviously my eyes won't work on this little task.

He took a pin out of his bag and closed his eyes, trying to remove the frustration from his nerves. Thinking once again of his Uncle Loiza, he concentrated his sense of focus and control, and then took a long breath.

Find the Magick I sensed was all he could focus on as he spun and released the pin into the air. The pin stuck into the wall, on the eastern part of the cave. Crux opened his eyes and ran over to it.

Of course, it's a Port Rune.

He had known of Supernaturals being able to use Witchbreed-enchanted Runes to do many things. These Port Runes were rare, to say the least, but were once used by Covens and an occasional Mancer court to travel across the planet. Humans couldn't see most of them, let alone understand the small markings. The Gypsy oracles used to tell stories of the runes, since they had been guardians of such Magickal markings in ancient times.

"How did those tales go?" Crux said aloud to himself, as his frustration began to rise again. He knew that a spoken word was the catalyst for the Port Runes. "Why can't I remember important stuff like this from the old tales? It was the Mancer who could travel through the Ether that was mocked by the Witchbreed. What was his name? . . . That's *it!*"

Crux placed his hand over the Port Rune, careful not to touch it until he made sure he had all of his pouches sealed completely shut. Taking in another deep breath, he thought to himself, *Humans have it easy.*

"Okay, here goes nothing," he said aloud.

Placing his small hand over the Magickal marking as ancient as the very rock that made up the foundation of this island, he began to say the name aloud: "Nergal!"

A wave of energy passed over Crux, and all of his senses went into overload. He could see the particles of his physical body fuse with his spirit, and separate just as fast in a roller coaster of movement. Constellations from deep within space appeared in the distance as a blur, then refocused as he stood still in what seemed like the middle of the cosmos, all alone, staring at a magnetar.

"Beautiful!"

Crux prepared to move. Then he was thrown across the universe so fast that he almost vomited.

Inside of the cave again, on his knees, he couldn't hold back the urge to throw up the little remaining food in his stomach. He cursed his luck again, then lifted a handful of the sea salt-scented sand, and wiped the bits of ration from his mouth. His facial expression changed in an instant from relieved to upset that he had remembered the word wrong.

He did his automatic pouch check as soon as his senses returned to him. Nothing was missing.

Damn it! Am I ever going to get off this island?

His eyes were still slightly fuzzy as he tried to adjust to the darkness, but he was happy to be back on Earth, even if only in a stupid cave.

He made his way out into the cool breeze. Dropping the handful of pebbles that he had held on reflex, he checked his pouches from the shock. Staring at the bright lights of a city, not the expected forest and mountains, he screamed into the cool air, "I *did* it!"

Gemini stood in the middle of the Japanese courtyard with his eyes closed in deep thought as Sky came up to him, keeping a thirty-foot distance between them. The last time she touched Gemini, she went into a trance, watching her past life as if she were at the movies. She wasn't sure what this test was about, but she was positive about what his touch could do.

After bumping into each other awkwardly in the hall, Blue and Maia walked into the court.

Sky instantly became a lot more comfortable as the silence between her and Gemini was now broken.

Blue pushed past his own hunger. He couldn't remember the last time he had actually eaten something. That bothered him as his stomach rumbled. He was anxious to learn what this test was about, and knew that he would demand food soon after.

Crux! What happened to the little guy?

"Have you seen Crux?" Blue absent-mindedly asked Maia while walking toward the center of the courtyard. "I'm starting to get worried about him."

Maia looked at Blue's T-shirt—clad belly and back up to his eyes. She almost forgot what he had asked until she saw that he was staring at Sky.

"No," she said, just slightly above a whisper, "I haven't seen him in days."

The breeze was biting her skin as she pulled her sweater close to her chest, realizing that she might be a little jealous of Sky, who apparently was in a staring match with Gemini.

The breeze was so cold that Blue wished he had worn something other than a leather coat.

If I had been smart, I would have layered, the way Maia always does.

Sky looked amazing in her purple corset top and short red skirt. Her hair was light brown, with blonde highlights and a red shine when the sun hit it.

Blue couldn't take his eyes off Sky as her exposed caramel skin, unlike his own, didn't seem remotely affected by the cold. He tried to stick his chest out and man up through the shivers.

Maia looked intently at Sky's outfit.

No wonder Blue's staring at her. She has no shame. Jayde said this was a test, not a fashion show.

Maia looked down at her own comfortable outfit made of her favorite pink-and-black striped cashmere sweater and black loose-fitting corduroy pants. She felt slightly embarrassed at the comparison, but figured she was better prepared for the cold weather in this outfit than if she were wearing something as skimpy as Sky's.

"I'm not sure where Crux is," Sky said. "But the rest of us are all here, so what's our test?"

As Blue and Maia came closer to Sky, they felt that the cold bite of the breeze was no longer there. Sky somehow controlled the weather around her to a perfect spring day in the middle of this winter-touched land. Maia was amazed, and Blue was relieved as he smelled her jasmine-oiled skin.

Gemini stood still with his eyes closed. His black hair blew in the wind as the three students stared anxiously at his statue-smooth features. The mountains that lined the horizon behind him only made him look more otherworldly in contrast. The long flowing cloak surrounded him and rustled in the wind like the breeze that would be chilling the students if it weren't for Sky's abilities. The three students tried to prepare for a sudden attack, but to their surprise, it never came.

The ground began to rumble, and the tiles that lined the inner courtyard shook the foundation. Rocks rippled and moved in place as if the stone garden were truly water.

The students watched as the sky changed from the winter blue to a dark and ominous shade of purple. The clouds moved as if they were reversing in time, and the Pagoda fell to pieces as if it were made of sand.

They all looked at Gemini, who was now staring back into their very souls.

Time stood still while they looked at their mentor's stern visage. No one dared to move, for fear of what might happen next. Instead, they all stood closer to each other, almost holding hands, with Blue in the middle.

"You thought this was a test of might or strength of body," Gemini said. "But it is indeed a test of your willpower. You must learn to accept who and what you are in order to become who and what you are *meant* to be."

Gemini faded into ash as soon as the breeze picked up. His voice was still lingering in the air around the three Mancers who had been in front of him.

"Learn from this, and you shall be victorious. You will fail if you choose to do otherwise."

Sky looked around and saw a familiar temple from the Pangaea flashback. A pyramid, older than the ones in Egypt, stood behind them in all of its glory. It was where she had made the decision to choose the Coven of Unity to cast the powerful Enlightenment spell.

"I'm guessing," she said, "we're supposed to go inside, in order for this dream sequence, which must be us in some sort of trance, to be done."

"I hate to say it, but I think she's right," Maia said, looking at the temple and then up to the sky, where the constellations had changed.

"Thanks, Maia. I'm glad I get your knowledge approval," Sky said sarcastically, looking over at Maia's soft features, which were staring up into the void above.

"Look," Blue said, "I don't know what this is, but I know we have to stick together, so let's just hope we're strong enough to make it through this. Agreed?"

"Fine," Sky said, gazing into his sapphire eyes.

"I agree," Maia said, almost as if she had seen a ghost. Then she slipped her right hand behind her back and held on to her left elbow, as she had always done when she was nervous. "This *is* Pangaea!"

"We kinda figured that by now," Sky said mockingly.

Blue shot her a glance that reminded her of the pact.

"Why are we here in Pangaea, though?" Sky asked.

"It's before the spell has been cast upon the planet," Maia said. "We don't have much time, according to the stars."

"Then, let's go witness the spell," Blue said, "if it's supposed to be our lesson."

"I'm cool with that. Let's go," Sky said, straightening her outfit as if getting ready to perform on stage.

Maia looked away from the stars in time to see Sky get ready, and then rolled her eyes.

Blue began walking cautiously toward the temple, but with enough speed to stay in a hurry.

Sky walked confidently beside him, and Maia took up the rear, slightly perturbed by the odd vibration in the air. The breeze felt and smelled different now. Sky noticed it, too. The air was a lot fresher, and she didn't need to change her environment at all. Everything seemed so peaceful, but it was the kind of peace that comes right before a storm.

Blue was aware of the vibration in the air, and recognized it as the Soulstream. He followed the feeling toward the source.

"Someone is channeling the Soulstream in a big way," he said. "I feel it, like during the fight with Jayde, except it's not coming from me. The source is somewhere close by. Follow me."

He ran toward the temple.

The entrance was not guarded. By the looks of things, the Witchbreed who constituted the Great Council had evacuated the place. The silence was deafening, to the point where Sky had to say something, anything, to break it.

"This place is like an Escher poster on drugs."

Maia understood her reference, and almost laughed out loud, because as blunt and crass as Sky's statement was, it was true. The stairs on the walls went in every direction, and there were lights that stood on random podiums throughout the inside of the gigantic structure.

The three Mancers looked around, trying to make sense of this labyrinthine building.

"I think I've figured it out," Maia said. "But, Sky, I may need your help."

The words came out truthfully, and Maia was amazed at herself for even uttering them.

Blue took a step back to watch the two ladies work together.

Maia's eyes darted methodically from one wall to the other. Pointing to a light, she said, "I figured as much. It's a path of constellations. That one is Circinus, which crosses Ara."

Sky flipped her hair with impatience. "Look, could you please speak normalese? Can't you tell by the 'duh' expressions on our faces that we don't have a clue about constellations? What do you want me to do?"

"I'm guessing 'normalese' means laymen's terms," Maia said, "so I'll keep it simple. You fly us to those lights on the podiums. Each one represents a constellation like the Compass, and the altar should tell me where the next step is. I can only imagine this is the security system for Supernaturals." Maia said all this to Sky with a little wrinkle on her forehead.

Before the Mancers could fly toward the first podium, they heard a familiar voice nearby.

Sky quieted Maia, as if shushing a child.

"There's someone coming," she said.

Kumarbi, from the Anu Coven, was speaking to Anshar of the Sinchimes. The conversation was hushed, but Sky could hear the entire thing as well as if she were standing next to them. She amplified it for the others.

"Of course," Anshar said, "she made a terrible decision to choose that group of ill-begotten outcasts to be responsible for such a grand ceremony! But either way, the wheels of destruction have been set into motion. Once the spell is completed, the world will be at war. My Coven will use the shards of every last dying bastard to exalt ourselves to rule this planet."

Anshar was gloating before the shocked Kumarbi.

"I didn't sign up for this type of blasphemy!" Kumarbi said. "You used me! You used all of us to start a war. The Enlightenment spell was your idea. You knew it would lead to this!" Kumarbi was speaking in his oracular tones, confirming through Magick what he speculated was the truth. "I must warn the others now."

"You'll do no such thing!" Anshar said, stopping Kumarbi with a gesture of his hand and laughing in his face as he telekinetically pulled him close. "You see, my love, your faith in me was the key to winning over the Great Council's trust, and your love blinded your Truth Sight. The world is mine, and there's nothing you or anyone else can do about it. The spell is going to be cast in a matter of minutes, and nothing will stop it. Not even you, my love. That fool Gemini was right. Humans were never meant to have powers such as ours, although their souls are as powerful as yours or mine. I may not have been the one to cast the spell, but it is too late now, and the world will pay."

Anshar slit the throat of the handsome Kumarbi as he struggled to live.

"Thank you for your sacrifice, Kumarbi. Your blood and soul will make me stronger."

As Anshar kissed Kumarbi on the lips, the life force left his body and was sucked into his own. Anshar's eyes began to glow. Kumarbi disappeared as if he never existed. Anshar made another gesture while laughing and phased out of the current reality.

Sky gasped at this scene of treachery, as she watched along with Blue and Maia. "This was all a setup," she said. "We were tricked into casting a devastating Apocalypse. It really is our fault for being such fools."

Sky was speaking in a whisper that only Blue and Maia, contained within her sphere, could hear.

"It would seem so," said Blue. "We must warn them. Maybe we can change the course of time." He looked at Maia for confirmation.

"It's possible, she said, "but it will be difficult." She looked at her palm, and then up to the podium. "We're running out of time!"

Standing in front of Maia and Blue, Sky asked, "Which one?"

"There," Maia said, pointing to the first light in the puzzle.

Blue watched as his feet left the ground. Then, at the speed of thought, he flew through the air and was on top of a podium made of pure light.

"We could use your help from this point," Maia said, looking at Blue.

"Um, what do you mean, you need my help?"

"Use your focus to spark this light pad and watch what happens."

Blue saw Sky shrugging. Maia was still looking at him as if she were looking through him.

"Okay, here goes!" he said.

Feeling the pain swelling up in chest, he bit through the intense stabbing tingle in his spine. Unlike the broken bones he had gotten from the mountain fall, this sensation was not going away. He found it easier to focus on the pain from the mountain than to focus on the shaking of his very soul. His hands began to sweat, then tremble. A bead of sweat rolled off his forehead as he tried to concentrate.

"I can't," he said, feeling defeated.

Sky put her hands on his face and looked into his eyes.

"You heard what has happened," she said. "You can do this. We have to stop them."

Blue looked into Sky's eyes, which were shifting colors from dark brown to hazel green. Her touch reminded him of the sacrifice she had made when she jumped off the ledge. He thought of all the people who had sacrificed themselves for this very moment. Smiling, he stood up straight, looking at Maia and Sky. Then he took a step back, subconsciously not wanting to hurt either of them with his power. But Sky was right. He had to do something.

Blue focused on his family through the pain, and the very reality around him started to shift and turn. The vibrations that his body released interrupted Sky's barrier, and even gave Maia an instant headache. The wave of energy was so raw and unfiltered that it boomed through the air in the form of a hum. Blue raised his hand, and a small portal opened. Sky and Maia could see through the portal to the Soulstream. It was breathtaking! Blue released its energy into the disc of light that they were standing on, punching directly into it.

The Compass constellation lit up.

Maia telepathically linked to Blue and Sky, to continue the path to the podium, where the Wicasht Coven of Unity was to cast the spell. To guide them, she fought through the disruption and pain in her head.

They did it! They made it to the podium, where there was a door leading outside to the open air, high up in the night sky. As they approached the door, two Witchbreed from the Sinchimes Coven barricaded the entrance.

"No one is to disturb the spell at hand!" one of them said. The blue marks on their faces and bodies matched those on Anshar. They were stoic, with robes draped over one shoulder, buckled by a large golden sun with a skull in the middle.

Blue took his hand out of the disc of light and focused on one of the Witchbreed.

"Move out of our way now."

"Or what?" one of the Sinchimes taunted.

"Or *this!*"

Blue released three blinding streams of light that invaded the hall. They looked like whips of pure energy tearing at anything they touched.

Maia and Sky stood behind Blue, watching as the Witchbreed cast a spell that looked like spinning runes in front of them. As the Sinchimes held hands, the runes spun faster.

When Blue's stream of raw energy hit the runes, it looked as if the Magickal shield were going to burst.

Sky thought for sure that the Sinchimes were going to die. The vibration in the hall made the walls quake, but the more Blue forced his energy upon the shield, the more the Witchbreed's eyes glowed a hot white.

Noticing the same thing, Maia read through the spell. "They are transferring the energy from the Soulstream into their own spellcraft! Stop, Blue, you are only making them more powerful!"

Blue didn't want to listen, as the burning power within him almost raged out of control. When he released his focus and put his hands to his sides, his skin was smoking in the cool air.

Looking at Maia, Sky asked, "Can you see their weakness? What is it?"

As Sky waited for an answer, the two Magick users unleashed a series of attacks in a wave of crushing force, attempting to knock the Mancers off the ledge behind them. Sky stood stalwartly in front of her friends, holding her ground with an invisible barrier, as sweat formed on her brow for the first time she could remember.

She felt her control slipping, just as Maia said telepathically: "Blue! You're going to have to punch them as hard as you can after Sky shocks their system with a sonic pulse. It will give me time enough to tangle their minds psionically."

Sky got the hint, and reversed the loud sound in the hall to penetrate the eardrums of the Witchbreed. In a frequency only the Sinchimes could hear, she started screaming. They, in turn, lost concentration of the wave of power they were casting.

Blue moved at a speed faster than thought, punching both of them in the throats.

Maia ran to stand within her telepathic range to assault them.

Both spellcasters went down with a thud, their eyes rolling in the back of their sockets, with the permanent looks of screams on their faces, as if they were being tormented in their sleep.

Impressed by what they had all just done, Sky said, "We have to go!"

Blue reached for the door, but realizing it was enchanted when his hand was repelled, he said, "Maia?"

She scanned the door, looking for its weakness. "Here," she said, twisting an invisible knob, and then running to the other side to perform the opposite motion.

The door dissipated into a mist, revealing the outside corridor.

Sky flew past Blue and Maia, carrying them both on an invisible current of wind. When they got to the patio, they saw Gemini standing outside the circle of the Coven of Unity, where Kaery was uttering the final words of the spell.

Sky tried to scream, as she had done in the hall, but it was too late to disrupt the spell. A concussive blast of light and wind blew past them. The Soulstream in the air around them felt like Blue's vibration when he had opened the temporal gates to the Soulstream.

Sky stopped in midflight and fell to the ground, slamming on her knees. Blue and Maia also fell, barely catching their balance.

As Gemini helped Sky to her feet, she began to weep.

"We've made a terrible mistake," she said. "It's horrible, what the Sinchimes are going to do."

Her tears and pain were so much of a shock to her that she could barely speak.

"She's right," Maia said to Gemini. "Anshar deceived us all. His Coven will use the chaos that is inevitable to destroy the world. The Coven of Unity must reverse the spell!"

Blue walked over to Kaery, trying to take her hands in his, but was stopped by an invisible barrier. Looking her deep in the eyes, he said, "You know I am telling the truth. I beg you to reverse the spell."

Kaery's golden eyes sparkled in the sunset. She didn't know what to say. Her entire Coven was looking to her for guidance when she turned to match their gaze. Looking back at Blue as he took a step closer, she smiled and said, "We will do our best, but we need a sacrifice. It is an energetic equivalent of time and space."

An immortal named Neflym and his Mancer mentor, Cronos, were watching the entire event next to a pregnant Inanna and fuming Kergal. They all stood next to Gemini, making an unsaid pact. Suddenly, the horizon split and shattered like a mirror. Then waves of destruction paralyzed the lands. Dragons flew from their posts, and blood poured from the sky onto the once peaceful Earth. Earthquakes shook the temple, and explosions littered the utopia that once knew only serenity.

Inanna looked over to Kergal, the beautiful Witchbreed holding her hand, and said quietly, "You know, Juno, I feel the pain of the world. I have to sacrifice myself and our son to save it."

"No! Let them take me. I would never let you do such a thing, Nina." Kergal called Inanna by her pet name, as her chocolate locks flew around her in the chaotic wind. The world was crying out for a savior.

Other Mancers flew into the sky to battle the Sinchimes, who were prepared, using the souls of the fallen and the dying to charge their Magicks. Absorbing the souls through their spinning Runes, they cast powerful spells of unparalleled force upon the Covens, the Mancers, and the Jreamers.

Maia stood in horror, with tears flowing freely from her eyes to the ground.

Sky shook her head in disbelief. "I didn't know!" she cried to herself. "I couldn't have known!"

Hugging Sky, Maia sobbed, "We must stop them!"

Nina walked over to hug both Maia and Sky, two of her favorite people in the universe. "I want to say goodbye formally," she said. "I can feel Gaia weeping and dying, and I cannot allow this."

Maia turned to tell the Witchbreed Coven to take her instead of sweet Nina.

"I will be your time and space sacrifice," Cronos said, looking first at Gemini and then at all the other Mancers he had trained so many years before. Gazing out over them all, a tall immortal with a long white beard and robes that were much too long, he said defiantly, "Do not weep for me. I have made my choice."

"And I will be your blood sacrifice," Neflym said to the group, as proud as any of the powerful entities in his presence. "I am only a human, who was born immortal because of my father, Cronos. But my blood is still human, nonetheless. Please use me. I want to save the world, no matter the cost."

Kaery looked long and hard at both of the immortals in front of her. Then she looked at the stars for an equally long while. "They are right," she said at last. "It will work."

Maia agreed with Kaery as she watched the constellations shifting before her eyes in the pool of space overhead.

"The stars are already changing," she said. "We don't have time to waste."

She held Inanna's hand until Kergal came over to kiss her on the forehead with a tear in her eye. "Thank you, Maia," said Kergal, "and thank you, Cronos and Nef."

Then Kergal walked her pregnant goddess away.

"Ahlina," Kaery commanded, "let them into the circle!"

Ahlina nodded, spoke a word, and the invisible barrier that surrounded her Coven opened long enough to allow Cronos and Neflym to walk inside the circle.

When Anshar, flying overhead, saw the Coven of Unity, he knew at once what they had in mind. He commanded a fleet of a hundred of his own Coven to attack the temple. As they flew through the high clouds toward the highest temple in the land, they used their spinning Runes of Transference as their shields.

Seeing them coming, Blue grabbed Kaery's hand, since the shield was temporarily opened to her.

"I won't forget this," Kaery said. "Don't forget me."

Sky watched Blue's loving touch to Kaery, and smiled with tears in her eyes. Then, flipping her hair, she turned to look at the Witchbreed flying toward her, and said, "I have a job to do. I know which one of us is going to die today. Are you in or not?" She looked over at Maia, whose fists were clenched.

Maia wiped away her tears and stared at the approaching enemies. "I'm tired of being scared and weak," she said. "Let's do it!" Her eyes glowed as she glanced at Blue, who was walking next to her.

"I'm in!" Blue said. "Let's kill all of them!"

As Blue began to focus on the Soulstream, Gemini grabbed his wrist. Blue looked up at the tall, ominous figure.

"You see how your bonds were created and what you lost that dark day," Gemini said. "This is the end of your test."

Chapter 23

THE FEAR

Something about the breeze in this forest had always been peaceful to Nina. She walked along uncharted paths, humming to herself, as if the world were standing still. Her only companion here was a squirrel that followed her every step, and listened as if it could understand her. In-between plucking flowers and admiring small stones, she found pieces of wood. Absent-mindedly, she began to carve them with a small knife that she had found along her travels. This was bliss to her, as she was away from the stresses of the world while on her hiking adventure. She had been out here so long that she couldn't remember how long it had been.

I used to come out to this forest when I was a small child. It's so peaceful. The trees smell exactly the same as then. I used to love leaning up against these trees and singing songs. The only things that ever heard me sing had be the woodland creatures. This really is a special place. I'm just happy to be back here.

As the breeze picked up a little, Nina realized that she was having the time of her life watching a small fawn follow its mother, soon after being born into the world. She carved a small fawn out of a redwood branch that she found on the ground. Her blonde hair had recently been chopped by this same knife. Her crystal blue eyes were a sharp contrast to the Earth tones surrounding her, but Nina could not feel any more at home than here.

"We are in position, Sir," Soldier 00901 reported back to the Control Panel. "If there are any Supernaturals here, we haven't found them. We still don't know what she's looking for. Our second sweep of this area, and still nothing."

"Keep looking," Shadow Harvester commanded. "She is headed in that direction, according to satellites, and we have stones that were compromised taken from that area."

"Yes, Sir! Over and out."

Deme leaned in and whispered, "Keep an eye on that area. Any sign of Juno, and we flush her out with Remote Black Hawks on standby."

"Yes, Sir," Shadow Harvester answered.

I know they're following me, but I don't care. I had to ditch the car a while ago, and have been on foot for a day. Thank goodness for the spells blessing my boots, making me just as fast on foot, anyway! At this pace, I should be in the general area. I've found a couple of pieces of Nina's handiwork. She seems to be up to her old habits of enchanting anything she feels worthy. These little bread crumbs are all the validation I need to know that she is alive. OZONE files were wrong for once. Very interesting. How did she somehow dodge every OZONE Agent, Tracker, and Soldier on her own, I wonder?

The brush here is so thick . . . . There's no sign of a hiking trail this deep in the woods, but she somehow survives as if she really belonged out here. Great way to hide your tracks, girl! I see you remembered the lessons from another lifetime, even though I don't know how. This is all too strange, even from my point of view. Mancers don't get their memories back.

According to the files, her father in this lifetime was a drunken carpenter. Could explain some of the carvings, but not the tracking skills. Her mother was a housewife who used to teach kindergarten. It's just not adding up, but I know I'm close.

Juno ran and jumped through the brush as if she were one of the woodland creatures herself. She was as agile as any predator that had ever stalked these woods, seeking her prey, and not stopping until she found the girl. Picking up speeds as fast as forty-five miles per hour for the past seven hours, and not slowing her pace, thanks to the enchantments on her gear, she continued her search. She had to get to Nina before OZONE Soldiers doing perimeter sweeps found her. Fear swelled up in her thoughts of Nina out here, helpless against armed Soldiers, giving Juno a reason to run even faster.

I haven't heard anything from Juno since the last transmission before psycho Rainbow lady went all horde on my laptop. Good thing I've been building these things since before I could form full sentences. It was back to normal . . . , well kind of . . . , by the time I got to the airport. Mom should be here soon, so maybe I should try to find Juno myself.

Still no answer. I'll log into OZONE base and look around from my connection that's still live . . . . Nice, it works! These people need to step up their security, I swear. If it were any easier, I would swear it was a trap. No way. If they know about this link, then they are onto Juno, which means . . . , oh, crap!

Great. It's Deme and his Technomages again. As far as I know, these Technomages are new occurrences of Supernaturals. They don't really get classified as Supernaturals, though . . . , because they are the product of OZONE. Apparently, they didn't even exist before the invention of the computer. Something triggered in a few random humans allowed them to see Magick through technology. They were instantly either recruited or killed off by OZONE, which is pretty much all I have on them, according to the files.

Well, I know they are following me, because I see their petty traps, but that won't stop me. I'll make it worthwhile to track me. There's a file they don't want me to have. Very nice . . . , the OZONE Agent list! It only took me six months to grab, with the help of Juno. I had to be connected to their intranet. I can read thousands of Agents' names and profiles per second. Let me blow that system data frame up here, and explode that router system there. They'll have a lot to fix, once I'm done with this place. I love being able to multitask! Reading the files while destroying everything I touch, like Ladytron. Wait! What's this? My PARENTS are OZONE agents?!!"

Surge stopped in her tracks to download everything she could, while everything she held dear had been corrupted worse than any hard drive. Her heart raced and her senses were paralyzed. Her multitasking functions ran on autopilot as she looked at the consistent file of her parents' missions and quests. Surge's heart raced even faster as adrenaline filled her veins with fear. She knew the Technomages were on her trail nearby, but didn't care as she analyzed the information on Magick tracking technology that her father had helped to develop with Braintech.

Crux looked around at the skyscrapers with a whole new respect for the civilization he had only briefly spent time in that night he arrived at the docks—the night he had met his new best friend, Blue.

This place looked so different that night!

Crux marveled at the concrete jungle in which he felt like a small, insignificant bug. He had felt more at home lost in the woods near Gemini's castle.

The people walk so fast here and speak so many languages!

Crux couldn't understand any of them, yet everyone seemed to understand everyone else. Walking neatly in lines, in order, as if trained to be this way, the people made Crux think of the old prophecies. Whenever he got scared, he went back to the old bonfire tales and the oracular short stories:

> *The people will lose themselves*
> *As they've lost the glimmer in their eye,*
> *And in the midst of the chaos*
> *A time for a new world will creep on them,*
> *Like a wolf on a sheep*

These words stood out in Crux's mind as he looked at the business men and women mixed in with the consumers and pedestrians, all mingling with tourists, and the beggars lining the sidewalks.

The place smelled of fresh food, saltwater, and sewage. There was something enchanted about this place, nonetheless. Crux didn't know how or why he was ported here, but he was destined to find the reason. He was on the run now, so the easy thing was to just blend in with the locals, if he just stayed quiet.

"Oh, yeah! That's why I'm here. Star has the diamonds! I have to find her."

He pulled out his lucky knives and kissed them.

"You're my only friend, Mr. Violet," Nina murmured to the small squirrel that was sitting on the tree knob next to her, eating a nut. "But you know I'm okay with that. You even let me give you a small purple yarn bracelet. Gosh, you're cute!" She reached into her backpack to grab an apple, took a bite, and smiled happily, looking up at the beautiful sky with puffy clouds above her.

"Nothing can ruin my day!" Nina exclaimed to her companion as she put her back against the cool bark and slid down the tree to sit at its base. "I wish I could sing, because I would sing to you, but I'll just hum while I carve a cloud out of this wood over here. Don't mind me. You just keep eating."

The squirrel stopped for a brief second as if it understood her, then stood up and looked around. Finally, it jumped up and down almost violently in a circle.

"Is that a new trick, Mr. Violet?" Nina started to say. Then she felt that something was extremely wrong. Panic came from the squirrel, which made Nina look around in a mirrored emotion. "What is it, Mr. Violet?" She stood up, dropping the half-carved cloud on the ground. With her mind racing over many different possibilities, she looked in all directions. In all of the years she had been out in the woods, she had never been attacked. A familiar wave of emotions flooded her senses—love, protection, hatred, and fear—as she suddenly realized that there were people nearby.

"Sir," said Soldier 00901, "I have a visual on a Code One. It appears to be a female, blonde, early twenties, and unaware of my position. After using the Magi-track technology, I've confirmed Magick on this target. I'm sending in video ops now."

The apprehensive Soldier had his finger on the trigger. He was still bitter about his partner, killed by a Supernatural many years ago. Since then he had enjoyed his job of sniping the threat to mankind. A quick button shift and the video from his gun camera was sent to OZONE Control Panel.

A Receptionist sent the transmission to Deme as fast as she could.

"Sir, we have a visual, and I have already cross-referenced the Code One with our files. She matches a Nina Hall, who was believed to be deceased three years ago, December 24th."

"So, *that* is who Juno was after. Destroy target!" Deme smiled as he gave this order.

"Yes, Sir!"

The Soldier took in a deep breath and said a silent prayer to his savior. Then his finger glided across the trigger, as if he had been born with the gun in his hands. He stared through the scope with what, on the surface, seemed like unflinching nerves, but underneath he was struggling with sudden panic. This marksman was one of OZONE's elite. He put the X on his mark's forehead and watched her expression of confusion and panic from two hundred yards away. She was so pretty, but a threat nonetheless.

Time to end her miserable existence.

This was the final conclusion from the Soldier while he worked through his own emotions.

A squirrel with purple yarn tied around its small paw jumped on the gun scope.

"What the—?!" the Soldier swore, taking his head off the eye hole, only to be attacked by the squirrel. The small claws and teeth tore into the Soldier's face and eye, making him pull the trigger unintentionally. The bullet destroyed the tree bark next to Nina's head.

Nina instinctively ducked down and looked up at the shattered bark of the once flawless tree. Then she looked in the direction she thought the shot came from, but was unable to see anything. She got down on her belly and hid behind the tree, with an old emotion she hadn't felt in a long time—fear.

When Juno heard the gunshot from a click north, her heart almost stopped. She changed directions and ran toward the shooter's position. OZONE Soldiers and Agents rarely missed, considering the vast majority were sharpshooters and marksmen from all over the world. Juno clenched her fists as she ran agilely through the woods. Her speed increased with every step, but she worked to keep her heart rate calm.

These trees were stunningly beautiful, so Juno could understand why Nina had chosen such a place to come for solitude and comfort. At this moment, she couldn't see anything but a blur as she stormed through the overgrown trails with grace, thinking about nothing but either saving or avenging Nina.

Juno didn't even bother pulling a weapon out as she continued her dash. She simply thought of better times and wished she had made it here earlier. It had been so long since she had even seen Nina's face that she had stared at the expired driver's license picture for hours before running out here in the woods. She thought of how OZONE had forced her to do unspeakable things to her own kind, and she felt betrayed and weak for not fighting against them sooner.

Her fear for Nina's life slowly twisted into hatred for her employer, a secret society that placed symbolism and subliminal messages through the media to keep humanity ignorant. That same organization controlled the medical industry, keeping the world at a chokehold, endlessly ill. It was OZONE that had created all governments and used them as pawns in what seemed like wars between conspiring country leaders to keep economies floating and fear rampant. OZONE also had developed new technologies that were solely meant for destroying Magick users. Juno knew that the use of the religion that OZONE had created over two thousand years ago was a way to deal with the human connection to the Soulstream. That connection could not be denied, so OZONE had twisted the connection to its own benefit.

Although humans have the Veil of Ignorance, the Soulstream still touched their dreams and their lives. OZONE tried to make them feel as if it were blasphemous to believe in Magick, and thus it slowly became so. The age of the rule of Magick users ended in bloodshed and destruction as OZONE put its stamp on the planet, taking over one village at a time until its oppressive blanket was felt everywhere equally.

Juno knew that she had made a terrible decision long ago, working for such an incredible network of deviants and spies, but it had all led to this moment when she would be reunited with Nina. The Supernaturals had failed to find Nina so many years ago that Juno had become bitter, working for the enemy to gather information. Now Nina could be lying in a pool of her own blood, wondering what she had done to deserve this fate. Juno felt helpless at the thought that Nina might already be dead. As she approached the sniper, she could barely see through her own rage.

✱

"What's going on, Soldier?" Deme asked angrily, watching the camera on the gun shaking back and forth and its unstable footage looking more like a cheap independent film than a proper mission file. "Give me a report *now!*"

"Get off me, you stupid pile of fur!" the Soldier shouted, managing to slice the squirrel with his hunter's knife and fling it into the brush. "My apologies, Sir," he said to Deme. "I was . . . , erm . . . , attacked by a squirrel, Sir. It was the weirdest thing I—"

"Shut up and kill the bitch!" Deme screamed.

At that moment, the Commander walked into the room. All Soldiers and Agents stood at attention as Deme turned to see the disapproving glare piercing his very existence.

"You seem to think," the Commander snapped at Deme, "that you have the authority to conduct missions without consulting me. You are overstepping your boundaries by playing cat-and-mouse with a hacker/ terrorist who is destroying half of our underbase's mainframes!"

The Commander was not in a bargaining mood and stood upright and glorified in the presence of this special unit of OZONE. He had been grilled by his boss earlier that day, after all of the military mainframes in four countries had been shut down for more than thirty minutes, for no apparent reason. The Commander knew otherwise, and walked straight to the Control Panel.

"Sir, I can explain—," Deme began.

"Dare to speak again without my permission, and see if you're not thrown in the brig for insubordination until you forget what a computer *is!*"

Deme's frustration was evident, but he stood seethingly silent, trying not to bring any more shame onto his already humiliated special unit of Technomages. He had fought for years to prove they were the future of OZONE, only to be constantly shamed by Surge-Overload, and now by the rogue Agent, Juno. Knowing that his luck was running out, he was desperately trying to prove that he could take down the biggest threat in the world, Surge-Overload.

"You!" shouted the Commander at Shadow Harvester. "Give me a report on that hacker, Surge-Overload . . . , *now!*"

Shadow Harvester looked nervously at Deme, who nodded in approval. The Commander noticed what had just transpired, and squinted, awaiting the answer.

"Sir, Surge-Overload—" Shadow Harvester could not believe his own brown eyes as he stared at the monitor in silence with a shocked expression on his face. He couldn't move at the news that had just been dropped in his lap.

"What is it, Receptionist?!" the Commander demanded.

Deme walked over to the monitor and began smiling maniacally.

"We've found Surge-Overload!"

With everything in her logical mind, Nina knew that she had to get up and run as fast as she could. She had been running her whole life, and this was no exception. When her father used to hit her mother, she had to run and hide. The night she woke up from the car accident, her parents were stuck in the car, and she was thrown out, not wearing a seat belt. After the explosion, she did what came naturally, and ran, not looking back.

She ran from Natasha and her psychotic abuse, along with verbal, emotional, and physical abuse. But for some strange reason, Nina's legs would not let her get up and run as far away from here as possible. She was tired of running. She was compelled to face her fear.

Finally, she stood up with her back to the tree. Her heart was still racing, and her mind was thinking of many things—to begin with, the cave that she had liked to crawl into near the ocean. It was her "tree house." She also thought of her many travels across the planet. She had been running this whole time without knowing why. She felt something, or someone, familiar. The wave of love and protection washed over her, making her feel that she was safe.

Moving from behind the tree directly toward the shooter, Nina worked up the confidence to creep in the direction the shot had come from, hiding behind one tree after another. She knew this was a stupid idea. Maybe it was her peaceful nature, but why not try to convince the person not to shoot her?

Maybe I'm just curious who I might find. Or maybe I'm just insane and suicidal.

At that moment, Nina didn't care, because of the strength of the pull on her.

Another bullet fired—this time not at Nina, but off in another direction. Nina's sense of urgency changed her pace. She boldly jogged toward the shooter, her adrenaline keeping her saturated with a false sense of confidence as she made her way north.

The Soldier regained his position, angry at himself and the stinging sensation in his face and his right eyeball from the rodent attack.

The guys back at the underbase are going to give me grief for this, for sure.

But first, he had a mission to complete. As he looked through the scope, his burning eye was almost useless. Everything was being recorded by the gun camera, so he knew that the underbase was already rating his every move and judging him. He was upset with himself for being distracted from his mission. Then, to his surprise, through the blood in his vision, he looked through the scope and saw the mark running blindly in his direction.

It couldn't be this easy!

He knew he had support and backup sweeping the area, and with his shots fired, they were already on their way.

I've gotta be quick, or another Soldier will steal my kill.

She was so close that he didn't even need his scope. As he placed his finger on the trigger again, his anger welled up in his gut. He could make this shot blindfolded—which was fortunate, considering the wounds on his eyelid and eyeball. He pulled the trigger, and his gun went off, but this time it shot straight up in the sky.

Juno was holding the barrel upward.

She smiled at him before pulling out a knife and stabbing his wrist, so he would never be able to fire a gun again. Then she stabbed him in the shoulder, which made him drop his weapon. When she kicked him, she sent him flying over twenty feet. Juno sensed three more Soldiers closing in on their location.

Nina watched all this in amazement, and then saw Juno turn toward her. Juno's chocolate colored hair was shining with raspberry highlights like sunlight breaking through the top of a forest.

Nina couldn't move. She didn't know why or how she knew this woman, but she felt that she had known her for her entire life.

Juno's face softened as she got a glimpse of Nina, alive and healthy. She almost forgot about the sweeper team flanking them. Running impossibly fast toward Nina and grabbing her hand, she said urgently, "Nina! Run with me!"

Nina regained her willpower to run just as Juno was running past her toward the tree that had been shot. When Juno saw the hole in the tree, she automatically thought of the boy, Isja, in Antarctica. She kept running, but not at her high speeds, so that Nina could keep up with her.

I don't know how she knows my name, Nina thought, *but she just saved my life, that's for sure.*

As Nina tried to keep pace, she noticed that the strange woman was wearing a tight-fitting black armor that sculpted her body like a glove.

The cat-suit makes her butt look perky!

At that thought, Nina tripped on a small rock in the brush, almost falling flat on her face.

Juno turned so fast on reflex to catch Nina that the girl, who had closed her eyes as she fell, didn't know that she had been caught, and was expecting the impact of ground to face.

"Stop staring at my butt!" Juno said teasingly, as she guided Nina back to her feet.

Nina blushed, since she couldn't deny the charges. All she could say was "Thank you for catching me."

She has the most beautiful eyes! Nina thought.

One of Juno's eyes was dark brown, and the other was bright blue—not a crystal blue, like Nina's, but a rich blue like lake water.

"How do you know my name?" Nina asked. "Who are you?"

Just then, there was another series of gunshots, this time from a semiautomatic weapon.

Juno threw a knife in the direction of the shooter. Although he was over one hundred feet away, she nailed him in the face.

"I'm Juno," she said to Nina. "We have to get to the waterfall. Do you know where it is? We don't have much time before they'll be on top of us."

Nina thought about what had just happened, trying to fathom the strength of this woman named Juno. Pointing in the direction of the waterfall, she said, "It's that way about three miles and down a ravine up ahead."

Juno whispered, "By the Sylphs of my cousins, please guide us!" Then she grabbed Nina's hand, jerking the little tomboy in the direction of the ravine. They ran so fast that Nina couldn't believe her feet were touching the ground.

Gunshots from another semiautomatic weapon barely missed Nina and Juno, hitting the trees around them. Nina didn't look back, more worried about the drop ahead.

"We're going to have to jump," Juno said. "They're right on top of us."

Nina's eyes widened in horror at the suicidal words of this strange woman, but she couldn't stop her momentum. She wanted to argue, but saw two bullets ricochet off Juno's back, and the distraction of that sight completely caught Nina off guard. As both women jumped, they literally flew over the ravine and dove downward to the trees below. As they were diving, Nina was grazed by a bullet from behind. Feeling the girl's pain, Juno spun her around in midair, shielding her as they descended toward the Earth like fallen Angels.

Crashing through the branches just before landing, Juno spun again to shield Nina as they hit the ground with enough impact to kill a normal human being. Juno's landing was not graceful as she cracked her shoulder into the ground, but she got up on her feet and whispered, "Regenerus!"

Nina watched in awe as Juno put her shoulder back into place. The shock from all of this—the fact that they had survived the descent, and Juno was not even flinching as her shoulder popped into place—was almost too much for Nina to take in at once.

Juno handed the girl a stone from a hidden pocket.

"What's this?" Nina asked, feeling tranquil as soon as the stone touched her palm.

"It's one of your calm stones," Juno said gently. "You used to use these when you felt anxious."

"I used to *what?!*"

Nina knew that she had touched this stone before, but she didn't know where or when.

"Trust me, Nina, it's yours. Your little bread crumbs led me to you."

Nina looked deep into Juno's mismatched eyes, but said nothing. Juno looked up at the sky. Her expression returned to the urgency it once had.

"Blackhawk 745!" Juno said aloud in alarm. "It will be hard to outrun, but we have to get to the waterfall."

She grabbed Nina's hand again and began running.

Random shots were hitting the ground around them from the cliff above the ravine. Nina didn't know what was going on, but she felt the danger and excitement, and, despite the calm stone, transferred her anxious emotions through her palm to Juno. The strange woman only smiled and quickened her steps. When she heard the waterfall, she was relieved that their salvation was close by. Like many other waterfalls across the planet, this one had an ancient Port Rune placed behind it.

Nina looked up in the air. On the horizon, there was a helicopter flying toward them. It had spinning barrels that unleashed dozens of bullets, tearing up the forest. Reaching the edge of a long drop to sharp rocks and splashing water, Nina looked anxiously at Juno.

"What's your plan?" the girl asked.

"To scale the wall and get behind the waterfall," Juno said, without looking at Nina, for she would have seen the fear in her eyes. "C'mon!" Juno said, starting to climb down the cliff. "We have to find Gemini."

Who's Gemini?" Nina asked.

"Great! I happen to find the only Mancer in history who doesn't know who Gemini is."

"I don't know what you're talking about or why we're going for a rock climb when people are shooting at us. Shouldn't we be getting out of here?"

"We *are* getting out of here," Juno said from the small ledge she had climbed down to.

Nina might have preferred a quick bullet over a fall to a rocky death, but she absorbed some of Juno's confidence and used her own rock-climbing skills to get down.

Juno watched the girl's skilled positioning and footing.

Her awareness of her body is that of a seasoned rock climber.

There was a gap between the small footing that they stood on and the waterfall. Juno could easily jump it, but Nina was stuck.

The Blackhawk 745 was now in position to aim right at the side of the cliff wall where they were standing. When the barrels began to spin,

Juno shouted to Nina, "Remember to say 'Nergal' when you touch the Port Rune."

With a firm grip on Nina's hand, Juno tossed her down like a rag doll. The girl landed behind the waterfall on slick, wet stone. There was a glowing symbol. As Nina went to touch it, she almost forgot what Juno had told her to say.

With her back to the cliff, Juno could see the pilot and recognized him at once. Using her Supernatural hearing, she knew that he was being ordered to open fire on her, but couldn't bring himself to do so. But then the Commander threatened to kill his entire family. Juno knew from the expression on the pilot's face that he had no choice. Using her hand gun, she shot one of his Gatling guns with uncanny accuracy, making it short-circuit. But the other was intact, and unloaded on Juno, destroying the stone around her.

As she jumped down toward the waterfall, bullets pierced her armor and followed her into the slick sanctuary.

Nina finally remembered the word and screamed it while touching the rune: "Nergal!" Her eyes were closed, and when she opened them again she was in a pure white light. Feeling serene, she heard a vacuum-like sound as she was thrown instantly through time and space. The molecules that made up her arm dissipated like mist and then resolidified as she landed on a hard cave floor.

Nina gagged for air, felt nauseous, and dry heaved. Unaccustomed to teleportation, her body went through a series of shocking shivers that made her subconsciously reach for the wall. She sat down with her back to the cold stone, finding comfort in the solid cool foundation. As she regained her proper breathing, she looked around.

At that moment, Juno fell onto her lap in a bloody heap, with gaping wounds littering her body. She smiled up at Nina through her own bloodied lips.

"You made it," she said. "Good. Now find Gemini."

Juno coughed, spattering blood on Nina's already dirty tank top.

"Who's a Gemini, and how am I supposed to find someone I don't know?"

"Just feel for him. You'll find him. I believe in you."

Juno smiled before convulsions racked her body and she fainted.

"Please don't die!" Nina cried. "I don't know what I'm supposed to do. I don't know what you're talking about. Please wake up!"

Nina's backpack was still intact. She had forgotten that she was wearing it. Now she looked hurriedly through it for something to help with the bleeding, but all she could find was a T-shirt. She shredded it and tied small makeshift tourniquets around Juno's wounds. The blood was flowing freely from this strange woman's formerly perfect body.

Nina stood up, knowing she had to do something.

"I've got to save you!" she said to the unconscious Juno. "I don't know what a zodiac sign has to do with all this, but I've got to find that Gemini."

When she walked out of the cave, she saw city lights.

"Where am I?" she asked aloud. "By the looks of that bridge, I'm in San Francisco. I would ask how, but I'm guessing that Port Rune is the answer." She stopped talking to herself and went into deep thought.

I don't know who Gemini is, but I'm guessing he's there.

She walked fast toward the city, looking over her shoulder at the cave once, to remember where it was, and then focusing on the task at hand. Gripping the stone that Juno had given her, she once more became calm.

I hate being around people, and the last thing I wanna do is be around MILLIONS *of them. But I must if I have any hope of saving Juno. I don't know what my connection to this woman is, but I know I have no choice but to help her. Dealing with my fear of crowds is the least I can do to pay Juno back.*

Crux took the knife out of the wall of a simple house. It looked similar to many others on the colorful block, but this was where his dagger led him, so it must be Star's home. He looked at the mailbox that had the name "Rouge" written in old-fashioned calligraphy.

My knives were right once again!

He smiled as he knocked on the door.

Eventually, Star answered.

"What do you want?" she said. "We're going to pay the stupid—"

She stopped in mid-sentence to stare at the familiar little boy. After a long pause, she said softly, "You're real!"

Chapter 24

GAME TIME

Using her tracking skills, Jayde made her way through the forest until she came across Crux's knife scars on random trees. He was clearly using his powers to find a way out.

How resourceful he is! He can navigate with probability. The only way he could've gotten out of here was through the Port Rune. But how would he know the word to get out? . . . The Gypsies must have told him.

As she walked into the cave, she thought of this group of Mancers that Gemini had specifically chosen to form an alliance. Crux was one of them, because of his skills in past lives, but she had no idea about his probability power. The boy had always been able to change the density of matter. In one lifetime they called him Atlas. He could lift things as if they weighed nothing, or make a pebble weigh as much as a mountain.

A very useful gift, but he used it for thievery and petty Gypsy crimes this lifetime. If he could only know his potential, that boy could be powerful. I must explain to him that this is not a game.

She looked at his footsteps all along the wall, which confirmed her suspicions. Then she walked to the Port Rune and saw his pin sticking from the wall. First, inspecting the technique he had used to throw the pin, she saw he had performed a martial arts twist to the floor while releasing in mid-spin. As she pulled the pin out of the wall, she smiled.

So he knows a lot more than he let on. I know where he is, then. Gemini will be interested in this revelation.

Jayde touched the Port Rune and focused on the point where she wanted to go. The Pagoda had a secret word to travel, *Cronos.* Jayde whispered the ancient name of the Mancer who had sacrificed himself for the greater good of the world. She remembered the stories that were told in his honor. Like all tales of the ancients told by humans, Cronos became something else, like Father Time and other messiahs.

The tale was misconstrued by OZONE . . . , but what else is new?

Surge got out of the taxi after scrambling the cab camera. The driver wouldn't notice until he got back to the shop for maintenance. He was a nice guy, in a creepy way, so she made him drop her off at a random stop as soon as she got the info from OZONE.

Those bastards somehow got to my parents. Okay, this is the part where my photographic memory is not so cute. Dad's been working for Sky's father to make weapons for those damned OZONE Agents. So my dad's known all along about Supernaturals.

And my mom sending me off to that camp was just wrong. Turns out it's a Stepford wife training camp for a secret society within OZONE called D.O.L.L.S., for the Daughters of Lilith's Last Scream. So my mom was pretty much programmed to be perfect. That's just great. Is there anything in this world that hasn't been totally messed up by those godforsaken chess masters?

So that means I can't go home, and I'm pretty sure those Technomages tracked my signal, so I can't use my laptop until I have some time to tweak a few routing/IP issues. They must've used Magick to distinguish which of the 8,572 IP addresses that randomly show up were mine. Process of elimination was the technique, I'm sure. If they are half as good as me, it must have taken them less than thirty seconds. Technomages are humans who've been broken by technology. Scary. I guess all of that TV isn't really so good for the kids.

But seriously, I have to get ghost . . . , and, like, NOW! So this should be easy. I think I'm gonna have to lay low. Pull my hoodie over my head and wear glasses like some kind of jerk. Give my luggage to a homeless person. I have to go where there are a lot of people, and distract them from locating me while I work out my laptop issues. Cool! I just made the bus.

Juno has issues of her own at the moment, so I can't call and ask her to get me to safety.

I'm kind of glad I've used the BART and MUNI system my whole life. I should be at the Fourth and Market exit soon. I wonder if I touch the bus . . . , yep, I can control the entire thing from sitting back here. Nice!

The electric-powered bus short-circuited for a brief second, then came back online. Even the driver didn't notice as he steered through traffic.

Oh, no! I don't need cameras looking at me, for sure. How about we make it zoom in on the homeless guy with the vomit on his shoes? Grossness!

Who can I trust? I can trust my followers on my site. I haven't been able to log in, so they must be worried. Okay, I'm so fourteen right now. I mean, listen to my thoughts, why don't you? I'm more worried about my online friends than I am of myself being tracked by the most powerful secret society the world has ever known. It makes all of those other secret societies look like medieval jump rope clubs.

I just hope that Union Square is crowded, because if it isn't, then I'll have to work some Magick of my own. It was all a game before, when I was taking marks off OZONE's checklist, but things are getting way serious, way quick.

★

"So that was our crash course?" Blue said to Maia after receiving the information for the first time about saving a girl in Union Square. "I mean, do Gemini and Jayde really think we're able to take on OZONE *already?*"

"Technically," Sky said, "we have to take on OZONE, Vampires, and Gypsy assassins all at once. Yay for us!" She said this sarcastically, looking at Maia.

"Why are you chewing *me* out?" Maia said defensively. "I was recruited just like you."

"Because you knew all along that we were going from dojo to dead serious," Sky answered. "Aren't you, like, Prophecy Girl or something? You could've told us when you read the stars or looked at your inner tumor . . . , or whatever it is you do."

"Sure, blame me for actually believing I have powers," Maia shot back at Sky and Blue. "I'm not the one masking my own insecurities behind fake logic or bravado. Just deal with it. If we plan on saving the world, then we have to save the girl." Her cheeks were flushed with a hint of anger as she crossed her arms and looked away.

Just then, Jayde walked into the room. When all three students focused on her, she realized, from the looks on their faces and from their body language, that she had interrupted a heated argument. "What's the problem?"

Blue looked at Jayde, realizing that she was ancient, even though she may have stopped aging physically in her late twenties. Her body was smoking hot and toned. She was always elegant in her movement, as if she didn't have to try to be so awesome. She just was.

"Is it true, Jayde?" he asked.

"Yeah," Sky added. "Is it true that we're supposed to go all comic book heroes on OZONE, Vampires, and Gypsy ninjas? I mean, seriously, after not even a week of so-called training, most of which felt like a drug-induced trance."

"You see what I've been going through since Gemini left?" Maia said to Jayde.

Jayde waited for them all to finish, then eloquently answered, "Yes, it's true. You will have to battle OZONE operatives, as well as encounter Gypsies who happen to be Vampyl assassins. As for your *training*, it was sufficient for the task at hand. No one has given orders to destroy OZONE just yet. Your mission is to save the girl."

"*What* girl?" Blue and Sky asked at the same time.

Then, realizing how awkward this was, they looked away from each other. Actually, Sky was still looking at Blue, but only with her special ability, keeping her face pointed in Jayde's direction.

"Maia will lead you to her," Jayde replied. "She will be in Union Square in four hours. Any more questions?"

"Ummm . . . ," said Sky, "only how you expect us to get from whatever fantasy island we're on now to shoppers' dream capital in less than four hours. Or is there another ability I have yet to find out about here?" Sky was genuinely trying to understand what was expected of them.

"We have ways," Jayde answered without a hint of worry or anxiety. "Maia, I need you to confirm something, please."

Shocked that she was being called upon in the midst of all this blaming and explaining, Maia put her right hand behind her back to grab her left elbow. Her blonde locks with black strips through them fell around her almond-shaped eyes and pale skin. As of earlier this morning, her red eyeliner was a new addition to her wardrobe.

"Sure," she said. "I mean, if I can help, I will."

"Is Crux in San Francisco?" Jayde asked.

Maia looked at Jayde, just as confused as Blue and Sky. "What? I mean, *what?!*"

"I asked, is Crux in San Francisco, California, right now?" Jayde repeated, taking a step closer to the girl. Her embroidered silk half-top revealed abdominals that Blue could not stop staring at.

Maia's eyes began to widen as she asked herself many questions before answering Jayde's question. Then she walked outside, and Blue immediately followed her. Jayde waited for Sky to walk past her before following Maia as well. They all walked almost in single file to the outside of the Pagoda. The walls had been repaired, and the stone garden brought back to its peaceful state.

It was slightly foggy outside as Maia looked up into the mist. Blue stood next to her in his black T-shirt, trying to condition himself to the cold air. As soon as Sky walked into the mist, she made it part. Now her invisible sphere wasn't so invisible. The circular gap in the mist revealed its exact size—thirty feet, as Jayde had predicted. The weather within the sphere was, as usual, a nice autumn day, based on Sky's favorite season.

Maia now had a clear view of the stars overhead and could see the constellation Crux. The sky was rippling like water, and then a reflection appeared to Maia.

"It's true!" she said. "He *is* in San Francisco, near the girl."

Blue's confusion was transferred to his new interest in saving the girl.

"Okay," he said, "it's game time. Let's go save the girl and get our first mission over with."

Sky looked at him, and then at Maia, and nodded. "I wanted to go shopping, anyway," she said.

"I'm guessing that's her version of yes," Maia said sarcastically, looking at Jayde. "I *have* to go, so there's no question. It's part of the prophecy. If all three of us don't go, then the prophecy fails. And if Jayde comes along, the prophecy fails. So it has to be us three."

"Do you remember your skills as a group?" Jayde asked. "You must always work together on the battlefield, no matter how unconventional that may be."

"I really don't have a choice," Maia said with a shrug. "I see everyone's unique powers and weaknesses."

Blue looked at Maia, intrigued. "I didn't know that," he said, smiling at her. Then, to Jayde, he said, "I only know that my powers hurt, but I can send out waves of raw energy from the Soulstream . . . . Oh, and I can cause explosions around me."

"You all can do much more than you think," Jayde said. "But don't forget your speed and position."

"What do you mean?" Sky asked. "I ran track, but I don't think that's gonna help me dodge bullets, will it?"

Jayde purposely walked out of Sky's sphere. Her black hair was blowing in the Japanese mist. Her green eyes stared at her students with focus and judgment. Then, in a flash, she moved back into the sphere to attack Sky. A fist punched at the girl's face, but Sky instinctively dodged it, seeing where it was coming from and anticipating the move.

"You see," Jayde said, pointing at Sky's head, "that is moving at the speed of thought. It's faster than bullets. You may be able to move even faster than that. It depends on your thoughts."

Sky stood in contemplation, while Blue smiled at her display of martial arts in a high-fashion pair of tights and corset top with poet sleeves from another time. Jayde noticed his relaxation, and before she began to move, Sky could feel her, but just watched to see her wipe the smile off his face.

Blue barely realized he was being hit until the strike crashed into his abdomen and sent him flying into the Pagoda wall. When he crashed, Maia and Sky grimaced, as if they felt his pain. Then Blue walked out of the dusty hole in the wall, wiping blood from his mouth.

"You don't have to accept the hit," Jayde said. "You can parry or dodge it. I've seen your speed."

"That's when things really get painful," Blue said. "I would much rather take the hit at this point. The Soulstream really tears me apart."

"Fair enough," Jayde said, "but you chose that path of fighting. The pain is your weakness and your blessing."

Then Jayde turned to attack Maia.

The girl looked as if she were dancing. Not one hit connected as she used her premonition to predict the moves before they came to her. She got so used to using her premonition automatically that when Jayde changed fighting styles and threw random punches, Maia was knocked into Sky, who was barely able to catch her in midair. Maia rubbed her throbbing bruise on her shoulder, subconsciously healing it.

Jayde knew that I was relying on my predictions of one of her smooth kung fu techniques, and switched to a more chaotic style, which happened so fast that it changed the lineage, and my body had to adapt. She definitely knows my weakness.

"You must remember," Jayde said, "to play off each other in this game . . . , as Blue calls it."

But Jayde was deadly serious, and they all saw the usefulness of her method of training. She knew she had connected to them on a level that they could understand for the mission at hand.

Jayde bowed to her students, and then walked away to look for Gemini.

"He's in the back forest," Maia said.

Turning back to Maia, Jayde said, "Thank you, Maia. Your skills are growing by the thought."

Then she bowed once again and headed toward the forest.

"We have visual, Sir," Shadow Harvester said to Deme. "Surge-Overload is in San Francisco's Union Square. We have sent some of our best on the mission."

"Give me the list of data that he went through the trouble to steal," Deme ordered, scowling.

"Yes, Sir. We have retrieved multiple files," the nervous Receptionist said to his violent boss. "What would you like me to review?"

"The most important," Deme said through gritted teeth, knowing that the list was probably as long as his own resumé.

"The last files taken," the Receptionist said, "were the list of Files' Agents, Sir. And—"

"*What!?*" Deme shouted, at the end of his patience. "I want that bastard dead! No other questions about it. Send Guardian, Grin, and that psychopath, Narles. Send a squadron wave of Soldiers and shut that area down. I don't want this guy getting away from us. I would send Agent 99, but his sense of justice would only end up with the guy in shackles. I need Overload dead!"

"Yes, Sir!"

I just cracked open this beer, Guardian thought, *and all of a sudden they need me at Union Square. The bright side of the whole thing is I get to take down Surge-Overload. It's all the buzz at the underbase. The bad side is, I have to work with not only one partner, but TWO assholes. Damn Juno for going rogue! I don't blame her completely. She made her bed, I guess. I'm just glad I don't have to hunt HER down . . . . Not yet, at least.*

Guardian drank the rest of his beer, anyway. Then he got his battle gear ready, his best weapons, including his favorite sound-barrier reverse force impact sniper rifle. The gun had been made specifically for him with his signature pad fingerprint trigger, which only shot when his hand touched it. The last time he used it was in Antarctica. He had never missed a mark with it.

He knew he didn't have much time to get to the location, so he set the bottle on the table and left in a hurry. His thoughts were researching everything he knew about Surge-Overload and what the guy must be thinking.

OZONE obviously didn't send Agent 99 on this one, so they want Surge-Overload dead. Fine with me . . . , the guy's a terrorist. I know that sounds like something the nutcase Narles would say, but it's true. And if OZONE wants him dead, there's no place on the planet he can hide.

★

This is the perfect spot to hide, Surge-Overload thought. *Tons of people to block my laptop review. Okay, I did put up a traffic jam as well. It's already sunset, and I don't know where I'm supposed to go after this. Maybe reserve a hotel under some random name? I can't call mom and dad until I know they're secluded on private lines. No wonder they never messed with my stuff. They were too busy doing their own thing as spies. First thing I need to do is send my computer an electrical overload to melt down the hard drive and make it impossible for them to retrieve it. It's all backed up on my private server anyway.*

Okay, so the computer is all brand new, but something isn't right. The news and OZONE activity in this area have been exceptionally low for this time of year. What am I, some OZONE weather analyst? Anyway, I'll send that overload, hence the name to my own desktop computer . . . . Done. Goodbye amazing computer I built from scratch.

Surge cried a single tear, then wiped her face before the mascara smeared.

This laptop will have to do until I ghost-touch another or build another desktop, whichever comes first. Hey I've never stolen anything except for information up till this point, but OZONE has stolen everything from me. I feel like one of the people I save on a daily basis.

Oh, no, they have my position! They know where I am. Those Technomages must know my signature with Magick by now. That's how they're tracking me. Not the IP. How could I have been so dumb? I'm tempted to destroy the economy and make them start over or give all our elderly a retirement fund. I just feel like doing something that will piss them off, since they're already aiming a gun at my head. Time to do my worst, then, and it is so ON!

✳

"Nice outfit, Blue," Sky said as he walked out of his room in a customized costume she had helped him to make. His fingerless leather gloves were of his own design, but she had created the reinforced motorcycle jacket and pants. Floating around him at the speed of thought, she tailored the parts she didn't quite like.

"Abuse of powers much?" Maia said, standing near the doorway, ready to go. "Why go through so much trouble with the clothes when they're probably going to get shot up anyway?"

"Gosh," Sky said. "Way to be a buzz kill, Ms. Misery."

She floated down slowly in front of Blue, coming face to face with him. Her light brown eyes sparkled, reflecting his oceanic orbs. The contrast of his black hair and rugged soccer model features, combined with his hands holding her small waist to guide her safely to the ground, made her forget that she was insulting Maia.

"Do I look good?" Blue asked both girls, showing off his new gear. "It's kind of tight, but I can still fight really well in it."

"I'm just being realistic," Maia said under her breath. Then aloud she said, "I didn't mean that I foresee you being shot, Blue. Sorry. And yes, you do look nice."

Sky smiled and blushed as Blue did a small spin. That was unnecessary, since she could and did check him at all 360 degrees. But she was flattered that he felt obligated to show her his new outfit.

"You look nice as well, Maia," Blue said. "I like your sweater all torn, and your pink-and-black striped jeans."

Maia started to shrink away.

Normally, Blue wouldn't care about what others were thinking or doing, but he found himself being really nice to these girls. They always had his back, and he swore he would protect them.

Sky half-smiled as she looked Maia up and down.

"I approve," she said. "I actually do like what you did with your makeup, but you gotta come out of this pink, black, and red thing. It's been done, girl!"

"Thanks, Blue," Maia said. "And thanks for that *almost* compliment, Sky . . . , I think."

A private jet landed at SFO Airport. It was solid black with matching windows and had security clearance. The passengers walked into the cool air with their beautiful black clothing on display. With cold demeanors, they glanced over their surroundings. Some of them sniffed the air, and others put on their sunglasses. They all spoke an ancient Gypsy tongue that sounded like a cross between bartering and singing.

The melodic tones were overwhelmed by sonic booms of the departing commercial carriers. The Shandor rarely traveled to America, but they were on a mission that could not be compromised. Their deadly pale skin made them look more unreal than they would prefer. The smoothness of their skin looked like Roman marble. The eyes of some of them reflected light like the eyes of a cat.

Their leader stepped out of the plane after receiving perimeter search details. The smell of Supernaturals was in the air, but they didn't mind that. Their leader was interested in only one scent.

To his entourage of Vampyl awaiting his orders, Chass said, "I want you all to go through this city and knock over every stone until we find that snake, Crux. Contact the bloodlines and ask them for a short time passage, now that we're here. How Crux got here and why we haven't heard anything about his whereabouts is what bothers me."

Chass looked over at one of the humans and snapped his fingers. The other humans instantly grabbed the luggage and put them into the limos.

Staring at the ocean from the top of the mountain with Gemini, Jayde reported, "Crux went through the Port Rune and is in San Francisco. Your sleeping giants are almost fully awakened. They did well today in realizing simple tasks in battle."

Continuing his rapt gaze at the endless body of water that reflected the stars in the sky just as Maia would see them, Gemini said, "The boy has learned much in his young life, but you must watch over him. Let the kids take on OZONE and the Shandor."

"Crux is looking for something," Jayde replied. "I believe he is seeking the Witchbreed Coven of Unity, for some reason. That is their domain and was where I took them home."

"I agree. It is his fascination with freedom. The kids are growing up, but as you know, they don't have much time to evolve . . . , unlike other lifetimes in the past, when they would have had formal training over thousands of years. Follow Crux and take care, dear Jayde."

"I know you are retrieving ancient items for them, Gemini. But do you think it will be enough to take down OZONE? We both know they are capable of a type of evil that these kids have yet to see in this lifetime."

"I am aware of that. I do believe that the plans set in motion are enough to assist them in their quest, and in their path of Destiny. I also believe, as I am sure you do, Jayde, in something deeper. I believe it is time for a new era."

"Game time, as Blue would say," Jayde whispered, smiling.

"Well said."

Blue, Sky, and Maia stood outside the Pagoda, as they had been instructed to do. They were one hour from the time that Maia told them was the deadline. None of them had a clue about how they were going to get to the city in time. But as soon as Gemini came up, towering over all of them, they knew he would explain the details.

"You are all very different from when you came here," Gemini said. "I say that in the most humble order. Even your spirits have changed as you unlock the mysteries of your own souls. If only most people were so privileged."

Gemini's smile was warm, which brought the kids to the reality that this was possibly a goodbye. That thought alone made all of them pay attention a little more.

Gemini continued, "Jayde will escort you back through the gates from which you came. She will use a simple spell that Cronos taught to the Wicasht, and they in turn use rampantly throughout many of their Covens. Gateways through time and space were the preferred methods of travel hundreds of thousands of years ago." Gemini watched the expressions of awe on the kids' faces. "You were all there, and used these quite often, as you did in your test. Remember the lessons you learned that day and to play off each other's strengths while protecting your weaknesses. Fighting Vampyl is hard to do at night if you are not prepared. They die, like everything else, but it's harder to kill them than the average person. You all are beyond average, so that is all I will say about that."

Sky had so many questions that she had wanted to ask earlier that day, but now that Gemini was here in the flesh, she had forgotten them all. Then she thought of how she hadn't been home and how much she missed that, but she didn't want to get her parents killed by some crazy spies, either. It was safer to stay away and have them remember her as she was, rather than have her institutionalized—or worse.

Maia knew that Gemini was not going away, but was needed elsewhere on the planet. He would reunite with them if they completed the mission. If they did not, then there was no point in saying goodbye, for the world would become a free-for-all for OZONE. She thought back to the flashback of Pangaea, when the world was in turmoil.

Blue said out loud what the other two were thinking: "I haven't been home in a while, so I'm guessing we can't hang out. And, as usual, I've forgotten what other questions I had for you. But I would like some confirmation. If we don't save the girl, then the world goes to hell as in the flashback, right?"

"Precisely," said Gemini.

"Okay," Blue said, "then I'm out of questions. Let's get going." He said this with as much optimism as he could muster, while hating all of the pressure on him.

Gemini walked into the hall and told them he would guide them across the wooden bridge that would place them into the warehouse district, where Jayde was waiting for them.

"Oh, *that's* my question!" Sky said. "How do we know which is the right girl?"

"You'll feel it," Gemini said, pointing at Sky's heart. She put her hand above her heart and looked up at him. "Trust yourself more," he said.

Taking this advice very seriously, the kids walked over the bridge toward a small fence. Sky went through it first and disappeared. Maia followed, trustingly, and also faded into the horizon. Blue stood back and looked at Gemini.

"Were we really that bad as rulers back then?" he asked.

Gemini patted Blue on the back, shook his head, and said, "You have no idea."

Blue realized that he had a lot more pressure to work through than he originally thought. His mentor was expecting him to be better than he had ever been before. He knew now, more than ever, that Magick was real, but he had never thought it was up to him to use it for the greater good of the world.

As he walked through the portal, he found himself standing in front of Sky and Maia, who were looking anxious.

"Jayde is outside with the car," Sky said, approaching the warehouse door. "She's probably more excited about this mission than any of us."

"Yeah, but it's not up to her," Maia replied gloomily. "It's up to *us*."

"And we won't fail," Blue said, pushing open the huge double doors. "See? Jayde's waiting in a green luxury car. By the way, we have thirty-nine minutes left."

✶

Surge laughed to herself as floods of people filled the large retail-rich Union Square.

A nice sale from every retailer within a few blocks of this place for eighty percent off everything should get more foot traffic. You won't get a clean shot if you know that's happening, you bastards!

She put out a bulletin for singles with laptops who wanted to date other singles with laptops, stating that they should meet right now in Union Square. As more than a hundred people showed up for that, Surge laughed. Then she invited all laptop-using gamers in the area to come and enjoy free game subscriptions for a year. Two hundred more people showed up.

It was quickly becoming a very interesting place. Surge knew that OZONE didn't have a clear shot, or even know what to aim at, so she basked in her epic win. She pulled off her hoodie and placed her sunglasses on top of her head. Then she kicked her feet up on the concrete block next to her, and placed her hands on her laptop.

"Surge-Overload reporting in to the Sanctuary. And, boy, do I have news! It appears that OZONE thought that they were going to grab me today. I simply raised the stakes in this little game of ours. All of you will be proud to know that I have collateral that they might want to trade for Supernaturals. I have the ultimate hack, their Agent list."

Surge smiled broadly as she gloated about her win. She didn't even notice the circle of Technomages using their laptops to form a spell.

✶

Narles was embarrassed. Not only was he belittled and tortured, like some terrorist of the state, but he was violated in more ways than he cared to admit. He did find out a lot about his threshold for pain and a bit about his sexuality, but other than that, he felt betrayed. To him the world was black-and-white. He followed the rules, and expected others to do the same. He did what he knew was right by turning Juno in. He wasn't sure what she was up to, but he didn't trust her, and look where that had gotten him? Probed in orifices by a Psiel with a fetish for torture.

Looking past his bruised lips and body, Narles told himself, *I'll be rectified because I've done the right thing. Now I'm finally working with the noblest member of OZONE, Guardian. That alias was bestowed on him after he completed so many missions. Most veterans get their nicknames that way . . . , like Juno, who's a feminist that moves like the wind . . . , and 99, who's taken ninety-nine of the most powerful Supernaturals into OZONE's custody. His prisoners are being held in a top-secret facility in Colorado Springs, being studied. That's where I'm from, so I wouldn't mind being stationed there again . . . . Oh, yeah, and there are other veterans who got the tags and aliases by default, like Grin. That Psiel bastard better stay away from me. God knows what kind of fetishes HE has.*

I'm not the only one who wasn't happy about him being here. It's so cool that Guardian and I are a team! I feel like we're brothers, even though he hasn't said much to me yet. But I'm a quiet guy, too. Only speak when spoken to. He kind of looks at me a little peculiar, but it's probably because of the bruises around my mouth and the way I'm walking. Either way, I'm gonna be known as the rookie who killed Surge. I have C-4 bombs in my pack, and I'm so ready to kill this bastard for my great country!

Look at all these weirdos and their laptops. I just wanna see some terrorist guts already. Just say the word, Commander, and its lights out for the terrorist, I'll make sure of that. Guardian is one of the best hand-to-hand fighters in the universe, but they have him on sniper duty. I can see him from here. I'm on foot patrol in somewhat civilian clothing. I'm dressed as a cop, securing the area. Easy enough disguise.

Grin is nearby with his yellow teeth gleaming at me, as if he could see what happened to me and got off on it. Maybe he talks to the other Psiel Agents, and they brag about it. Sickos! Either way, the laugh is gonna be on them when I take down Surge-Overload. They might tag me "Kill-Overload." That would be cool.

Okay, I can see by my compass that the Soldiers in the area are surrounding the outskirts of this area, so that Surge doesn't leave. I guarantee he's not leaving. I think I see him. The older guy scanning through pages way too fast for a human has got to be Supernatural. Oh, yeah, he looks exactly like the profile description of Surge-Overload! I'm looking over his shoulder, and he keeps logging into some high-level stuff. I think I have an ID on him, but I don't want Guardian to get the kill.

I'm gonna take some initiative and get this guy.

"See," Blue said to Jayde, "this is the part I don't miss about the Bay Area, the traffic. We're only a few blocks away, but we don't have much time. We should just get out and run there."

He tapped his hands impatiently on the dashboard, hating that he wasn't behind the wheel.

"It's your choice," Jayde said, "but I do agree that you would make it faster on foot."

"Why does it seem like a parade?" Sky asked. "You would think that all the clothes in the city are on sale or something."

Maia pointed to the side of a building off Market Street that read:

ALL CLOTHES IN UNION SQUARE 80% OFF

Sky shrugged, her mouth open in awe. "I swear," she said, "that wasn't a power thing. I can just smell a sale in the air."

Maia rolled her eyes.

When Blue got out of the car, Maia ran after him, yelling, "Wait for us!"

Sky was still gazing at the sign, imagining a shopping spree. Then she shook her head to clear her senses. That's when she finally caught sight of Blue and Maia crossing the street in the bumper-to-bumper traffic.

"Bye, Jayde," Sky said. "Wish us luck!"

She hopped out of the car before Jayde could even respond.

"You don't need luck," Jayde whispered.

The sidewalk was littered with all kinds of people. More tourists were around than normal, a lot of them with cameras and videophones to enjoy the fiasco that downtown San Francisco was quickly becoming.

Blue made his way through the crowd as the locals usually do, keeping his fast pace toward Union Square, still a few blocks away.

Sky could see Maia's blonde hair with black strips bouncing, as she walked a few yards behind her friend.

To add to the disruption, a male fan who had cried on the blogs over Sky's kidnapping spotted her and was almost killed by a trolley as he crossed Market Street to see if it were truly her. His bangs were cut like hers, and he had dyed his hair brown with blonde and red strips in it.

As Sky got to the crosswalk, and stood with the people as she had done many times before, her fan boy ran up to her, screaming and weeping like a mourning child.

"It really is you!"

He reached out to grab her wrist and sniff it, but she quickly pulled away, looking down at the petite teenager.

"Please don't do this! Not right now!" Sky pleaded.

Blue looked back disapprovingly. Maia rolled her eyes as she stared at the crying teen.

This kid has problems! she thought. *I can see all of his mental ailments. It's funny . . . , humans are easier to read.*

When the traffic light turned red, the people at the crosswalk halted, cautiously taking pictures of Sky and downloading them to their personal sites. In one block alone, there were more than two hundred uploads.

The fan boy grabbed again, this time for Sky's legs and her skirt. She smacked him, but he only grinned gleefully.

Blue was the first to see the OZONE Soldiers.

It's because of the Sky uploads.

He put his head down to see what was about to happen.

There's only twenty-two minutes till deadline!

The Soldier pushed past Blue, reaching for Sky. But before he could grab her, she was instantly thirty feet in front of Blue, and walking fast through the crowd.

Her fan boy continued to look for her as if he couldn't fathom how she had disappeared so fast in the thick crowds that filled the sidewalks. He jumped up and down until her saw her shining hair flying in the wind.

Maia watched Sky's movement. It looked like teleporting, but it wasn't. She followed behind Blue, making sure not to lose him.

A Soldier grabbed Maia. "Do we know you, young lady?"

As he said this, a bio-scan was sent to OZONE for a visual on her file. A Receptionist confirmed a Magi-track scan with his goggles. From default, the Soldier saw a strange aura permeate from the young Latina. He reached to pull out his gun, but before he had time to move, Blue punched the side of his head, knocking him out.

As he kicked the Soldier over and over in the ribs of his Teflon chest plate, a homeless man shouted, "Yeah, screw the man! That girl wasn't doin' nothin'!"

Blue pulled Maia out of the crowd before she could stop the homeless man from beating the Soldier.

"We don't have time for that," Blue said. "How did he recognize you?"

"His goggles were . . . , I can't explain . . . , enlightened," Maia said. "I mean, they could see the enlightened. It's a new technology that OZONE is using to track us, I'm sure."

Sky was first to get to the corner of the crosswalk to Union Square. As she looked back, she didn't see Blue or Maia.

Oh, well.

She crossed the street, noticing the thick traffic coming into the intersection from every direction. She also saw that hundreds of people with all sorts of laptops were running around, flirting with each other.

What is this, some kind of nerd convention?

More people recognized Sky, which created chaos in Union Square as fans ran up to her, crying and happy to see her, even though she had never met any of them. She just smiled.

I hope Blue and Maia can get to the girl, whoever and wherever she is.

Blue and Maia got to the corner just in time to see Sky mobbed by countless youngsters and older people alike, who were asking for her autograph and telling her how her parents must miss her so much.

Maia rolled her eyes again, scanned the area, and then looked up at the stars.

This is a trap! Maia said, forming a telepathic link with Sky and Blue. *There are other Supernaturals here, but they work for OZONE, and they're here to kill a female.*

"That female is our girl," Blue said aloud, looking around. "But which one is she? I don't know how they expect us to see Supernaturals in a crowd this big."

As soon as Blue said this, the people in the crowd looked gray, whereas Sky was a bright and beautiful flood of colors, and so was Maia.

There were five people sitting in Union Square, surrounding a girl who looked like Maia and Sky on the color scale. She was young, maybe ten years old, and she was typing on her laptop, looking as if she were in a trance.

"It's her!" Blue told Maia as he nodded toward Surge. Maia focused her vision. All of a sudden, she was able to see the Supernaturals in the crowd. Sky appeared to be made of Magick. Blue looked like a constellation of stars. But Maia could definitely tell who the girl was—a fourteen-year-old Mancer with the ability to manipulate machines.

"You're right," Maia said to Blue. "Look, she's surrounded by those humans casting a spell. It's a binding spell. Maybe that's why she can't move. How are the humans able to break through the Veil of Ignorance that the Coven of Unity cast on the world?"

Maia looked nervous as she shot a look up to the stars.

"Death is coming!"

Guardian lay on the balcony of the sixth floor, pointing his favorite sniper rifle at the busy crowd.

They don't seem to understand the danger they're in. Soldiers were commanded to stay away from Union Square and guard the checkpoints leading in and out of it. Narles is patrolling the streets in the guise of a traffic cop. And Grin has yet to make his appearance, always preferring to smoke from the shadows.

Good, as long as he isn't smoking near me . . . . Wait, there are undercover Technomages here, trying to filter out the computer crowd. Good idea . . . . Deme's, no doubt . . . . Just give me a target, so I can blow his head off and go home to finish my beer. It's probably still cold. I'm gonna miss the game if I don't hurry up and get rid of this Code One.

Guardian scanned the crowd, trying to sense any Supernaturals with his other senses. He felt multiple ones here, and they were strong. Before calling in to the underbase, he got a transmission from OZONE.

"Guardian, we have a match! Surge-Overload is near the center of the courtyard. The undercover Technomages have the mark trapped in a binding spell."

"Affirmative. Which one is it?"

Listening to the incoming call from the Receptionist, and turning it off before he could hear any more, Narles crossed the street, aiming his gun at an older gentleman who was staring at his computer monitor. He was sitting on a wire frame chair outside of a coffee shop at the top of a stairway.

His monitor has spells on it in languages that humans shouldn't know. I'm not going to let Guardian steal any more glory.

"Freeze, freak!" Narles shouted, putting on his Magi-track goggles.

He's definitely a Supernatural.

The Technomage didn't move because he was in deep concentration. If he stopped to tell Narles of his mistake, Surge would be freed and would destroy all of their laptops in an instant. His sweat beaded on his forehead as he continued to focus on Deme's orders.

"Put the weapon down slowly," Narles commanded. "Your laptop is a weapon, and if I see one more screen change, I'm going to open fire."

The Technomage decided to break his concentration, in order to avoid being shot. As he reached to close his laptop, he was suddenly shot ten times in the back, and four times in the head.

As the crowds ran hysterically around in chaos, Narles announced into his transmitter microphone, "I got him! I killed Surge-Overload! I just neutralized the target. I repeat . . . , Surge-Overload is dead!"

Guardian laughed. But then the transmission crackled, "Surge-Overload is the female in the sweater with the skull on it. All parties have confirmed."

Looking through his scope, Guardian quickly spotted the female with a skull on her back.

How fitting!

As he placed his finger on the trigger, like a thunderbolt he realized she was only a child. Once again, he felt the inner turmoil of killing that innocent boy in Antarctica.

"Remove the threat, Guardian! *Now!*" Deme barked into the microphone.

Guardian knew that this was his job. He was fully aware of all of the damage one Supernatural could do. He didn't want what he was about to do recorded, so he turned off the camera.

At that moment, the girl turned around, looking confused.

Guardian's jaw dropped as he stared at her in horrified silence. *Surge-Overload is my niece!*

As Blue saw the Soldiers running in his direction, he felt the Soulstream well up in his gut. Immediately, he unleashed a small spark, which blasted a Soldier so hard that he flew across the street, smoking, before he crashed through the window of a pizza restaurant on the corner.

People near Blue didn't understand what had happened.

"That soldier was struck by lightning!" one man said.

"I think an electric cable swung around and shocked him," a woman said.

"No," a boy said, "he touched the trolley cable, and was electrocuted."

Maia looked at Blue with wide eyes. "Wow!" was all she could manage to say.

Sky watched the Soldier fly through the air, as people continued to pester her for autographs. Some asked for strands of her hair, or made other ridiculous requests. Sky was tempted to knock them all away, but she kept her cool, and was extremely nice to them. Actually, she had been missing all the attention.

Gunshots went off as a cop started shooting a middle-aged man with a laptop. Then he shot the laptop, using the rest of the bullets in the clip. He was smiling, as if he had done something amazing.

Blue recognized the goggles, and so did Maia.

"OZONE!" they said simultaneously.

The people in Union Square ran away from the seemingly crazy cop, falling over each other in their panic.

Still dazed a little, Surge looked up and realized she was in the middle of a broken circle of people. Technomages were sitting around her, still concentrating on her binding. She touched her laptop screen, and in a flash, all of their laptops exploded in their faces.

More screams came from frightened people, falling over themselves, trying to escape the lightning bolts that had already killed five people, and get away from the crazy police officer.

"He's trying to kill Sky in Union Square!" some shouted.

With his goggles still on, Narles saw Sky standing in the middle of the crowd, which was trying to pull her in different directions. They would have torn her clothes if she hadn't pushed them back with an invisible force.

Narles ran toward her.

"Freeze, freak!" Narles shouted.

I must have shot the wrong guy. The transmission said I'm supposed to be looking for a girl. She must've taken off her sweater to lose us, but she's Supernatural, nonetheless. I know for a fact that I'm gonna bag Surge-Overload now.

The Magi-track goggles made Magick in any form show up as an aura like a black light. But the goggles were only fifty percent accurate, since sometimes they indicated that microwaves and cell phones were Magick. This girl had a huge aura around her, so Narles was doing the right thing by eliminating the threat. As he pointed his gun at Sky, people standing near her instantly posted this on the web.

It was all over the news that "a crazy cop was pointing a gun at Sky."

But Sky put her hands up as if she were under arrest, which made Narles's gun fly into the air.

"Oops! Mr. Officer, please don't shoot me!" Sky said, acting as if she knew that cameras were on her. "Please! I just want my daddy!"

Maia sighed at Sky's performance, then looked at the police officer. "His weakness is large crowds and frogs?"

Blue said, "Let me see if he's weak against a couple of these!"

His hands began to glow just as a Soldier grabbed him from behind. Blue released the blasts into the Soldier's face, sending him into a passing trolley. Then he turned to looked for Maia, and saw a Soldier behind her, who was about to shoot her.

But Maia saw this coming, and dodged out of the way, so that the bullet hit another Soldier in the chest.

Maia kicked the shooter hard in the genitals. As he bent over, she used her knuckles to hit him in the throat, knocking him out instantly.

Blue looked at her with wonder.

"His weak spot," she said.

"This place is getting crazier by the second," Blue said, fighting his way through the crowd toward Surge.

Seeing him coming, Surge ran toward an alleyway.

Blue glanced back at Maia, shrugged as if wondering why Surge had run away, and then ran after the girl.

Sky was watching Narles take a C-4 bomb out of his pants pocket.

Since people were still viewing this all over the world through a live feed, OZONE quickly pulled the internet plugs to stop all news footage.

Deme was screaming for Blackhawk reinforcements, although he knew he couldn't authorize another bloodbath. He had already lost five of his best Special Ops Agents to stupidity.

Sky walked toward Narles, totally unafraid. When she came close, she did a simple "shoe fly" motion with her hand, and he soared past Surge into the alleyway.

I can't believe I'm actually doing this, Nina thought. *I have her blood all over me, and I don't know where I'm going. I can feel the angst*

of the people in this city, and it makes me want to curl up in a ball and shake myself to sleep.

Nina continued to walk down the street as people ran past her, screaming and talking about lightning bolts, and crazy cops killing innocent people. For some reason, Nina, who wanted to run more than anyone away from here, kept walking *toward* the riot. She felt pain and fear as vividly as if she were shot herself. Her stomach ached and her head hurt even worse, but she pushed through it.

As she turned a corner, she saw a police officer pointing a gun at a little girl.

"So, you're Surge-Overload," the officer said. "You messed up my career, and you're only ten years old. Evil comes in all ages, I suppose. There's nothing else for me to do but rid the world of you."

"Sir," said Surge, "I don't know what you're talking about, and I'm fourteen."

She was lying to get the man to calm down and let her go.

Nina's heart rate increased as her anger level began to rise. She could feel the people around her change from panicky to furious as they stared at the police officer.

"I wouldn't do that if I were you," Nina said to the deranged man.

"She's evil!" he screamed. "I'm just doing my duty. Everybody back!"

"Leave her alone!" Nina screamed right back at him.

But before the words came out of her mouth, a group of bystanders walked behind Nina and glared at Narles. They all ran toward him as he pointed his gun at them.

"Stand back!" he shouted again. "I'm warning you! I'm a special Agent, and I don't want to hurt you!"

As he fired a warning shot into the air, an older woman grabbed a trash can lid and hit him in the back of the head with it. When Narles turned around, he pointed his gun at her just as a bottle hit him in the forehead. Then six other people jumped on him. He shot one in the shoulder, and tried to aim at another, when someone finally hit him with a four by four.

As Narles was mobbed, Guardian put his gun in his pack and jumped from one building to another until he could get a good view of his niece.

"Guardian reporting . . . , Surge-Overload is on foot. I am in pursuit."

Nina held her arms outstretched toward Surge, and the girl ran to her and gave her a hug. Nina felt warm and protective. Surge had never felt that way before, not even from her own mother and father. A wave of security hit her, making her never want to let go.

Guardian jumped onto an iron balcony as if flying from one building to another. His fearless leaps were animal-like, and his landings were equally graceful. He never lost his balance, even high above the city streets, where he now got a direct view of Surge. She was hugging a Supernatural blonde who looked familiar. Although she had bloody and grimy clothes, Guardian was certain that he knew her from somewhere.

Nina Hall! he thought. *The file that Juno had is where I know her from. She's definitely Supernatural. I don't need to use my own Supernatural senses to tell that. She seems to be protecting Cindy.*

As Guardian looked through his sniper scope, he saw a Soldier sneaking up behind Cindy and Nina. When he pulled the trigger, the Soldier died instantly. Guardian looked through his scope to check the scene in the distance, where he saw Vampyl scaling the rooftops, looking for something, but jumping in his direction. He pointed his gun at one and blew his leg off, which sent the Vampyl falling to the street below, crushing a car.

This is getting nasty! Guardian thought as he aimed at another Vampyl. But then he was suddenly hit with a wave of anxiety, sensing that a bomb was about to go off. He automatically thought of Narles and the C-4.

Nina stared at the sniper who was shooting in her direction.

I'm tired of being shot at.

As she pointed at him, she thought of the anxiety of losing Juno, and the anxiety of being around these people. She thought of running, as she stared at Guardian.

Almost as if she commanded it, he jumped from the fourth story into the alley trash, leaving his gun up on the balcony.

As Blue, Sky, and Maia ran around the corner, they found Surge hugging Nina.

"Nina?" Sky said.

As Surge saw Blue standing in front of Sky and Maia, she stood behind Nina, convinced that this woman would be able to protect her from anyone.

Nina looked at the trio in front of her. They all felt familiar, but she knew none of them, as far as she could tell.

How do they know my name? And why is this girl so afraid of them?

"I'm just looking for a Gemini to save her," she said.

"We are here to save her," Blue answered.

"Are you a Gemini?" Nina asked, realizing how silly she sounded, but not knowing that astrology had nothing to do with anything.

"We know Gemini, yes," Maia said. "The girl has to come with us." Looking at Nina through her new vision, she said telepathically to Blue and Sky, *She's Mancer.*

I can see that they BOTH are, Blue answered telepathically.

How can both of you tell? Sky asked, looking at Nina's filthy outfit. *All I see is a homeless looking tomboy with a cute haircut under all that grease, blood, and grime.*

Okay, conveyed Maia, *that's a start. Look deeper at her.*

Sky looked harder, and then scent came into play. *Oh, my god! She stinks, too, and that's fresh blood. I swear I know her from the past life, but she didn't respond when I called her name.*

"She may not know who she is," Maia said aloud. Then she asked, "Nina, who are you trying to save?"

Nina looked down at Surge, then back up to Maia. "Juno," she said.

"Follow them," Chass said to his entourage, "and tell me if you find Crux. They are Supernatural, and I have a feeling they know our little stowaway snake."

They were standing high above a building, listening to the conversation below. Chass's abnormally handsome face smiled as he added, "I can smell him on them."

Chapter 25

LOOSE ENDS

There comes a time in everyone's life when they question the reason why they're even here. I ask myself that every single day. Until recently, I couldn't have cared less, but I got the metaphorical bomb dropped on me that I have the power to save the world . . . . Well, a few of us do. We just choose to use that power. As per my mentor, Gemini, we are Mancers and we chose to be this way before we got to the planet, just as you chose to be the way you are. I chose to lead, and that's not a job, it's who I am.

Your bodies are only a shadow of your true potential. After my family died that night, I struggled with this simple truth. Keep reading, and you will see how even the smallest use of your powers is better than not using your powers at all. My friends and I have a world to save. We will meet others who feel the same way. The questions you should be asking yourself are, "Do I want to know what power lies within me, and will I use it?"

I am Blue and I am Mancer. If you exist, then so do I.

✳

As Blue, Sky, Maia, Nina, and Surge walked out of Union Square through the rioters and the fearful, Blue turned to look at the psychotic cop, Narles, on the ground. His gun had been taken away from him by a crazy lady, and he was being kicked in the ribs and the stomach by an angry businessman. Sky's fan boy was trying to grab the C-4 from Narles's clasped, unconscious hand.

Blue shrugged and kept walking with his friends. When they turned a corner, a few seconds later, a loud explosion set off car alarms for blocks around. Screams split the air as Maia looked up at the stars through the haze and glow of the city lights.

"We can't save everyone," she said, "but the world is safe tonight."

Nina could feel the chaos and panic as sharply as if she were looking at the explosion up close, even though she was blocks away from it. She used the explosion as her signal to walk faster back to Juno. As she looked at all the kids around her, she wondered what they could do to help the beautiful woman who was dying in the cave.

They're no older than I am, and the young one is still clinging to my cargo shorts.

Sky could feel the energy radiating off Nina like a wind that she needed to control.

Everyone's emotions seem to be filtered through Nina, she thought. *It's a wonderful thing to witness. I can't see Nina in some intensified color, the way Maia does, but I can feel her powers more than the others can, since she's in my sphere. I can only guess that the girl we're supposed to save is Nina. She's the one from my past life. The little girl is a Mancer. Not a very powerful one, based on the energy she's releasing, but most certainly a Mancer.*

"I'm going to bet that Nina is who we're supposed to save," Sky whispered to Blue while walking next to him.

Blue nodded, but then looked at the small girl next to Nina and reconsidered. "I still think it's the small one," he said. "Maia, what do you think?"

"I think that our first mission is a little too easy," Maia said, looking up at the stars as they all headed into a forest. "I also know we're being followed."

"I was thinking the same thing," Blue said. "Too easy . . . . Wait! Did you say we're being followed?"

Sky stopped in her tracks to look over the darkness of the horizon as they left the downtown area, heading toward Golden Gate Park. The large trees were doing a wonderful job of hiding whoever it was Maia thought was following them.

"I can't see anyone," Sky said. As she looked around in all directions at once, she could only see her friends searching the area as well. Even Nina had stopped to look around as she held on tightly to the young girl.

"The death I spoke of is here," Maia whispered.

"What about Juno?" Nina erupted anxiously. "We have to save her!"

She looked from one kid to the other, desperately trying to find out why they were talking about death. She didn't want Juno to die.

"Yeah, Nina," Sky said with her arms crossed. "I'm not too excited about saving the woman who tried to kill me."

Sky remembered the flashback, and how Juno had loved Nina. She remembered blessing their baby and promising their unborn son a Kingdom. The disappointment on Nina's face, and the energy of her helplessness, made Sky rethink her attitude.

"I'll only do this for you, Nina," she said. "Let's go, guys. If they're following us, they'll have a hella chase on their hands."

Blue smiled at Sky's generous words to Nina. He could see she was trying. He could also see that she must have remembered the flashback as she looked into Nina's ice blue eyes, and simply couldn't be her normal blunt self.

That was a twig breaking in the distance, Blue thought. *Whoever is approaching us is close by.* "You all go ahead," he said, "and I'll keep them busy."

Maia looked at Blue, then up at the sky. "The stars are changing," she said. "If we are to help Juno, we need to hurry. Her life is slipping away. Blue, there are four of them following us."

"Please . . . , um . . . , be careful, Blue," Sky said, turning to face him.

He nodded tenderly at her, and began to focus on the Soulstream.

Sky could feel the vibrations all around her. They completely disrupted her concentration. It was the most uncomfortable sensation she had ever felt, and it was tingling every sense she had.

When Blue ran out of view, into the darkness, Sky looked after him.

Nina pointed up to a high ridge through the tall trees near the beach. "She's up there," she said. "How are we going to reach her in time?"

Surge knew who Sky was from her extensive OZONE files. She also knew Nina, with the help of Juno. Juno was right to find such a Supernatural. Surge could feel Nina's power seeping through her skin and into the air as well as she felt the breeze lifting her feet off the ground. An invisible force was allowing them all to defy gravity.

This is new! Surge thought.

Sky said to Nina, "You just point us in the right direction, and I'll take us there."

Maia linked Sky's thoughts with Nina's, and in a brief moment Sky knew exactly where they were supposed to go.

Nina's mouth was open in shock, as was Surge's.

Sky was enjoying her new control over her powers as she held them all in an invisible bubble and flew with them through the large trees as fast as she could think.

Dodging the trees at the last minute, feeling like a roller coaster at a theme park in Southern California, Surge sensed her adrenaline rushing through her as each branch barely missed ripping off her face.

Sky had amazing precision. This trip was like nothing any of them had ever felt before.

Maia looked back and saw a faint shadowy darkness with a darkening light within it. "So that's what a Vampire looks like to me!"

Sky heard Maia, but concentrated on getting to the cave in her surface thoughts. She knew that her life had been blessed before she met any of these kids, but she had no idea how blessed she truly was. Sky only believed in the books and pantheon that her parents had told her to believe in. She never really questioned her own faith until she realized that a secret society had placed those religions in specific demographics in order to confuse the helpless humans. Now she was questioning everything, and it made her feel guilty as she flew through the forest.

Nina felt the wave of guilt coming from Sky as she tried not to close her eyes that were almost pierced by random branches hanging in the night like barbed wire.

They all split around trees with as much ease as running past them, even though they were traveling at least fifteen feet above the ground.

Sky spoke to Maia telepathically, *Are you sure Blue will be okay out there?*

No, but I do know that Juno is losing her essence of life.

I couldn't care less about that evil cat-suit-wearing bitch!

Sky realized that her thoughts were cold, but she also felt a sense of fear. Something about Juno didn't sit well with her.

Maia felt the same way, but tried to calm Sky anyway.

Well, we can't bring Nina to Gemini without Juno, so we have to make a decision. I'm not sure if we can heal her. You saw all that blood on Nina.

Yeah, like a horror film. But we need to get Surge to Gemini, as well. I'm not sure which one of them we were meant to save.

Maia agreed silently and looked back. *We have a dilemma. Blue will need our help as soon as we save Juno.*

Unaware of the private conversation between Maia and Sky, Surge could not get over her own addiction to this flight. It was like a video game she had never played. Suddenly, she accidentally dropped her backpack with her laptop in it, but as it flew off her arm, an invisible force brought it right back to Surge's hand. Surge looked at Sky, who was smiling at her, even though she was looking with her peripheral vision.

How cool it must be, Surge thought, *to embrace your powers like these people*. She smiled. But not for long. *Whoa! Now, THAT's a creepy looking cave!*

As all four landed gracefully on the cave floor, Nina looked at Sky in wonder. Then her senses changed as she saw Juno, dying on the stone floor.

"Please help her!" she cried.

Blue ran into the darkness, knowing that eyes were watching him. He squinted as he looked through the trees. His speed never changed as he ran toward the danger.

I think I saw a moving shadow . . . . I'm sure I'm being followed.

He slowed his pace.

A dark figure almost fell from high up in the trees in front of Blue. Its eyes were a glowing silver, and its fangs were vampiric.

Blue smiled at it, which probably made it quite upset. Its cool features snarled into a grimace as it charged Blue with claws on its pale hands.

Blue got out of the way just in time to see the front of his new jacket get gashed by the claws.

Stepping back to look at his ruined jacket, Blue glanced ruefully back up at the predator. It was almost what Blue had envisioned a Vampire would be like—smooth pale skin, fangs, glowing eyes, and model looks, in fashionable clothing much too expensive to be worn in the woods.

"Look, I don't know why you're attacking us," Blue said reasonably, although he was slightly annoyed.

The Vampire swung for his face, but Blue easily dodged out of the way with a simple step backwards.

Just then, Blue felt a sharp pain in his back as a pair of claws sliced through his flesh from behind. He fell forward, almost onto the silver-eyed Vampire, before a knee to his chin struck him in the air and knocked him on his bleeding back, which caused a small dust cloud.

"Okay, maybe you're serious about attacking," Blue said, still on the ground, while considering getting back up to his feet.

A pair of stilettos fell from the trees above and landed on his chest. The impact crushed his rib cage, and the stiletto from the right shoe pierced his left lung.

"Why are you playing with the meat?" a female voice said to the two males that were standing near Blue.

He tried to breathe through the fluids filling his lungs and the blood in the back of his throat, which reminded him of the mountain.

"Sorry, Sasha, we just thought—"

"That's your first problem," Sasha spat out in the most threatening tone she could muster. "Chass doesn't expect us to think, Emilian. Now, get your act together and finish him. I will go after the females."

Her dark brown hair was pulled back in a bun, and her purple eyes were shifting into a blood red as she glared at her subordinates. Then she jumped high within the darkness of the trees, and was gone.

Emilian walked over to Blue with his silver-tipped boots and custom-made spurs. His walk was similar to Blue's, sending out a message that he didn't care too much about his surroundings. He watched Blue's eyes studying his boots as Blue's face was planted directly on the fertile soil.

"You like these boots, do you?"

Emilian shot out a swift kick, which Blue saw coming, but couldn't dodge through his pain. He heard a snapping sound from inside his chest and realized it was his body healing.

If I can only have a few more moments, I can heal enough to take these guys.

Emilian picked Blue up by his jacket with one hand and held him high above the ground. Blue knew these Vampires were strong, but Jayde had never told him he would be treated like a small child. A claw stabbed into Blue's wound in his chest, and he could feel the claw digging around inside. The pain almost made him black out.

The Vampire laughed as he held Blue in the air. Pulling out his claw, he said, "I wonder what you are, and how you taste?" Bringing a bloodied finger up to his mouth, Emilian sniffed the blood like wine.

"Emilian," the other Vampire said, "you heard Sasha. Just kill him and be done with it. The others have Crux's scent on them as well."

A loud hiss came from Emilian's red lips and fanged mouth, as his eyes changed to a blood red.

"Don't *ever* speak to me like you are my sire, Yanoro!"

He placed his finger in his mouth and tasted the blood, which was richer than ordinary human blood. Emilian's eyes glazed over as he tasted the most potent blood he had ever drunk in all of his five hundred years. When he opened his eyes, Blue was smiling.

"I feel a little better now," Blue said, looking down at Emilian.

A loud thunderous crackle and a flash later, Emilian was blasted into the forest, set on fire, as Yanoro watched three lightning bolts strike his comrade.

Yanoro threw a globe of darkness around Blue, which was a natural gift of the Shandor. Then Yanoro ran over to Emilian, and bent down to inspect his comrade, whose torso was hollow, and whose arms were completely gone. Yanoro stood up in terror, looking back toward the globe of Magickal darkness that surrounded Blue.

Sasha wants us to kill him, but if he can do this to Emilian, I'm not sure what I am supposed to do.

Blue focused on the Soulstream until the vibration rang around him and into the forest. A burning light from within him shook his flesh and made him cringe in his already wounded state. He could hear his sister's voice as the light canceled the false darkness around him.

Yanoro was getting ready to attack with a machete. But then he stopped in his tracks as he watched the lightning crackle in the air with a deafening thunder. His globe of darkness was no longer his advantage, as it disappeared into thin air. He took a step back, and thought of fleeing for his life, but he couldn't face the alternative. Rushing in with a precise kill strike for Blue, Yanoro leaped with his Vampiric speed to kill his prey.

Blue felt a slice tear through his chest and held the arm that was responsible for piercing him. Eyes still closed, he let the burning he felt within him now be transferred to the Vampire's arm. Yanoro let out a scream that could be heard at the cave.

✶

"What in the hell went wrong?" Deme yelled furiously at the Receptionists, Technomages, and Soldiers in the Control Panel. "We had more Agents and Soldiers there, including some of our best, and no one was able to get an ID on Surge-Overload besides the ones that are sitting in Union Square with their heads blown to bits by their own laptops?!"

He stared at the footage and studied it.

Guardian must have turned his gun cam off before an ID was made. Narles went fucking AWOL and is virtually responsible for the biggest epic fail in my career. Guardian was attacked and not responding while three Soldiers were dead or injured with electric burns. Sky was most definitely a Supernatural, based on the footage OZONE had to pull from the net and live TV. The public may have seen her as a victim, but I've seen the footage and reviewed her through the Magi-track goggles. My suspicions about her were confirmed, even though she has been off the radar since dodging an interrogation. Her father was useful to OZONE as one of the most influential minds in human history. He had to be tortured and interrogated by the Psiel profilers to find out the information they needed on her location.

This was becoming more of the war that Deme had signed up for. Before the Commander could walk in and berate him in front of his special unit again, Deme decided to send out other teams to sweep the area, and Cleaners to falsify reports and clean up the city.

"I am going to destroy you, Surge, and you will pay for this! Just make another mistake, and I will personally be there to see the life leave your eyes, little girl!"

Sky spun around when she heard the scream. Her wits were temporarily paralyzed by fear for Blue's safety, until she concluded that it was not his voice. She did hear the hum in the air, though, and figured he was handling his own, as she knew he could.

"She's lost a lot of blood," Nina said through strained tears as she looked at Juno. "We have to get her to a hospital. I can't sit here and watch her die."

She tried to pick up the armor-clad woman delicately, but her strength was already drained from the long day. She tried to understand how she had gone from playing with Mr. Violet to being shot at, all in the space of a few hours. As she looked down at the strange woman at her feet, she still felt the familiar emotions resonating inside her body.

"She will die soon if we don't do anything!" Maia said, looking at the cave wall. With a light that came from her palms, the constellations from space showed up on the walls for the girls to see.

Surge-Overload looked at the wall in absolute awe. "Wow!" she said aloud. "That's Ursa Major . . . , and that's the Pyxis constellation. How did you make them change like that?"

Maia looked at Surge with surprise, both excited that the young girl knew the names of the constellations, and confused that she knew they were shifting.

"We have to save Juno," Maia said, "or the constellations will shift again."

Sky looked at the sparkling lights on the wall as if she were staring at a bunch of random dots. With a shrug, she asked, "What do you want *me* to do?"

"Please help her," Nina said, walking over to Sky.

"Sky," Maia said, "you have the ability to heal her. Just believe it, and it will be so. I will assist you."

Sky walked over to Nina and placed her hand on her shoulder. "I am only doing this for you. Juno tried to kill me. But since she means so much to you, I will try."

Sky's smile warmed Nina's worry-stricken face as she felt the truth in Sky's words.

Why is Sky helping me? Why did Juno try to kill her?

Sky studied Juno with disgust as she searched for body parts that were not too bloody to place her hands on.

Maia stood behind Sky, her eyes beginning to glow a soft sun yellow.

For Surge, this was one of the weirdest days she had ever encountered, and she had seen some shocking things on the web. But never before this day was she the one being saved.

As Sky concentrated on the wounds, she could see the muscles and tissues gaping out of Juno's skin.

"Repair the flesh with your thoughts," Maia said. "I can only heal so much."

Sky looked into Maia's glowing eyes.

How am I supposed to do all this stuff? It's one thing for Gemini to think I'm somehow supposed to save the world, but for Maia to be so sure, as if she were Gemini or Jayde, is pissing me off! And what about Blue? He's counting on me.

Seeing the look in the scared little girl's face, Sky decided to try her best, as she had promised Nina.

Sky watched with bewilderment as one cell after another began to reform in Juno's wounds. She was actually able to heal the terrible holes all over the tattered and gory body beneath her warm palms! As

Sky thought of the cells forming faster, they actually did. The muscles regenerated at an accelerated rate as Surge took a step forward with a hand over her mouth. Nina stood next to Surge in disbelief, looking at the back of Sky's healthy head of hair.

Suddenly, Juno gasped and screeched for air. Her body was still weak from the loss of blood and from her scattered thoughts trying to return to her toned body. Her matted blood-soaked hair fell back onto the floor as her pain-inflicted body fought to survive.

Looking at Juno's energy, Maia said aloud, "She was poisoned by OZONE, I can see it." Showing Sky telepathically what she could see, she added, "We're going to have to extract the poison from her veins. It looks like a control serum of some sort, and is somehow linked to Magick. What has OZONE been up to?"

"You have *no* idea," Surge said under her breath.

But only Nina paid attention to her. Only now was she starting to realize what was going on.

As Maia felt the blood on Juno's head, her powers lit Juno's body with a soft light.

Juno convulsed again, causing a dark green fluid to spew from her eyes and mouth.

Maia concentrated, forcing the fluids to pour onto the cave floor, and then, looking at the moving fluids as if they were a living being, she bit her right index finger.

"What are you doing?" Sky asked.

"I'm destroying whatever it is," Maia said as a drop of her blood dripped onto the puddle of green fluid. Everyone watched in fascination as the fluid began to twist in on itself in a chaotic swirl, then bubbled and disappeared, as if in agony.

Nina felt the conflict that had just happened on the floor, but decided not to pay any attention to it. Instead, she looked with wonder at Juno's miraculously healed body. Then, as Sky and Maia took a step back, she knelt down beside Juno.

Maia lifted her hand to the wall, and the constellation of the Phoenix showed its fiery wings.

Surge smiled, knowing that the Phoenix symbolically represented rebirth.

Chass punched the side of Blue's head with such force that Blue thought his neck and part of his skull had been shattered.

As Blue slammed against a tree, Chass walked over to the injured Vampyl on the ground.

"Get up and grab what's left of your dignity, Yanoro. Emilian was a fool to mess around with a Mancer."

Chass shrugged at Yanoro, who was holding his singed arm.

"So this is who saved Crux from the docks?" Chass said contemptuously as he walked over to the nearly unconscious Blue. Then he turned Blue's head so he could get a better view of his face. "Zeus!" Chass stood up, half from fear and half for his luck. "Prince Lord Ka will be pleased!"

Chass looked over at Yanoro, who was trying to heal his wound.

"The blood won't heal it," Yanoro said, frustrated.

"You have survived an encounter with one of the most powerful beings on the planet. Just be glad you can say that. Emilian can't say that much." Chass spun around with the grace of a dancer, his eyes sparkling with ambition. "Tell Sasha to come here, and we will take this one with us."

Standing in her gladiator pumps in the shadows of a large tree, Sasha scoped out the cave. She knew they were inside. The moon overhead was beautiful and nearly full, and she was already nervous to be in this city. It was the constant battleground of Vampyl Bloodlines and Spiraar Packs.

The classic Vampire versus Werewolf war that plagued most human populated areas was evident in this place. Chass always demanded the best of the best to accompany him, and Sasha was honored that he had chosen her. She had proved her skills in many battles and assassinations worldwide. She knew spies and she could smell an OZONE Agent in the cave. This group was not to be underestimated. They had rounds in their guns that could destroy Vampyl, and since they were notorious for killing her kind, she kept her position, waiting for one of them to slip up.

There was fresh blood in the air and tainted blood, too. The aroma almost sent Sasha into a ravenous bloodthirst. She controlled her willpower long enough to stop the bloodthirst from taking over, the way it tended to do with the handsome idiot, Emilian.

Someone's coming out of the cave!

Watching with the ferocity of a sleek huntress, Sasha saw the small girl who was with them.

Why did they let her come out by herself?

Sasha was intrigued, and looked for ways to circle the girl, to move in for the kill.

"How did we do that?" Sky said, looking at Maia.

Turning her gaze from the stars, Maia simply replied, "It was meant to be." Then, feeling the presence of another Vampyl, she said, "Where's the girl?"

Sky saw no sign of Surge. She looked back briefly at Nina, who was holding Juno on the ground, then said to Maia, "She's outside getting some fresh air."

"Fresh air?!" Maia said, suddenly afraid for the girl. "With Vampyl on the prowl? That's smart!"

Maia was proud of how she and Sky had healed Juno, but there was no time for that now. She had to deal with the issue at hand.

"Blue's in trouble, too," she said. "And I thought this was too easy. Next time, remind me to keep my mouth shut." She walked out of the cave.

"Oh, I will. Don't worry about that," said Sky, following Maia outside.

They saw Surge sitting on the rocks, looking out at the horizon.

"So this is what it feels like to lose your human life?" Surge said. "And I thought I couldn't sympathize with Sky or the others. Now look at me."

Maia said telepathically to Sky, *There's a Vampyl about fifty feet away, behind the tree with the "I Love You" scar.*

I can see her, Sky replied, surprised that her sphere had grown. *I can move to her right now and surprise her. Damn, I'm jealous of her shoes!*

Sky was still facing Surge's back and looking down at her own bloodstained shoes.

"I don't know why this war started or how," Surge continued, "but I was born into it, and I just lost everything today. What am I supposed to do now?"

Before Sky vanished, Maia said to her telepathically, *Her weakness is her heart. She has a glimmer of a Shard within her. Her blood is tainted, but it's her strength.*

Then Maia sat down next to Surge and looked out at the horizon. "We will take you to our mentors, Gemini and Jayde," she said aloud. "They will explain everything a lot better than I can. I'm kind of the useless one in this little bunch."

Surge looked over at the pretty Latina in the moonlight. "You call being able to read the stars and heal people and exorcise Demons, or whatever that was, useless? God, I wonder what you must think of *me*? Don't answer that, please . . . . Man, I sound like one of those demotivating blogs." Surge looked back at the moon. "By the way, I'm Cin . . . . Surge-Overload . . . . Nice to meet you."

"I'm Maia, and the pleasure is all mine." Maia was truly proud of the compliments from the young girl. "By the way, I really like your eyeliner."

✴

Blue felt the pounding in his head as he tried to do something simple, like open his eyes. His face ached and his body was numb. What had hit him seemed like a truck coming off the freeway. There was that crunching sound again that always made him sick to his stomach when he heard it. He also knew what it was now—his bones regenerating. The ringing in his ears from the busted eardrum was so loud that it made Blue grunt in discomfort.

When he could open his eyes, he saw Chass standing nearby, talking on a cell phone. He couldn't hear what the Vampyl was saying, but he did see him hang up and start to walk toward Blue's broken body, which was lying at the base of an old Blue Gum Eucalyptus tree.

"So the rumors of your invulnerability are true," Chass said politely in his proper European accent. His features were even more striking than those of the Vampyl who had attacked Blue earlier. "That was enough impact to even kill immortals. But I can't let you get your consciousness."

Blue looked past Chass's head and grinned. At least he thought he did.

"I have to save you *again*, Blue?" Sky said, floating in the air behind Chass. "Hey, pretty boy, if you want your two losers here to stay alive, I suggest you stay away from him."

Yanoro and Sasha were floating next to Sky with arms outstretched as if they were going to be crucified.

Chass laughed aloud. "This is an unfortunate turn of events," he said. His seductive voice was dripping with something he hadn't felt in a long time—happiness. "It would seem the boy has found some powerful friends to fight his battles. Bravo. You can let them down, please, Madame. They will do you no harm, and we will make our departure."

His polite words surprised Sky as she floated to the ground and tossed the Vampyl hostages to Chass's feet.

Blue rubbed his head as Sky walked toward him, not directly facing Chass. "Are you okay, Blue?"

"Only if you have some painkillers. I think I'll be fine." Blue managed a weak smile.

"I wouldn't take that stuff if I were you," Chass said as he turned to walk away. "I know the guy who started that industry. Not really a nice guy."

What was left of Chass's entourage were following closely behind him, tending their bruised egos and flesh, as he walked into the darkness, laughing.

Sky touched Blue's head and looked back at the Vampyl, who had already disappeared into the shadows. Seeing how hurt Blue was, she wanted to dash after them and tear their dead limbs from their sockets. But as she tried to focus on Blue, her healing powers didn't work. "I swear, I was able to heal a few minutes ago," she said, still holding her smooth hand on Blue's bashed head.

"Don't worry about me," Blue groaned. "I'll be fine. Thanks for the assist." He smiled at Sky as his hand held hers over his wounded skull. She could feel his bones regenerating under her fingers, so she held very still.

He's regenerating himself! So that's how he survived the fall off the mountain the first time.

Feeling the warmth from Blue's skin, she made sure the temperature in the air was just fine for his recuperation.

That's the least I can do.

Looking up at her, Blue said, "I actually wanna feel the real breeze, if you don't mind. I kinda miss it."

Knowing what he meant, she stopped her control over the environment as she sat next to him, still holding his head.

Blue realized at that moment that he made her feel like the girl she used to be.

✹

Juno opened her eyes. "I knew you would do it, Nina," she said. "Never once did I doubt you." She reached up to caress Nina's face. "You're going to have to explain to me, one of these days, *how* you did it."

"It wasn't me," Nina said. "I just watched. Sky, I think her name was, and Maia did it." Nina still didn't know exactly how they did it or what they had done, but she felt extremely lucky to have found them. "Oh, and you didn't tell me Gemini was a person. I was asking people if they were Geminis, thinking their Zodiac sign was going to save you somehow." Nina blushed.

Juno tried to suppress her laugh because it hurt her chest. By reflex she looked around the cave to check for any possible danger. Then she sat up.

Nina stayed on her knees, looking at the tough woman. She felt the strength from her returning quickly, but she also felt the sting of pain and decided to give Juno back the "calm stone."

"Thank you, this helped," Nina said, holding the stone in front of her.

At that moment, Maia walked into the cave. The sight of Nina kneeling before Juno as if she were a knight to a queen made her giggle at the irony.

When Maia stopped, Surge bumped into her back.

Oops! I think I just ran into Maia. I'm not paying attention to my own steps. I guess I'm not as graceful on my feet as I am online.

"So, what next?" Surge asked the puzzled-looking adults. She was tempted to log into her computer and update her site, but decided not to.

"We go back to Gemini and tell him about our mission," Blue said, walking into the cave with Sky behind him, smiling.

When Sky looked at Juno, for a moment the uncomfortable silence was felt not only by Nina, but by all the others. Nina walked over to Sky and gave her a big hug. Sky didn't know what to do with her hands still at her side as she looked at the smiles on Maia's and Surge's faces, so she gave Nina a small hug—the minimum that etiquette would require.

Please don't get blood all over me! I'll have to burn these clothes later.

As Juno stood up, the holes in her armor exposed her flesh. But she didn't seem to care as she walked over to the Port Rune. "I'm guessing this is the fastest way to get to him," Juno said, pointing at the Magick marking on the wall, which looked like a snake and a spiral with a star in the center.

Maia walked over to inspect the Rune, then said loud enough for everyone to hear, "Cronos! This is his marking. I remember it from the flashback. It was on his robes and on the podiums . . . . Juno's right. It's our way back home. I think we should be quick about it. Gemini is back from his mission."

Lost

She sat in the white hospital room, crying and sore. Her name was Aiel, and she had just given birth to a baby boy. Aching from within and shivering in her cold, sterile bed, she wept uncontrollably as she stared at the door, hoping to see her child. This would be a miraculous and amazing moment if she weren't thirteen years old.

After carrying the burden of her pregnancy for the last nine months, she was used to being judged. However, she didn't care as much about what people thought anymore as she did about the fate of her newborn. Somehow she couldn't bring herself to look into the large mirror on the other side of the room as she thought back to how all this had happened.

Aiel had grown up in an orphanage, not knowing who her real parents were. The religious teachers taught her a lot about the world through their strict eyes. She had read the scriptures more times than she could count.

Just ten months earlier, she had been a happy child who did volunteer work around the church. The sisters would have her teach the younger children lessons about the scriptures, and her mind was set that this was the order of things.

But after Sunday school one day, she ran to the bathroom to vomit. The sisters blamed it on the food she had eaten, and encouraged her to rest. Aiel knew from the very first moment that something was different about her body, and very wrong.

Three small boys and a priest were the only males in the church. The only other males were priests who visited from time to time.

When, after three months, the sisters noticed something different about Aiel's shape, they tested her for pregnancy. When they discovered that she was positively fertile, they shunned her and forced the other children to stop speaking to her. All of that time, Aiel wondered how this was possible. She had never even kissed a boy, let alone had sex with one. But no one would believe her, no matter how many times and how forcefully she pleaded.

During the many months that she was alone at the orphanage, waiting for the baby boy to come (for she knew all along that it was a boy), she recited poetry to him as she washed the floors on her knees. Aiel somehow knew the baby loved it when she sang to him. Now, without him in her arms, she felt empty and detached, more confused than ever.

She had read many times about the Virgin Mary and other miraculous virgins who shared a similar story. She knew that immaculate conceptions were incredibly rare, so she prayed to god, asking why he had done this to her.

Am I chosen . . . or lost?

Aiel never received an answer to her question, but she always felt the love from her unborn son. It was a love that was beyond words and comprehension, but clearly came from another place. This boy was special, and Aiel knew it. Having this baby was her purpose in life, although she was still only a child herself.

As tears stained her tanned cheeks, Aiel stared at the hospital door through puffy eyes, even though no one walked past her room. Not a sound came from the hallway on the other side of the door. The silence scared her even more than the glares of the incensed sisters.

✦

"We can see the child, but she cannot see us, right?" Reynolds said to his wife.

As Lisa looked at the young girl in silence, a single tear fell from her eyes.

"Why do I get the feeling that she knows we're here?" Reynolds asked. "Look, I know she reminds us of Cindy, but you understand we have a job to do."

"She was a virgin," Lisa said, still staring at the innocent girl in the bed. "How is this possible? Even the doctors reported that this must have been a miracle birth. There are definitely Supernatural workings here."

"That's why we have to report to our boss, Lisa," Reynolds said with a smile, looking at the soft features of his wife. "I will call this in right now."

"No, let *me*," Lisa said, pulling out her late-model Braintech cell phone. Then she sighed and voice-dialed the underbase: "Agent Lisa, reporting in. The baby is perfectly healthy. Code four and awaiting orders."

✦

"Okay, I demand you guys give up eavesdropping," Maia said to Surge and Sky as they tried to listen in on the conversation behind the wall.

"You're no fun!" Sky retorted. "Aren't you even a little interested in what Gemini asked Blue, Jayde, and Juno to talk about in there?"

"Well . . . ."

Maia found herself at a loss of words, since she was just as interested as the others, but knew that everything was happening for a reason. After a minute of thought, she said, "Okay, maybe I *am* curious. But you know as well as I do that if Gemini or Jayde wanted us to know, they would tell us. Besides, Sky, you can't even use your powers to hear what's on the other side of that wall. And Surge over here can't even use her techno-stuff to penetrate the barrier of the door for a single peep."

"I don't even feel Juno anymore," Nina said in a whisper.

The other females looked at her with surprise, for Nina had hardly said a word since they arrived at the Pagoda earlier that night.

"What do you mean?" Sky asked, floating over to Nina. "Like as in she's not even there?"

Nina looked at Sky, Surge, and Maia, who were staring at her. She blushed as she remembered how shy she was.

"I . . . I don't know *what* I mean," she stuttered. "I . . . umm . . . just feel things, and I don't feel her presence here anymore."

Nina sat down and became very quiet.

"See," Maia said, "if they wanted us to know what they're talking about, they would invite us into whatever kind of energy cocoon they're in. So, I guess we'll have to find other things to keep us occupied."

"O-M-G!" Surge-Overload said out loud. "I thought you'd never say that." Her short pigtails, which still complemented her cyberpunk makeup, bobbed as she ran down the hall to grab her backpack from the other room.

Sky looked at Maia with a shrug. "Maybe she has to go to the restroom?" Sky's long legs moved gracefully as her feet touched the ground. Contemplating why Gemini would bring Juno into the locked room, she crossed her arms over her chest and placed a manicured hand on her chin.

"It's useless, Sky, so let's do something else," Maia said as she helped Nina to her feet.

Suddenly, Surge screamed from down the hall, "Come check *this* out!"

Sky flew down the hall at the speed of thought. Seeing Surge's hands meld into her laptop, she said, "Okay, kinda creepy. But what am I supposed to be looking at?"

"I'm gonna hack into the OZONE database," Surge said enthusiastically, "to see if there are any other Supernaturals to save. Kinda like the night I tried to warn you that they were on to you, and you kept dropping the phone like some dumb chick in a cheap horror movie."

"Shut up!" Sky said, pouting. "How was I supposed to know that this was all true, and some secret society was gonna send supersoldiers to stormtrooper my house and try to kill me?"

"Well, sometimes the voice on the other side of the phone is really there to give you the sign you need," Surge said, looking over her shoulder to smile at Sky. Her computer screen was flashing so fast that Sky had no idea what was going on.

Nina and Maia ran into the room, out of breath.

"What's going on?" Maia asked frantically.

Nina, realizing that no one was in danger, calmed down and touched Maia, who relaxed instantly.

Sky noticed this exchange of power, but kept her thoughts to herself. *So, she can change people's emotions when she touches them, can she?*

"Shhh!" Surge hushed the other girls. "I'm intercepting a live call right now."

"Your orders are as stated," a Receptionist said clearly. "Tell the girl that her newborn didn't make it. Switch the baby with the woman down the hall, whose child actually had cerebral complications and died. Keep an eye on the new family and place the girl back in a new orphanage under watch. Am I clear, Agents?"

"Clear!" Reynolds said.

Lisa was staring at the girl through the mirror, placing her hand on the glass. "She's not even Cindy's age. How could this be?" She was whispering, so that only her husband could hear her. She saw that the young girl was shaking, with only thin white blankets covering her from the waist down as she mumbled something—perhaps a prayer—in the empty room.

Reynolds held up the phone to signal his wife to answer the Receptionist.

"What?" Lisa said. "Oh, yeah . . . . Clear!"

Lisa realized that she had zoned out, trying to imagine what her young daughter would be doing in this situation.

Surge stared blankly at the computer, her smile long gone since she first heard her parents' voices in the hospital with the poor young girl. As if her skin weren't pale enough, she seemed to lose the little color she had. Hearing the concern in her mother's voice, she knew these missions must be against her will.

"What's wrong with you?" Sky said, looking down at the hacker. "You look like *you're* the one who's in that room with your baby taken away from *you*."

"Yeah, something is definitely wrong, Surge-Overload," Maia said. "Are you sure you're okay? Do you know that girl?"

"Umm, no . . . ," Surge mumbled. "I . . . I don't know her."

Maia telepathically linked to Sky, *She's lying.*

Yeah, I don't have to be psychic to tell that, Sky linked back. *Do you even know if this spying stuff is safe? I mean, if they found out we were hacking into OZONE, Gemini would give us some cryptic speech, and Jayde would probably punch us in the face.*

"Look, Surge," Maia said aloud, "we have to be careful, is all. Gemini has been hiding us off the grid from OZONE for months. What's your connection to that girl?"

Surge sat up straight. "Look, I'm a professional. You all haven't seen me work. Sometimes I take these things personal. So what? I *hate* OZONE more than both of you combined. They're monsters! And what they're doing to that girl is no different than what they would have done to either of you. Now, are you going to let me get back to work, or are you going to just sit there and silently judge me?"

Sky raised an eyebrow at this sudden attitude. "I'm not James or Bond," she said. "I'm not feelin' the spy thing. So I'm outta here. I need some fresh air." Instantly, she disappeared, leaving behind a faint breeze and a hint of jasmine.

Maia looked at her own palm, where a small constellation was starting to form.

I wish I could tell Sky, but who knows where she is now? We're supposed to know about this girl for some reason. She's important. I wish Gemini would just tell us what to do.

Nina had been quiet this whole time, studying the girl on the screen. There was a passionate energy hidden beneath Aiel's young skin. She was an old soul, and Supernatural. How Nina knew this, she had no idea, but she could feel it through the monitor. The girl was definitely terrified, and Nina felt that she had every right to be.

As Aiel trembled in fear, she fought through the numbness and the pain from giving birth. She was crying uncontrollably now, but had the urge to get up and find her baby. She didn't know how, but she could tell that someone was watching her. As a matter of fact, multitudes were watching her.

"Why are you doing this to me?" Aiel said, looking around the room, but finding no cameras. As she threw off the sheets, she noticed that her legs were still numb, as if they had fallen asleep.

I can't stay here. Something is terribly wrong.

As she tried to lift one leg, she winced from the pain in her abdomen. A sharp jolt stung her temples as a migraine suddenly plagued her.

"God, why are you doing this to me?!" she prayed aloud. "Have I forsaken you? I have loved you more than anyone else could. You've been my only friend, dear Lord. Is this a test? Please just let me see my baby one more time."

When she finished her prayer, Aiel opened her eyes, and the headache instantly went away. She continued to fight through her pain, but she did so willingly, with thoughts of her baby in her mind.

Just then, a doctor walked into the room. His dark hair was neatly brushed, and his lab coat was immaculate. He seemed to radiate the warmth of a young father.

"I have bad news for you, Aiel," he said. "Your baby didn't make it."

Down the hall in the hospital, Lisa walked into the cold room where a mother was crying. Expecting terrible news from her doctor, the woman sat up in her bed when she saw Lisa come through the door.

"Is my baby alright, nurse?" she asked, studying Lisa's every movement. She knew that something must be terribly wrong when her husband fainted at the sight of their newborn. It was also a bad sign when there were no cries coming from the baby as the nurses rushed him out of the room to an incubator.

"Please tell me that my baby is going to be okay!" the mother pleaded, becoming annoyed with her own sweaty locks, which kept falling in her face. "I know I shouldn't have tried so late in life, but this is a miracle baby, I can feel it."

Lisa looked at the sink to take a moment to straighten her thoughts, as she had been trained to do. Using her subterfuge, she polished her face with a bright smile as she turned to meet the mother's gaze. "Your baby is going to be fine. You're right, he *is* a miracle baby."

The lady sobbed and prayed. "Thank you! Thank you, god!" She sat back on the hard pillows and asked with a nervous smile, "When can I see him?"

"Soon after you rest, we'll bring you to him," Lisa said in a calm and sweet voice. "We need a name to put on his crib, if you don't mind."

"I don't know where my husband is, but he hated the name when we spoke about it. At this moment, I don't care what he thinks, because the baby must be a blessed boy, like the blessed child in Carthage in an old tale from my great-grandparents' land. I'm sorry I'm ranting. I will name him . . . ."

✳

Maia studied the palm of her hand for a long time, and then ran to the window to see the constellation in the sky. As the clouds and the spaces between them began to ripple like water, she smiled because her predictions were becoming more accurate. "Isja!" she said out loud.

Surge-Overload didn't even interrupt her trance to look at Maia. She was engrossed in the scene at the hospital, wanting to know how OZONE planned to play this one out. Her palms were literally fused into the keyboard. Although across the ether she knew she was playing a dangerous game, she continued to spy on the most powerful of all secret societies.

Nina felt terrible for Aiel as she watched her baby being given away to some random woman down the hall.

If this is what OZONE is capable of, no wonder Juno was searching for me to get me away from them.

She sat up, brushed her blonde hair out of her ice-blue eyes, and shuddered a little as she looked over at Maia, who was still staring out the window.

✳

Sky was sitting in the woods, a few miles away from the Pagoda. This was an unusual spot for her, but she didn't particularly want to be found in one of her normal thinking haunts.

Life was so much easier at home when all I had to think about was what I was going to wear to school the next day. I miss my closet! I miss daddums and mum. Now I'm surrounded by the freaks I used to ignore in school. No wonder! I'm gonna tell Gemini that I wanna go back home.

I can risk it. I feel like I've lost everything anyway. If OZONE wants to deal with me, then so be it!

"Freeze! Don't move!"

An Agent from OZONE was pointing a huge gun at Sky. At his signal, an armored platoon surrounded her. Their Braintech gear reflected the moonlight, telling Sky there were at least a dozen of them.

"You've gotta be kidding me," Sky said as she stood up, noticing that she had nowhere to run.

"Make a move, young lady, and the castle goes up in flames," the Agent said, holding up a detonator in his hand.

"Please don't!" Sky pleaded as she took a step. "There are innocent people in there."

"I told you not to move!" the Agent said, pressing a button. A large explosion boomed in the distance.

"NO!" Sky screamed in horror. *What have we done?!*

(End of Book I)

NEVER SAY NEVER

The rain was just as refreshing as the news that Gemini had to deliver. He walked through the intricate maze of tunnels without missing a step. He had never been here before, and he couldn't say he would ever return. The world was one step closer to becoming free of the true tyrant that controlled it.

This place was fashioned after temples long forgotten by the world, with pockets in the hieroglyphic-carved ceiling that allowed rain to flow into the halls to provide water for the lush plant life down here, which grew by artificial light. It was underground, but smelled of fresh rain from above.

The test with the kids triggered a realization in Gemini that he hadn't thought possible before. This temple was almost an exact replica of a place he once knew very well. He had gone over the scenario countless times, but it was nothing like the last time. The key to OZONE was right in front of him. He was one of the oldest beings on the planet, and he had his notions that there were others at work here.

Walking past guards who dared not halt or even approach the immortal, Gemini kept his stride toward the large double doors. He used his ability to sense other Supernaturals to track this one from across the planet. His senses were nearly flawless, but he had never tried to search for this particular Supernatural, believing him dead long ago.

The door opened with a slow, dramatic, creaking sound. Gemini waited patiently for it to open, so he could pass. His audience was waiting for him, and he was interested in seeing the one responsible for OZONE. This was a predestined meeting, and Gemini knew, after so many millennia, what he must do.

"Hello, Gemini," said the one. "I've been waiting for you, as I'm sure you know. I see you've been busy as well, finding the old Mancers to do your work to destroy my OZONE."

Neflym smiled his handsome smile.

Author's Bio

Geo Ivery was born in Benton Harbor, Michigan, in 1978. He is a professional graphic artist, comic book character developer, and computer game designer with a B.A. degree in Computer Animation. Raised all over the world in a military family, he has been influenced by many cultures and places, which has added a fantastical twist to his stories. He sees everyone as a comic book character and loves to find both the gifts and the flaws that make people unique, so that the world can see Magick through his vision. With thousands of original characters in his head, he has created worlds parallel to our own, but so much brighter and more vivid. Geo has worked with private editors nationwide, has ghostwritten graphic novels, and has developed back stories of characters for multimillion-dollar companies. His work has been compared to *Percy Jackson and the Lightning Thief*, *Harry Potter*, *X-Men*, *The Matrix*, and *The Da Vinci Code*.